Waterloo Sunset

Books by Martin Edwards

Lake District Mysteries
The Coffin Trail
The Cipher Garden
The Arsenic Labyrinth

Harry Devlin Novels
All the Lonely People
Suspicious Minds
I Remember You
Yesterday's Papers
Eve of Destruction
The Devil in Disguise
First Cut Is the Deepest
Waterloo Sunset

Suspense
Take My Breath Away

With Bill Knox
The Lazarus Widow

Collected Short Stories
Where Do You Find Your Ideas? and other stories

Waterloo Sunset

Martin Edwards

Poisoned Pen Press

Poisoned Pen Press
6962 E. First Ave., Ste. 103
Scottsdale, AZ 85251
www.poisonedpenpress.com
info@poisonedpenpress.com

Printed in the United States of America

Dedicated to Bill Grice

The First Day

In Memory
HARRY DEVLIN
Died suddenly,
Liverpool
Midsummer's Eve

Chapter One

Harry Devlin stared at the announcement of his death.

The sheet of paper came from an envelope bearing his name. No covering note, no explanation. He turned it all around and upside down, feeling like a volunteer confronted by a stage illusion. No clues leapt out, no hint of the author's identity. Nothing but those stark words in between the black borders.

His brow furrowed. Not even 'In *Loving* Memory'.

The sun sneaked behind a cloud, and his swish new office slumped into shadow. A fortnight in, he still didn't feel at home. The room reeked of paint, the comfort cooling dried his throat and the computer's state-of-the-art hum set his teeth on edge. It might be healthier to crowbar a window open and inhale exhaust fumes wafting up from the Strand.

He swallowed a mouthful of black coffee from a mug that insisted *Old Lawyers Never Die—They Just Lose Their Appeal.* On his way back from court, he'd stopped off to down a couple of pints of Cain's after a torrid morning before the magistrates, trying to make crime pay. If his head swam, blame strong ale on an empty stomach, not a weird anonymous message.

A hoax, it had to be. He had nothing to fear.

And Midsummer's Eve, what was all that about? He glanced at the desk calendar; a gift from a client who owned a funeral parlour. One page for each day of the year, accompanied by a motto in Gothic script above a logo of a setting sun.

Change your thoughts and you change your world.

Monday 18 June. Not quite Midsummer.

He'd fed the envelope into the jaw of a tall box marked 'For Shredding and Recycling—Guaranteed Secure, Environmentally Friendly and Confidential'. A child of two could have taken off the lid. He reached down, as if into a lucky dip, and fished out his prize. A cheap, crumpled envelope, bearing his name in bold type. No stamp, no postmark. It hadn't been sent by the solicitors' document exchange. Hand delivery, must be.

The puzzle provoked him. Someone had invaded his life, and he wanted to find out who, and why.

He grabbed the sheet, and raced down the corridor to an airy space with a welcome desk and chairs that squelched when you sat down. Double glazed windows looked out over the Parish Church gardens and city beyond. A slim woman in a uniform of green jacket and skirt was watering bamboos and weeping figs in pots of fired earth. He might have strayed into the Palm House at Sefton Park instead of Crusoe and Devlin's reception area.

The woman swung round to face him, flicking tendrils of dark hair out of her eyes. The leafy logo of Green and Pleasant Plant Care was embroidered on her jacket breast. Her cast of features spoke of Chinese origins, but her accent was born-and-bred Scouse.

'Posh new premises, Harry. How are things?'

'Good, thanks, Kay.' Her full name was Ka-Yu Cheung, but she preferred Kay. 'And you? '

Her cautious smile revealed perfect teeth. She said she was fine, and he thought she was about to ask a question, but a glance at the woman behind the desk seemed to change her mind. The receptionist had frizzed blonde hair, a solarium tan and the pout of a spoilt child. Her nose was stuck in a dog-eared Danielle Steel and she didn't favour Harry with a glance until he spoke to her.

'Suzanne, that letter I picked up when I came back from court.' He nodded towards an alcove where the post trays squatted. 'Who brought it in?'

The receptionist sighed, a low gust of patience tried beyond endurance, and book-marked the paperback with her nail file. She screwed up her face in a dumb-show of brain-racking before the inevitable admission of defeat.

'Haven't a clue.'

'It wasn't with the rest of the morning mail. Someone must have delivered it specially.'

'I'm only just back from my break.' A mutinous note crept into her voice. 'People are always coming and going. Juniors with files, folk filling up the water cooler, tradesmen hammering so loud you can't hear yourself think. I might as well be sat on a traffic island in the middle of Lime Street. This isn't like the old building, you know.'

Harry glanced outside. The windows in their last office had been encrusted with grime, so that the city outside was tinted sepia, like an Edwardian photograph in a dusty junk shop. Now the glitzy hotels and apartment blocks of twenty-first century Liverpool shimmered like a mirage in the summer light. Cranes swivelled like sentinels, and drills roared as they churned up paving stones. He'd lived here all his life, yet sometimes he lost his bearings amid the road-works and the fenced-off sites, with their hard-hat signs and blood-red warnings to put safety first.

'No,' he said, 'it's not the same.'

A gawky figure in St Nicholas Gardens caught his eye. Wasn't that Tom Gunter? Tom was Kay's boyfriend. A skinny, dark-haired young man in a black tee shirt and jeans, his gait was energetic but jerky, as though a puppeteer dangled him on twisted strings.

'Are you all right?' Kay asked.

In Kay's eyes, Tom could do no wrong. He might be moody, but he was misunderstood. A year ago, he'd been charged with stabbing a neighbour to death and Kay persuaded him to ask Harry to conduct his defence. Trouble was, Harry suspected that Tom had stabbed the woman in a cocaine-fuelled rage when he tried it on with her and she'd said no. The psychiatric reports blathered on about anger management issues, and when Harry asked if he'd consider pleading to manslaughter, Tom flew into a temper and sacked him on the spot. He hired another lawyer with fewer scruples and more friends in the underworld, and within weeks the main witness for the prosecution withdrew her evidence. The case collapsed and Tom walked free. Even so, he was the sort to bear a grudge. Maybe he'd dropped in that cryptic note about Midsummer's Eve.

'I can see Tom down in the gardens.'

Kay bent to place the watering can on the floor, giving herself a few seconds to decide what to say.

'It's sunny for once, so this morning we walked into town together.'

'You walked?'

Last time he'd heard, they lived out in Halewood, miles away.

'We've…we've moved to an apartment at the Marina.'

The Marina? That wouldn't come cheap. She sounded embarrassed rather than proud and a flush came to her olive skin. Harry wondered if she knew about the note. He was seized by the urge to confront Tom, and find out if he'd written it. A spur of the moment decision, no time to stop and think. Best catch up with him before he vanished from sight. With a nod to Kay, Harry shimmied between a pair of palms and thumbed the lift button marked with a downward arrow.

'Harry…'

As the receptionist leaned forward, ears pricking up, Kay's voice trailed away. Maybe she meant to warn him not to do anything rash. But it was too late to break the habit of a lifetime.

Harry liked Kay. She had a blind spot about the man who shared her life, but her naivete was part of her charm. Even if Tom made trouble for him, it wasn't fair to drag her into it.

'Can I catch you later?'

'Yes, you're busy. I'll see you soon.'

As the lift doors closed, she turned to a yucca with leaves like scimitars. He leaned against the side of the carriage and rubbed his eyes. At one time, he could have downed a liquid lunch and felt none the worse. He contemplated his reflection in the mirror. A baffled face stared back at him.

Died suddenly?

◇◇◇

The burly ex-docker who guarded the entrance foyer was deep in conversation with a wrinkled crony who resembled the late W.H. Auden. If a masked gunman ran into John Newton House, Harry rated the odds of his being spotted at evens.

With scant hope, he asked, 'Have you seen a feller in a black shirt go up to the fifth floor in the past hour?'

'Search me, mate.' The concierge shook his head in sorrow. He was an amiable man who was glad to help if it didn't cause him inconvenience. 'We get all sorts in and out of here, don't we?'

The crony clicked his false teeth by way of confirmation. An aroma of cod and vinegar clung to him; he was a fish and chip supper in human form.

'You know how it is, Harry. Hard to keep track.'

'Don't you issue everyone with visitor ID?'

'Run out of badges, mate. New office, landlord cutting corners. Bound to be a few glitches.'

Thanks for nothing. Harry headed through the side door and out into a small courtyard. A narrow pathway led in one direction through gardens stretching towards the lantern spire of the Parish Church, and in the other to the six-lane highway of the Strand. Harry checked the benches that faced the waterfront, and spotted his quarry.

Tom Gunter sat alone, scanning the horizon in a spaced-out way. His eyes were bloodshot and glazed. Harry strode over to the bench, the announcement of his demise squeezed between thumb and forefinger.

'Hey, Tom. Long time, no see.'

Tom Gunter gazed into nothingness, paid him no heed. Harry flourished the sheet under his nose.

'Did you write this?'

Tom blinked, like a time traveller adjusting to Planet Earth.

'Uh?'

'Midsummer's Eve,' Harry snapped. 'Sounds familiar?'

Tom bared his teeth. Spots of anger reddened the pale cheeks.

'What…are you talking about?'

He sprang up and snatched the piece of paper from Harry's hand. He gave it a quick glance, then screwed it into a ball.

'Died suddenly? Is that right?'

He wasn't faking ignorance, there was no point. Besides, the message was enigmatic, and Tom didn't do enigmatic.

'If it's nothing to do with you, fine,' Harry said. 'My apologies, I'll see you around.'

A black Swiss army knife appeared in Tom Gunter's palm. It came from nowhere, flourished with a magician's sleight of hand. A small blade glinted in the sun.

'Bastard,' he said.

Harry gritted his teeth. People said he was too impulsive for a lawyer. One of these days, recklessness would be the death of him. But not today. Tom wasn't that stupid.

'Look, I made a mistake.'

'Dead right.'

Harry glanced around. A minute earlier, half a dozen people were strolling around the garden. Now they had disappeared, perhaps into the church to say a little prayer. They'd better put a good word in for him.

Tom Gunter stood up, caressing the blade as if it were a woman's cheek. Harry didn't move. He'd acted for enough criminals to know better than to give an inch. They often made threats they didn't mean to carry out.

'Put the knife away, Tom. No need for any grief.'

Tom's laugh was packed with scorn.

'No need for grief? Bit late for that. You have no…'

His words were drowned by a peal of bells from the church tower. Three o'clock, there must be an afternoon service. At the same moment, a siren rang from the building on the other side of the iron railings that enclosed the garden. Within seconds, a swarm of men and women in business suits buzzed out of the canopied front door. A firm of stockbrokers, observing a fire drill.

Tom lunged forward and Harry lost his footing. He clutched at a black litter bin, but couldn't save himself from falling. The breath smashed out of his lungs as he hit the ground. Tom's shadow towered over him. Steel-tipped size ten boots loomed an inch from his forehead

This was Liverpool. Anything might happen.

Harry shut his eyes. His body was taut.

'Lucky for you I have to…' Tom muttered. 'Next time..'

The boots clattered into the distance and when Harry looked, Tom was disappearing into Chapel Street. He hauled himself to his feet and limped over to pick up the screwed-up notice with the report of his death. The chattering stockbrokers took no notice; the grubby stains on his Marks and Spencer suit and scuffed shoes didn't mark him out as a prospective client of high net worth.

He shielded his eyes. The gardens were full of maritime artefacts and memorials to people who died in the war. The church was dwarfed by the shiny towers of a new Liverpool that knew nothing of the past. Curvy glass buildings winked and preened in the sun, as if to say *Do ya think I'm sexy?*

He rubbed his hip. It felt tender, and tomorrow he would have a bruise. Otherwise, no harm done.

Still five days to go before Midsummer's Eve.

Chapter Two

'Did you get my message?'

Harry spun round as Wayne Saxelby clapped him on the shoulder at the entrance to the church gardens. Had Wayne written the note about Midsummer's Eve? He couldn't guess why a management consultant might foretell his death. Some kind of trendy motivational tool?

'Sorry?'

Wayne's smile showed lots of expensively whitened teeth. 'This morning I popped into your office and asked Amazing Grace if you'd spare me five minutes after you came back from court.'

Grace was the temporary substitute for Harry's secretary, a long-suffering paragon whose arthritic knee had been replaced a month ago. As far as he was concerned, Lucy couldn't hobble back to work too soon. Grace hadn't grasped that the prime requirement of a gatekeeper was to keep the gate shut, at least to management consultants.

'Love to,' Harry lied. 'But actually…'

'Let me buy you a cappuccino at Kaffee Kirkus. Or an Americano, mocha, whatever you fancy. Did I mention the manager is a personal friend?'

Typical Wayne. He loved to be loved, but most of all, he loved to impress. Once upon a time, he'd practised as a solicitor, drifting from firm to firm until he finished up with Crusoe and Devlin. His career came to an end when he couldn't face telling a client that he'd lost her case. He said he'd negotiated a handsome pay-out and sent her a cheque from the firm's client account. He meant to take out a loan and refund the money, but that wasn't the point. The moment Harry and his business partner Jim Crusoe found out, not even Wayne's gift of the gab could save him. He resigned to save being sacked and struck off the Solicitors' Roll.

But Wayne's creative approach to the truth, so hazardous in the law, proved a blessing when he left town and re-invented himself as a consultant. By the time he returned to Liverpool, he drove a limited edition BMW, sported a black Tag Heuer chronograph and a Prada mobile that did everything except make afternoon tea. He was seldom seen without his state-of-the-art laptop and he dropped the names of celebrity chums like other folk scattered litter. The buzz word in the city was *regeneration*, and no-one had regenerated his life more extravagantly than Wayne Saxelby. His new girlfriend Tamara had risen to stardom on *Celebrities without Shame* and rented one of the two penthouse flats at the top of John Newton House. Wayne had moved in, and although she'd disappeared to film in the Caribbean, there was no escaping him. The only option was to give in with good grace.

'All right, lead the way.'

Wayne had acquired a mid-Atlantic twang since his lawyering days, along with a fashionably shaven head. He boasted that his tan came courtesy of a fortnight in the Maldives with Tamara, and his cream cotton suit was a Paul Smith limited edition. The *braggadoccio* was wasted on Harry, whose favourite holiday destination was Anglesey, and who confined his clothes shopping to a quick annual foray in the January sales.

The ground and first floors of John Newton House were reserved for retail and food and drink outlets. One unit was occupied by a Bavarian coffee shop, another by the property agents tasked with selling the upstairs flats; the rest was steel-shuttered silence. Half a dozen metal tables squatted on the pavement; Continental café culture had arrived here with a vengeance. Everywhere you looked there were coffee houses and swanky bistros. Lychee martinis were all the rage, and a restaurant near Lime Street sold the best sushi outside London. You might imagine you were walking the boulevards of Paris or the avenues of New York, if not for the squally showers and the wind blasting in from the Mersey. Soon global warming would take care of them too.

Harry sat outside while Wayne went in to be served. Across the road, a fat man was playing a penny whistle. What he lacked in musicianship, he made up for with ruddy-faced gusto. The moment he finished 'Mull of Kintyre', he launched into an onslaught upon the chordal complexities of 'Alfie'.

What's it all about?

Good question. Harry wished he knew the answer.

'All right?' Wayne asked as he returned with the drinks. 'You were panting like a pensioner.'

'Out of condition, that's all.'

'Nothing to do with the skinny guy dressed in black, then? Or that piece of paper you picked off the grass and stuffed in your pocket.'

'Ah,' Harry said. 'You noticed.'

'And the bloke who was about to kick your head in? Hard to miss.'

'He used to be a client.'

Wayne winced. 'You over-charged?'

'It's a long story.'

'No offence, Harry, but with you, it always is.' A gleam lit Wayne's eye. 'Risky to challenge him, if there's bad blood between you. So what was so special about the scrap of paper you rescued?'

'Nothing.' Harry wasn't in the mood to confide in a man with a mouth like the Mersey Tunnel. 'I got my wires crossed, that's all. The man in black is Tom Gunter. Last year I defended him on a charge of murder.'

'And he's walking the streets already? Is the early release scheme even more generous than we've been told?'

Harry tasted the coffee. 'You might remember hearing about the case on the regional news. A woman who lived two doors away from Tom was stabbed to death. Her body was found in an alley-way. Three years earlier, Tom was convicted of breaking an ex-girlfriend's jaw. This time, the police reckoned he'd propositioned his neighbour and took it badly when she turned him down. He and I argued about his defence and he instructed someone else. '

Wayne leaned his elbows on the table and bent closer. His aftershave had a spicy tang. It probably cost more than Harry earned in a week.

'Who got him off?'

'A witness who placed Tom at the crime scene changed her mind. A week later she jetted to Disneyland with her kids, all expenses paid. Very nice for a single mum on benefit. Tom waltzed off without a stain on his character. If you don't count his previous convictions, that is.'

'So justice was cheated?' Wayne shook his head. 'You know something, Harry? That's why I decided I couldn't stomach the law any longer. It has nothing to do with justice.'

'Unlike management consultancy?'

'Trust me, you're wasting your time with criminal law.'

'I like a challenge. Defending habitual drunks on the basis they suffer habitual thirst.'

'I'm not joking. I've taken a long, hard look at your business model. The practice needs to change.'

Wayne had come back into Harry's life when he rang to offer a fortnight's consultancy funded by a government grant. Jim Crusoe reckoned they had nothing to lose, but Harry wasn't so sure. Wayne never missed a chance to remind them that quitting the law was the best career move he could have made.

'Defending criminals is what I do.'

'You could do something else.'

'I handle divorce work too, don't forget. County court cases. Accident claims.'

'I mean something more ambitious than demanding compensation for people who trip over pavements. Don't you ever yearn to do something fresh?' Wayne gestured expansively and nearly knocked over Harry's mug. 'Your life can change in a moment.'

Harry pictured Tom Gunter, stroking the knife's blade. 'Yeah, that's what I'm afraid of.'

'You know what they say, Harry? Feel the fear and do it anyway.'

'Moving office was bad enough. What if I want my life to stay the same?'

'You're kidding.'

Harry frowned. 'It's not so terrible.'

'We all want something more. Come on, admit it. Where's the fun in defending dyed in the wool rogues and trying to persuade the judge that a fourth generation burglar is one of God's lost children?'

'None of my clients deserves to be stigmatised as guilty. It's needlessly discriminatory. I like to think of them as…differently innocent.'

Wayne tutted. 'A sense of humour is all very well, but it doesn't bring down the overdraft.'

'All right, if you want the truth. No two days are alike in this job, that's the appeal. Tomorrow I'm before the City Coroner. Representing the son of the deceased at an inquest.'

'What hourly rate will you charge? Please tell me you didn't quote a fixed fee.'

'Aled Borth reckons he was duped out of what little money he was expecting to inherit. He may work in the movie business…'

'What?'

'…but we're not talking Steven Spielberg or Martin Scorsese. Aled plays the Mighty Wurlitzer at the Waterloo Alhambra. The cinema dates back to the age of silent movies, but these days it's run by a charity.'

Wayne shook his head. 'Crusoe and Devlin aren't a charity, Harry. You need to apply your mind to profit and loss, debtor days and cashflow.'

'In the small hours of the morning, I think of little else.' Harry wiped his mouth and got to his feet. 'Thanks for the coffee. Catch you another time.'

◇◇◇

Lou the concierge was still in conference with his wrinkled chum as Harry waited to take the lift back upstairs. Pan pipes fluted from concealed speakers, the bland music spreading across the foyer like mayonnaise. Facing the welcome desk was a huge plasma screen television. A DVD played in a never-ending loop, featuring exquisitely groomed young architects with public school accents who conjured up virtual images of a futuristic Liverpool. Harry doubted if they'd ever set foot north of Watford. When they extolled his home town, he scarcely recognised the warts-and-all city he loved.

'Vibrant sustainability…construction initiatives…catalyst for economic growth…'

He hurried up to the office, keen to talk to Kay and find out what she'd meant to say to him. Maybe she knew who had dropped off the note about Midsummer's Eve. But she was nowhere to be seen.

In reception, he spoke to Sylvia, Jim Crusoe's secretary, who doubled as their office manager.

'Is Kay around?'

Sylvia was a softly spoken woman in her late forties who had worked for Harry and Jim Crusoe since they'd first set up the firm together. No crisis ever bruised her calm good humour and Harry sometimes puzzled over what they'd done to deserve such loyalty. It certainly wasn't down to how much they paid her.

'Taking an interest in plant care, all of a sudden?'

'Are you questioning my green credentials?'

'Of course. You're a serial killer of spider plants and mother-in-law's tongue. Kay said goodbye ten minutes ago. She'd finished here and was off to her next job.'

'Did she leave any message?'

Sylvia raised her eyebrows and he guessed she thought he'd taken a shine to Kay. She was a would-be match-maker, determined to pair Harry off with a woman more reliable than those he'd been mixed up with in the past. The snag was, reliability didn't turn him on.

'What message did you expect?'

'She said she wanted to have a word. Maybe about Tom Gunter, I don't know.'

'Tom Gunter?' Sylvia's grimace made clear what she thought about Kay's boyfriend. 'Sorry, she didn't say anything to me. How about you, Suzanne?'

The receptionist shook her head. 'By the way, I meant to tell you. That Aled Borth rang. He was due here at four o'clock, but he's cancelled the meeting.'

'Did he speak to Grace?'

'No need,' the girl snapped. She detested Harry's new secretary and never communicated with her if she could avoid it.

'But the inquest into his mother's death is tomorrow. We were going to discuss the evidence.'

'He said he didn't want to see you, after all.'

She made it sound like a good decision. Harry had meant to talk Aled Borth through the witness statements taken by the coroner's officer. He was desperate to persuade his client not to turn the inquest into a fiasco by accusing an innocent man of murder.

'Surely…'

'He's coming in tomorrow at nine sharp before you both set off for court, so what's the problem? I said it was fine if he wanted to cancel. No point in running up costs if there's no need. Client care, you know?'

She beamed in triumph. At least she was cheap, and on a good day, her Scouse wit was sharper than anything on the telly. For Harry and his partner, employing Suzanne had become a bad habit, like drinking more than was good for you or supporting a football team that never repaid your devotion. She'd long ago become part of the furniture at Crusoe and Devlin—and now she'd outlasted the furniture. The old desks and chairs would never pass muster in slickly refurbished John Newton House. A fortnight ago, they'd been sold for firewood.

◇◇◇

Back in his room, he propped his feet on the brand new desk. John Newton House was named after an eighteenth century slave-ship master who saw the light after being appointed tidal surveyor for the Port of Liverpool. He became a clergyman and writer of hymns, including the one which gave Amazing Grace her nickname. The building dated back to the age of King and Kaiser, when Liverpool was second city of the Empire and gateway to the New World. Once the headquarters of a long-sunk shipping company, it remained for decades a soot-blackened relic of past glories. The wind whistled through broken windows and rain seeped in through holes in the roof. It was supposed to be a listed building, but the list probably consisted of blots on the waterfront.

But that was then. Once Liverpool was named European Capital of Culture—eat your hearts out, Milan and Barcelona—investment flooded in. John Newton House had become a landmark in a mini-Manhattan skyline, at least according to the agents' brochure. A developer ripped out its guts to create office and retail space, coupled with luxury apartments on the top floors.

Harry knew he should be grateful for his corner office, with its panoramic views of river and town, but it felt as homely as a hotel lobby. Crusoe and Devlin had moved from a block resembling the Leaning Tower of Pisa minus the charm. Last week a demolition crew had reduced it to rubble. It would be foolish to say he preferred its cramped and cobwebbed ambience. Jim Crusoe would never forgive him. And yet…

As he closed his eyes for a moment, the door swung open and his partner marched in. Jim was a broad-shouldered man whose confident stride never became a self-important swagger. He considered Harry's indolent pose and unleashed a theatrical sigh.

'Taking a well-earned break?'

'Power-napping,' Harry said. 'Two or three naps a day increase production, wellbeing and longevity. It must be true, I read it in a self-help book Wayne Saxelby lent to me.'

'You were asleep.'

'Blue-sky thinking. Trying to see the big picture. You were right, these management consultants know a thing or two.'

Jim's eyes swept over the jumble of files and papers scattered over desk and floor and came to rest on a tottering pile of back issues of *The Law Society's Gazette*, still in their virgin, shrink-wrapped state.

'We agreed on a clear desk policy. Touch each piece of paper only once?'

'It's not a mess, just an eclectic design scheme.'

'Shouldn't you catch up on your reading? Keep up to date with what's happening in the profession?'

'True.' Harry gazed sadly at the magazines. 'Trouble is, the *Gazette* isn't quite the gripping read it used to be.'

'We need to talk about practice development. Wayne says we should give up on legal aid. You can re-invent yourself as a specialist in civil liberties. Harry the human rights lawyer, it has a ring to it.'

Harry groaned. He'd understood business consultants to be people who spent endless time and money writing down what you told them and then regurgitating it in jargon-ridden reports to be filed in the waste paper basket. Any hope of relying on Wayne to preserve the status quo was misplaced. Since he'd blipped off Crusoe and Devlin's radar, Wayne had metamorphosed from clueless solicitor into a dynamic evangelist for change. He fizzed with energy and ideas; every time he consulted his laptop, he came up with something new. Clear desk policies were only the start. Soon management-speak and documented processes would encroach on every aspect of Harry's working life like Japanese knotweed, smothering him with bureaucracy.

'Bloody Wayne. When I heard about his new career and glamorous girlfriend, I thought he must be suffering from delusions. Now it looks like pure unvarnished grandeur.'

'Don't be negative. He was at pains to assure me he isn't a seagull consultant.'

'A what?'

'Someone who flies in, craps over everything and then flies out again.'

'I'm not reassured. Let's talk another time.'

'All right. I'll schedule a meeting.'

Harry rolled his eyes. Another shortcoming of their upgraded computer system. Anyone could trespass into your diary or your email inbox. The tyranny of technology. Your life wasn't your own any more.

'If we must.'

'What's the matter with you?'

'Somebody wants me dead.'

Jim was as inscrutable as a warrior from First Emperor Qin's Terracotta Army.

'So what's new?'

◇◇◇

He was right, that was the scary thing. While Jim scrutinised the black-edged message, as though trying to decipher the Enigma Code, Harry mulled over the people who might bear him a grudge. In this line of work, you couldn't help treading on toes. Nothing personal, he assured himself. But then again…

Jim tossed the slip of paper back on to the desk.

'You may be looking peaky, but I still say the report of your demise is exaggerated.'

'You're all heart. Who could have sent it?'

Once upon a time, Jim had grown his hair long and shaggy, and every time he shook his head, the locks fell to mask his eyes. Now he had much less hair, and not simply due to the passage of time. His new barber was as ruthless and expensive as a high class hit man.

'Face it, Harry. The list must be endless.'

'Actually, I liked you better when you were unsuccessful.' Harry cast his eyes around the bare white walls. One of these days he'd pin up his framed posters of *Casablanca* and *North by North West*. 'Before you hit the big time.'

'If I'm that successful, why am I still in partnership with you?'

'You don't have long to wait to be rid of me.' Harry pointed to the sheet. 'Midsummer's Eve.'

'Doesn't say which year.'

'Always look on the bright side, huh?'

'Listen, someone's winding you up. Don't lose sleep over an out-of-season April fool. Just make sure you've paid your insurance premiums and written your will.'

Harry ran his hand through his hair. At least he still had plenty of it, though lately he'd discovered several strands of grey. Soon he'd have to stop kidding himself it was simply due to the stress of defending the indefensible. The cracking of his knees when he ran up stairs wasn't simply caused by a touch of damp in the air. He was getting older, though he wasn't confident he'd truly grown up.

'The envelope must have been delivered by someone close by. But Suzanne didn't notice anyone.'

'Maybe it came from someone who works for us.'

Harry shook his head. 'Can't see that.'

'You haven't upset Amazing Grace?'

'She wouldn't do something like this.'

As soon as he said it, he wondered why he was so sure. The secretary was their newest recruit. He hardly knew her.

'Have you asked Lou if he spotted anyone suspicious?'

'Old Hawkeye, are you serious?'

'Not really.'

Jim loosened his tie. It was made of silk and discreetly patterned; long gone the days when he favoured psychedelic designs and polyester. His dress sense had transformed since his wife's death after a short and terrible battle with kidney cancer. After six months of numb denial, he'd moved in with a woman young enough to be his daughter. He'd lost weight, and his suits these days were tailor made. Not like the shabby tweeds he'd favoured when a stone and a half heavier.

'So what's special about Midsummer's Eve?'

Spreading his arms, Harry said, 'Your guess is as good as mine.'

◇◇◇

Aled Borth might have cancelled their meeting, but Harry supposed he ought to look at the papers before the inquest opened in the morning. The Liverpool coroner, Ceri Hussain, was legendary for her efficiency and she expected lawyers appearing in her court to be fully prepared. Besides, he wanted to give a good impression. One evening a few weeks earlier, he'd fallen into conversation with her at a lawyers' networking event and they'd finished up having a drink together. She was recently widowed and, he guessed, as lonely as he had been after the death of his wife Liz. They hadn't met up again. But you never knew.

He picked up the phone. 'Grace, any idea where the Borth file might be?'

'Oh, sorry! I meant to put it back in the cabinet last night and ….I'll bring it in right away.'

She'd put down the phone before he could say there was no rush and within a minute she was in the room, thrusting the buff folder into his hand with stammered apologies.

'No problem, don't worry.'

She gave him a hesitant smile. A slim woman in her thirties, with dark waist-length hair, high cheekbones and anxious eyes. Her skin was pale, and the slits in her sleeveless black cotton dress revealed glimpses of white, unshaven legs. The magenta lipstick matched her nails.

'Would there be anything else?'

'Thanks, that's fine.'

The door closed behind her, shutting out the muskiness of her perfume. Grace had been with him for three weeks and he still couldn't make her out. She didn't wear a wedding ring and dropped no hints about her private life. At lunchtime she would be hunched over *The Road Less Travelled* rather than a word puzzle in *The Daily Mirror* or a sex-and-shopping blockbuster. You couldn't imagine her joining the girls who sunbathed out in the church gardens. She seemed to have nothing in common with the other secretaries, whose conversation—in the bosses' hearing—revolved around the shortcomings of the men in their lives, and their next holiday in Spain.

He couldn't settle to the chore of ploughing through the Borth file. At least he had an excuse. He sneaked another glance at the crumpled announcement of his death. The print and layout resembled a facsimile clipping from the *Liverpool Echo*. Someone had taken trouble to make it look like the real thing.

Might as well dig out the newspaper for comparison. He'd bought an early edition on his way back from court. The vendor had bellowed about a body on a beach, but Harry's mind was elsewhere. He was lost in wonder that he'd talked the magistrates into giving that career car thief a community sentence. He couldn't claim too much credit; the lad had the authorities' zealous pursuit of law and order to thank. The prisons were crammed to the rafters with recidivists paid to play Scrabble as a means of keeping the peace, so there was no room for anyone else. Chances were, his client was half way home to Runcorn now, scattering traffic cones on Speke Boulevard in someone else's Saab.

He pulled the *Echo* out of his briefcase and thumbed through the classified advertisements. The In Memoriam section ran to six columns of sorrow, without mention of his name. Of course not, it would be absurd. Today wasn't even Midsummer's Eve.

As he folded up the newspaper, the front page headline screamed at him.

WOMAN MURDERED AT WATERLOO.

Chapter Three

Some men were changed by murder, some men were suspected of murder, for some men murder was all in a day's work. With Harry Devlin, it was a mixture of the three. Years ago, his wife Liz had been stabbed to death and he'd stayed in the frame until he uncovered the truth. Since then, murder's cruel finality had obsessed him. Whatever Wayne Saxelby said, even twenty years in the legal profession hadn't killed off his yearning for justice. More than once, he'd come face to face with murderers, determined to confront them with their guilt. But he'd made himself a promise—leave detection to the detectives. He'd only bought the *Echo* to find out about this goal-hungry Italian striker the Reds had signed. The news story was a distraction. Yet he had to read it, couldn't help himself.

◇◇◇

The remains of a young woman had been discovered on the beach at Waterloo, just up the coast. Someone walking a dog at daybreak had stumbled across the body and raised the alarm. A detective superintendent described the crime as shocking and savage and said it was vital for the perpetrator to be caught before he struck again. He appealed for anyone in the vicinity of the beach the previous evening to come forward as a matter of urgency. It was too early, he said, to rule out the possibility that this death was linked to the killing of Denise Onuoha.

Denise came from New Brighton on the other side of the Mersey. A seaside resort that for years struggled to compete with Margate, let alone Marbella. First, the Tower was burnt down, then the pier went, finally they ripped out the open air pool that Harry and his mates swam in as kids. Lately New Brighton had checked in for regeneration therapy, but Denise's murder hadn't done any favours for its tourist appeal. Her remains were discovered on a tide-washed strip of beach below Egremont Promenade. There was enough left to make it clear that she hadn't died of natural causes.

In the absence of a quick arrest, the murder was soon relegated to a line among reports of bust-ups in the city council. The snap of Denise was fuzzy and out of date, but Harry recalled a pretty dark-haired girl in school blouse and blazer with buck teeth and the eager-to-please smile of a contestant in a talent show. She was eighteen years old and said to have dreamed of a career on the catwalk. The reports spoke of her as bubbly and fun-loving, a piece of journalese that covered a multitude of sins.

Harry had heard gossip about the Onuoha case over at The Latte of the Law, a swish café opposite the courts in Derby Square. Rumour merchants insisted that Denise's body had been mutilated in some bizarre fashion, prompting prurient speculation over countless espressos and blueberry muffins. What astonished Harry was that the full story hadn't leaked out. Some insider usually talked. Murder wasn't unknown in Liverpool, for all the statistics proving how safe the city was compared to supposed havens of tranquillity. The police would never keep things so tight without a good reason. There must be something out of the ordinary about the killing of Denise Onuoha.

And now another young woman had been found dead on a beach.

Another life wasted, another corpse left to moulder in the wet and wind. At the mercy of the sea, prey to tiny creatures with cruel appetites.

How could you do that to a fellow human being? He would never understand.

The story in the *Echo* ran to four terse paragraphs; the media conference must have finished minutes before the early edition went to press. Harry knew that if the police were unsure of a connection with the Onuoha case, they would never risk sparking hysteria. Something must link the killings; perhaps the murderer had a particular signature. Any time now, the city would echo with the newspaper vendors' hoarse cry.

'Serial killer on the loose!'

And people walking the streets would be shocked and frightened, but excited too.

Read all about it…who could resist?

'Serial killer on the loose!'

◇◇◇

'Any preferences for funeral arrangements?' Jim poked his head round the door to say goodnight. 'Flowers, donations? Just in case, I mean?'

'Piss off,' Harry said amiably.

'Remember, old son. That which doesn't kill us simply postpones the inevitable.' Jim nodded towards the Borth file. 'Doing plenty of spadework for the inquest, then?'

'I like to be prepared.'

'Liar. I suppose you want to make a good impression in front of the Coroner?'

'What do you mean?'

'Come on, Harry. You fancy the pants off her, don't you?'

'Ceri Hussain?'

Jim tapped the side of his nose. 'I'm not blaming you. Very attractive woman.'

'She's the Coroner!'

'No need to sound so indignant. Anyone would think I accused you of peering up the Queen's skirt. I wasn't the only one who saw you sloping off to the bar with her after that Legal Group meeting at the Adelphi.'

'We had a quick drink, that's all.'

'Oh yeah? Mind, she's a bit intense. You'd be good for her.'

'As light relief?'

'Why not? She spends her working life deciding how people came to die. Can't be a barrel of laughs.'

'The drink was a one-off. I didn't even ask for her phone number.'

'She's not long since lost her husband.' Jim's grin wavered for a moment. He knew about coping with the death of a spouse. Though his wife, unlike Harry's, and Ceri's husband, had died of natural causes. 'Makes sense to take it slowly.'

'I'm not taking it any way. This is just your fevered imagination.'

Jim smirked. 'Suit yourself.'

Harry put up two fingers as the door swung behind his partner. Nothing pleased him more than to see Jim putting the ravages of bereavement behind him. Carmel was doing him good. But his relentless humour was becoming a pain.

He switched off his computer and wandered to the window. Across the road loomed the Liver Building, its twin clock towers topped by giant birds resembling malevolent cormorants, each clutching a sprig of seaweed in its beak. One faced out to sea, supposedly watching for sailors' safe return, the other gazed towards the city, checking to see whether the pubs were open. People said that if ever the Liver Birds were to mate and fly away, Liverpool would cease to exist. Just as well they kept their backs turned to each other.

A faint noise from outside caught his ear. The grumble of vacuum cleaners had long since died down. He strained to listen. Was someone sobbing?

He poked his head out and looked up and down the corridor. The air was heavy with the tang of floor polish, pungent enough to make your eyes water. No-one was in sight. He listened.

Then it came again. A low, insistent sound. A young woman crying, he was sure of it. To both left and right, the corridor zig-zagged drunkenly, an elaborate designer touch to justify high rents. The idea was to relieve the monotony of long straight lines, so at regular intervals the corridors veered around kitchen areas, walk-in cupboards and spaces housing photocopiers, laser printers and other essentials of modern office life. As a result, you couldn't see far whichever way you looked.

The woman must be one of the night cleaners. Harry had glimpsed several of them since arriving here, a ghostly troop who wielded their mops like weapons. Often they chatted together in a foreign language he didn't recognise. The sensible thing was to keep his distance. Or better still, sneak off in the other direction and get away for the night. Let her sort herself out, whoever she was. But she might be in pain. If someone had hurt her….

He took a few steps in the direction of the lifts and called softly, 'Are you all right?'

Stupid question, but he didn't know what else to say.

Silence.

'It's Harry Devlin. What's the matter?'

He could hear sniffling, but she didn't reply. With a couple of strides, he rounded the bend in the corridor. The door to the kitchen was open. He moved forward, so that he could look into the room.

A young woman he'd never seen before was standing between the sink and the water cooler. He wasn't sure he'd ever encountered anyone looking quite so forlorn. She had short blonde hair, a pale tear-stained face and a handkerchief bunched in a small fist. It was as if misery had washed all the colour out of her. Even her linen overall was plain white, except for three tiny blue Cs on the breast. He recognised the logo: *Culture City Cleaners.*

'Is there anything I can do?'

'Nothing.' A local accent, for once. 'I'm fine.'

He thrust his hands in his pockets. At least the woman in white had answered. It was a start.

'Hey, I don't think so.'

'I didn't mean to disturb you. Sorry.'

He took another pace towards her. If nothing else, twenty years in the Liverpool courts had taught him not to fret about stating the obvious.

'You're upset.'

She dipped her head. Her hair was a mess of tangles. Dark roots showed.

'I cry easily.'

'Can I make you a cup of tea? It usually helps.'

A pause. 'You can't help, believe me.'

'But…'

'I have to go!'

She brushed past him and hurried down the corridor, sandals clacking on the wood-block floor. He watched until she disappeared out of sight, leaving a scent of room freshener in the air. A tang of cinnamon to remember her by.

◇◇◇

Ground level of John Newton House was deserted. From the lift, Harry saw the welcome desk was vacant, the bank of CCTV screens unwatched. The only hint of 24/7 security was the blinking red eye of the alarm. The plasma screen was blank and the pan pipes had fallen silent. All he could hear was a low electric hum and the eternal gush of the stainless steel waterfall. Black leather tub chairs formed a crescent facing the lifts. He'd never seen anyone sitting in them. Prints of modern artworks covered the walls, frantic splashes of red and yellow and green. With the interior lights dimmed, the leaves of giant palms cast spiky shadows. Through the curtain of foliage he glimpsed the world beyond the locked double doors. The Strand was a blinding pool of light.

He stepped into the foyer. The carpet smelled new, its soft clutch was like quicksand. The desk was light Scandinavian wood, vast enough to make a colossus of industry feel like a midget. On the wall, a shiny brass plaque listed the three small businesses resident in John Newton House. An image flickering on the surveillance screens caught his eye. He sneaked behind the desk to take a closer look.

One camera was trained on the entrance to the underground car park. The developers had carved it out of an ancient basement and only the priciest apartments in the building came with the right to a space, though until they were all sold there was room to spare. The BMW belonged to Wayne Saxelby; the only surprise was its lack of personalised number plates. But Harry focused on a sporty yellow Mercedes. Or rather, the woman clambering out of the driver's seat and fiddling in her bag for a key.

Juliet May.

Juliet, here? Impossible.

His heart thudded and he slammed his eyes shut, but when he opened them again, she was still in view. Striding towards the exit, bag tucked under her arm. Head held high, eyes gazing straight ahead. She moved like a woman who knew precisely where she was going. In the years since they'd last met, her red hair had been restyled and acquired blonde highlights, but it was Juliet, all right. The contours of her body were as familiar as if he'd embraced her only yesterday. In his mind he heard her gasps and cries when they were together in bed and she let herself go.

He hurried to the back door and let himself out into the courtyard. The brightness dazzled him and he shaded his eyes. The exit door from the car park swung open and Juliet May emerged. When she saw him, she stopped in her tracks and did an extravagant double take. Yet her gaze was steady, as if she wasn't in truth so surprised to see him.

'Harry.' He'd always loved her voice, cool and smooth as the touch of her skin. 'It's been a long time.'

He nodded, not sure what to say. She looked different some-how, and it wasn't just her new haircut. The lips, that was it. They were bigger than when he'd last kissed her, as if some cosmetic surgeon had got carried away with the collagen implants. Why had she bothered?

'I suppose it was only a question of time,' she murmured.

'We've moved our office here. The bulldozers have flattened Fenwick Court.'

'I saw your firm's name on the sign at reception.'

'You're visiting someone?'

Her smile tantalised. 'No, you and I are neighbours.'

'What do you mean?'

'I live here, of course.'

His heart missed a beat. 'In one of the flats?'

'What would you expect, the car park? I'm in one of the penthouses on the top floor. There's a balcony, with wonderful views. Sometimes I sit out in St Nick's Gardens, when they aren't packed with office girls eating their sandwiches. But it's not the same as lazing high above the city. I need to find time for a bit of sunbathing. Want to know my guilty secret? My tan comes courtesy of the sun centre in Rumford Street.'

She pretended to sniff with self-pity. She was slimmer than ever; at a distance, she might have passed for thirty. He didn't know much about fashion, but he guessed the grey business suit and matching handbag were her favourite, Donna Karan. And she was talking rapidly, not letting him get a word in edgeways. A tactic he recognised, to buy time while she gathered her thoughts. Not that he wanted to get a word in edgeways. It was enough to drink in the sight of her. Better take care to avoid intoxication.

'I heard about you and Casper.'

He didn't say he was sorry her marriage had broken up; she wouldn't have believed him. Her ex-husband was an entrepreneur whose charity fund-raising made gossip columnists drool, and whose wealth had politicians queuing up to trade honours for donations to party funds. What nobody dared mention was how Casper May made his very first million. He was a hard man and people who got in his way found themselves crushed. Literally, since he retained an interest in a scrap-yard near the river. One business rival was rumoured to have been fed to a metal-shearing machine, though the official line was that he'd skipped to Spain to escape the taxman. By sleeping with Juliet, Harry had taken his life in his hands. The madness of lust, how else to explain it? Splitting up with her had saved his skin.

'It was bound to happen. Didn't you once tell me that yourself?'

'You should have dumped him years ago.'

'You know something, Harry? I never did dump him. There's no point lying to you, he found this kid, a waitress working in a club he owns. Face of a fourteen-year old and heart of a whore. After all his affairs, he did the one thing I never expected. He fell in love.'

'It won't last.'

Casper May must be mad too, he didn't know when he was well off. Juliet studied him for a moment, before breaking into another smile that revealed perfect teeth. Even more perfect than before, like the delicate shape of her nose and the jaunty tilt of her breasts. She'd once told him that she didn't intend to grow old without a fight.

'You still wear that puzzled look. As well as permanently crooked neckwear.'

She bent close to straighten his tie. Soft hair tickled his face. He shrugged away his embarrassment, prayed that his face wasn't reddening.

'People don't change.'

'That's a depressing observation.'

'True, though.'

'Not of me, Harry. I've changed, haven't you noticed?'

'You look as good as ever,' he said carefully.

'You're too polite. Nature's had a bit of help, I don't mind admitting. Though the lip implants didn't work. An allergic reaction, I'm taking the clinic to court. But I wanted a new beginning. Please don't be offended that I didn't ask you to take up my case. Or handle the divorce.'

'It wouldn't have been a good idea.'

'I mean, we did agree on a clean break.'

He nodded. When the time came for them to part, they'd made a promise to each other. No recriminations and no further contact. At the time he'd feared he wouldn't be able to honour the bargain. But he'd stayed strong.

'Actually, I met someone else. His name is Jude. No jokes about obscurity, please. Only twenty-seven, but quite a hunk. He has a flat in the Colonnades, a stone's throw from your place.

We keep our own bolt-holes, though I spend nights there when he isn't away working. He's an actor, he's had a few small parts in films.'

'Am I allowed jokes about small parts?'

She grinned. 'Don't provoke me. Come to think of it, you may have seen Jude in *Coronation Street*.'

'Must have been an episode I missed.'

'I'd forgotten you're so sarky. No need to be nervous. I haven't breathed a word to Casper about you and me.'

'I guessed not. Otherwise I'd have been buried under the foundations of the Paradise Project long ago.'

Her eyes sparkled. 'We all need a little danger in our lives.'

'I'm too old for danger.'

'Casper's very respectable these days. His company's a major sponsor of culture in the city. But you look as though you could do with some fun. How are things?'

Should he mention the warning of death on Midsummer's Eve? Perhaps not.

'Same as ever.'

'I wanted to say, I'm so sorry about your brother.'

Harry's half-brother had died unexpectedly the previous autumn. He'd been visiting a friend in Bangor when he'd suffered a massive brain haemorrhage. Dead on arrival at Ysbyty Gwynedd. The two of them had never been close; in fact, they'd only known each other for a few years, so Harry had never been able to fathom why grief clubbed him like a back street mugger. Something to do with opportunities missed, he supposed. It had taken months to free himself of the gloom with which the news had enveloped him. Some days, he wasn't sure if he was rid of it yet.

'Thanks.' A thought struck him. 'How did you hear?'

'I like to keep in touch. It must be hard for you. Losing your parents in a car crash when you were a kid. Then your wife. Now this.'

His gaze settled on the solid bulk of the Liver Building. Maybe he was one more Liver Bird, powerless to tear himself away from the city, no matter what went wrong. Wind rippled the flags on the hotel across the road and blew his hair into his face. He brushed it away, telling himself she didn't mean to twist the knife, she was only trying to be kind.

'Well.' She checked her watch. Cartier, wasn't it? He recalled the care with which she placed it on the bedside table before they last made love. 'I'd better be going. It's lovely to see you, Harry. Now that we're so close, I'm sure our paths will cross again soon.'

Before he knew what was happening, she'd leaned forward and pecked him on the cheek. And then she was gone, rushing towards the door that led to the private lift for residents, rummaging in her bag for her security fob and key. She disappeared into John Newton House, leaving him with the memory of her plump new lips. They had never felt so cold.

Chapter Four

He'd meant to head back home to his flat in Empire Dock, but the encounter with Juliet changed his mind. He wasn't hungry or in the mood to cook. Besides, his idea of cooking was to rip the clingfilm from a ready-made meal in a box and sling it into the microwave. He'd wander into town for a drink. Maybe two.

Half a dozen middle-aged Japanese men dressed up to look like John Lennon boogied across Water Street. A bus screeched to a halt in front of them and the driver waved his fist, but they took no notice. There was a Lennon convention this week and the city was packed with tourists singing *Give Peace a Chance*.

◇◇◇

He crossed the road and headed for the Stapledon Bar in Drury Lane. It was frighteningly trendy, and the prices chilled his spine, but they served good beer. Accountants and bankers packed the place at lunchtime and for the first couple of hours after work, but now they'd be speeding home to their luxury barn conversions, making way for people from apartment blocks on the waterfront. Later on, chances were you'd be shoved aside by the bulky minders of rock singers and football stars *en route* for the VIP lounge, accompanied by a swarm of slinky blondes. Flashbulbs kept popping; the bar staff must have a hot-line to the paparazzi. The celebrities basked in the free publicity and the Stapledon boosted its reputation as a happening place. In the fame game, everybody played to win.

The entrance to the Stapledon was inconspicuous, but the bar area was much larger than you would have guessed from outside. The walls were covered with huge murals depicting a graphic artist's lurid interpretations of scenes from sci-fi classics. A kraken waking alongside a horde of extra-terrestrials wielding ray guns, a troop of triffids that looked like refugees from the foyer at John Newton House. On half a dozen TV screens suspended from the ceiling, Tom Cruise fled from Martian invaders in *The War of the Worlds*. A synthesised buzz hummed in the background; Harry recognised the theme from *Blade Runner*.

A notice by the door explained that the bar was named after a Thirties sci-fi novelist, Merseyside born and bred, yet boasting the unlikely first name of Olaf. He wrote novels about forms of intelligent life beaten down by an indifferent universe. A theme refined, Harry suspected, during Olaf Stapledon's wage-slave years, spent clerking at the Blue Funnel Line's office, round the corner from here.

Someone tapped Harry on the shoulder. The way today was going, he half-expected to come face-to-face with something slithery out of *Alien*. Not quite, but a short balding man with a wispy moustache and protuberant eyes between small rimless glasses. If he hadn't been wearing a blue and white football shirt, he might have been mistaken for a cryogenically unfrozen Dr. Crippen. This was Victor Creevey, the building manager from John Newton House.

'What will you have, Harry, my old friend?'

They weren't old friends. Harry doubted they ever would be, and not only because Victor supported Everton Football Club, but where was the harm in a drink or two? This evening he could use the company.

'Pint of Cain's, thanks.'

'You were last out?'

'From our office, yes. There was a cleaner…'

'I don't count the cleaners,' Victor said. 'The supervisor has a key to the alarm system so they can come and go as they please. Usually they knock off half an hour early, but I turn a blind eye.'

'This girl seemed in distress.'

'Lithuanian, was she?' Victor asked, as though this explained everything. 'The agency keeps sending kids from places you'd never believe. Estonia, Latvia, wherever. Illegals mostly, but it's not for me to ask questions if the contract price is right. Most of the girls don't speak proper English, you know.'

Harry knew plenty of English people who didn't speak proper English, but he let it pass. 'She's not Lithuanian.'

Victor shrugged. 'You know what these kids are like, Harry. She'll have rowed with her boyfriend or one of her mates. Happens all the time. I only hope she hasn't hung around after the rest of them have gone and triggered off the alarm.'

'She left before I did.'

'There you are, then. Nobody stays later than you and Jim Crusoe. The other folk usually scoot out the door by half five. The developers have only signed leases on a couple of other offices. You rattle around like peas in a tin. At least it makes my job easier.' His grin revealed small discoloured teeth. 'That's why it doesn't hurt if I play hooky once in a while.'

'The flats are moving, aren't they?'

Victor wrinkled his snub nose. 'Seen the prices they're asking? You could buy a five-bedroom detached in Woolton Village and still have change. When the agents released the first phase of flats, two dozen were snapped up. Buy-to-let speculations. Take a gander at John Newton House from the Strand one night. You won't see many lights. It's like the *Marie Celeste*.'

'I ran into someone who lives on the top floor this evening. Woman called Juliet May.'

'Keep your hands off, mate,' Victor leered. 'Do you know who she used to be married to?'

Harry was all innocent surprise. 'Mr. May?'

'Not any old Mr. May, my friend.' Theatrical pause. 'Casper May himself.'

'Ah.'

'Not a man to cross, Harry, take it from me.' The drinks arrived. 'Good health, mate.'

'But you said they are divorced?'

'Casper still likes to keep a close eye on her. Trust me.'

Harry tasted the beer, torn between the urge to find out and knowing that it was prudent to keep his nose out. Of course, there was only one possible outcome.

'How do you mean?'

'Why else would he install his ex in a penthouse at the top of a building he owns? Nice arrangement, if you ask me. Saves on alimony and if he fancies a trip down memory lane, he has a spare key. If you follow my drift.'

Harry winced. '*Casper May* owns John Newton House?'

'Didn't you realise?'

No, Harry didn't have the faintest idea. Casper doled out work to half the lawyers in Liverpool and Jim was among those who traded properties on his behalf. Jim didn't know about the affair with Juliet, but he'd sensed that Harry didn't care for Casper and never discussed what his client was up to. Harry's idea of hell was reading leases or balance sheets and he left the business side of the practice to his partner. Suddenly he understood how they could afford the rent. Jim must have done a deal on his fees to secure the premises on favourable terms.

'We signed an agreement with the developers.' He reached back into the trivia warehouse of his memory. 'Culture Capital Holdings, something like that?'

'Spot on. Casper May is chairman.'

Harry took a swig of beer as an aid to digesting this news. Jesus, he'd cuckolded his own landlord. For all he knew, this was a breach of one of the covenants spelled out in the small print of the lease that he'd never bothered to read.

'Bad day, mate? Why don't you come over and join us? Barney will be wondering what's happened to his dry martini.'

Victor gestured to one of the plush semi-circular booths at the back of the bar. The lighting was sepulchral, but Harry made out a tall, skinny figure in a dark suit, cradling a glass beneath a scene of manic book burning inspired by *Fahrenheit 451*.

'Don't let me interrupt your evening.'

'No problem, Barney will be made up to meet you.'

This seemed unlikely, judging by the tall man's languid pose, one long leg hooked over the other, but Harry followed as Victor bustled over. In the background, Vangelis had given way to Richard Strauss. *Also Sprach Zarathustra*, definitely the only tone poem Harry had ever stored on his iPod. As he exchanged cagey smiles with the man in the booth, he caught a pungent whiff in the air. A strange and unpleasant smell, yet somehow familiar.

'Didn't I tell you that Harry Devlin had moved into John Newton House? Meet the man himself! Harry, this is Barney Eagleson.'

Barney didn't stand up to shake hands. His grip was weak, his palm moist. Long dark hair flowed on to his shoulders and a nose stud glinted in the gloom. He wore a raffish black velvet jacket and had the hollow-eyed look of someone who'd just stepped out of a poem by Baudelaire.

'Harry Devlin himself, eh? Victor tells me you've been mixed up in lots of murder cases.'

'I'm a criminal lawyer. It's part of the job.'

'You're supposed to be a bit of a detective yourself.'

'That was a long time ago.'

'You'll have heard about the murder?' Victor asked.

'The body at Waterloo?'

'They say a serial killer is at work. Is that right, Barney?'

Barney put down his glass and raised a finger to his lips.

'Trouble is, Harry,' Victor sighed, 'This chap's an oyster, the soul of discretion. He won't say a word about what's happening with the investigation, even though he does have the inside track.'

'You work with the police?'

'Not exactly.' Barney's nose stud twinkled.

Victor leered. 'He's a mobile embalmer.'

A wild vision sprang into Harry's mind. Barney driving a van emblazoned with the slogan *Stop Me and Bury One*.

'I prefer to call myself a freelance restorative artist,' Barney said. 'I'm not tied to any particular undertaker. I'd rather be self-employed. I like the freedom. The hours aren't bad and weekend working doesn't worry me. Sorting out the tax and pension side is a small price to pay. You're in the service sector, Harry, you know what I'm talking about.' He dug into his trouser pocket. 'Take my business card. The website address is on there as well.'

'Website?'

'It's all about marketing these days, isn't it? Public relations. Have a look at my blog. I like to reach out beyond the embalming community. As a matter of fact, I've tidied up one or two of the corpses in cases you've been involved with.'

Harry didn't want to talk about the past. He tucked the card into his wallet and took a swig of beer.

'The body on the beach won't have been embalmed yet.'

'You're right. Denise Onuoha, though, she was one of mine.'

One of mine. The words hung in the air.

'Don't bother trying to persuade him to let on what the murderer did to her,' Victor said after a pause. 'Waste of breath, he's not telling.'

'I have to keep mum,' Barney said. 'Once an embalmer gets a reputation for…a loose tongue, he's finished.'

He gave Harry a cheeky wink, as though daring him to participate in a secret game. But Harry didn't know the rules

'They were saying on the radio that a serial killer's on the rampage.' Victor's small eyes shone with excitement. 'I heard an interview with Professor Maeve Hopes, the profiler. She says the first crime is the key. That's when the murderer makes most mistakes, before he's honed his skills. Fascinating, huh?'

'Victor is passionate about crime scene and forensic stuff,' Barney murmured. 'Can't get enough of it, he's a walking encyclopaedia. You name it—bite mark analysis, decoding the pattern of scattered bloodstains, Victor is your man.'

As he exchanged a grin with the building manager, Harry again sensed that he'd been excluded from some private joke. He gulped down the rest of his pint. A fascination for forensics was fine for a bloke who resembled Dr. Crippen, but Harry didn't fancy an evening in the company of a murderer's look-alike.

'I'd best be going. Must prepare for court tomorrow.'

Victor wagged an admonitory finger. 'You work too hard!'

'Lovely to talk,' Barney said. 'I'm sure we'll meet again.'

Harry shook hands again. No question, the man reeked of something strangely distinctive. He felt a *frisson* of repugnance.

'Don't worry, he's not sizing you up for a cold slab,' Victor said. 'Barney often drops into John Newton House. In between bodies, so to speak.'

When Harry reached the pavement outside, he halted to take in a lungful of evening air. Victor Creevey's words reminded him of that terrible morning all those years ago when he'd first encountered the smell that clung to Barney Eagleson.

In a chilly mortuary, gazing down at the waxed features of his dead wife.

The man stank of formaldehyde.

◇◇◇

The light on the answering machine flashed as Harry walked into his flat. He wasn't expecting a call. It was bound to be bad news. Those clients who weren't in trouble with the police were having their lives shredded by divorce or being ground into dust by the mills of litigation. They'd have to wait.

The flat was in sore need of a spring cleaning. Harry was a hoarder, though he couldn't explain even to himself why he was so reluctant to throw things away: books he'd not read for years, music seldom played, shirts too unfashionable even for him. He walked under the shower, sluicing away the stench of the morgue. His waist was thickening; it wasn't imagination that his suit trousers felt tight. In days gone by, he'd knocked back the pints and scoffed the chip butties without a second thought. They never made any difference. But things had changed.

'You're getting old,' he said to the misty bathroom mirror.

His reflection glowered back at him.

Not exactly Tom Cruise, he was forced to admit. He'd never been vain about his appearance. Too lazy to bother too much about it. Somehow he'd attracted Liz, and later Juliet May, and they were women who could pick and choose. In the end, they both chose to live with someone else.

Was Jim right, did he fancy Ceri Hussain? Irrelevant; he was out of her league. She'd taken a first at Cambridge, shone at both medicine and law, and written a learned treatise exploring obscure crannies of the Coroner's Rules. Close to forty, she was as glamorous as she was successful. When conducting an inquest, she was calm, sympathetic, patient, mistress of her own emotions while relatives of the bereaved succumbed to tears and rage. He'd learned from their chat that they shared a few things in common. Ceri might be keen on ballet, *Battleship Potemkin* and Bartok, none of which set Harry's juices flowing, but she also confessed to a weakness for Dionne Warwick, *Don't Look Now*, and Dashiell Hammett. For an hour in the bar at the Adelphi, she'd seemed at ease in his company, but he'd made no attempt to see her again, or even contrive a chance encounter that might lead to something.

'Feel the fear and do it anyway?' he asked himself.

His reflection cringed. Had it come to this, Harry Devlin quoting a management consultant? And what did management consultants know about fear, come to that?

He towelled himself dry and flung on a tee shirt and shorts. The flat looked out on to the Mersey and he opened the double window and spent ten minutes gazing at the river. It was the closest he ever came to therapy. He and Liz had flown inside the Grand Canyon and been serenaded in a gondola under the Rialto. But no question, this was his favourite view in the world. He loved to watch at sundown, when it seemed to him that the shades on the water differed subtly every time. Bathed in a peach-yellow haze, even the oil depot at Birkenhead on the opposite shore took on a mystical splendour. Not long ago the United Nations had categorised the Mersey as a dead zone, because of pollution rather than the homicide rate. But their statistics were thirty years out of date; maybe they should concentrate on securing world peace. These days salmon leaped in the Mersey, although Harry wasn't sure he was ready to swim in it.

He wandered into the kitchen, but didn't have the appetite for a proper meal. Grabbing a jumbo sized bag of hand-cooked sea salt and crushed black pepper crisps from the cupboard, he poured himself a glass of Coke. Healthy living could start tomorrow. Though if he was to meet his end in a few days' time, really, what was the point?

As he snacked, he took another look at the Borth inquest file. Aled Borth had come to him for advice following his mother's death. The late Nesta Borth, widow of a long-deceased bus driver, had been seventy-nine years old and suffering from enough ailments to provide a warning against the downsides of extended life expectancy. Yet her death at the Indian Summer Care Home in Crosby came out of the blue, according to Aled. He'd visited her the evening before her death and said she seemed as fit as a flea. A flea on extensive medication, but not at death's door. Aled's suspicion that Nesta had not died of natural causes was fuelled by the discovery in her bedside table of a codicil to her will executed a month before her passing. She'd left ten thousand pounds to Dr. Malachy Needham, who owned the Home. Aled, her only child, was incandescent, especially as her little terraced house had been sold to fund the care fees. Once the legacy was paid, there would only be buttons left for him. But there was nothing unusual in people becoming embittered about inheritance. It was when the post-mortem revealed unexpectedly high doses of morphine in Nesta's body, far in excess of therapeutic treatment levels, that Ceri Hussain insisted that the police started asking questions.

It didn't look good for Needham. Yet it didn't make much sense, either. He'd trained as a medic, and his wife was a nurse, but for years he'd focused on business ventures. Years ago he'd made a quick buck by retailing fake Beatles memorabilia, nowadays he had a finger in innumerable pies. He owned holiday homes in Tuscany and the Caribbean and drove a silver Rolls Royce, so he would scarcely risk life imprisonment for the sake of a measly ten thousand quid. Although hadn't Dr. Shipman, having successfully murdered countless patients, come to grief through forging a will which sought to cheat a daughter of her proper inheritance? Foolish, given that the daughter was a solicitor. Harry presumed Shipman must have wanted to be caught.

Needham had spent a small fortune proving his innocence, Harry reflected, as he sifted through the papers. He'd hired a shit-hot firm of London lawyers and their first move had been to threaten Aled with an injunction if he said anything defamatory about their highly respectable client. Their master-stroke was to instruct an expert in pharmacokinetics to examine the toxicological evidence. Professor Afridi from Edinburgh, a man with more qualifications than you could shake a stick at, had established that Nesta Borth's fondness for gin—testified to by everyone other than Aled—had turned her liver into a sodden, malfunctioning mess. As a result, her body had been incapable of excreting the opiates at the usual rate. The damage to her metabolism produced misleading toxicological results. She had indeed been given the right morphine doses and Needham was in the clear.

If Harry hoped Aled Borth would be glad to learn that his mother hadn't ended her days at the hands of a rapacious poisoner, he was soon disabused. As far as Borth was concerned, there were lies, damned lies, and expert medical evidence. Needham was guilty and that was that. When the Crown Prosecution Service sat on the file for month after month, he persuaded himself that the net was closing in on Needham. Once the CPS announced that no charges were to be preferred, he reacted with fury.

An inquest could now be held and Aled made clear to Harry that he intended to accuse Needham of murder in open court. Not a good idea, and this afternoon Harry had meant to talk some sense into him. A lawyer's job was to tell clients truths that they preferred not to hear.

Maybe one of those clients was behind the prank with the death notice. Surely it wasn't Borth?

He closed the file and flicked on the TV. There wasn't much on. He couldn't face yet another concert by rock stars with big cars and even bigger fortunes protesting about climate change and poverty, but the countless channels he zapped through with the remote offered nothing better. *Showbiz Darts, Amazing Traffic Cop Videos, Footballers' Wives Makeover Tips, Zoo Vet, Extreme Cosmetic Dentistry,* a repeat of *Celebrities without Shame*…no, no, too demoralising. He wasn't in the mood to watch Wayne Saxelby's girlfriend frolicking in the wet tee shirt that had made her reputation, and frankly hoped he never would be. Time to chill out with soft soul music. Drop down on the sofa and see what the shuffle came up with.

James Ingram. *This is the Night.*

But he couldn't settle. His eyes strayed to the answering machine. It sat uneasily on a wonky table that proved there was no such thing as simple home-assembly. Its monotonous blinking was a silent reproach.

With a sigh, he ambled across the carpet and pressed *play.*

A couple of clicks, followed by silence. Christ, don't say he'd been called up by a heavy breather…no, what was that?

Even though he strained his ears, he'd missed it. He turned the volume to maximum and played the tape again.

A distant, throaty whisper. Gender indistinguishable.

'*Midsummer's Eve.*'

The Second Day

Chapter Five

Sun streamed through the blinds as he awoke. Clothes lay scattered across the bedroom carpet. The previous evening had ended in a blur of canned beer and an old rock concert on TV. His throat was parched, but he felt much better than he deserved. It was summer, and the world wasn't such a terrible place. No need to be spooked by this Midsummer's Eve stuff. He luxuriated in a languorous stretch. New day, fresh start.

Someone was having a laugh at his expense. Nothing to fret about. When clients were sent to prison, some blamed their brief, even if their DNA was smeared all over the crime scene. If they walked out of court with not the faintest stain on their good name, police and prosecutors were equally pissed off. He turned on the shower and blinked water out of his eyes. Maybe he should have listened to Victor Creevey. All work and no play was a big mistake. Better get out more. If all else failed, he'd overcome a lifetime's prejudice against exercise for the sake of it, and join a gym.

He shaved with infinite care and chose his smartest suit. Not a time-consuming process, since his wardrobe boasted only one smart suit. The tie challenge was trickier, but he settled for something silky in blue by a designer he'd never heard of. Juliet had given it to him years ago as a birthday present after wondering aloud if he'd signed up for a Hideous Tie Convention. She had exquisite taste; that she'd married Casper simply proved that nobody gets it right all the time. He kept the tie for special occasions, and appearing in Ceri Hussain's court counted as a special occasion. He gave his shoes an extra shine.

Wandering into the kitchen, he trod on the crumpled mock-up of the death notice from the *Echo*. Last night it had spilled from his pocket and on to the tiled floor. He smoothed it out, shook his head, and tossed it into the waste disposal. Its destruction was accompanied by a satisfying roar.

Died suddenly? On this particular June morning he felt as if he'd been transported back to his student days, when he still believed he might live forever.

Drenching his muesli in milk, he half-listened to local radio. The headline item was the body found at Waterloo. A breathless reporter said that the police refused to discuss a possible link with the murder of Denise Onuoha. A dour DCI's muttered insistence that the police weren't ruling anything in or anything out, she took to mean that a madman was on the rampage.

He switched off and flipped down a TV screen mounted under the wall unit. A studio discussion about fear of crime. The guest was an expert on all matters criminal, a leather-clad woman with the bright eyes and body language of Squirrel Nutkin on speed. Professor Maeve Hopes, Victor Creevey's heroine.

'Should we be frightened? Of course not, Nemone. We need the maturity to dismiss these scare stories about social decline. The homicide figures speak for themselves.'

'But there are far more murders than half a century ago?'

The professor gave a smile of triumph. If she'd had a bushy tail, she would surely have wagged it. She'd stock-piled enough statistics to reduce Nemone to a pouting silence.

'We really must avoid clichés or knee-jerk response, Nemone. Let's put the data into perspective. The Home Office estimates that our proportion of murder victims per hundred thousand people is only a tad over the European average. And for goodness sake, compared to Finland...'

So that was all right, then. Harry picked up the remote and vaporised Squirrel Nutkin with a swift ruthlessness of which

Old Mr. Brown could only have dreamed. Time to venture out and witness poor old Nesta Borth's name being scrubbed off the murder list.

◇◇◇

'Mr. Borth's in reception.'

'I'll have ten minutes with him in meeting room one. Can you ask Grace to make a quick coffee for us, please?'

As he walked down the corridor, he clamped on an emollient smile, but the moment he reached reception, he saw it would take more than bonhomie to soothe Aled Borth. His client's eyes swam like reproachful goldfish behind spectacles whose cracked frame was mended with tape. At the best of times, rosacea gave his skin an unhealthy flush, and today his nose and cheeks were so empurpled that Harry half-expected him to keel over with a coronary the moment he clambered to his feet.

Two heavy canvas bags squatted at Borth's feet. A bad sign. Clients with their own bulging files of paperwork reckoned they knew more about the case than everyone else. Even if they did, it never helped. They researched the law with fundamentalist zeal, haunting dusty libraries until late at night, heedless that the books they studied were years out of date. Litigation became a passion, even if it afforded no pleasure. Aled Borth was single and worked irregular hours at the Waterloo Alhambra. He'd had too long to brood on his mother's death, and on the man he held responsible for it.

'Shall we be off, then?' he asked, ignoring Harry's proffered hand.

'Let's have a quick word before we leave for court.'

'What's the point? I cancelled the meeting yesterday because we've said all that needs to be said between us.'

Harry groaned inwardly. A solicitor and client engaged in a long-running court case that was coming unstuck resembled an aged couple in a loveless marriage. You'd stuck with each other for so long, it made no sense to part. Divorce was too much trouble, but it was a joyless journey as you struggled on together until the inevitable unhappy ending.

'I'd like to make sure I'm clear about your precise instructions.' Harry caught Suzanne raising her eyes to the heavens at his ersatz breeziness. She could spot a last throw of the dice when she saw one.

Before Borth could protest, he led the way into the first of the partitioned interview cubicles. He heard the Welshman's heavy, reluctant footfalls behind him and enjoyed a rare moment of smugness. First part of the mission accomplished.

'Fancy new offices you've got,' Borth said, scowling at an abstract print on the wall. It was captioned, enigmatically, *Synthesis*. Harry had to accept that it deserved to be scowled at.

'Thanks very much.'

'It wasn't a compliment!'

'Ah.'

'I mean, where does the money come from but law-abiding folk like me paying inflated fees? Daylight robbery, Mr. Devlin. What was wrong with your old gaff?'

'They knocked it down.'

Borth snorted, as if the demolition of Fenwick Court proved incompetence on Harry's part. He unzipped one of his bags and pulled out a ring binder. Settling down in his chair, he rested an elbow on the table as though about to start arm-wrestling. Instead, he flipped open the file. It was a confection of coloured tabs, careful highlighting and footnotes in a tiny hand. More artistic than *Synthesis*, Harry thought. How many hours had it taken him to put this stuff together, all in a lost cause?

'You're well prepared.'

Borth looked as though the words *One of us needs to be* trembled on the tip of his tongue. 'I know what has to be said today, Mr. Devlin. By myself, if you're not willing or able to speak for me.'

'My role is to act on your behalf. We discussed this when we met the coroner's officer and he talked you through all the statements.'

Borth hadn't even had any right to see the statements, but Ceri Hussain didn't want rabbits jumping out of hats at the inquest. She had authorised her officer, Ken Porterfield, to disclose to Borth the evidence obtained following the decision not to charge anyone in connection with his mother's death. Ken was a good-natured former vice cop, whose career had ended when a pimp high on heroin stabbed him in the thigh. Nothing much fazed him, but even Ken's affability was taxed when Borth insisted that any evidence that conflicted with Needham's guilt was tainted by skulduggery.

Borth puffed out his red cheeks. 'His mind was made up from the start, it was written all over his face.'

'Ken was a detective for twenty five years, and it was a textbook investigation.'

'The police were blinded by science.'

'We can't ignore the science,' Harry said gently.

'I'm not prepared to let this rest.'

'The coroner won't allow you to call Needham a murderer. That's not what inquests are for.'

'This is my Mum we're talking about, Mr. Devlin. Needham was responsible for her death. Call himself a doctor? Half the staff in the place can barely speak a sentence of proper English. There's been a cover-up, I'm telling you!'

'The Coroner will only want to hear from you on matters that cast light on how and why your Mum died.'

'I'll say what I like.'

'Please don't,' Harry said. 'It won't do you or your Mum any good.'

The door opened and Grace trotted in, bearing a tray of coffee. To his astonishment, Borth was transfixed by her appearance. As she bent to set the tray down on the table, she caught his eye and at once her cheeks, normally devoid of any trace of colour, turned as red as a Liverpool soccer strip.

She twittered something incoherent. It might have been an apology for the lack of biscuits, or something else entirely. And then she fled from the room.

◇◇◇

Liverpool Coroner's Court occupied part of the old Cotton Exchange. The building had once boasted a magnificent classic frontage, but after surviving the Blitz, it fell victim to an adversary deadlier than the Luftwaffe, the nameless planners who devastated the city in the sixties. They ripped off the façade and replaced it with a concrete carbuncle, in an act of vandalism that would have made Attila blush. A huge weathered statue that once sat upon a tower at the top of the building now squatted on a pavement outside a glass-fronted cafe, looking as lost as an old tramp.

Harry led the way into the inner courtyard. Borth hadn't uttered a word during the short walk from John Newton House, through the church gardens where he'd confronted Tom Gunter, along Chapel Street and into Old Hall Street. Usually he found it a challenge to keep his mouth shut for more than five seconds. Harry had no doubt that he and Grace recognised each other, and that the encounter had proved an unpleasant shock for both of them. He couldn't help indulging in wicked, fanciful speculation. Might they be former lovers, the fey woman and this frankly unpleasant middle-aged man? Strange bedfellows, for sure. Judging by their reactions, if there had been an affair, it hadn't ended happily.

A question nagged him. If the pair did know each other, why had Grace failed to recognise the name from the client file? Merseyside surely wasn't overflowing with Aled Borths.

'So where do we go?' Borth panted with the effort of lugging his two canvas bags through the streets. Serve him right. Twenty years of court work had taught Harry to travel light. The world was full of litigators with curvature of the spine.

'Turn right, there's a room where we can wait.'

'You think the inquest is a foregone conclusion,' his client said as they walked into the waiting room.

'Well, you never know.' Harry hoped this was kinder than a simple yes. 'But…'

'I tell you, the bastard's getting away with murder,' Aled hissed.

At that moment, his bête noir marched past the door, followed by a retinue of well-groomed young people who must be the team sent up by the shit-hot London firm of lawyers. They reminded Harry of Pod People from *Invasion of the Body Snatchers*: uncannily similar to human beings, but stripped of all passion. Malachy Needham glanced in and gave a brisk nod, the gesture of an important man, acknowledging his inferiors. Needham was tall, greying and slightly stooped, as though carrying an outsized ego through the years had angled his shoulders and bent his back. According to his statement, he was fifty seven years old; he would have started out in medical practice at a time when even a humble GP took deference as his due. And Harry would take a lot of persuading that Malachy Needham had ever been humble.

'Mr. Borth, we've been through this. The decision has already been taken. Dr. Needham will not be prosecuted. The coroner has no power to contradict what the investigators have decided.'

'My mother wasn't a secret drinker!'

Borth's face was so red, Harry was afraid he might burst. He put a restraining hand on the man's arm.

'No, Mr. Borth, that's the whole point. I'm sorry, believe me. There was no secret about it.'

As a single tear slid down the baggy, disfigured cheeks, Harry couldn't help it. His heart went out to the man.

◇◇◇

The coroner's court in Liverpool was large and airy. Harry had seen photographs of the old trading hall from which it had been carved. Ceri Hussain's chair occupied the place where, years ago, the cotton merchants' fireplace had stood. She looked thoughtful as her flunkeys organised the technology to permit the experts' evidence to be presented in such a way that laymen could understand. Even Harry, who was to IT what King Herod was to child care, recognised that the gleaming equipment was state-of-the-art. The video visualiser had a camera on top to enable the learned witness to demonstrate his point on screen.

Pictures could be shown on the high white walls, with power-point displays to help make sense of all the medical jargon. And there would be jargon, a lot of it.

The courtroom was crowded. Borth sat beside Harry, his cheeks dried but his breathing laboured. Most of the seats were taken by Needham's staff, advisers and miscellaneous flunkeys. The man himself had composed his features into an expression of benevolent concern. Care homes didn't flourish if questions were asked about the deaths of their residents. He was on his best behaviour, whatever his anger about the police investigation. And Harry guessed that this was a man capable of serious anger. The difference between him and poor Aled Borth was that Needham knew how to control it.

In charge of it all, quiet and unobtrusive, was Ceri Hussain. She was wearing a dark suit and blouse, well-cut but scarcely striking. She was so different from Juliet May; he had no sense that she yearned to be admired, far less desired. She acknowledged Harry with a nod as soon as she took her seat. He knew she'd be relying on him to make Borth behave and was anxious not to let her down. Easier said than done.

When she called Aled Borth to supply the short essential facts about his mother, she treated him with such kindness and encouragement that Borth seemed nonplussed. As he was when the questions suddenly stopped.

'Thank you very much, Mr. Borth, that will be all. I know this is difficult for you, but I am most grateful for your help. You may go back to your seat now.'

Borth was off the stand before he knew it. Harry allowed himself the luxury of a sigh of relief. So far, so good.

The toxicologist, a Gene Hackman look-alike with a Derbyshire burr, talked a lot about the half-life of drugs and exponential decay. Half-life, Harry reflected, as a variety of Delphic equations scrolled down the screen, was quite a phrase. So many people only lived a half-life. Maybe he was one of them, maybe he ought to do something about it before the decay went too far.

Ceri Hussain's gaze flicked from witness to screen. Evidently she understood everything the man said. Not even an Oscar-winner could feign such interest, or be confident that she was nodding in all the right places. She was scarily bright; he remembered that she'd qualified as a doctor before turning to the law. She'd made partner in a national firm before giving it up to become Coroner of the City of Liverpool. To live with such a woman must be daunting. How could you hope to compare? Was this, he wondered, the reason behind her husband's death—had he yielded to a sense of inadequacy as overwhelming as a tidal wave?

Ricky Hussain had committed suicide earlier in the year. One evening he'd swallowed some whisky and pills and pulled a plastic bag over his head. Ceri had returned home to find his body slumped in an armchair. He was a salesman who had set up his own business and the rumour mill suggested his finances were over-stretched. What the full story was, nobody knew. It hadn't come out at his inquest, that was for sure.

Ceri had spent years consoling the bereaved and now she had to come to terms with her own loss. He guessed that she felt guilty, it was common enough. But she was dealing with her husband's death in the way she knew best, by throwing herself into her work.

'Professor Afridi, would you be kind enough to take the stand, please?'

The guru sashayed over to the box, a Hollywood star strolling on set to meet a chat show host in front of an audience of hand-picked admirers. As he took his seat, he surveyed the court and gave a slight shake of the head, as if to still an imminent outbreak of applause. Harry rolled the word *pharmacokinetics* around on his tongue as the professor occupied five minutes by describing his degrees, honours, publications and miscellaneous achievements. He was an immodest man with a lot to be immodest about. As he explained the data, Harry had no doubt that Nesta Borth hadn't quite managed to drink herself to death before her heart gave out, but it had been a close run thing. There was no case for Needham to answer.

Nevertheless, a lawyer has to earn his corn. As he rose to his feet, Harry felt uncomfortably like a schoolboy invited to bowl a few off-breaks at an Australian Test batsman. He cleared his throat.

'Now, Professor, you're clearly one of the world's leading authorities…,'—on second thoughts, he still wasn't quite sure how to pronounce pharmacokinetics—'in your field…'

'Thank you.'

'Is it not possible, though, that there might be room for doubt here? Another way to interpret the evidence?'

'Such as?'

'That Nesta Borth died of an injection of morphine improperly administered and in excess of the therapeutic dose and that the liver damage we have heard about has merely confused the facts?'

The professor sucked in his cheeks as he considered this. Harry was suddenly gripped by excitement. Was this his Clarence Darrow moment? Hadn't the great attorney said that lost causes were the only ones worth fighting for? What would Ceri Hussain make of it if, with a single casual question, he cracked the case wide open?

The professor cleared his throat. Harry found himself leaning forward, waiting for the reply.

'No, Mr. Devlin, I fear it is you who may be confused. As you might have gathered from listening to *and understanding* the evidence I have given over the past twenty minutes, your suggestion represents a fundamental misreading of the data. With respect to those who had care of the late Mrs. Borth, it would amount to a calumny as illogical as it was unfair.'

Afridi allowed Harry the glimmer of a smile. Harry winced. Darrow, he recalled, had also said this: *I have never killed a man, but I have read many obituaries with a lot of pleasure.* Right on, Clarence.

Suddenly, Aled Borth sprang to his feet.

'I've had enough of this farce! Call this British justice? My mother wasn't some old dipsomaniac. A touch of sherry on special occasions was her limit. She was murdered, I tell you! Poisoned by that man!'

He pointed across the courtroom at Malachy Needham as the London lawyers quivered with outrage like reeds in a gale. The toxicologist cringed in embarrassment. Needham alone seemed unmoved, his face a mask.

Harry hissed, 'Please, no more. This isn't helping.'

Ceri Hussain half-rose in her chair. 'Mr. Borth, I realise this is distressing for you and I'm anxious to afford you latitude as the only child of the deceased, but I cannot allow you to indulge in wild accusations. Please resume your seat.'

And it was her words, rather than Harry's, that silenced Borth.

◇◇◇

'They had us for breakfast!' Borth said bitterly back in the waiting room. 'I wasted my money on you. What chance does an ordinary working man have, up against the likes of Needham and his bank balance? Professor Afridi versus Harry Devlin. It's a bit of a mis-match, frankly.'

Harry didn't point out that he was a solicitor, not a magician. The client is always right. Or, at least, should always be allowed the last word.

'The coroner listened carefully to what you had to say.'

'For the sake of appearances. You professionals, you all stick together, you're all in the same club.'

Harry stood up and offered his hand.

'I'll see you at the Alhambra tonight.'

'I shan't be there. I'll be going through the file. Work out grounds for an appeal.'

Harry smothered a sigh and headed for the door. In the passageway outside, by the reception counter at the coroner's office, Ceri Hussain was in conversation with a secretary. When she saw Harry approaching, she detached herself.

'How is Mr. Borth?'

Harry glanced back towards the waiting room. 'He'll get over it. But this case has been his life for months. It'll take time.'

'You did your best for him.'

'Thanks. I only wish he felt the same.'

She arched her eyebrows. 'Not expecting gratitude, are you?'

He grinned. 'Not really.'

'It's good to see you again.'

'And you.'

He was wondering about this conversation. Ceri Hussain didn't bother with idle gossip. Should he ask her out? That smooth operator Wayne Saxelby would know by instinct what buttons to press. Maybe this was the area in his life where he needed the input of an expert consultant. How to build a relationship to last.

'I enjoyed our chat at the Adelphi. We must do it again sometime.'

Jesus. An opportunity, to be grabbed with both hands.

'May I give you a ring?'

'Do.'

He beamed. 'Great. Well…see you again.'

As he turned to go, she laughed and said, 'Don't you need my number?'

'Oh, yes. Please.'

She took a business card from her bag and jotted on the back. 'Here, that's my mobile.'

'Thanks.' A thought struck him. 'You don't happen to like Polanski, by any chance?'

'As a film director, yes. *Chinatown* is one of my favourites.'

'Mine too. It's a long shot, but if you're free tonight, they are showing a new print of *The Tenant* at the Waterloo Alhambra.'

'The Alhambra? Isn't that where Mr. Borth…'

'He won't be there,' he said quickly.

'Well, I doubt he'd be very pleased to see you and me together at the cinema today of all days, but if you're sure…'

'That's what he told me.'

'I have a few reports to prepare, but apart from that, I'm at a loose end. What time are we talking about?'

'Ten o'clock. It's a late night screening, a series the management calls Just Because You're Paranoid…'

'As in…it doesn't mean they're not still out to get you?'

'Spot on. I'll be honest, if you're looking for a feel-good movie, *The Tenant* is to be avoided. It's not exactly *The Sound of Music*.'

'Can I confess a guilty secret? I always loathed the Von Trapp kiddies and their do-re-mi. Give me a bit of darkness any time. Shall we meet outside at a quarter to?'

'How about half past nine, and we can have a drink at the bar?'

'Perfect.'

Knowing that Wayne Saxelby would advise against a show of excessive delight, he contented himself with a brisk nod and left her at the counter. On his way out, he bumped into a red-faced man in his fifties whose navy blue suit struggled to contain his bulk. Ken Porterfield, the coroner's officer, was in his customary affable mood.

'Bad luck, Harry. You were never going to pin anything on Needham. More's the pity. He's a snake, that bloke.'

'You took a dislike to him?'

'Not simply over this, though he was an arrogant shit to interview. I'd have sympathised more, if I hadn't come across him before. Not that he remembered me, thank Heaven, I was too insignificant to register on his radar.'

'When was this?'

'Must have been ten years ago. He was in the porn business then.'

'Seriously?'

'Yeah. Nasty stuff, under-age girls, supposed snuff movies imported from the Continent. Even more lucrative than the medical profession, no wonder he hung up his stethoscope. As for residential care, it's a neat way to launder the profits as well as providing a legitimate source of income. I expect he still has his finger in a few dodgy pies. You can usually judge a man by the company he keeps. Present company excepted, Harry.'

'You don't think it's possible one or other of them murdered dear old Nesta?'

'Do me a favour. Ten thousand is loose change for people like that. Needham's hand in glove with Casper May, you know.'

'No, I didn't know.'

Ken Porterfield patted his paunch with inexplicable pride. 'Mind, if he knows what's good for him, he won't get the wrong side of Casper. People who make that mistake tend to finish up dead. Ever crossed swords with Casper yourself, Harry?'

'Not exactly.' A vision swam into Harry's mind of Juliet May's bare body, stretched out beneath his. He made a performance of checking his watch to cover his confusion. 'Well, good to have a word. See you around.'

He strode out into the courtyard, keen to escape. Standing on the pavement of Old Hall Street, beyond the wreath-laden war memorial, was Aled Borth. He must have scurried out while Harry was talking. In his hand was a newspaper and he was staring at the front page, open-mouthed.

Harry waited until Borth had moved on and then strolled to the nearest news vendor. There was only one story on the posters, only one of any consequence on the front page.

WATERLOO MURDER—WOMAN NAMED.

Chapter Six

What's in a name? Harry asked himself. Specifically, what's in the name of Lee Welch?

He'd stopped off in a café opposite Exchange Flags to study the newspaper. The office could wait. He was sure Aled Borth had been shocked by something he read. The man seemed even more startled than by his puzzling encounter with Grace in the office. His hands shook so much that Harry half-expected him to let the tabloid sheets slip from his grasp and fall to the ground.

Yet the story didn't say much, apart from naming the woman found dead at Waterloo as Lee Welch, aged 21. The report was accompanied by a holiday snap apparently taken on the beach of some Spanish resort. She had shoulder-length bleached blonde hair and a neck tattoo. An unnamed neighbour described her as bubbly and fun-loving. The same epitaph as bestowed upon Denise Onuoha, and, it sometimes seemed to Harry, upon everyone young who met a tragic end.

The senior investigating officer kept it vague: 'Police inquiries are continuing and we are following up a variety of leads.'

In other words, they didn't have a clue. The SIO dead-batted suggestions of a link between Lee's death and Denise's, while appealing to the public for fresh information. Nothing there to set Aled Borth's pulse racing. Could something else have spooked him? Unlikely that Liverpool FC's latest activity in the transfer market would provoke such a reaction. There were a few small box advertisements, for sofas, digital hearing aids, and Mediterranean cruises, and that was it.

It must be the name. The only explanation Harry could conjure up was that Lee Welch herself meant something to Aled Borth.

Perhaps she was a patron of the Waterloo Alhambra? Harry struggled to believe that he and the dead girl had been friends. Even allowing for mood-darkening effects of bereavement, anyone less bubbly and fun-loving than poor old Aled you wouldn't meet in a day's march.

He checked his watch. Time to get back. It was chilly for June, with the threat of rain, but his mood was jaunty as he strode down Chapel Street. Of course, he knew better than to expect that anything serious might develop between him and Ceri Hussain. She was just interested in his company, without strings; but she'd given him something to look forward to. Since he'd split up with Juliet, he'd had a few flings, but none that meant much either to him or the women. It suited him to be beholden to nobody once he retreated to Empire Dock and locked his door on the world outside. When he'd heard that his half-brother was dead, he hadn't wept, though there was so much that the two of them had never said to each other. But the loss of the last close member of his family deepened his sense of isolation when he sat in his flat and watched the river swirl by.

By the time he reached the cut-through at the Parish Church, he'd persuaded himself that things were looking up. He'd rid himself of the Borth case. Tom Gunter wouldn't cause any more trouble if he wasn't provoked again. Maybe it was time to give his life a makeover. If Liverpool could reinvent itself, why couldn't he?

He strolled into the gardens where he'd confronted Tom Gunter. Twenty-four hours later, everything was quiet. This was the oldest corner of Liverpool, but few guessed its bloody history. During the Black Death, it served as a burial ground for plague victims, and in the Civil War the church served as a prison for both Cavaliers and Roundheads. Two hundred years back, the old spire crashed into the nave, killing a group of girls from a charity school. The Luftwaffe's bombs destroyed the church, but it rose again from the wreckage. Now the graveyard was a quiet oasis of shrubs and trees strong enough to withstand the salty wind. The planting had a Biblical theme: wormwood, laurel and a Judas tree.

He paused by one of the benches. It wasn't sitting-out weather and there were few people around. A young black woman in a business suit typed with two fingers on a laptop, an elderly couple poured hot drinks from a Thermos flask. In the eighteenth century, a coffee house had stood in the corner of the churchyard. It was a place of business as well as for relaxation. Shackles were fixed for slaves who were auctioned, and the successful bidders shipped them across the Atlantic in return for cotton, sugar and rum. Before abolition, Liverpool was the centre of the slave trade. The city grew rich from the sale of human lives.

◇◇◇

'Harry!'

Juliet May stood at the iron gate to the gardens, swinging a bag from hand to hand. She wore a sleek grey single-breasted jacket and low-cut blouse, with spotless high-waisted white pants. After a moment's hesitation, he walked towards her.

'I've not seen you for years, now it's twice in two days.'

'Now I live in the same building where you work, we're bound to bump into each other.'

'I suppose.'

'I hoped you would be pleased, that the two of us are so close again.' That familiar, tantalising smile. 'At least in terms of geography.'

'I hear Casper owns the building.'

'Of course. Didn't you know?'

'Not until last night.'

She laughed. 'I told you, Casper knows nothing about you and me. Just as well. He's very proprietorial.'

'Even now, when your marriage is over?'

She sighed. 'We were more than husband and wife. We've been business partners for years. It's a tax thing, I don't understand the details. He still needs to keep me sweet. It's in his financial interest.'

'And in return, he keeps you in the style to which you're accustomed?'

'A sensible business arrangement. A win-win situation.'

'So where does Jude fit in?'

Her brow clouded. 'Who knows? He's away in London for an audition.'

He cleared his throat. 'I need to clear my desk for the day.'

Again she laughed. 'You're special, Harry, do you know that? I never met anyone quite like you.'

Probably she meant it in a good way, but it wasn't the right time to find out. 'Good to see you, Juliet.'

As he walked towards the path that led to the Strand and the main entrance to the offices, she called after him.

'The penthouse is lovely. Views to die for. On a clear day, I kid myself that I can see America. Come up and have a look sometime.'

He glanced back over his shoulder. The glossy, plumped-up lips formed a smile that didn't seem quite natural. Her eyes followed him, their expression impossible to read.

◇◇◇

His room was in chaos.

Hands on hips, he surveyed the scene from the doorway. It was as if some demented conceptual artist had created a tableau of bureaucratic disorder as an entry for the Turner Prize. Someone had pulled all the buff folders out of the cabinets, and strewn their contents all over the floor. Court documents, legal aid forms, fliers from recruitment agencies and expert witnesses. And there were business cards, magazines, the framed certificates he kept on the wall. Nothing left untouched.

Jim wandered towards him, heading for the kitchen. He'd forsworn caffeine and kept consuming endless cups of water. Since Carmel had moved in with him, she'd persuaded him of the need to cleanse his colon and lymph glands of all impurities.

She'd even lent Harry a book about extreme detox diets, but the first couple of chapters had set his bowels trembling, and he'd decided to remain impure.

◇◇◇

'What's up?'

'Someone's trashed my room.'

'How can you tell?'

'Very witty. Take a look.'

His partner joined him at the door and contemplated the mess.

'So much for the paperless office, eh? Couldn't you find something? Did you have to turn the place upside down?'

'I haven't laid a finger on it.'

'This isn't your secretary's new filing system?'

'I know you're not a member of Grace's fan club, but…'

'She's weird, admit it.'

'No, she's…interesting.'

'You think weird *is* interesting.'

'She had nothing to do with this. It's so pointless. Who would want to wreck my room?'

'You tell me.'

'I need to check whether anything has been stolen.'

'You left your wallet here?'

'No, of course not.'

'Don't take this the wrong way, Harry, but why would someone steal anything from you other than cash or credit cards?'

'Someone may have been searching for something. Rummaging for confidential information in one of the files.'

Jim's pitying look said it all. 'You think that's likely?'

'Not really.'

'It's kids.'

'Kids?'

'Some little bastards who were excluded from school, and wanted a break from vandalising phone booths and spraying graffitti on garage doors. Thank your lucky stars they haven't pissed all over your file notes.'

Harry hadn't considered that possibility. He sniffed the air cautiously. Nothing.

'Why choose my office?'

'Be honest, old son. You set a gold standard in attracting trouble. It's a wonder we can still get insurance.'

'This is the fifth floor. It's not as if you can peer through the window from outside and make sure I'm not around. Breaking into my office makes no sense.'

'Nobody broke in. You never lock up.'

'There must be twenty rooms on this floor alone, not counting cupboards. An intruder could have been disturbed at any moment.'

'It's quiet at this end of the building. Most of it's lying empty. Where's the fun in trashing a vacant office?'

'Maybe they aren't far away.' Harry took a couple of paces down the corridor. 'Suppose they're hiding somewhere close by?'

'Where are you going?'

'To find whoever did this.'

'Waste of time.' Jim pointed to the door opposite Harry's office. 'That room connects with a couple of others. None of the doors are locked during the day. Fitters wander in and out every five minutes. Plumbers, electricians, you see them all the time. The prankster who messed up your room will be long gone by now.'

'I'll nip down to reception and see if Lou spotted anything out of the ordinary.'

'You'll be lucky. We could be subject to asteroid attack and Lou wouldn't bat an eyelid unless it interfered with reception on his portable TV.'

'Even so.'

Harry raced down the corridor. He gave the lift a miss, wanting to see if an intruder lurked on the stairs. The carpet muffled the sound of his pounding feet as he headed down from floor to floor, but he didn't see another soul. By the time he reached the ground he was out of breath.

Up on the vast plasma screen, an architect as glossy as one of the Stepford Wives preached the glories of Liverpool redux.

'*Reinvigorated docklands....multi-faith street furniture...a cultural logarithm with conference facilities...*'

Behind the welcome desk, Lou was resplendent. Casper May's company had kitted him out in a smart navy blue uniform with extensive brass trimmings. He might have passed for a rear-admiral, but for the sign on the desk labelled *Concierge* and his ceaseless gum-chewing. He was conferring about prospects for the next World Cup with an asthmatic crony with a scary wheeze. Like all Lou's friends, the crony had a characteristic smell. He reeked so strongly of boiled cabbage that, for all the lavish décor of the foyer, Harry was transported back to the school canteens of his youth.

He coughed and Lou glanced up, allowing his grizzled features to fold into an expression of concern.

'All right, mate? You're all flushed. Out of condition? You don't want to overdo it, you know. We're none of us getting any younger.'

'Have you seen an intruder in the building?'

Lou's bushy eyebrows wouldn't have looked out of place in a border at Croxteth Park. They jiggled slightly, the closest that Lou came to indicating intense reflection.

'Sorry, mate. What's the problem?'

'Someone has turned over my room.'

Lou chewed more slowly as he considered this.

'Much gone missing?'

'Not as far as I can tell.'

'You dropped lucky, then.' A mournful sigh. 'It'll be teenage scallies, bet your bottom dollar. Bring back national service, that's what I say. Give them some backbone. Discipline.'

The asthmatic friend gave an affirmative gasp, but before he could confirm that the country was going to the dogs, Harry said, 'So you haven't seen anyone suspicious?'

'You get all sorts in here at the moment. Talk about Piccadilly Circus. It's not possible to keep track.'

'But surely…'

Lou gave a reproachful shake of the head. 'I don't have eyes in the back of my head, Harry, do I now?'

'I suppose it's too much to expect that the CCTV…'

'On the blink, isn't it? I was telling Victor, they'd have done better to invest in Japanese technology.'

'You can't beat the Japanese,' his aged pal croaked.

'Not these days, anyhow,' Lou said. 'Makes you wonder who won the bloody war, eh?'

Harry gave up and took the lift back to his room, to discover Grace bending to pick up a couple of sheets of paper. When she heard his footfall, she gave a start and a little shriek. Her cheeks were tinted crimson.

'Sorry. I thought I ought to help. Mr. Crusoe told me what had happened.'

'Don't worry. I'll sort it all out before…'

His voice trailed away as he caught sight of the PC monitor on his desk. The screensaver had vanished; presumably Grace had touched the mouse by mistake in her hapless attempts to tidy the room up.

Someone had opened his calendar. Normally he set it so as to view a week at a glance, but the setting had changed so as to show a single day. The whole of it was blocked out.

The date wasn't today, but 23 June.

And to make sure the point was not missed, someone had typed in two words.

Midsummer's Eve.

◇◇◇

Grace offered to stay late to help him clear up, but he shooed her out, promising she could leave it to him to get the room straight. But he didn't say when.

Through the window he watched the black hands of the clock on the Liver Building. With every minute that ticked by, Midsummer's Eve drew closer.

'*The Big Clock*,' he muttered to himself. Another film that fascinated him, the story of a man called Stroud, hired in a race against time to find a witness to murder, so that he could be silenced. His boss didn't realise that Stroud was the witness. He was hunting himself.

Jim was right. He'd fallen victim to a joker with a childish sense of humour and too much time on his hands. He didn't fret about the cascade of emails from spammers cluttering his inbox, urging him to invest in Viagra or share his bank account details. He'd pay no attention to this, either. Getting on with life was the best retaliation. He deleted *Midsummer's Eve* from his calendar, together with an email from the Law Society urging him to be vigilant to detect money laundering.

Or too much time on *her* hands? The joker could be anyone. You never knew.

Enough. He must stop dwelling on it.

He yanked the Borth file out of his briefcase and started tidying up the loose ends so that the papers could be archived. Better not think about how much time and money he'd written off through agreeing the fixed fee. Wayne Saxelby would be aghast if he knew. He was muttering into his dictaphone when he heard a gentle tap on the door. The timidity of the sound caught him by surprise. Usually people marched straight in without a second thought.

'Come in.'

The face of the cleaner he'd met the previous evening appeared round the door. Her cheeks still had no colour, but at least they were no longer wet.

'Can I empty your bin?'

Before he could say yes, she took in the state of his room and exclaimed in dismay.

'What's happened?'

He climbed to his feet and spread his arms. 'Someone decided to reorganise my files.'

'A burglar?'

'I don't think so. No-one in their senses would come here to steal.'

'But this is a solicitors' office.'

'Exactly. Not worth robbing. We don't keep sacks of cash on the premises. Any thief would only get the slimmest pickings.'

'Then why…?'

'I must have upset someone.'

'You, Mr. Devlin?'

He wasn't sure why she sounded so astonished. 'It happens. And do call me Harry.'

She blushed and, as if to cover embarrassment at his familiarity, bent down and picked up a set of documents tied together by a treasury tag. 'The supervisor asked me to look after this side of the building. Your usual girl is off sick.'

'Sorry to hear that.' A meaningless response. He hadn't yet registered who the usual cleaner was.

'Don't be. She probably smoked one joint too many, that's all.'

'You needn't worry about all this.' He waved at the floor. 'It's not your job to clear up after trespassers.'

'No problem. I like cleaning.'

'You do?'

When she frowned, he realised his question might have offended her. He hadn't intended to scoff, all he meant was that he couldn't imagine anyone enjoying having to clear up after others.

'Sorry, I didn't…'

'It's all right. Even the supervisor thinks I'm off my head. But it's true. I get a kick from sorting out. Rearranging stuff, putting things in order, making sure they are all in the right place. Does that sound strange to you?'

Harry cast his mind back to the night cleaners at the old offices, a bunch of cackling harridans whose day job was probably as warders on Walton Jail's maximum security wing. They had once skived off early and locked him in the building after he'd had the temerity to ask them to mop up a spillage on the kitchen floor.

'Different, yes. But I'm not complaining. By the way, I don't know your name.'

'Gina.'

'Okay, Gina, let me give you a hand.'

He joined her on hands and knees, scrabbling around on the floor and scooping up the sheets and trying to find the folders where they belonged. She still had a tang of cinnamon. After a couple of minutes they backed into each other and both burst out laughing. He turned to face her.

'I'm glad you've recovered from whatever upset you yesterday.'

She coloured. 'I wouldn't say I'm over it. Thanks all the same.'

'Do you want to talk about it? Whatever was on your mind?'

She pointed to the pile of correspondence they had amassed. 'You didn't want to talk about your problem.'

'This isn't a problem.' When she raised her eyebrows, he realised he'd spoken too sharply. 'I don't know who did this. It's a minor inconvenience, that's all.'

'Yeah, right. Someone picked on you for no reason?'

'Why not? Teenagers playing truant, I expect.'

'This is the fifth floor, Mr. Devlin. Why would any teenagers wanting to cause trouble flog all the way up here?'

'They didn't run much risk of being caught. With so many empty offices…'

'Why bother? It doesn't add up.' She pursed her lips. 'If you ask me, someone did this deliberately to cause grief for you.'

'Thanks,' he said. 'That's cheered me up.'

'Sorry, Mr. Devlin…'

'Harry.'

'Sorry, Harry, but it won't do any good telling lies to yourself, to make you feel better.'

She had located his calendar among the debris. She dusted it off and handed it to him. Today's message wasn't encouraging. *The best thing about the future is that it only comes one day at a time.*

He put it back on the desk and gazed down at her. Something impelled him to say, 'Is that why you were crying last night? Because you refuse to lie to yourself?'

She hauled herself up off the floor and looked him in the eye. 'Why do you ask?'

'Tell me to mind my own business, if you like.'

She closed her eyes. 'If you must know, a friend of mine died yesterday.'

Self-loathing stabbed him. Why did he always have to keep prying? 'Christ, I'm…'

'You weren't to know.' When she opened her eyes again, to his horror he saw that tears were forming. 'But what happened was terrible. It wasn't an ordinary death.'

He caught his breath. 'Is any death ordinary?'

'Not this one, for sure. She was murdered.'

'Not the girl they found on the beach at Waterloo? Lee Welch?'

'How do you know her name?'

'They printed it in the *Echo*. Someone has identified her.'

'Not me, thank God.' Gina stared at her trainers. 'I couldn't have gone to the morgue and seen her there, all waxy and lifeless. It would have broken my heart to see her dead.'

For a while neither of them said anything. At last Harry said, 'If ever you do want to talk about it…'

'I wasn't in the mood yesterday, for sure. But you were kind to me. So, thanks.'

'Anyone would…'

'No, you're wrong. I haven't been cleaning offices for long, but I soon learned that most people look straight through you. The moment I put on this overall, I become an invisible woman. At least you spoke to me like I was a member of the human race.'

He didn't know what to say.

'All right, what have I got to lose? Besides, there's nobody else I can talk to about Lee. Nobody else who cares.'

◇◇◇

Forty minutes later, he was trying not to spill his beer or her vodka and lime as he sidled through the crowd on his way to a booth at the back of the Stapledon Bar. After finishing work, Gina had changed out of her overall and poured her boyish figure into a sky blue tee shirt and impossibly tight jeans. She was checking out the mural behind her seat. Doctor Morbius, introducing Robby the Robot to the crew visiting the *Forbidden Planet*. Above their heads, Tom Cruise raced across the TV screens, this time fleeing from the pre-crime cops in *Minority Report*. Harry stole another look at Gina as she picked up her glass. Her face was so fresh she might have passed for sixteen. Only that wariness in her eyes was a giveaway, a clue that she'd been hurt before and was determined not to be hurt again. She was as luminous as Agatha in the film, the pre-cog with a terrible gift. Agatha foresaw murders before they were committed.

But, Harry reminded himself, he definitely wasn't Tom Cruise.

'Cheers.'

'Thanks…Harry.' She took a sip and then giggled. 'Oh my God, the look on Victor's face when we walked past him!'

On his way past the desk in the foyer of John Newton House, with Gina at his side, Harry had nodded at Victor. When the building manager glanced up from a chunky paperback, his straggly eyebrows almost hit the ceiling.

'Don't worry about it. There's no rule against a tenant taking one of the contract cleaners for a drink.'

'I'm not worried about him. He's a bit of a joke. The girls are always calling him names. Victor Creepy is as nice as it gets.'

'They don't like him?'

'God, no. I was warned to keep my distance, my first day on the job.'

'What's wrong with him?'

'I don't know for sure. But they say he's strange. He runs the building like his own personal empire. When we're at work, he struts around like the Duke of bloody Edinburgh, inspecting the troops. And then there's the way he goes on about murder.'

'Murder? You mean forensics, crime scene stuff?'

'Yeah, he's obsessed with it. Crime scene stuff, forensics, you name it. See that book he is reading? One of the girls had a look at it last night. It's about what happens when maggots make a breakfast out of dead bodies. Lovely.' Her face darkened. 'And when I think about Lee…'

'He's harmless, I'm sure.'

'Last week, he told the supervisor he was reading the life story of the German cannibal killer. This bloke met someone on the internet and talked him into letting him eat his bits. I mean, can you imagine?'

'I'd rather not.' He savoured the bitter. 'So tell me about yourself.'

'Not much to tell.'

'People always have something to tell. More than you might imagine. Let's start with your second name.'

'It's Paget. Gina Paget.'

'How long have you been cleaning?'

'Since January. From ten in the morning, I work in a sand-wich bar in Covent Garden. We finish at three and then I start cleaning. I do an hour at a travel agent's and then I'm due at John Newton House.'

'Busy schedule.'

'I need to pay the bills, same as everyone else.'

'And Lee Welch was your closest friend?'

'It doesn't say much for either of us, I suppose. We've only known each other eighteen months.'

'So you didn't meet at school?'

'I'd guess Lee spent even less time at school than me. She was a Scouser born and bred too, but we met in London, would you believe? Soho, actually.'

'Dare I ask what you were doing in Soho?'

She drank some vodka and lime. 'Let's just say she and I discovered we both shared the same dream. We wanted to be actresses and we met at an audition.'

'For what?'

'Not what we were led to believe, that's for sure. This pervy bloke and his mates said they wanted us to star in a movie. Porn, of course. I'm not proud of it. But Lee and I hit it off. Two kids from Liverpool, trying to make it in the big bad city. We found we had a lot in common, and not just that our mothers both sold cigarettes in the Co-op. For a few months we shared a flat.'

'And the film career didn't work out?'

'My only starring role was as Harriet Houdini, would you believe? I was an escapologist who was tied up by a master criminal while my co-star was tortured to reveal government secrets. You'll get the idea if I tell you he was cast as James Bondage.'

Harry laughed. 'So you both got out alive?'

'But stark naked, needless to say.' She grinned. 'Oh well, it was a life experience. Last Christmas, Lee and I came back to Liverpool. We thought there might be less competition up here. We knew we could pick up cleaning work and stuff like that to earn a few quid while we traipsed round the agencies. Waiting for a break.'

'And you're closer to family?'

'Makes no difference, that wasn't why we came back to the north. Lee's parents were dead, her older sister works for the social services. My mum and dad split up when I was a kid and he emigrated to Australia. Mum's dead now and the old feller might as well be for all I know or care.'

'I suppose the sister identified Lee's body?'

'Your guess is as good as mine.'

'Did she have boyfriends?'

'Plenty. They couldn't get enough of Lee, she had more touch-sensitive features than the latest mobile. But whenever anyone got too serious, she gave them the elbow. Said she was too young to settle down. What she meant was, she was looking for a man with money. Of course, blokes like that are always married and only looking for a bit on the side.'

'Did she find a man with money?'

'I'm not sure. Lee loved being a woman of mystery, it gave her a kick. She enjoyed having secrets, hugging them to herself.'

'What sort of secrets?'

'If I knew that, they wouldn't be secrets, would they? All I can tell you is that she had a secret, there was something she wasn't telling me.'

'How can you be sure?'

'For the past few weeks, she kept dropping hints that things were looking up. The moment I showed any interest, she changed the subject.'

'Was she doing it just to amuse herself? Make herself seem important?'

'I suppose so. I didn't want to give her the satisfaction of seeming bothered. But she did start spending money. The sort of money she'd not had before.'

'You think this might have had something to do with her death?'

'How can it? Sounds like she was killed by some maniac. Another woman was murdered a few weeks back, wasn't she? So it was nothing—personal. Not that it makes things better. People are saying there's a Liverpool serial killer. Some of the Lithuanian girls say they'd be safer going back home. Poor Lee. To think she would finish up…'

She started to sniffle. He rested his arm on her shoulder and she buried her face in his jacket.

'I do hope you're not causing this young lady distress, Harry?'

The words were spoken lightly, but all of a sudden the temperature had plunged to freezing. Harry disengaged himself from Gina and turned to face Juliet May. She was standing in front of the booth, accompanied by a tanned, bulky man. For all his cream suit and bling, his cold eyes reminded Harry of the soulless Borg in the mural of *Star Trek*. This was someone Harry hadn't seen for a long time and had hoped not to encounter again. His new landlord, Casper May.

'Evening, Juliet.'

'Evening. You've met my former husband before, I think?'

Harry nodded. Casper didn't react.

'Harry's a partner in the law firm that's moved into John Newton House. Crusoe and Devlin, remember, there was a time when I helped with their marketing?'

A grunt. 'I've used Jim Crusoe.'

Juliet's perfume spiced the air. Although it was early, Harry realised that she'd already had a few drinks. 'You do use rather a lot of people, don't you, darling?'

Next to him, Gina stiffened. Harry noticed her glance from Juliet to Casper, trying to fathom what was going on. Harry wished he knew.

Juliet's arched eyebrows said: *she's half your age, you must be out of your mind.* Her voice was honey-smooth.

'Well, Harry, aren't you going to introduce us?'

'Sorry. Gina Paget, this is Casper May and Juliet…'

'May,' Juliet said. 'I haven't changed my name since our divorce.

'Gina, how lovely to meet you.'

Juliet extended a slender hand. Exquisitely manicured, as ever, but could Harry detect a hint of not-quite-concealed age spots? 'And what do you do, exactly?'

The girl shook hands and treated the older woman to an all-innocence gaze.

'As a matter of fact, Mrs. May, I'm an executive in the premises regeneration sector.'

Chapter Seven

'So what's the story with you and Mrs. May?' Gina asked as Juliet and Casper strolled off in the direction of the restaurant and VIP lounge, accompanied by the theme to *Close Encounters of the Third Kind*.

'Story?'

'Why did she want to muscle into our conversation when her husband obviously couldn't give two shits? Is she after your body, or what?'

'My expense account couldn't compete with Casper May's.'

'But she's not married to him any more, is she? And what's that all about anyway? Why divorce a bloke, then swan around posh bars with him?'

'Juliet's a lady with expensive tastes. She likes the lap of luxury.'

'She won't be dropping into your lap, then?'

'Not any time soon. Her boyfriend is some hunk who acts in a soap.'

'I don't get it. There's something between you.' She moved closer, scrutinising his face for clues. 'Come on, I saw it in the way she looked at you. Like she'd been rummaging through a cupboard and found a pair of shoes she'd forgotten she ever had.'

'Thanks for the ego boost.'

'Listen, women like that are crazy about shoes. Can't see it myself, give me a pair of Nike trainers any day.'

'Women like that?'

'You know. Glossy, upmarket. Women who can afford to spend a small fortune on a nip and tuck whenever something starts to sag or droop.' A bitchy grin. 'Shame about the trout pout. She looks as though she stuck her gob in a wasp's nest.'

He couldn't help flinching.

'Go on, then. Do you and Lady Muck have…a past?'

He had no intention of telling her or anyone else about his affair with Juliet. Some doors needed to stay shut forever. 'You're a scary cross-examiner. More like leading counsel than a cleaning lady. Or, should I say, a premises regeneration executive?'

'You liked that?'

'Loved it.'

'I couldn't resist. Anyway, there's your image to think about. It wouldn't do for a respectable solicitor to get a name for buying drinks for humble cleaning ladies.'

'Who said I'm respectable?'

'Oh my God, are you denying it? Lee and I agreed, you can figure out everything you need to know about the people you clean for. I don't mean earwigging at doors or snooping through their wastepaper baskets. It's about the way they treat you.'

'Tell me more about Lee.'

'What do you want to know?'

'What sort of woman was she? Did you like her?'

'What do you mean? I told you, she was my closest friend!'

Her voice became strident and a grey-haired man in the next booth with his arm round a fat girl in a very low-cut top looked round to see if anything was wrong. Harry glared and he turned back to contemplating his companion's milky cleavage.

'Sorry, Gina.' His cheeks were burning. 'I shouldn't have said that.'

'I mean, yesterday evening, you found me crying after I heard the news. I couldn't take it in. And you ask if I liked her?'

Protesting too much? 'I'm sorry.'

'No.' She swallowed hard. He could see her mind working; he'd seen the same expression on a thousand clients' faces. How much to say, how much to conceal? 'You don't need to apologise. I mean, you're smarter than you look.'

He waited, said nothing.

'Matter of fact, you're right. I never thought about it before. Because you should like your friends, shouldn't you? Nothing else makes sense. And I did like her, most of the time, of course I did. But…she could be difficult.'

'How?'

'Lee was ambitious. She told me that, every night since she was a kid, she'd dreamed of becoming an actor. And nothing was going to stop her. All she needed was a stroke of luck.' Gina bowed her head. 'Won't happen now, will it?'

'When did you find out Lee was dead?'

'Shaz texted me yesterday afternoon. She was Lee's supervisor. When I rang her back, she said the police had spoken to her and they had a preliminary ID. There was stuff in Lee's handbag that told them who she was. And a payslip from the cleaning company.'

'So whoever killed her didn't rob her?'

'Some money was taken, according to Shaz. And her Rolex.' Gina's face crumpled. 'She was so proud of that watch, it was brand new.'

'Not a fake?'

'She said not. But most of her bits and pieces were left with…the body.'

'Have the police talked to you?'

'No reason why they should. There's nothing I can tell them.'

'You're her friend.'

'But I don't know anything about the murder, do I? Anyway, Shaz didn't give them my name. Cleaners and the police don't mix. A lot of the girls work under false names. It's the tax, you know.'

He grinned. 'And do you have an alias for the taxman?'

She burst into a fit of the giggles. 'Harriet Houdini, who else?'

'Never thought I'd get to buy Harriet Houdini a vodka and lime. Care for another?'

Her face was flushed, her voice growing louder. The alcohol had ironed out her inhibitions. 'Trying to get me pissed so you can have your wicked way with me?'

'Would you believe me if I said no?'

She considered. 'Know something? I think I would. Anyway, who cares? Same again.'

When he came back from the bar, he caught sight of the grey-haired man in the next booth putting his hand up his girlfriend's tent-like skirt. The man's face had disappeared in his companion's hair. Her eyes were fixed firmly on Tom Cruise.

Gina asked, 'You're not seriously trying to get me pissed, are you?

'No, promise. See, I'm on grapefruit juice already.'

'Very restrained.'

'I'm out later tonight.'

'Oh, yeah? Hot date?'

He shook his head. 'Not exactly.'

'You're not married, are you?'

'How did you guess?'

She fingered the rim of her glass. 'Mmmm. You don't have the shifty look of a married man on the make. I could almost believe you're interested in talking to me for the sake of it.'

'It's true.'

She shot him a heard-it-all-before glance. 'Not entirely true, though? I mean, why are you asking all these questions about Lee?'

'Once upon a time, I was married, but my wife left me for another man. I always dreamed we'd get back together, but one night someone stabbed her to death.'

'Shit.'

'For a few days the police suspected me of killing her. I made it my business to find out why Liz died. It was a sad story. The reasons for murder usually are.'

'That's terrible.' Her hand crept across the table to cover his. Her touch was soft and warm.

'It was a long time ago. But ever since, I suppose I've been obsessed with murder. The people who commit it. And their victims.' He withdrew his hand. 'Hard to explain better than that. You probably think I'm as bad as Victor Creevey.'

'Honest, you're nothing like him.'

He sipped his juice, the grapefruit sharp on his tongue. 'The smart money says that Lee and Denise Onuoha were killed by the same man.'

'Racing certainty, isn't it?' She gave a theatrical shiver. 'Serial crimes…'

'Does the name Aled Borth mean anything to you?'

'Should it?'

'I saw him reading the report which identified Lee this afternoon. The news seemed to shock him. As if her name meant something to him.'

'Who is he?'

'Around fifty, works as a cinema organist. Single, never been married, as far as I know.'

'A loser?'

'Why do you ask?'

'No reason.'

'Ever heard Lee speak about Borth?'

'Never.'

Her voice was flat and emphatic. He'd heard that tone so many times before in police interview rooms. She was holding something back about Lee, but he guessed that if he pushed too hard, she'd walk out and refuse to talk to him again.

'You can't protect her now, Gina. She's beyond that.'

She flushed. 'You think I don't realise? I've never heard of Aled Borth, let's leave it at that.'

'Okay. Sorry, I know it's hard, the loss of someone you were close to. Whatever their faults, however angry they made you feel.'

She shook her head. Not listening, following her thoughts. 'You wouldn't believe it, would you? It was Lee's idea to come back to Liverpool. She said if we weren't careful, we'd finish up on the game, working to keep a gang of Albanian pimps in cocaine.

Lee said we'd be safe back home.' Gina turned to him, her pretty face twisted with pain. 'How fucking wrong can you be?'

◇◇◇

The Waterloo Alhambra was a mock-Moorish palace shoe-horned between a car repair workshop and a doctor's surgery in a narrow street that ran down to the waterfront. Harry contemplated the ornate carved red brickwork and the elegant columns, mentally transporting himself to the sun-splashed hills and terraces of Granada. The illusion was shattered by a slap of wind from the Irish Sea and the smells from a kebab house half a dozen doors away.

Built in the days of Cecil B. De Mille by an architect with a similar fondness for the epic, the Alhambra had shut its doors when movie-going fell out of fashion in the seventies and suffered an inglorious reincarnation as a bingo hall and bar. When the owners called time on bingo, a group of enthusiasts had set up a charity to lease the premises and restore the Alhambra to former glories. Five years later, to everyone's amazement, including their own, the venture flourished. Sidney Rankin, the chairman of trustees, and universally known as El Sid, was a friend of Harry's from days when they'd played together in the same student football team. Sid had recommended Aled Borth to consult Harry for legal advice, something all three of them had come to regret.

In the foyer, Sid's favourite song was playing. He'd picked it as a signature tune for the Alhambra after reading somewhere the—no doubt apocryphal—story that Ray Davies had been inspired to write the lyric by the Mersey, not the Thames, as everyone thought.

> *'But I don't need no friends,*
> *As long as I gaze on Waterloo sunset,*
> *I am in paradise.'*

From a vantage point outside the bar, he spotted Ceri as she walked into the foyer. Green silk blouse and chiffon scarf around her neck, black trousers and sparkly sandals, casual chic for a summer evening. A couple of heads turned in her direction. She must be accustomed to attention, both in and out of court, but it didn't seem to mean anything to her. Their eyes met and she smiled.

'This place is amazing, isn't it? Ten years I've lived in Merseyside and I've never come here once. I feel ashamed. Thanks for inviting me.'

'What would you like to drink?'

'Just an orange juice, please. I'm driving.'

The bar was an extravaganza in marble, the walls festooned with black and white stills from films dating from the Alhambra's hey-day. Harry contemplated a shot of Robert Donat handcuffed to Madeleine Carroll in *The Thirty-Nine Steps*. He'd travelled here by cab, so he could allow himself another beer. He joined Ceri at a corner table beneath a picture of Claude Rains twitting Bogart in *Casablanca*. She was studying a what's-on leaflet with the concentration she devoted to everything she did.

'So you have a season ticket for a series of films for paranoiacs, Harry? What should I read into that, I wonder?'

'Last week I saw *The Parallax View*. A man driven to his doom by this sinister and ruthless, all-powerful organisation. An allegory for the Legal Services Commission's campaign against legal aid?'

She laughed. 'You really do think the bad guys are after you, then?'

'It's been one of those days.' He considered. 'One of those weeks. One of those careers.'

'Borth was asking the impossible, expecting you to cross-examine Afridi into confusion. What he doesn't know about pharmacokinetics isn't worth knowing. You did your best.'

'It's not that, it's…well, never mind. Thanks for keeping me company this evening.'

'My pleasure.' She considered him. 'If something is on your mind, why not share it with me?'

'It's nothing. Forget it.'

'Harry, you're troubled. It's as plain as if you'd scrawled a message on your shirt. Don't bottle it up, that's always a mistake.

Work problems, relationship problems, money problems, you mustn't let them get on top of you. Believe me, I know what I'm talking about. My husband…'

Her voice trailed away for a few moments as she became lost in thought. Harry didn't know what to say.

'You'd be amazed at the lengths people go to when they are desperate.'

'You must see a lot of bad stuff.'

'You've no idea. In the past two or three years alone, we've had death by antifreeze poisoning, by circular saw, even by a home-made guillotine, would you believe?'

Harry shuffled his feet. Time to shift the conversation away from suicide.

'I remember a poem from when I was at school. Talked about work as a toad, squatting on the poet's life. Who wants to sell their soul to a toad?'

She laughed. 'The snag is, you can't adjust your work-life balance like twiddling a knob on a thermostat. I know I take my own work to heart too much. It's just that I love my job. I'd never want to do anything else. So—is it life at Crusoe and Devlin that's bugging you?'

'Not exactly.' He took a breath. 'On Monday someone warned me that I'm about to die.'

'You're not serious?'

'On Midsummer's Eve.'

She stared. 'These are threats you're receiving? Hate mail? Have you informed the police?'

'Jim Crusoe reckons it's kids, playing tricks. Possibly he's right. And yet…it's getting under my skin.'

So, he'd made his confession. Until this moment he had refused to admit that he was rattled, let alone that there was anything to be rattled about. A master of the art of self-deception. But at the back of his mind, two words nagged away.

Midsummer's Eve, Midsummer's Eve, Midsummer's Eve.

'What's happened?'

He told her about the announcement of his death, the message on his answering machine, the trashing of his room. As he talked, he was struck by the triviality of the incidents that had turned his life upside down. Nobody hurt, no damage done. The police would laugh in his face if he asked for help, let alone for protection from some unknown foe. He should have kept his mouth shut.

'What is so special about Midsummer's Eve?'

'God knows. I don't dance around Stonehenge naked to celebrate the summer solstice, that's for sure.'

'Glad to hear it,' she said. 'Do you know of anyone who bears you a grudge?'

'Leaving Aled Borth aside?'

'If he wanted to take revenge on anyone, Malachy Needham would be the obvious candidate.'

He shrugged. 'Tom Gunter?'

'Gunter?' Her eyes opened very wide. 'Your former client? But...what makes you mention him?'

'I saw him yesterday. He was in a weird mood. Maybe he'd taken a line of cocaine. He gave the impression he had something to do, something on his mind.'

'Such as?'

'At the time, I wondered if he'd nipped into the office and dropped off the mock-obituary. When I saw him in the gardens, I made the mistake of asking him if he'd written it.'

'Why would he bear you a grudge?'

They'd talked about Tom Gunter the last time they'd met. Ceri had conducted the inquest into the death of the neighbour he'd been acquitted of killing and it was clear to Harry that the experience rankled. She'd called Tom to give evidence, but on the advice of his new lawyers, he kept his arms folded and his mouth shut. Most witnesses could be wheedled into answering questions, even after they had been cautioned about self-incrimination, in the mistaken belief that they were smarter than the person asking them. But Tom Gunter was too street-wise to fall into that trap. In the end, Ceri had to resort to a narrative verdict, outlining the factual circumstances in which the woman had met her death. No question of pointing a finger at Tom. The law said he was innocent, and what Ceri or Harry might think about justice counted for nothing.

'I don't think he forgave me for suggesting he should plead guilty to manslaughter. He's violent, unpredictable.'

She shook her head. 'He kept himself under perfect control at the inquest. Cool as ice.'

'He had time to prepare. If things don't go as he expects, who knows how someone with a temper like Tom will react? My guess is, that's how he came to kill his neighbour. He lost it, simple as that.'

She almost choked on the last of her juice. 'Better be careful what you say, Harry. Don't forget, he was acquitted.'

The rebuke was gentle, but it stung him. Better change tack.

'All right, you've convinced me, I need to get this Midsummer's Eve nonsense into perspective.' He swallowed the last of his drink. 'Come on. Time to watch Polanski losing his mind.'

◇◇◇

'Mr. Devlin!'

Harry's heart sank as he recognised the voice. He and Ceri were in the throng jostling for the exit. It was past midnight and he was ready for home. But Aled Borth was right behind them.

Harry turned. 'I didn't expect to see you here.'

'Changed my mind. They might not need me to play the organ when they show this late night foreign muck, but I thought I'd show my face.' Borth smelled as though he'd spent the past two hours in the bar. 'And I didn't expect to see you squiring the lovely Coroner. No, I certainly did not.'

Ceri gave him a civil nod. 'Good evening, Mr. Borth.'

'I mean, I'm entitled to wonder, aren't I? This man Needham got away with murder, but what do you two care?'

His voice was becoming louder. People were glancing towards them and nudging each other. Sid Rankin, red-faced and portly, was queuing a few feet away. Harry caught his eye and the chairman pushed through to join them.

'Harry, Aled. Nothing wrong, I hope?'

'My friend and I are just leaving,' Harry said.

'It's a scandal!' Aled called out. 'They are hand in glove, all of them. Conspiring to hide the truth. It's a cover-up.'

Sid Rankin seized Aled's arm. After he stopped playing football, he'd taken up refereeing and earned a name as an old school disciplinarian. The least murmur of dissent saw him whip out the red card; he'd once sent off a whole team.

'Aled, you've made your point. These good people have come here for a pleasant evening. Let it go.'

Aled shrugged off Sid's grip. He was stronger than he looked. He stared at Harry and Ceri with contempt.

'You haven't heard the last of this. You let justice be cheated, and you'll have to pay the price!'

The scrum in front of them was clearing. Harry gave Sid a quick nod of thanks and guided Ceri through the doors and into the street.

'Sorry about that.'

'Don't worry.' She stared at the pavement. 'He needs time. Obviously I failed today. I should have helped him come to terms with losing his mother.'

'You can't blame yourself.'

'No? But that's my job, as coroner.'

'All you can do is decide how the deceased came to die.'

She shook her head. 'You don't understand. My business is not with the dead, but the living.'

'You take too much responsibility on yourself. You're a perfectionist.'

'It's a curse.'

'I wouldn't know. But I do know this—life is good, but it's never perfect.'

She mustered a rueful smile. 'I've always struggled to come to terms with that. Good isn't good enough. Anyway, you came by cab. Can I give you a lift home?'

'I don't want to take you out of your way.'

'It's only a ten minute detour. I'm parked over there.'

Driving back to the city, they talked about the film. How much of the conspiracy was in Trelkovsky's mind, how much was real? Everything Ceri said was logical, persuasive, intelligent, and yet he sensed her thoughts were elsewhere. With the memory of her dead husband, he guessed. The man who had destroyed his own life, just like Trelkovsky.

Even sitting next to each other in the cramped cinema seats, they'd kept a distance. It was enough to inhale her sweet perfume; to touch her would have been a betrayal of trust. He supposed she must like him, but she wasn't in the market for romance. Still grieving. And he wasn't sure he was ready for a new relationship. Ceri was as safe with him as Gina had been.

'Here you are,' she said, pulling up in the car park at Empire Dock.

'Thanks.' He thought for a moment about pecking her cheek. Decided against it.

'Take care of yourself,' she said. 'And if you hear any more about Midsummer's Eve, tell the police. Please.'

'Will do.' He grinned. 'If I make it past Midsummer's Eve, maybe we could do this again sometime?'

'Maybe.' Her smile was as enigmatic as the film they had seen. 'Goodnight.'

The Third Day

Chapter Eight

'Harry, I need to talk to you.' Kay Cheung said. 'It's urgent.'

He'd been back from court for five minutes when Kay's call was put through. A client who'd spent years claiming disability benefit on account of an allegedly dislocated hip had been charged with obtaining money under false pretences. His mistake was to take part in a televised Thai kick-boxing contest in which his athleticism earned the judges' admiration, before coming to the attention of the social security's fraud squad. A suspended sentence counted as a good result, and Harry was pleased with himself. But Kay's voice shocked him. She sounded terrified.

'What's wrong?'

'I can't say on the phone.'

'But…'

'He might be back any minute,' she hissed.

'Tom?'

'Who else?'

'Is he in trouble?'

'It's not Tom I'm worried about. At least, not…'

'What, then?'

'I need to see you, there's nobody else I trust.'

'How about the police?'

'He'd kill me,' she whispered.

Harry sat up. In Kay's eyes, Tom Gunter walked on water. Never before had she acknowledged that her lover was dangerous.

She refused to believe he'd murdered that neighbour. When she'd pleaded with Harry to take his case, she said Tom would be condemned simply because he had a record, because he'd made mistakes in his younger days. The police had no proof he'd killed that woman; therefore he couldn't have done it. Why persecute Tom instead of seeking out the real culprit?

Tom never wanted Harry as his brief. Joe Pipe's firm had acted for him since he'd been old enough to be arrested, but Kay had persuaded him to change lawyers. Like Sid Rankin, she must wish she'd never bothered. Tom preferred to swim with sharks.

'Do you want to come in to the office this afternoon?'

'Too risky. He mustn't find out I'm seeing you.'

'Sure.'

'It's serious, Harry. Promise me you won't say a word. Not to anyone. I want you to swear it.'

'Of course. I'll do whatever I can. When would you like to see me?'

'Six o'clock tonight?'

'Where?'

'Runcorn Gap, underneath the bridge. On the Widnes side of the river, the West Bank. A long way from the city. Nobody we know will see us there.'

'Do you need a lift?'

'No!' She was alarmed. 'I don't want Tom to spot us together. There's a chance he might follow me. I'll pick up a cab.'

'I'll be there.'

'Thanks, Harry. You're…a good man.'

Harry heard a clicking noise.

'What do you…?'

Kay rang off before he could finish his question. He banged the phone down in frustration. Impossible to ring back; what if Tom Gunter answered? Had someone been listening in?

So many questions. Among them, a wild piece of guesswork. Might the envelope containing the death notice have been delivered, not by Gunter, but by Kay? He felt an adrenaline rush. Come six o'clock, he might find out the truth behind the messages about Midsummer's Eve.

◇◇◇

Half an hour later he was glancing over a Law Society circular, not taking any of it in. He couldn't shove Kay out of his mind. For as long as he'd known her, he'd wondered how someone so decent finished up with Tom Gunter. It wasn't something he could ask outright, but in a dozen conversations, he'd teased out clues to the answer.

Kay only spoke English and had never felt part of the city's Chinese community. Once she'd told him she was caught between two worlds; that was why she preferred to be called Kay, rather than Ka-Yu. People from Chinatown knew at a glance that she wasn't full Chinese, while a gang of kids at school bullied her because she didn't look like them. In her teens she'd developed a passion for plants and wanted nothing more than to work with them. Her lack of ambition disappointed her parents; now they were dead and she'd never got on with her older sister. She'd lived briefly with a twice-divorced man, but walked out when she realised all he wanted was a submissive home-maker, a mail order bride on the cheap. Within weeks she met Tom Gunter. He fixed the computers at one of the offices where she tended the potted palms. He was good at what he did, when he was minded to work, and even Harry had to admit, he wasn't bad looking. But she'd fallen for a man with a violent streak. Now it was hard for her to escape. She was on her own.

Except for me, Harry thought. *There's nobody else I trust.* A sad admission from a woman he cared for, but couldn't claim to know well. But he felt she'd made him responsible for her well-being. He owed it to her to give whatever help she sought.

He exhaled. The circular sermonised about the need for solicitors to practise effective risk management. Apparently this was achieved by issuing dozens of policy documents on everything from health and safety to how to manage trans-gender issues in the workplace without falling foul of discrimination law.

A noise made him look up and he saw his door creep open half an inch. From out in the corridor came a throaty whisper.

'Beware Midsummer's Eve!'

He sighed. 'Carmel, is that you?'

A woman with a mass of untamed dark hair bounced in and deposited herself on the chair opposite him. Carmel Sutcliffe was too big-boned and gawky to claim beauty, and her dress sense was as haphazard as her coiffeur. But even in a beige business suit that had seen better days, her outrageous exuberance made her seem unlike any other lawyer and all the more desirable for that. Harry thought for the hundredth time that Jim Crusoe was a lucky man.

'Spoilsport. You recognised my voice?'

'The cruel humour gave you away.'

'Thought I'd look in while I wait for Jim to sweep me off for lunch. He's up to his eyes in small print about rights of way across a housing estate. Life's too short for that stuff, I told him, the client should stop mithering and go up the back passage.' She patted her stomach. 'I expect nothing less than a gourmet meal. Something expensive and filling, so he won't expect me to cook tonight. Between you and me, I'm not sure my idea of domestic bliss coincides with his.'

'The amount of weight he's lost since he started seeing you, give him six months and he'll have faded into thin air.'

She wriggled out of her jacket and slung it on the back of the chair. Her blouse, as usual, was firmly buttoned but far too tight.

'Simply a matter of keeping him exercised.'

'Just make sure his heart can take it. He's older than me, you know.'

'I'd hate to be unkind, Harry dear, but don't you think he might be wearing better?'

'True.'

Carmel Sutcliffe had spent eighteen months as a junior solicitor with Crusoe and Devlin before, like Wayne Saxelby, moving on to better things. She'd joined a larger and more affluent competitor and later reached the giddy heights of Chief Adviser on Corporate Governance in the legal department of Liverpool Police Authority. Harry had always relished her zest for life and her flirtatious wit; now Jim was enjoying them even more.

The blossoming of their relationship took everyone by surprise. Probably including both of them. While Jim's wife was alive, Carmel was pursued by a long succession of admirers, pushy young lawyers who fancied themselves almost as much as they fancied her. Yet for all her sexy banter, Harry thought her heart was never quite in the thrill of being chased. After Jim's wife died, he and Carmel found something in each other they'd never even realised they were searching for.

'So what's with this Midsummer's Eve malarkey? Are the Ides of March too classical for you?'

'Jim should have kept his mouth shut.'

'We're concerned for you.' She grinned. 'I mean, nemesis isn't far off. When is Midsummer's Eve, the summer solstice?'

'Saturday. Strictly speaking, the summer solstice is Thursday, the longest day of the year. The difference is down to Pope Gregory, fiddling about with the calendar.'

'Your command of trivia never ceases to impress. Remind me to pick you for my team next time we enter a pub quiz.'

'If only I knew as much about the law, eh?'

'You said it, Harry. So who do you think is after your blood?'

'According to Jim, there are dozens of suspects. Possibly hundreds.'

'You will tread on people's toes,' she scolded, pointing at the leaflet on his desk. 'Risk management? You've never been too hot at that, have you?'

He didn't want to talk about Tom Gunter. He'd promised Kay he'd say nothing and he had an old-fashioned attachment to keeping his word.

'Jim reckons someone's taking the piss.'

'Always a temptation, I'm afraid, Harry. Not to worry, if someone meant to bump you off, they wouldn't give you such a precise warning.'

'Thanks for the reassurance.'

'Don't mention it. Any chance of a coffee?' She stretched like a pampered Persian cat as he rang Grace for drinks. 'What else is new, or are you exclusively focused on staying alive until next week?'

'I've discovered our cleaning lady was best mates with the late Lee Welch.'

She rocked so hard with laughter that he feared her blouse buttons might pop. 'You can't help yourself, can you? Where there's a murder, you're never far behind.'

'A gift,' he said modestly.

'A curse, more like. And you wonder why you ruffle feathers? Even if you make it past Midsummer's Eve, don't bank on cashing in your pension.'

'All I've done is talk to the girl over a drink.'

'Attractive, is she?'

'She's half my age.'

'Who cares? I'm a lot younger than Jim.'

'She was crying. I felt sorry for her.'

Carmel shook her head. 'The amazing thing is, I believe you. You're too innocent for this world, Harry.'

'I'm a hard-bitten lawyer.'

'The only thing hard-bitten about you is your fingernails. Don't scowl, it's a sort of compliment. You know I wouldn't change you for the world. So you took pity on this young cleaner without an ulterior motive darkening your pure heart? What did she murmur into your ear as she wept on your shoulder?'

Putting his feet up on the desk, he recounted Gina's story about meeting Lee in London before returning north. Carmel sat back and kept quiet; on the rare occasions she stopped talking, she was a good listener.

'Gina doesn't know Denise Onuoha. At least not under that name. I'm assuming the same person killed Denise and Lee Welch?'

Carmel's eyes narrowed in a parody of suspicion. 'You wouldn't try to pump me for privileged information? Given that I chew the fat with senior police officers every day of my working life?'

'Perish the thought.'

'Harry Devlin, you're a lying toad. So you'd take advantage of our friendship to satisfy your curiosity?'

'You know I'm the soul of discretion.' Harry picked up the Law Society circular and idly fashioned it into a paper dart. Did such flagrant disrespect constitute professional misconduct? 'Reading between the lines in the Press, the police believe the crimes are linked. We're talking about a signature killer?'

'How much does your cleaner know about Lee's murder?'

'More than she's told me, I'd guess. Lee may have been her mate, but I'm not sure how much she really liked her.'

'Maybe she disapproved of Lee's lifestyle.'

'On the game?'

'Did the friend say so?'

'No, but Lee was a wannabe actress, short of money, not too scrupulous. It doesn't take an Einstein.'

Carmel sighed. 'All right. Lee worked as an escort. So did Denise.'

'And the murders reveal the same M.O.?'

'My lips are sealed. Don't look like that, there's a first time for everything. I'm not even supposed to know myself.'

'But you overhear stuff at the water cooler?'

'They keep the details tight. The last thing the powers-that-be want is copycat attacks on working girls. Sorry, Harry, much as I love you, I'll keep my mouth shut for once.'

Lips sealed. Mouth shut. A fuzzy image of Barney Eagleson, the mobile embalmer, drifted into his mind. He saw again the knowing wink, heard that fluting voice: *Once an embalmer gets a reputation for… a loose tongue, he's finished.*

People gave things away, it was human nature. He couldn't resist a long shot.

'Does he cut out their tongues?'

She flinched, as if he'd flourished a pair of secateurs in front of her eyes, and he knew he'd struck lucky.

'Does your cleaning lady know, did she tell you?'

'Just a wild guess.' He grinned. 'Or ingenious deduction. Take your pick.'

'Harry, you never cease to amaze me.'

'If I've figured out his signature, there's no point in your being mysterious for the sake of it. How were the girls killed?'

She sighed. 'All right, he strangled them. Manually, he didn't use a ligature. Which might suggest it was a crime of impulse.'

'Forensic clues?'

'Nothing worthwhile in Denise's case. With Lee, it's too early to say. As far as we know, neither of them was raped. Maybe he can't get it up, God knows. One more pathetic man, taking his inadequacies out on defenceless women.'

'I suppose he keeps the tongues as souvenirs? Isn't that how serial killers amuse themselves?'

'No, he dumps them near the scene.' Carmel pulled a face. 'Miserable piece of shit that he is.'

'So why does he do it?'

'Search me, I'm not a psychiatrist.'

'Presumably the girls were murdered by a client?'

'Your guess is as good as the Senior Investigating Officer's.' She shook her head. 'By the way, I don't think you mentioned your cleaning lady's name?'

'Told you I was discreet. She doesn't want to talk to the police.'

'Charm her into changing her mind, will you? But if you have qualms of conscience, I can ask Sylvia. She knows everything.'

Something in Carmel's tone puzzled him.

'I thought you liked Sylvia.'

'I do, very much. But she doesn't approve of me.'

'Bollocks.'

'It's true. Not since I moved in with Jim.'

'She's thrilled that he's found someone to take care of him.'

'Not sure I do that, really. But you're missing the point. She had her eyes on him herself.'

His mouth opened, though for a moment no sound came.

'You're kidding.'

'Never said a truer word.'

'But she's married.'

'Oh, Harry…'

He stared. 'You're serious, aren't you?'

'Would I lie to you?'

'If it suited you.'

'All right. But this is gospel, take it from me. Sylvia's husband has been going through a mid-life crisis for years. He keeps embarrassing himself over trollops who make him feel he's twenty again. Sylvia would dump him like a shot if she had a better offer.' She gave him a foxy grin. 'Don't panic, she sees you as too much of a challenge. As for Jim, typical man, can't see beyond the end of his nose. He hasn't the faintest idea she's lusted after him for years. And I mean to keep it that way, all right?'

He shook his head in wonder. 'Did you manage to fit in any work when we employed you, or was all your time taken up with salacious gossip?'

'I'm a people person. I love trying to understand what makes them tick.'

The door swung open and Grace arrived with the coffee. She was wearing a navy blue smock with a deep V-neck that, when she bent to pour, left nothing to the imagination. Carmel chatted with her as though to a long lost friend, reminiscing about her days as a junior lawyer skivvying for Jim and Harry. Grace smiled, but said little. The moment she left the room, Carmel turned to Harry and chuckled.

'So that's Amazing Grace?'

'Jim's prejudiced, don't listen to what he says about her. She isn't his type.'

'Glad to hear it.' Carmel smiled. 'Is she your type, by any chance?'

He frowned. 'Are you joking?'

'She's not bad-looking, in a fey sort of way. Nice pair of tits and she didn't miss the chance to remind you of their existence, I noticed. Does that happen a lot?'

'Once or twice,' he admitted. 'But it's summer. Nobody wants to be over-dressed.'

'You ought to introduce a cleavage display policy. I favour a cover-up—recruit more hard-working Muslim women in burqas and you'll beat your diversity targets for good measure. I don't want Jim's attention to wander when I can't keep my eye on him. As for Amazing Grace, you could do worse.'

'Thanks, but I'm not interested.'

'Perhaps you ought to be,' she murmured. 'It's a long time since you had someone special.'

He shrugged. 'I get by.'

'Getting by isn't enough. Even your desk calendar says so.' She pointed to the latest motto: *Life is ours to be spent, not to be saved.* For a couple of seconds she hesitated, as if about to skip along a tight-rope. 'Tell me, do you see anything of Juliet May these days?'

'Juliet?' He felt as though she'd doused him with a bucket of iced water. 'What do you mean?'

'Come on, Harry. You had a bit of a thing going with her at one time, didn't you?'

'Do you know who she was married to?'

'Casper May, yes. I always thought you were either brave or foolhardy. Probably both. I keep telling Jim, he needs to be choosier with his clients. And his landlords. There are cabinets overflowing with paperwork devoted to Casper May at Police Authority HQ. Never mind, I hear he and Juliet have divorced. So she's footloose and fancy-free.'

He didn't like deceiving Carmel. But sometimes a lie felt safer than the truth.

'You've got the wrong idea about Juliet and me.'

Her smile spoke louder than words. 'Calm down, Jim doesn't have a clue. Men never do. Me, I saw it on your face the first time I saw you and Juliet together in the office.'

'I don't follow.'

'She was discussing marketplace perceptions and you were hanging on to her every word. Utterly out of character, it was obvious you were besotted.'

He'd spent a career advising clients not to admit guilt and he wasn't about to make a confession. Better not protest too much. He'd take refuge in evasion.

'Carmel Sutcliffe, you've got a dirty mind.'

She waved this away. 'I'm not blaming you, Harry. She's a classy lady, whatever I might think about the company she keeps. But on this subject, I promise, my mouth is zipped.'

Harry groaned inwardly. 'I'm not debating it with you. As for Casper May, he's supposed to have turned over a new leaf. According to *The Daily Post*, he's a candidate for Northern Entrepreneur of the Year.'

'Here's a bit of insider information. Don't bet your life savings on Casper winning the prize. I wouldn't fancy his chances of stepping up to the podium once the news gets out.'

'What news?'

'Denise and Lee worked for Cultural Companions. Upmarket name for an escort agency, don't you think? And guess who owns fifty per cent of the business?'

Harry's stomach churned. 'Casper May?'

'Spot on.'

'Casper thinks culture is something that grows on damp walls.'

'So what? I doubt many of the girls discuss Shakespeare with their clients. Casper doesn't have a hands-on management role, if you'll pardon the expression. But he has a half-share in another joint venture you've come across.'

'Namely?'

'Culture City Cleaners.'

He groaned. 'Oh shit.'

'Seems like he and his partner are cornering the market in female-dominated work sectors. A lot of girls they employ are from countries in Eastern Europe. Cheap labour, very profitable. There's even a rumour that the cleaning company is a recruiting ground for Cultural Companions. You earn a lot more as an escort for a night than as Mrs. Mop for a month. Especially if you're willing to offer a few extras as well as the pleasure of your company and conversation.'

'I suppose that management keeps a safe distance from any suggestion that they are hiring out call girls?'

'You bet. Merely to hint at impropriety would have Casper calling in m'learned friends. The operation is carefully set up, the girls are given strict instructions not to enter into any private arrangements with the clients. They have policies and procedures coming out of their backsides. Health and safety, rest breaks. Dignity at work, even. What that means for an escort girl, I shudder to think.'

'Is Casper a suspect?'

'He's been interviewed in connection with the deaths of Denise and Lee, of course. I gather he was concerned but co-operative. PR-speak for privately furious, but too smart to show it. He even offered to put up a reward to find the culprit.'

'Maybe the girls angered him. Wouldn't do what he wanted, made him lose his temper.'

'The way I hear it, people who get on his wrong side simply vanish off the face of the earth.'

'Does he have an alibi for the murders?'

'Watertight. So does his business partner. Though frankly, there's no reason to believe that either of them would murder the girls. You don't make fat profits by killing your own staff. Casper agreed to let the team sift through details of the agency's client base, with particular reference to people who had hired the services of Denise and Lee. It's left us with plenty of people to interview. There are a lot of lonely men out there.'

'Who is Casper's business partner, then?'

He thought she was bound to say it was Juliet. Despite the divorce, she and her ex were still bound together by something that meant more than love. Money, money, money.

'It's not who you might think.' Carmel gave him an encouraging smile. 'He's in partnership with another dodgy capitalist of culture city. Name of Malachy Needham. Small world, eh?'

Liverpool wasn't a city in the same mould as Manchester or Birmingham, Bristol or Leeds. Its communities were small and closely-knit, and Harry knew the old saying was true; Liverpool was the largest village in Britain. So many relationships inter-twined.

'You know I have a client who accused Needham of murdering his mother? She was a resident at a care home Needham runs.'

'Yeah, I heard the story from a mate in the CPS.' Carmel's network was formidable. 'Apparently they were thrilled that he might have poisoned this old dear. He's not popular, isn't Malachy Needham. Then it turned out she'd drunk so much gin, the toxicology was messed up and Needham was squeaky clean. The CPS clung on to the file a couple of months longer than necessary, just to make him sweat. But there was no doubt. He didn't kill the old woman.'

'At the inquest yesterday, Ceri Hussain recorded a verdict of death by natural causes.'

'And she's never wrong, isn't our Ceri.'

The sardonic note surprised him. 'What do you mean?'

'Oh, take no notice. I shouldn't be such a mean bitch.' Carmel fiddled with her bracelet. 'Truth is, she used to make me feel inadequate whenever I bumped into her at Legal Group meetings.'

'I thought it was flabby corporate lawyers who turned you off?'

'It's easy to feel superior to people whose sad lives revolve around banking deals and mezzanine finance. Ceri's different, she's no expense account zombie and I bet she doesn't play golf. You know, I thought she had it all. Successful and glamorous, quite frankly, I'd hate her if she wasn't always so nice. But her husband's death changed things. I found myself pitying her. She devoted herself to her job, body and soul, and forgot to take care of what mattered most.'

'She wasn't to blame for his suicide,' he snapped. Much as he loved Carmel, once in a while, her confident certainties grated.

'How can you know?'

He glared at her. 'Ricky Hussain was a salesman. Not a very good one, by all accounts. His business was going down the plughole, I heard he was due to meet his bankers the day after he killed himself.'

'Spent too much of his time chasing women instead of working, is my guess. Ever meet him?'

He shook his head. 'You?'

'Ceri brought him along to a Legal Group social event. Good-looking bloke, but he obviously fancied himself. By the time she introduced us, he'd already had a few drinks. Five minutes after she wandered off to chat to the President, Ricky was stroking my bum and asking for my phone number.'

'Did you give it to him?'

'I trod on his foot and disappeared to the loo, actually. When I got back, he was making a fool of himself with the social secretary from Liverpool Lesbian Lawyers. There was something desperate about the way he pawed at her. If you ask me, Ceri didn't pay him enough attention.'

'You can't blame his wife because he was a Lothario. Or because he couldn't face carrying on.'

'She's a workaholic, famous for it. Imagine, she trained as a medic and then started all over again to become a lawyer. Someone so ruthlessly driven must be bloody difficult to live with. I mean, Jim works long hours, but he has a life as well. He's a real person.'

'Ceri is a real person. And I've not noticed a ruthless streak. She's focused, that's all.'

Carmel sniggered. 'Oh yeah? Jim tells me you have a soft spot for her.'

'For Chrissake. Do people have nothing better to do than talk about my supposed love life?'

'From what I hear, over the years your love life's been a bit of a soap opera.' She grinned. 'You can't blame your friends for wanting to tune into the next instalment.'

'Actually, my love life is more like a long-forgotten sitcom with no repeats.' A rueful shake of the head. 'I read this article about a tiny sea creature, a bdelloid rotifer, it's called. It hasn't had sex for one hundred million years and I know how it feels.'

She laughed. 'And Ceri?'

He took a breath. 'Her husband had a history of depression.'

'Probably because so many women found him sleazy.'

'I heard he was on Prozac, but that didn't help balance the books of his business. It wasn't Ceri's fault that despair overwhelmed him.'

She hung her head. 'Sorry, I'm a cow. You were telling me about your client?'

'Aled Borth lives in Waterloo. He's a cinema organist at the Alhambra. Never married. But he knew Lee Welch, I'm sure of it.'

'Perhaps they shared a packet of popcorn at the pictures?'

'Lee doesn't sound like a devotee of art-house cinema. So how did Aled get to know her?'

'Might be worth checking. I'll have a word.' She leaned across the desk and patted his hand. 'Thanks.'

The door swung open and Jim bustled in. He wrapped a proprietorial arm around Carmel's shoulder. Harry couldn't remember a time when his partner looked happier.

'Ready, sweetheart? Hope she's not distracted you, Harry.'

She pecked Jim on the cheek. 'We've just been passing the time of day.'

He grunted. 'With you two, I scarcely dare think what that means.'

'Just the usual, you know.' A wicked grin. 'Sex and scandal and sudden death.'

◇◇◇

On his way out of the office, he bumped into Gina Paget. The lift doors were open and she was shining the mirrored walls of the cab as though her life depended on it. Her back was towards him, but her reflection gazed at him. Her face was drenched with misery.

'I know how Lee made her money,' he said.

'Oh yeah?'

'Does the name Cultural Companions mean anything to you?'

She swung round to face him. 'Never heard of it.'

She wasn't a bad liar, but he'd seen better. Some of them were clients of long standing. 'She was on their books as an escort girl.'

Gina hung her head. 'All right. So maybe she made a few quid that way.'

'She told you about it?'

'If you must know, she invited me out for a drink one night and tried to talk me into signing on with them myself. I wasn't interested. Like I told you, we'd come back to Liverpool to get away from gangsters on the make. No point in jumping from the frying pan into the fire.'

'You argued about it?'

'Yes, I told her she was making a huge mistake. She said she didn't have to do anything with the clients that she didn't fancy, and how many girls made a fortune out of trudging round offices with a mop and bucket? That seemed to amuse her, she pissed herself laughing. I shouted at her, said she was cheapening herself. The barman told us to button our mouths. We were disturbing the fellers watching football on satellite TV.'

'Was that the last time you saw her?'

'No, we met up a couple of times afterwards. She said she was sorry for upsetting me, and promised that soon she'd give up escort work. I didn't believe her. Lee was heading down the slippery slope and nothing I said could save her.'

'I hope you're not blaming yourself for her death?'

'Who else should I blame?'

'The man who killed her.'

'But I don't know him, we'll never meet.' Her face crumpled and she dabbed at the corners of her eyes with the duster. 'You mean well, Harry, but you don't understand. It's so much easier to blame myself.'

◇◇◇

'In a hurry?'

Barney Eagleson had his feet up on the reception desk and his hands behind his head. The whiff of formaldehyde still clung to him. His smile was coy, complacent, verging on conspiratorial. You might have believed that he, not Casper May, owned the building.

Harry wasn't in the mood for a cosy chat with a mobile embalmer, but he couldn't help succumbing to curiosity.

'Lou's gone home?'

'In-growing toenail, would you believe? He nicked off a couple of hours early to see his doctor. Victor's not happy. I called in to see if he fancied a pint and he asked me to keep an eye on things. He's a bit of a slave-driver, if you ask me.'

His teeth were pointed, like tiny tombstones. Harry felt sure Barney was taking the piss. He had never noticed Victor's obsession with the work ethic.

'And where is Victor?'

'In the back room, on the phone to the idiots who installed the CCTV.' Barney chortled. 'For all poor Victor can tell, John Newton House is swarming with masked intruders at this very moment.'

'If any of them want to fill in a few legal aid forms while they're here, point them towards my office.' Harry hesitated. 'The girl who was murdered, she had her tongue cut out, didn't she?'

Barney's smile vanished. 'I didn't say that.'

'You hinted that…'

'I'd had a few drinks,' Barney interrupted. 'I didn't mean any harm.'

On the plasma screen, two more Stepford Architects rhapsodised about the new Liverpool.

'Helicopter views…wilful unorthodoxy…energy pathways…'

'Can you tell me…?'

Barney swung his feet off the desk. 'Listen, Harry. This is police business. I'm on the edge of the case. You're not even that close. Take my advice, don't interfere, don't even hint about what I said. Otherwise your own tongue might be cut out too.'

◇◇◇

Harry hit trouble the moment he set off for his meeting with Kay Cheung. The Strand was blocked by a procession of tractors, combine harvesters and assorted farm vehicles. A cabinet minister was visiting Liverpool and a pressure group called Farmers4Justice had organised a demonstration. They kept finding fresh ways to cause maximum inconvenience in their campaign. They were fighting against the way the government favoured the city at the expense of the countryside. At least in their opinion.

Horns honked, tempers frayed, as the police tried to divert the protesters away from the main road so that the rush hour commuters could escape the city centre. Harry sat behind the steering wheel, listening to local radio for a traffic update. On the drive programme, a historian claimed to have found proof that Adolf Hitler stayed with his half-brother Alois in Liverpool during his teens. It didn't seem to Harry to be something to boast about, and he switched on the CD player. Dusty Springfield just didn't know what to do with herself, and he understood the feeling. He'd be late for his appointment, but there was nothing he could do. He couldn't call Kay to let her know. He'd have to hope that she waited for him.

When at last the gridlock eased, he put his foot down, but it was impossible to make up for lost time. Speke Boulevard was a maze of traffic cones and cars and vans were bumper-to-bumper. Further on was a lengthy tailback from the Silver Jubilee bridge. Harry took the last exit for Widnes. In his teens he'd dated a pretty girl from the town. She lived in Farnworth, where Paul Simon once sat at a railway station with a ticket for his destination and wrote 'Homeward Bound'. Harry hummed the tune until he found himself in Waterloo Road, driving past the Waterloo Centre.

Waterloo, Waterloo, everywhere…

He eased his MG over the humps in the narrow terraced streets that twisted into a dead end. A wide stretch of the Mersey blocked the way. Up above, the approach to the river bridge squatted on fat grey concrete legs tattooed with purple graffiti about the sex lives of unknown teenagers. He parked in their shadow.

During the journey, he'd speculated about what Kay wanted to tell him. She'd sounded more fearful than when Gunter was on trial for murder. Someone had snatched the comfort blanket of childish faith in her man, leaving her defenceless and bare.

Twenty to seven. He locked the car and started to walk. A stiff breeze made him shiver. He wandered down to the river's edge, and stared at the gleaming mud. A flock of gulls wailed as they flew by.

No trace of Kay.

Overhead, the traffic roared. A hundred thousand vehicles a day crossed the Mersey, but down below it was peaceful. A couple of kids kicked a football, old men walked their dogs. The London to Liverpool express set off from the station on the Runcorn side of the water and blasted through the wrought-iron spans of the railway bridge. But Kay herself was nowhere to be seen.

'*The Lady Vanishes*,' he muttered to himself, walking under the viaduct through a vast brick arch. A stretch of the river was fenced off by spiked iron bars and he peered through them like a convict. A boat chugged towards the docks. In the distance, the steel towers of an oil refinery glistened in the pale brightness of evening.

He turned and headed for Victoria Promenade, past a pub and a sandstone church. Notices along the river bank urged him to *Stay Safe*, and warned that hidden things might trap him. Beware of deep water.

Maybe she'd given him up and gone home, maybe her taxi too had been delayed as a result of the demonstration of bucolic wrath. He'd wait another half hour, he owed her that much. Before meeting Kay, he'd killed off spider plants and kalanchoes by the box-load, but she'd taught him moderation and consistency, that it was as fatal to over-water as to starve a plant. It baffled him that someone so gentle could bear to live with a brute like Tom Gunter, but what women saw in violent men he found impossible to understand. Take Juliet, for instance; what ties still bound her to Casper May? This was the twenty-first century, but some women seemed as shackled as the Africans who'd been bought and sold in the grounds of the Parish Church.

His mobile sang the theme to *Shaft* and he whipped it out of his pocket.

'Kay?'

'What's that? Harry, are you there?'

Wayne Saxelby, for God's sake. Panting as though he'd run a four-minute mile.

'Sorry, Wayne, this isn't a good time.'

'Harry, nothing's more important than this. I had to phone you.'

He'd never heard Wayne sound like this. Exhausted and panic-stricken.

'What is it?'

'Jim…Jim Crusoe.'

'What about him?' Harry felt his stomach muscles tighten. Was that a siren he could hear on the phone?

'He's been attacked. Hit over the head.'

Harry swore. 'Is he hurt?'

'The ambulance is here now. So are the police. I thought you ought to know.'

Suddenly Harry was shouting. Never mind Kay, she'd have to take care of herself. Only one person mattered now.

'Are you telling me he's in a bad way?'

'Yes.' Wayne's voice was muffled. Was he on the brink of weeping?

'How bad?'

'Harry…I think he's going to die.'

Chapter Nine

Harry hated hospitals. Yes, he knew they were good places, where wonderful work was done, where some lives began and others were saved. But he hated the echo of footsteps as they slapped the tiles of those echoing, sterile corridors, hated the stench of antiseptic scouring his sinuses, hated most of all the fear wasting the faces of those who waited for a word from the doctor. Reason and logic had nothing to do with it. For him, hospitals were places of pain, places where everyone suffered and too many died.

If only Wayne would stop pacing up and down, clicking his tongue every couple of minutes as he consulted his watch. Even when he sat down for a moment, he fidgeted like a child, crackling the pages of tonight's *Echo* or leaflets explaining how to spot the signs of a heart attack or a stroke. But Harry and Carmel owed Wayne so much. If he hadn't ventured into the basement of John Newton House to collect his car, chances were that Jim would already be dead and gone.

'Carmel's a long time,' Wayne muttered.

'She'll be waiting for news.'

The surgeon was operating on Jim in the Neurosurgical Unit. No word yet about his chances of pulling through. Harry had called Carmel as soon as Wayne had rung off, but on arriving at the hospital he'd only seen her for a couple of minutes before she rushed away to be with her man. Harry had never seen a woman's appearance change so much in the space of a few short hours. Terror and despair had washed away the *joie de vivre* of the morning, leaving her as shrunken and gaunt as a patient in a wheelchair they'd passed outside the cancer ward.

'Don't you think,' Wayne said, 'that hospitals are like prisons? I mean, you just feel desperate to escape. Last time I was in one of these places, all I could think of was when I might get out. I felt like a lifer, ticking the days off, one by one. Do you know what I mean?'

Harry nodded.

'It's no good.' Wayne put his head in his hands. 'I can't help blaming myself. If only I'd turned up ten minutes earlier.'

Harry ground his teeth. 'Thank God you turned up at all. Was his body…hidden from sight? '

Wayne breathed heavily. He stared at the ceiling, making a visible effort to concentrate. 'I saw him lying in one of the marked spaces for cars. Whether he'd been dumped there or managed to crawl, I can't say for sure. A few spots of blood led from the main lift shaft, but I didn't notice them when I first reached the basement. I was late for a meeting with a prospective client, my head was buzzing with business stuff. I ran straight to my car, and as I drove past the bays on the other side of the lifts, something caught my eye. Someone spread out on the ground in the shape of a star. I didn't realise it was Jim, I thought some tramp had sneaked into the car park and then collapsed in a drunken stupor. I slammed on the brake and jumped out to see how he was. When I recognised Jim and saw that gaping wound in the back of his head…I mean, it obviously wasn't an accident.'

'Was he conscious?'

'I knelt beside him and felt for a pulse. The faintest flicker. I spoke to him, begged him to hang on. All he could manage was a muffled groan.'

'He didn't say anything?'

Wayne shook his head. He gnawed at his lower lip, trying to contain himself.

'Not a word.'

'Did you see the weapon?'

'Tell you the truth, I didn't hunt for it. The first thing that went through my mind was: *suppose whoever did this is still here?* Frankly, I almost pissed myself.'

Harry could imagine. He'd always thought of Wayne as deeply shallow, but it must have cost the man something to admit that.

'I couldn't hear a sound, just the clanking of a lift on the floors above. Nobody was in the basement, and nobody else came down. It's always deserted. Only a handful of people park their cars under the building, since it's not fully let.'

'So you dialled 999?'

'I stepped outside, to get a better signal. Poked my head round the door very warily, I can tell you, but I didn't see anything suspicious. The path from John Newton House runs behind a wall to the Strand. Whoever hit Jim could have made a dash for it and never been seen. I rang for an ambulance first, then the police. After that I called you, then Victor. We'd spoken barely ten minutes before. I dropped by at the desk to let him know we had a flood in the bathroom…shit, this puts leaking taps into perspective.'

'Victor was on duty?'

Wayne puffed out his cheeks. 'If that's what you call chatting with his mate Barney.'

'Barney was there too?'

'As usual. Victor grumbled about Lou skiving off, and being left to do everything on his own. Though the workload doesn't stop him racing through books about CSIs.' A harsh laugh. 'Well, he has his own crime scene to contend with now. Right under his bloody feet.'

'Too much to hope that either Victor or Barney saw anything suspicious? No-one lurking around the doors to the car park?'

'Are you serious? The security's a joke.' Wayne flushed as he fought to keep emotion in check. 'You'd think that whoever set it up actually wanted to give intruders the run of the building. When I think of the rents they charge…'

'Victor joined you in the basement while you waited for the emergency services to arrive?'

'He took some persuading. I suppose he was terrified that whoever bashed Jim over the head might still be around. We left Barney at reception to keep an eye on the ground floor. Victor thought he'd said goodnight to Jim a quarter of an hour before I came back for help. The bastard who attacked Jim couldn't have been long gone before I arrived on the scene.'

'He'd gone out through the side door?'

'Or even the exit for cars. It's not overlooked. If the cameras had been working, it would have been different. As it is, anyone could have marched in or out. The chances of being spotted are minimal and once you're outside, you can head off in any direction.'

'You assume it was a man who hit Jim?'

Wayne stared. 'What are you suggesting?'

'If Jim was hit with a brick or a cosh or an iron bar, it wouldn't need a lot of strength.'

'I suppose not.'

'Someone hiding behind the lift shaft might have jumped out and hit Jim the moment he stepped out into the car park. Before he had chance to turn round.'

'Or had time to identify his attacker.'

Cogs whirred in Harry's brain. 'It would have been over in a matter of seconds…'

'What's up? You look as though…'

'Nothing.'

It was a lie. A question had slunk into his head, like an unwelcome guest at a funeral.

What if the attacker meant to kill me?

◇◇◇

It made no sense, he told himself as Carmel thanked Wayne Saxelby and said goodnight, this had nothing to do with that puerile nonsense about Midsummer's Eve. Nobody who wanted to harm him would skulk down in the car park of John Newton

House. He'd never once ventured into the basement, let alone brought his car there. There was no point, when he lived a few minutes' walk away.

Carmel came over to him. Her eyes were bloodshot, her skin's bloom faded to grey.

'You might as well go home.'

'I'm staying.'

'There's nothing you can do.'

'I can keep you company.'

She took hold of his right hand and squeezed it hard. 'Thanks. But one of us needs to stay grounded.'

'That's you.' He lifted his hands, placed them on her shoulders. 'I'm here to make sure you don't forget it.'

She leaned forward, breathing hard, letting him bear her weight. Tears welled up in her eyes. Harry clenched his fist. Any moment now Carmel might break. He had to make sure she was strong for Jim, so that she could help him make it through the night.

'He'll never forgive you if you don't look after the office. Till he's fit and well again.'

'Sylvia will take care of the office. I'd better call her, let her know what's happened. You've spoken to the kids?'

'They're checking for flights.' Jim's children were students, each travelling the world, Thailand and South America. 'They both want to come back and be with him.'

'Shall I talk to them?' Jim hadn't said much, but Harry had once picked up a hint that the kids were unhappy about his relationship with Carmel. They thought it had come too soon after their mother's death.

'No, it's my responsibility. We must stick together, for Jim's sake.' Carmel exhaled. 'Harry, who would do such a terrible thing? To Jim, of all people?'

She didn't say it, probably hadn't even thought it, but he guessed what must be swirling around her sub-conscious. If disaster had befallen him rather than his partner, nobody would have been too surprised. He was accident-prone, famous for it. Jim was different.

'I haven't a clue,' he said. 'But I'll find out. Promise.'

◇◇◇

Sylvia was fighting back tears as he rang off. Carmel had been right. The woman's devotion to Jim was even fiercer than he'd realised. To hear that he teetered on the brink between life and death was more than she could bear.

He hurried down the corridor to the small square room set aside for the families of patients with head injuries. There was a recess with tea and coffee making facilities and a cheap sofa. Through the inner door was an even tinier room equipped with a narrow bed for overnight vigils. A lavender scent made the place smell like a granny's sitting room. A watercolour of Snowdonia hung on the wall, facing a dusty sofa with a floral pattern that might have been fashionable twenty years ago. A Bible squatted on a corner table. He sat down next to Carmel on the sofa and put his arm around her. She hadn't changed out of the tight blouse she'd worn that morning. He felt her shoulder-bone and her soft flesh beneath the cotton. She was shivering.

'Sylvia will mind the shop tomorrow. Keep an eye on things until Jim is back.'

Carmel wriggled out of his grasp. She fished a tissue from her handbag and blew her nose loudly.

'He won't be coming back, Harry.'

'Of course he will.'

'No, he won't. Not ever.'

She clutched at him and dissolved into misery. Her face was wet, her heart pounding. He felt sucked into a quagmire of sadness; the more he struggled, the harder it was to escape. He'd never had a child—a regret so deep-seated that he never acknowledged it—but this must be how a father might feel if his daughter plunged into disaster. An urge to keep her safe from harm, coupled with a sense of inadequacy as overwhelming as a tidal wave.

'Jim will make it. Are you listening to me?'

A minute passed before she spoke and said, distinctly but without rancour, 'You're a fucking liar.'

'The scan says his brain isn't dead. The doctors are fighting for him, all he needs is time.'

'They told me he has an extradural haematoma.'

Harry didn't know how bad this was. Whenever stuff about hospitals or operations came up on TV, he made a grab for the remote control. He squeezed her hand.

'It's a blood clot, to you and me. They have to lift the flap of his skull to squeeze it out.' She made a face. 'The consultant in A&E said that before they put him to sleep, he was semi-conscious for a few minutes. But he was agitated and talking gibberish.'

'Could he move his limbs?'

'Yes, but there's no telling the extent of his injuries. They've stuck a tube into his lungs, they were afraid he might swallow his tongue.' She sucked in air. 'I see it on their faces, Harry. The way they dodge the questions. He's going to die.'

'No.' Losing Jim Crusoe was impossible. 'They have to take it one step at a time. He'll be okay, we must keep faith.'

The door opened and an acne-plagued police constable peered round it. His name was Cusden and Harry had seen him earlier, talking to Carmel and then a nurse. He kept fiddling with a hangnail. Harry felt sorry for him. Carmel was a serious player in the Police Authority. No young policeman would want to mess up in a case which meant so much to her.

'Mr. Devlin, can you spare a moment?'

Harry joined him out in the corridor. 'Any more news?'

'No trace of the person who attacked Mr. Crusoe. But we've found the weapon. Stuffed into one of the mobile waste containers in the basement of the building. An iron bar.'

Harry flinched. 'You can do a lot of damage with an iron bar.'

The DC fingered an angry red spot on his chin. 'A glancing blow is all it took. Your partner's lucky to be alive.'

'Fingerprints on the bar?'

'Looks as though it's been wiped.'

'A mugging gone wrong?'

'Funny sort of mugger who leaves his victim's gold watch and wallet full of cash and credit cards. Of course, he might have panicked, but…'

'Any other leads?'

'Nothing at the moment, sir. That's where you come in. Ms Sutcliffe says you've received a number of threats yourself.'

'There's no way anyone could have mistaken Jim for me.'

'You both work in the same office.'

'But I never use the car park. Whoever threatened me knows a bit about my movements. If they were planning to attack me, the car park is the last place to choose. Especially when I was out of the city.'

'You never know,' Cusden said. 'Shall we have a cup of tea while you tell me what's been going on?'

◇◇◇

Harry didn't mention the call from Kay. It would only complicate the inquiry and make her situation worse. Whatever her situation might be. Tom Gunter had no reason to batter his partner and the attack wasn't a case of mistaken identity. Jim was taller and broader, even after the slimming effect of life with Carmel. He dressed better, his stride was longer. Even from behind, even if you were psyching yourself up to beat out your victim's brains, you could spot the difference in a nanosecond.

Besides, he didn't want to believe that whoever had smashed Jim's skull had intended that he, rather than Jim, should die. He dared not believe it. The guilt would be too much to bear.

DC Cusden didn't seem impressed by the messages about Midsummer's Eve. 'In your line of business, you must come across plenty of oddballs.'

'I suppose so.' Harry was tempted to add that some of them were police officers. 'So you don't think there's a connection?'

'Why wind you up with these messages and then batter your partner?' A fair point. 'What I'd really like to know is, who might have a grudge against Mr. Crusoe?'

Harry frowned. The lad had to ask, but the idea that someone would wish to kill Jim was absurd. Wasn't it? The man worked hard, he was respected by other lawyers, well-liked by his staff. Even his relish for everything that, in Harry's eyes, was mind-numbingly tedious—property law, probate work, profit and loss accounts—was admirable. Indispensable, actually.

But what if Carmel was right, what if Jim died? What would he do?

He banished the questions the moment they slid into his head, ashamed by the pang of selfishness at a time like this. All that mattered was getting Jim fit and well.

'Was there something?' Cusden pressed. 'Dissatisfied client? Tempers can fray in legal disputes.'

'He bought and sold buildings and looked after the estates of dead people.'

'Nice work if you can get it. The deceased don't make any fuss.'

'Very few of his living clients complained, even about his bills. People came back to Jim, time and again, they liked dealing with him.'

I'm already talking in the past tense. Stop it. Think positive.

Cusden rubbed his eyes. He looked tired, out of his depth. 'Um…I have to ask about his private life. Were there any…'

'His wife died a fortnight before Christmas. Carmel came to the funeral, she used to work for us. She stayed in touch and one thing led to another.'

'There hadn't been anyone else?'

Years ago, Jim had had an affair. Moments of madness. His lover was a police officer. In the end, they'd gone their separate ways; the last Harry had heard, the woman had transferred to the North East. He was as sure as he could be that Jim's wife had gone to her grave without finding out.

'Nobody else.'

A woman passed them, pushing a trolley whose wheels squeaked on the floor tiles. Cusden cringed at the sound, or perhaps at the difficulty of deciding what to do next.

'So nobody had a grudge against him through his legal practice, or his private life. Yet someone lay in wait for him under your offices and hit him so hard on the head that it's touch and go whether he'll make it through the night.'

Harry nodded. 'It doesn't make sense.'

'No.' Cusden chewed at his nail. 'Perhaps you wouldn't mind telling me exactly where you were at the time of the attack?'

◇◇◇

He still didn't mention Kay, simply said that he'd planned to meet a prospective client and was obliged to keep her name confidential. Cusden didn't like that and wasn't mollified when Harry said that if the CCTV at Empire Dock wasn't as useless as that at John Newton House, there would be evidence on film of his car in the queue for the Strand when Farmers4Justice blocked the road. Of course, it didn't prove his innocence. He might have parked out of sight and hurried back to the office building, to hide in the basement until he had the chance to bash Jim over the head. For all Cusden knew, he might have lost the plot altogether and sent the Midsummer's Eve messages to himself. Harry could only hope that they wouldn't call in the psychiatrists. Even if they found no hint of homicidal tendencies, they were bound to have a field day.

He rejoined Carmel in the room for families of patients at death's door. She was trembling and wouldn't look him in the eye.

'What's the latest?'

'They've removed the blood clot. The next forty eight hours will be crucial.'

He squeezed her hand.

'Harry, I don't…I don't know what to do. What if he pulls through and spends the rest of his life as a fucking vegetable?'

She dissolved again.

◇◇◇

At four in the morning, Carmel said, 'Go home. You'll need to be up before long. Off to work.'

'I don't want to leave you here on your own.'

'I'll be fine. I've stopped feeling sorry for myself. For the moment, no guarantees long-term. Go back to your flat. You need to be at the office first thing. Taking charge.'

'The office can take care of itself.'

'No. You know what you have to do. It's what Jim would want. No point both of us sitting here moping. He'd expect you to make yourself useful for once.'

'I suppose he would.'

'No suppose about it. In the nicest possible way, Harry, piss off.'

He stood up, dropped a kiss on her hair. 'I'll call you later.'

'Look after Sylvia, will you? Losing Jim will crucify her.'

He paused at the door and wagged a finger in admonition. 'We're not going to lose him.'

She stared at the white-capped peak of Mount Snowdon on the wall, but didn't say another word.

The Fourth Day

Chapter Ten

It wasn't worth going to bed. Exhaustion weighed down his limbs, and to make a cup of black coffee required a gut-clenching effort of will, but he knew sleep would never come. Slumped on the sofa, he flicked through the TV channels and found himself watching Harold Shand's world fall apart in *The Long Good Friday*. Sid Rankin should have found a slot for the film in the Alhambra's paranoia season. Calamity after calamity hammered the iron cladding of the little bulldog's self-confidence until you almost felt sorry for him. Even when Shand hung people from meat hooks in a vain attempt to figure out what was going wrong.

'Who's having a go at me?' Harold Shand demanded. 'Can you think of anyone who might have an old score to settle?'

Good question. Or was it?

Maybe the wet-behind-the-ears DC Cusden wasn't so naïve after all. What if Jim was the real target? Might he, like Harold Shand, have made dangerous enemies without even knowing?

Juliet's soft voice slid back into his brain, her warning as sinuous and deadly as an uncoiling snake.

'Casper isn't a man to mess with. Don't ever make him angry.'

◇◇◇

He was in the office before half seven. Lou was on duty, chewing gum with much solemnity. When he saw Harry walking in through the double doors, he cleared his throat, as if about to embark on extensive commiserations, but Harry gave a brief nod and made straight for the lift. When he rang Carmel from his room, her voice was hoarse; she hadn't slept either.

'What's the latest?'

'No change. He's in intensive care, dead to the world.'

'So his condition is stable?'

'They've dedicated three nurses to him, on eight-hour shifts. I've been talking to the woman who's on duty this morning. She says that even those who survive this kind of injury sometimes wake up with their personalities changed.'

'He's in good hands. Liverpool General is one of the best hospitals in the country. The league tables…'

'Mean nothing,' she said, and he knew she was right.

'Let me know the minute you hear more.' She didn't answer. 'Please, Carmel.'

'Even if he doesn't die, he won't be the man I fell in love with. There isn't going to be a happy ending here, Harry.'

'You can't know that. We must keep hoping. Talk to you later.'

He turned the page on his desk calendar. *The way to love anything is to realise that it may be lost.* In a fit of temper, he ripped off the sheet, and threw it into the wastepaper basket. Not that it made him feel any better. For once, the calendar was right.

At nine, he summoned everyone to the brand new boardroom and broke the news. He'd never known a staff meeting like it. No jokes, no back-chat. Grief spread like a stain, disfiguring pale and fearful faces. Most of the women wept. Not Sylvia, though; she'd had time to come to terms with the shock. As soon as he'd finished speaking, she became brisk and business-like, explaining how Jim's work was to be delegated, who would do what.

As he walked back towards his own room, Grace caught up with him. She was wearing a sleeveless summer dress and strappy sandals. Her bare arms and legs were white, as though the sun hadn't shone for months.

'I just wanted to say, if there's anything I can do…'

'Thanks, Sylvia will organise…'

'No, I meant for you.' She bent close to him and the musky perfume assaulted his sinuses once again. 'I'd visit him in hospital, but the last thing he would want is to see me at his bedside.'

Harry stared at her. 'I'm not sure…'

'He doesn't like me,' she said softly. 'No, it's nothing that he's said, but I can read it in his eyes, hear it in his voice whenever he speaks to me. But it doesn't matter, I'm not offended. We haven't had a chance to get used to each other yet.'

He wanted to tell her she was wrong, of course Jim didn't dislike her. Trouble was, he'd be lying and she'd know it. As he groped for words, it struck him how little he knew about the woman. Nothing unusual in that, nobody checked out a temp in depth. You waited to see what the agency came up with. If they turned up on time and worked with a semblance of competence, who in their right mind would ask too many questions?

'This is about believing,' Grace murmured, and she disappeared in the direction of the secretaries' room before he could conjure up an answer.

◇◇◇

He spent an hour at an appointment before the district judge in the new county court building. His client, a woman in her fifties whose vivid red wig matched her temper, was a serial divorcee. Her size 44 DD chest attracted plenty of admirers, but all too often she ended up throwing plates at them; occasionally kitchen knives. The last time he'd acted for her, she'd sent him a perfumed thank-you card, expressing her appreciation for his ridding her of a slobbish limp-dick and promising to hire him again if her next marriage broke down. Within eighteen months, she proved as good as her word. Harry was grateful for repeat business, though he worried that if her aim ever improved, he'd finish up defending her on a murder rap.

Back at John Newton House, Sylvia's mask of calm competence was glued on. He could only guess at the emotions swirling behind it.

'As luck would have it, Jim completed half a dozen deals during the past fortnight. The staff can cope for the time being, we don't need to bring in a locum.'

'Do we have any work on the go for Casper May's companies?'

The mask twitched. 'Casper May?'

'You know. Our illustrious client. I gather he owns this very building.'

'I wasn't sure that Jim had mentioned it.'

'As a matter of fact, he didn't. Someone else let it slip.'

'It wasn't a secret.' At once she was on the defensive, determined to protect her boss from criticism, real or imagined. 'I think he might have wondered if it…bothered you.'

'Why should it?'

She gave him an old-fashioned look. 'Let's not go there, Harry.'

Shit. Was there anyone in the city who didn't know he'd carried on with Juliet? Whatever happened to personal privacy?

'I'd better take a look at our lease.'

Her eyebrows arched. Of course, he should have studied it before signing. But he trusted Jim. Would trust him with his life.

'There's nothing to worry about. The deal's a good one. We have a break clause after five years.'

'But?' He'd known her long enough to realise there must be a 'but'.

'No such thing as a free lunch, Harry. I warned him about Casper May. It's not a good idea to get in hock to a man like that.'

'And?'

'A few days ago, they had a row.'

'I never heard about it.'

'It was our second day here. You were in court with that footballer from St Helens.'

Another matrimonial client with violent propensities. He'd married a precocious sixteen-year-old in a shotgun wedding and when he'd come home unexpectedly eighteen months later to find his wife in bed with his team's goalkeeper, he'd initiated an airgun divorce, peppering the couple's naked backsides with a dozen pellets each.

'So what did Jim and Casper quarrel about?'

'The client wanted to pay cash for a nursing home. Jim was worried that Casper was using the deal to launder dirty money. He didn't want to touch the deal, but Casper reckoned he was owed a favour.'

'What happened?'

'Jim refused. Of course. Nobody is straighter.'

'How did Casper take that?' He remembered Casper's bleak manner when they met at the Stapledon.

'He didn't make a song and dance about it. Simply said he never forgot anyone who let him down.'

'Jim never mentioned it to me.'

'He didn't want to worry you. And....'

'What?'

She bowed her head. 'I encouraged him not to bother you with it.'

He stared at her until the explanation stole into his mind. 'Because of Juliet?'

'I thought your life was complicated enough without having to worry about Casper May all over again.'

He stifled a groan. 'I suppose I should say thanks.'

She shrugged. 'There are plenty of lawyers out there who are happy to turn a blind eye when rich crooks want to be looked after. The only surprise is that it took so long for him to try it on with Jim.'

'Yeah, he must have known how hard it would be to persuade Jim to break the rules.'

'I thought he would take no for an answer. My mistake. And now...'—all of a sudden, Syliva's mask collapsed—'..and now that bastard has taken his revenge.'

◇◇◇

'Green and Pleasant Plant Care,' a posh woman trilled, 'how may I help you?'

Harry introduced himself and said, 'I'd like to speak to Ka-Yu Cheung. Can you tell me where to find her this morning?'

'I'm afraid I can't, Mr. Devlin. She didn't come into work today.'

'Is she off sick?' His hopes lifted. Perhaps some bug had prevented her from keeping the appointment at West Bank.

'I'm afraid I can't say.' Posh, but also pissed off. 'She didn't have the courtesy to let us know. Although company rules do require...'

'That's not like Kay.'

'No.' A sigh. 'But these young women...'

'Do you know how I can get in touch with her?'

'I'm afraid that I can't disclose employee details to clients, Mr. Devlin, no matter how valued.' How afraid could one woman be? Harry wondered. 'It would be a breach of the Data Protection Act. As a solicitor, you will understand.'

Harry understood that the Data Protection Act had become a convenient excuse for keeping people in the dark. He told a few fibs and within five minutes had prised out both Kay's mobile number and the address of the flat she shared with Tom Gunter at Liverpool Marina.

The mobile went straight to voicemail and the familiar soft voice said: 'Hi, this is Kay. Please leave your name and number and I'll get back to you.'

He muttered into the phone: 'This is Harry. Please ring me as soon as you can. Just to confirm you're all right.'

But, like the posh woman at Green and Pleasant Plant Care, he was afraid—afraid that Kay would not return his call.

◇◇◇

He needed to get out of the city for half an hour. Clear the fog in his head. He hurried over to Empire Dock and jumped into his car. He drove on auto-pilot, trying to squeeze out of his brain the memory of Tom Gunter in St Nicholas Gardens, caressing his knife. After twenty minutes, he reached Waterloo and turned off the main road, parking as close as he could to the beach.

From here it was only five minutes' walk to the Alhambra, but he hadn't come to watch a film.

A stiff breeze slapped his cheeks as he followed the path skirting the lake. Clouds had gathered and he felt drizzle on his skin. A man in a black wetsuit clinging to a gaudy sail drifted across the water. Gulls squealed overhead, as if in derision. Soon Harry reached a board warning THIS BEACH IS HAZARDOUS and beyond it the vast expanse of yellow sand.

Hazardous for Lee Welch, that was for sure. She had died here, though he didn't know the precise scene of crime. You couldn't chalk the outline of a corpse on the beach.

The Seaforth radar terminal loomed to his left, beyond it the rattle and boom of the container port. Wind turbines twirled on land and sea. Crosby beach wasn't a conventional beauty spot. Harry had read some snooty Southern journalist describe it as a long channel of estuarial sludge. An old lady tapping a stick on the asphalt made her way towards him, an obese dachshund grunting at her feet.

Harry walked on to the beach, shoes squelching in the damp sand. The old lady halted, intrigued by the sight of someone in an office suit wandering out to sea. Perhaps she imagined him stripping off by the water's edge and then moving forward until he was submerged by the waves. Even the dachshund was sufficiently intrigued to hold its tongue.

A tall naked man, feet buried in the sand, had his broad back to the land. Harry stopped beside him. The man took no notice. A weathered penis dangled between his legs, blind eyes stared out towards where sea and sky merged into a slate-grey horizon.

He must have witnessed Lee's murder, he knew the truth of her fate. But he'd never tell.

He was made of cast iron.

Chapter Eleven

This was Another Place.

Another Place, where one hundred iron men stared out at sand, sea and sky.

A sculptor named Gormley had created the pensive figures, moulded from his own frame, and arranged them along the beach, stretching for a kilometre towards the sea. You could have been forgiven for thinking the Iron Men were emissaries from a distant planet, taking part in some eerie ritual in a bleak and futuristic setting. At high tides, water submerged the Iron Men, but nothing fazed them, nothing shook their sombre calm. A notice said they were merely a particular body. No hero, no ideal, merely the representation of a middle-aged man trying to remain standing and trying to breathe.

Another Place obsessed Harry. He often slipped up here to stroll among the rusting statues, asking himself if they saw what he saw, if they dreamed what he dreamed. He might not know much about art, but he did know that the Iron Men meant something to him, perhaps something different to whatever they meant to anyone else. Too many people hated the disruption to their environment: coastguards, conservationists, fishermen, hobby-sailors, they all wanted rid of the Iron Men. But Harry rejoiced that they had been allowed to linger here, gazing out towards—God knows, America? Striving to make sense of a mysterious world.

Like him.

Questions tumbled down the helter-skelter of his brain. Who had beaten Jim, what had happened to Kay, how could he fathom the significance of Midsummer's Eve? Leaning against the cold hardness of the sculpture, he murmured, 'What do you think?'

No answer.

The old lady with the fat little dog watched his lips move, then bent down and instructed her companion to get a move on. No doubt she thought Harry was a madman, possibly a fugitive from Ashworth Hospital. The drizzle eased, but once she hobbled out of sight, he was the only living being on the beach.

He pictured Jim lying on his bed in intensive care. Eyes shut, tubes poking out of him. Frozen on the ledge between life and death.

Until now, shock had numbed Harry. But as he acclimatised to the horror, he was beginning to feel something else. Hot and smothering rage.

He clenched his fist. Time to fight back.

◇◇◇

The sun peeked from behind the clouds as he reached Liverpool Marina and the paintwork of the boats sparkled in its rays. Outside the bar and restaurant, the car park was crammed with BMWs and Volvos. Portly men in smart sailing gear, accompanied by stick-thin second wives thronged the pathways. Tall blocks of houses and flats spilled along the riverside. Harry checked out the house numbers on Ballance Boulevard and made his way to the address the posh woman had given for Kay.

All very different from the mean streets of Halewood. Tom Gunter and his girlfriend had come a long way up in the world. Harry wondered what Tom was up to these days. There was money to be made in IT, but even so. Besides, he couldn't be working full-time, otherwise what was he doing in St Nick's Gardens?

Harry pressed the entry buzzer. No reply. He dialled Kay again on his mobile. Voicemail once more. This time he didn't bother to leave a message.

'Can I help you?'

He turned to face a woman wearing too much lipstick, her arm entwined with that of a bearded bloke in a peaked cap. A sceptical gleam lit their eyes. Harry's suit was shinier than his shoes, even though he'd scraped off most of the sand, and his tie had seen better days. Not a Liverpool Marina person, really.

'Do you know when Tom and Kay are likely to be back?'

The woman frowned. 'The new people in Number Seven? We don't really know them.'

'We hear them more than see them,' Captain Pugwash snorted. 'Playing their music all hours of the day and night. This rap stuff. Bloody rubbish, if you ask me.'

'You haven't come across Kay in the last twenty four hours, then?'

'I had to knock on their door last night,' the man said, ignoring the question. 'Asked him to turn down the racket. Bloody rude, he was.'

'And Kay?'

'Didn't see her.'

'Was she in the flat at the time, do you know?'

The woman jabbed him in the stomach with a bejewelled forefinger. 'Why do you ask?'

Might as well tell the truth. 'Kay is a friend of mine.'

'And is this chap of hers a friend of yours?'

'No.'

She turned to Captain Pugwash with a smirk of triumph. 'Told you so!'

'What?' Harry demanded as the man belched in disapproval.

'He's a bad lot,' she said. 'I know the type. Years ago...well, never mind. Let's just say that the moment I clapped eyes on him, I knew he was a brute. All this music, I don't think he plays it for entertainment.'

'What, then?'

'If you ask me, he hurts her. And he turns up the music loud enough to drown out her crying.'

◇◇◇

Lou was behind the desk on the ground floor of John Newton House, gossiping with the crony who resembled W.H. Auden. From the way they fell silent as Harry approached, it was clear that the attack on Jim had replaced soccer as the topic of conversation. A Stepford Architect on the plasma screen waxed lyrical about *vibrant sustainability* and *key deliverables*, but Lou silenced her with the flick of a switch.

'This is a bad business, Harry.' he muttered. 'Any news from the hospital?'

'He's still on the danger list.'

'If you ask me, we should bring back capital punishment,' the crony said.

Harry resisted the urge to snap that he hadn't asked him. 'Where's Victor?'

'In his flat.'

'I'll have a word.'

Lou lifted the phone as Harry moved towards an inconspicuous door at right angles to the waterfall. 'I'll let him know you're on your way.'

Now why would that be necessary? Had Victor told Lou to let him know whenever anyone wanted to call on him? Perhaps it was reasonable if he wanted to sleep during the day. Even so.

Through the door was a small windowless landing. Even in the middle of the day the light was on, illuminating a flight of steep steps down to the basement. Facing the steps was another door marked BUILDING MANAGER. Harry pressed the buzzer, heard it squeal. His skin prickled; he was sure someone was peering at him through the spy-hole. Ten seconds passed. A key screeched in the lock and at last the door swung open.

Victor wore a navy blue vest and denim jeans that had seen better days. His eyes were bleary and he smelled of stale sweat. Harry had never seen his skinny arms before. Each bore a tattoo of a bad-tempered griffin.

'Harry.'

'Sorry to disturb you, Victor.'

The building manager took a breath. 'How is he?'

'Not good.'

'Fucking hell, Harry. I mean, like, fucking hell.'

'Yeah.'

Victor folded the bare arms. No sign that he was about to invite his visitor in.

'A bad do.'

'Are the police finished in the basement?'

'Uh-huh.'

'I'd like to take a look round.'

'What's the idea?'

'I want to see where Jim was attacked.'

Victor frowned. 'Doing your amateur detective stuff, eh?'

'You don't mind?'

A moment's hesitation. 'No...of course not. I'll come down with you.'

'No need. You should catch up on your sleep.'

'After what happened last night, I haven't been able to do more than doze for half an hour at a time.'

'Seriously, I don't mean to mess up your resting time. If you let me have the key...'

'It's not a problem. Won't be a moment.'

Victor turned on his heel and disappeared into the room where soft music played. Harry thought he heard muffled voices, but if Victor had company, he wasn't about to make introductions. Within a minute he was back, a fat bundle of keys bulging in his fist.

'Follow me.'

He locked the flat behind him, as if to emphasise that nobody remained inside. Protesting too much. Harry wondered why.

'Can't be too careful after last night.'

'I suppose not.'

Victor's chin jutted forward. 'You okay?'

'I've felt better.'

A heavy sigh. 'It was grim, Harry. I'm glad you weren't here to see him in such a shocking state. It'd have broken your bloody heart.'

Harry followed him downstairs. The steps were ancient and worn and Harry picked his way with care. It would be so easy to lose your footing and pitch headfirst down to the basement and break your neck. No wonder Victor kept the light on. The walls were whitewashed and fringed with spiders' webs. The interior designers who had transformed John Newton House hadn't made it below ground level. No thick floor coverings deadened the echoing footfalls. There was no climate control. The temperature in the stairwell was a couple of degrees lower than in the entrance lobby.

'You know the basement was part of the original building on this site? Dates back three hundred years. Mind, that's nothing compared to Tower Building next door. The first Tower was built in the twelfth century. It was a prison. So was this place, in a manner of speaking.'

'What do you mean?'

Victor arrived at the bottom of the stairs. He pressed a switch and smiled, his gold tooth gleaming in the fluorescent glow as he unlocked yet another door that led to the car park.

'The slave traders kept their goods here until the ships were ready to sail to Jamaica or wherever. Look closely at the walls and you'll see the fastenings for the chains.'

'The property agents never mentioned this.'

'Part of our history, mate. Why should we be made to feel ashamed of it? These days people say we should apologise for what happened generations ago. Fucking barmy.' Victor waved at a series of indentations in the brick wall. 'See those marks? Makes you think, eh?'

They stepped through a tall arch, one of a dozen spanning the basement and a movement-activated sensor flooded the car park with light. To their right was a floor-to-ceiling metal roller shutter, ahead of them two rows of marked bays for cars. On the left stood three large blue waste bins on wheels; beyond them a passageway led to a row of large, hollowed-out spaces. Harry glanced into the first alcove. Dusty metal shelving ran the length of its back wall.

Victor nodded. 'Over there was the old telephone exchange. Not used since the sixties. You can still see some of the bits and pieces. There's an electricity sub-station at the back.'

Harry pointed to the roller shutter. 'And behind there?'

'Part of the floor inside is missing. The health and safety people ordered us to shut it off. I asked the landlords if I could get a quote to have it fixed, but they want to flog a few more flats before they shell out any more money on the building. At least on the parts that the tenants don't see.'

'Any chance that whoever hit Jim could have hidden in there?'

'None. The police asked the same question, but there's only one key and I keep it with me.' He jangled the keys in his hand. 'You can't be too careful these days. The insurers wouldn't pay up if anyone had an accident.'

Ahead were the vast double doors of the car lift and beyond them the passenger lift shaft. Only one of the three carriages came down to this level. Apart from the stone staircase, the remaining entrance to the basement was the door which gave on to the outside path. High on the walls hung two CCTV cameras, sited to command a view of the entrances and exits. When they worked.

Harry noticed a few dark smudges on the stone floor. Traces of Jim's blood left after the police had taken samples. He couldn't shut out the vision of his partner, groaning as life seeped out of him. He flinched as he imagined the pain, dug his nails into his palm as he strove for calm.

The police hadn't moved Jim's car. No reason to do so, once they'd checked it hadn't been broken into or tampered with. Of the three other vehicles, Juliet's and Wayne's luxury motors were parked next to each other, as if keeping a snobbish distance from Victor's rusting Fiesta, tucked into a corner marked RESERVED—BUILDING MANAGER.

'Jim always left his car in the same place,' Victor said. 'He was a creature of habit.'

Past tense. Harry ground his teeth. 'Aren't we all?'

Victor clicked his tongue as he surveyed the scene. 'Who would have thought it? A crime scene in my own bloody back yard.'

'You talked to the CSIs?'

'Only the DC who took a statement from me. Not that I had much to state. I was on the desk and didn't have the faintest idea what was happening down here.' Victor shuddered. 'I tell you, Harry. It's one thing to read about crime scene stuff as a hobby. Something else entirely when you know the victim.'

Tell me about it.

'Did the police press you for an alibi?'

Victor frowned. 'They asked a few routine questions, that's all. I'm hardly likely to do Jim in, am I? Decent feller, always happy to pass the time of day. Besides, Barney can vouch for me.'

Very convenient. Not that Victor was a prime suspect. As he said, why would he wish to do Jim harm?

'We were chewing the fat when Wayne Saxelby raised the alarm. I rushed down here to see what I could do, while Barney kept an eye on the desk. Wayne had already dialled 999 and inside five minutes, the place was crawling with medics and coppers. Jesus, what a night.'

'Anyone else in the building around the critical time, other possible witnesses?'

Victor shook his head. 'The other tenants had all made themselves scarce by half five. As per usual. Same with your staff. Apart from the Mays.'

'The Mays?'

'Casper and Juliet, of course. They came down about twenty minutes before Jim Crusoe.'

'Together?'

Victor leaned against a sign on the wall that said in big red letters NO SMOKING. NO NAKED FLAMES. 'There's no law against it, mate. Just because they're divorced, doesn't mean that…'

'Did they go down to the car park?'

'No, through the main entrance. When Wayne called me downstairs, Mrs. May's car was parked in its usual spot. So either the pair of them went off on foot or took a cab.'

'Unless Casper drove.'

'He never leaves his car here. Told me once, he has a private garage next to his office in Rumford Street.'

'You didn't happen to see which direction they took?'

'Christ, Harry, what do you think I am? Some kind of voyeur?' Victor assumed an improbable haughtiness. 'I mean, you can't possibly imagine Mr. and Mrs. May had anything to do with the attack on Jim Crusoe.'

'No, but…'

'It was some scally, trust me. Somehow he's sneaked into the basement and decided to lie in wait, see who he could mug. Maybe someone forgot to lock the external door. It happens, no matter how often I remind people about the need for security. Poor old Jim drew the short straw. But even a mugging gone wrong is still murder as far as the law's concerned, eh? No way could anyone have clobbered him by mistake.'

'Jim isn't dead.'

'No, no. Sorry, mate. No offence. But you know what I mean? Such a decent bloke. You'd never think he had an enemy in the world. It's a crying shame.'

Harry thrust his hands deep into the pockets of his suit trousers. 'Thanks for your time.'

'No problem.' Victor glanced at his watch. 'Seen all you want to see?'

◇◇◇

Harry waited in the lobby for the lift to take him to the office and wondered whether Victor's furtiveness was suspicious or merely habitual. After the attack on Jim, he would take nothing for granted. How much did he know about Victor or his mate Barney the mobile embalmer? How much did he really know about anyone, come to that? You only saw the sides of people that they wanted to show, learned the details of their lives they were willing to reveal. Everyone kept secrets. Even conventional, conservative Sylvia.

The lift doors slid open and Juliet May stood in front of him. He took in the smoothness of her ski slope nose. The startling fullness of those lips. She was wearing a blouse and cream trousers so simple that he knew they must have cost a fortune.

'I heard the news about Jim.' Her eyelids flickered. 'Is he…?'

'He's in intensive care. God knows whether he'll pull through.'

'It's dreadful. Casper's furious. The police have even questioned him.'

'Really?'

'They aren't impressed that the CCTV is fucked. Neither is Casper. I suppose the contractors cut corners. There will be hell to pay when Casper catches up with them. The last thing he wants is to be interrogated by some wet-behind-the-ears plod who doesn't know who he's dealing with. This has caused Casper a lot of grief.'

'My heart bleeds. I suppose he has an alibi for the attack on Jim?'

'He was in a restaurant, if you must know, for a drink and a chat with a business colleague. I joined them later, once they'd got the boring stuff out of the way. I went for a walk along the riverside.' She gave him a teasing smile and he guessed she had been drinking. 'So I'm afraid I don't have an alibi, Harry.'

'You don't need one.'

'Thank you.'

'Was the business partner Malachy Needham, by any chance? I came across him the other day in court.'

'Your client accused him of murder.' She leaned forward and he could smell alcohol fumes on her breath. 'Though the City Coroner was never going to find him guilty, that's for sure.'

'Coroners aren't allowed to name people as guilty of murder these days.'

'Whatever.' She shrugged. 'The legal details don't matter. It was all taken care of.'

Harry shook his head. 'What are you talking about?'

'Casper and I may be divorced, Harry, but we still speak to each other every day. He's tired of his little waitress, I'm sure of it.'

'In the meantime, you're another of his business partners. Like Malachy Needham.'

'There's no comparison between Malachy and me. Casper's relationship with him is entirely professional.'

'They run an escort agency together.'

'Cultural Companions, yes. Good name, don't you think?'

'Until two of the escorts got themselves murdered.'

'Nothing to do with Casper.'

'Can you be sure?'

'Stone cold positive.' Her expression hardened. 'Both those girls cut private deals with their clients. The stupid kids do it all the time, just to save the agency fees. More fool them. At least Casper would protect them.'

'Heart of gold, eh?'

'You may scoff, but I promise you. Casper didn't have anything to do with their deaths. All he cares about is that the killings have messed up his precious business plan.'

He shook his head. 'Christ, Juliet, how can you tolerate a man like that?'

'Don't tell me you're jealous?'

'It's not that. He has a score to settle with Jim.'

'What on earth are you talking about?'

'He and Needham had money to launder and he wanted Jim to handle the deal. When Jim said no, Casper wasn't happy.'

'You're not suggesting Casper arranged for Jim to be attacked last night?'

'How could anyone prove it? I'm sure he wouldn't dirty his own hands, now he's snuggling up to the great and the good.'

'Harry.' Lowering her voice as if someone might eavesdrop, she leaned towards him. 'Don't say such things. Even to me. It's dangerous. Whatever you've heard about Casper, you haven't heard the half of it. Trust me, you wouldn't want to know.'

'You know something, Juliet? After what's happened to Jim, I don't care any more. Less than twenty four hours ago someone left my oldest friend for dead. All that matters to me now is discovering who and why.'

'Leave it,' she said. 'The police will find the bad guy and lock him up. That's what we pay our taxes for.'

'Like they locked up Casper each time he did something wrong?'

She shrugged.

'And what did you mean about the City Coroner?' he demanded. 'Why so confident that Malachy would get off?'

'Oh, Harry. Twenty years a solicitor and you're still not wise to the ways of the world. Malachy had the best advice that money could buy, but he and Casper had something useful tucked up their sleeves. They gave it to me for safe keeping, to tell you the truth. With all this trouble over the murdered girls, they're worried about having their homes and offices searched.'

'What are you talking about?'

'A photograph. I keep it in my magazine rack. Bold as brass.' She laughed, and he realised she'd had even more to drink than he'd thought. 'Shades of that story by Edgar Allan Poe.'

'I don't understand.'

A mischievous smile. 'Come up to the penthouse and take a look for yourself, if you don't believe me. I don't mind telling you the story, entre nous. Look, I'll be back here in an hour. I'll make us a pot of Earl Grey. Have you learned to drink it with lemon yet, rather than milk?'

'Thanks, but I have work to do.'

'You need a break.'

'Sorry, Juliet.'

'Come on, you know you want to.' She retrieved a key from her bag. 'Here's the spare for my front door. I had Casper change the locks as soon as he told me that dreadful Creevey man has a master key to everywhere in the building.'

'Including our office?'

'Don't look outraged. It's only a precaution. Casper likes to keep in touch with what goes on in his properties. Don't worry, I can't imagine he'd ever want to rifle through your drawers.'

'We'll change our locks too.'

'Calm down, it's no big deal. Shall I see you in an hour? Casper's out on business this afternoon.'

He shook his head. 'Seriously, it's not a good idea.'

'Take it.' She slipped the key into his jacket pocket and skipped off towards the main doors before he could hand it back. 'See you shortly!'

'But not this afternoon,' he said to himself as he stepped into the lift. Their affair belonged to the past and he meant it to stay there.

The lift stopped at the fifth floor. He said to himself that if there was anyone around, he'd get out and go to work. If not, he'd carry on up to the top of the building and have a scout around for himself.

The doors opened. Nobody was to be seen. He pressed the button and the doors closed again.

The two penthouses on the top floor each covered more square feet than the average semi-detached. Across the landing lived Tamara Dighton and Wayne Saxelby. He tried the key in Juliet's lock and the door eased open at a touch. He found himself in an airy hallway, its centrepiece a wrought-iron spiral staircase. Each wall was covered from top to bottom with framed abstract art, wild splashes of purple, green, yellow and black.

The stairs led to a vast entertaining room. A dozen cushions in intricate patchwork covers were scattered over a U-shaped sofa. Wherever you sat, windows afforded an outlook of the Strand, and the river beyond. The glass was tinted; when the sun was high, the room would flood with light. A narrow balcony ran outside the picture windows. There was a deck chair styled after the green Penguin edition of *The Big Sleep*, and oak containers filled with blooms as lurid as the paintings in the hall.

The magazine rack stood close to a TV screen worthy of a small cinema. Stuffed between copies of *Cosmopolitan* and *Vogue*, he put his hand on an A4 brown envelope. Reaching inside, he found a photograph and slid it out.

Why did Juliet think the fuzzy picture might be useful to Malachy Needham? It looked innocent enough. Hand in hand, a man and a woman strolled up to the well-lit front entrance of the Adelphi Hotel. The photo had been taken at night, perhaps in haste. The man wore a well-cut business suit; he was around forty, and his expression was so smug and satisfied that it might have belonged to Wayne Saxelby. But it wasn't Wayne. Harry had never seen him before.

The man was admiring his companion's figure. Her face was half-turned away from the camera. Again it was someone Harry didn't recognise. Not Ceri, for sure. This was a younger woman in a skimpy top and short skirt, her face creased with laughter. Perhaps her companion had cracked a joke, perhaps she enjoyed him peering at her chest. On closer inspection, something about the woman struck Harry as familiar, but he couldn't place her.

He sank into the embrace of Juliet's sofa and scoured his memory. The Adelphi, did that have any significance? He'd had a drink there with Ceri, but Juliet couldn't know that. By tradition the Adelphi was the finest hotel in the city, and though it now faced competition from upstarts on the waterfront, none could match its history. It once served passengers of the White Star Line; the Legal Group met in a suite modelled after the *Titanic's* smoking lounge. The Beatles stayed there, so did Roy Rogers and Trigger. During the war, the *White Mischief* murder suspect, Jock Delves Broughton booked in after his return from Kenya and took a fatal overdose in his bedroom. Yet Harry saw nothing sinister in this photograph of two people relishing each other's company.

Juliet had fooled him. She knew curiosity was in his DNA. Did she realise he fancied Ceri? She'd found a way to tempt him up to the penthouse. He wondered why she had taken the trouble.

The penthouse doorbell rang, a sharp and unforgiving yelp.

Shit. This couldn't be Juliet—why sound your own front bell? He pushed the photograph back into its envelope and stuffed it back into the rack.

The doorbell squealed again, as if in pain.

'Juliet, you in there?' Casper's voice rasped out of the entry-phone speakers. 'We finished early. Come on, get off your arse, save me digging out my key.'

That was the *nouveaux riches* for you. As bone idle as the old rich, with all their mansions and servants. Harry shut his eyes, scarcely daring to breathe. It could have been worse, Casper might have returned home to find him in bed with Juliet. But this was bad enough.

A sigh of disgust at the lack of response wafted from the speakers. Harry prayed that Casper would piss off and come back some other time.

From downstairs came the thud of a door thrown open. So much for the power of prayer.

Harry's heart hammered as he looked round. A pair of glazed doors gave on to the balcony. He tried his key in the lock and one of the doors slid open. Footsteps crashed on the iron treads of the spiral staircase. Any second now, Casper would be up here.

No choice but to step on to the ledge outside the room and pull the door shut behind him. A stone balustrade separated him from a seven floor drop to the street below. The Liver Building was in deep shadow, but the sun had reappeared, high over the heads of the Liver Birds. A yellow open-top tourist bus drove by, and *Ferry Cross the Mersey* blared from speakers on a deserted upper deck.

Clinging to the outside wall of the penthouse, he clambered past the planters. A pool of greasy water had collected and his feet gave way under him. He found himself sliding, but somehow he stayed upright. Inching forward, he made it beyond the last window on the front elevation of the building. Rounding the corner as the balcony took a ninety-degree turn, he halted. He was out of sight of the entertaining room, not a moment too soon.

Juliet's phrase echoed in his memory. *Views to die for.*

As he looked down on St Nicholas Gardens, unwanted memories of *Vertigo* flooded into his mind. Jimmy Stewart, the investigator haunted by a fear of heights, and betrayed by his obsession with a beautiful woman, roaming the rooftops of San

Francisco. In his head he heard Bernard Hermann's Wagnerian soundtrack rise to a terrible crescendo. To break the spell, he glanced over towards the Strand. Not such a good idea. The trucks and cars were tiny, the pavement a dizzying distance away.

The flower beds outside the church blazed with geraniums and marigolds, but when the sun dodged behind a cloud, the wind had a terrier's bite. A shiver ran down his backbone. Impossible to hang around here for hours, waiting for Casper to go on his way. The flags above the hotel across the road flapped like albatross wings. It was only a question of time before a cold blast from the Mersey whipped him off his feet.

He heard a click as the door to the balcony shut. In his haste, he'd left the key in the lock and Casper must have noticed. No chance now of waiting for the man to leave and then stealing back inside.

Breathe deeply, count to ten.

Half a dozen strides ahead, the balcony came to a dead end. The way beyond was blocked. No gate, no stairs, not even a ladder. Wonderful, absolutely fucking wonderful.

He was trapped.

Chapter Twelve

He reached the end of the balcony, and levered himself up. The wind blew his hair into his eyes and the wet soles of his shoes slipped when he tried to stand upright, so that he had to grab for the cold little balustrade to avoid toppling over. The unnatural movement tweaked a muscle in his shoulder and he let out a cry of pain.

There must be a way out of here.

Gripping the low stone wall, he eased forward and peered over the end of the balcony. Six feet below was a wooden deck, guarded on the left by a railing that ran along the outside of the building above the gardens. To the right of the deck was a deep rectangular light well. Harry peered down into it and saw a couple of the big blue waste containers at ground level. There was no safety rail on that side of the deck. Harry recalled Victor showing him round on the day they moved in; he'd mentioned there were four light wells in John Newton House, designed into the structure to afford natural light to rooms that lacked outside windows. Nice idea, unless you happened to fall down one of them.

The wooden deck ended beneath a balcony identical to the one that enclosed Juliet's penthouse. Even though Tamara Dighton was filming in the Caribbean, Wayne Saxelby might be inside; he was self-employed and could come and go as he pleased.

A gull landed on the balustrade and peered at Harry with the mild distaste of a respectable householder confronted by someone selling clothes pegs from door to door. If he could make it across the deck, there were two small ledges cut into the old stonework that he could use as footholds to lift himself up on to the opposite balcony. Once there, he could attract attention.

If Wayne was at home. If not...

He'd go for it. The deck wasn't so far below the balcony that he was likely to break his neck. Take a chance and aim for a soft landing. Failing that, he'd rather plunge to his doom in the churchyard than finish up headfirst in a container of rubbish.

He scraped his shoes dry on Juliet's penthouse wall, an act of defiance that gave him a small surge of pleasure. With infinite care he hauled first one leg over the wall at the end of the balcony and then the other. Taking a breath, he launched himself on the short drop. His feet slipped as they struck the decking, but he seized the iron rail and steadied himself.

Moving at the pace of a nervous nonagenarian, he edged along the deck until he reached the opposite wall. Climbing up to the balcony proved tougher than expected. He'd put on too much weight. Twice when he tried to pull himself up, he slid back and for a heart-pounding moment feared he would trip and plunge down the light well. His shoulder hurt where he'd pulled the muscle, and his head ached with the concentration. Things they never trained you for at college. Given the week he'd had, it was a pity that survival skills didn't form part of the Law Society's programme of compulsory continuing professional development. At the third attempt he managed to scramble on to the low barrier. Jumping down on to the balcony that crept around the second penthouse, he could scarcely suppress a roar of triumph.

What if the penthouse was empty? Wayne might be anywhere. At Jim's bedside, for instance. If nobody was around to help him escape, he might have to indulge in a little breaking and entering. Just his luck if the security systems that had betrayed his partner in the basement car park functioned to perfection on the top floor.

At the window overlooking the gardens, the blinds were drawn. Harry swore and knocked on the glass. No reply.

Two teenage girls in cropped tops and skimpy skirts were walking along the path that led from Chapel Street to Tower Gardens. One caught sight of Harry and grasped her friend by the arm, pointing up at him. They burst out laughing and waved. Nonplussed, he waved back and, grinning with delight, they strolled out of sight. Did they think he was a daredevil pin-striped burglar whose enterprise deserved appreciation, encouragement even? Only in Liverpool.

He turned the corner of the balcony. At the picture windows, again the blinds were drawn. No sign of life at all. He rapped hard: once, twice, three times.

Was that a noise from inside? The double glazing deadened sound; the property agents bragged about it. He held his breath and started counting. At seven, a hand parted the blinds and a pair of wide eyes looked out.

Harry had never imagined that the sight of a management consultant would send him weak at the knees with joy. He had to restrain himself from kissing the glass.

The blinds opened. Wayne Saxelby stood motionless, as if confronted by a three-headed creature escaped from the murals in the Stapledon. His amazement was forgivable.

He mouthed, 'Can I come in?'

For a weird moment, it seemed that Wayne was deliberating whether or not to open the sliding doors. He must think he was hallucinating. Harry Devlin lurking on your upmarket balcony? Not what you paid sky-high rents for.

'All right, Wayne?'

Wayne snapped out of his trance, as if at the click of a hypnotist's fingers. He disappeared from sight and Harry was seized by a sudden terror that he wouldn't come back. But within ten seconds he returned, key in hand.

'I don't know what to…to say,' he said as the doors slid apart.

In the background, the Stone Roses were belting out *I Wanna Be Adored*. Typical Wayne, but Harry didn't care.

He felt light-headed, almost delirious with relief. The temptation to dance and sing was overwhelming. He had to restrain himself from bursting into a chorus of *I Will Survive*.

'I mean, for fuck's sake, what were you doing out there?'

Wayne sounded as though suspicion might quickly turn to anger, as though Harry had been spying on his private quarters. Snooping around for intimate secrets of law firm management. Or, perhaps, of the lovely Tamara Dighton.

'Sorry, I didn't mean to intrude.'

'It's unbelievable. When I heard the tapping, I thought it must be a window cleaner. The last person I expected to see was you.'

'I can explain.'

As soon as he spoke the words, he regretted them. He didn't want to tell Wayne about his affair with Juliet. The man had done his best to save Jim's life, but he'd never been the soul of discretion. Better fob him off. Yet how to account for his wandering around the penthouse floor balconies when he ought to be at work? The truth it must be. Or rather, a heavily censored version of it.

'You'd better.'

'Mind if I sit down? I must be getting old.' He rubbed his sore shoulder. 'Ten minutes' exercise and I'm knackered.'

Wayne nodded towards a black leather sofa. The décor in the flat was minimalist. No pictures on the walls, no little touches of luxury. No sign even of Tamara's legendary wet tee-shirt. His cherished laptop squatted on a small table, along with a couple of railway magazines. His father had been a railwayman and Wayne's knowledge was encyclopaedic. At the slightest provocation, he would harp on about the dockers' umbrella, the overhead railway that skirted the waterfront until it was dismantled half a century ago. Who would have thought that Tamara Dighton would team up with a train-spotter? It might be true love, though Harry couldn't help wondering if it had something to do with Wayne's new-found wealth.

'What's this all about, then?'

Harry sighed. 'It's a long story.'

A grin crept across Wayne's face. He was regaining his composure.

'I've got plenty of time.'

◇◇◇

'I've shared a lift with Mrs. May a few times,' Wayne said five minutes later. 'Pleasant woman. Must have been quite a babe in her younger days.'

The patronising tone riled Harry. But what could he say? All he wanted was to make good his escape and get back to the office, without mentioning the photograph that he'd found in Juliet's flat. He would rack his brains for the name of the woman in the picture, though identifying her might leave him none the wiser.

'Suppose so.'

'When Tamara bought the penthouse, Mrs. May had this younger bloke in tow. Looked like an Australian beach bum. All medallions and bleached hair. But he seems to have vanished.' Wayne took a long draught of Fosters and wiped his mouth with the back of his sleeve. 'As for her ex, I've seen him around. But one thing puzzles me. If they are divorced, why panic at the thought of his finding you there, waiting for her to show up?'

'He's pathologically jealous.' It sounded lame. Time to improvise. 'I'd guess he never wanted to break up with her. Why do you imagine the beach bum made himself scarce?'

'You're just good friends?' Wayne didn't bother to disguise a smirk.

'She used to help Jim and me with our marketing,' Harry said hastily. 'She specialises in P.R. and we hired her services for a while some years back. Before your time with us.'

'I don't mean to be unkind, but she didn't exactly transform the firm's image, did she?'

This wasn't the moment to leap to her defence. The last thing Harry wanted was Wayne telling all and sundry that he carried a torch for Casper May's ex-wife. He shrugged and said nothing.

'Casper May's a client of Jim's, isn't he?' Wayne murmured. 'You didn't want to tread on his toes, I guess.'

It was a lifeline and Harry grabbed it. 'No, of course not.'

'He has a dodgy reputation. You don't want to get mixed up with people like that. Especially after what's happened to Jim.'

'How do you mean?'

'Well, you're on your own now, aren't you?' Wayne studied the subtleties of the pattern in the cream and grey carpet, as if trying to arrive at a decision. 'By the way, there's something I ought to mention. Just between you and me, if you don't mind.'

'Sure.'

'That policeman has spoken to me again.'

'Cusden?'

'Yeah.' Wayne exhaled. 'There's no easy way to say this, Harry, but he pressed me hard about the call I made to you after I found Jim. He wants to know where you were at the time.'

Harry scowled. 'I hope he isn't suggesting that I battered Jim?'

Wayne spread his arms like a scarecrow. 'Search me. I didn't tell him anything, Harry.'

'Nothing to tell. I was out on a…on a wild goose chase, that's all.'

Wayne bowed his head again, said nothing.

'What?'

'He asked if I'd noticed anything unusual about your behaviour.'

'Such as?'

'I didn't let anything slip.'

Through gritted teeth, Harry said, 'There was nothing to let slip.'

'Sure about that?'

'Absolutely.'

Wayne fiddled with his watch, didn't look Harry in the eye. 'It's just that…you haven't seemed like your normal self these past few days.'

'How do you mean?'

'The women in the office have noticed it. I overheard Grace telling Sylvia she is worried about you. You seem jumpy, neurotic.'

'Neurotic?' Harry gaped at him. He'd been accused of many things before, but this was a first.

'Face it, Harry, this is what people are saying. Something odd is going on in your life. I saw it for myself when I spotted you in the gardens, with that bloke who was on the point of kicking your head in.'

'I explained about Tom Gunter.'

'Time to cut the crap, Harry. Admit it, your life's out of control. Your mind is elsewhere. You seem bowed down. Little things have been getting on top of you. Like when some kids trashed your office.'

'That wasn't kids.'

'How can you be so sure?'

Kids wouldn't leave a message about Midsummer's Eve.

'God knows,' he said wearily.

'Grace thinks you've been working too hard.'

'Me?'

'Amazing, huh? Sylvia's worried about you too, it's written all over her face. With Jim gone…'

Harry stood up. 'Thanks for your concern. I'd best get back to the office before anyone else starts fretting that I've metamorphosed into a panicky workaholic.'

'All right.' Wayne put out a hand. 'Best of luck, Harry. I have this feeling you're going to need it if you keep sticking your neck out.'

As the door to the penthouse closed behind him, a phrase from their conversation drummed in Harry's ears.

You're on your own now.

◇◇◇

Back in his office, he dialled Carmel's number, but the call went straight through to voicemail.

'Just wondering how he is. Give me a ring when you have a moment.'

As he rang off, Sylvia put her head around the door. He'd never seen her face so ashen.

'Have you checked your emails?'

Bad news from the hospital? Out on the balcony, he'd felt cold and shaky. But nothing compared to this.

'Is it…?'

'The police want to talk to you.'

'What about?'

'There's been another murder.'

He stared. 'What's that got to do with me?'

'I've no idea.' She sounded angry, as though she blamed him for bringing the roof down on all of them. 'I only take the messages around here.'

'Who's been murdered?'

To his horror, a tear trickled down Sylvia's cheek. She stifled a sob.

'I can't believe it…'

'Who?' he demanded. 'Tell me.'

She cleared her throat.

'Kay Cheung.'

Chapter Thirteen

Harry recognised Detective Sergeant Stan Sibierski's pock-marked features the moment he walked into the interview room at police HQ. Sibierski was a morose Mancunian who reeked of cheap cigarettes and was famous for hating lawyers. According to Carmel, his wife had left him for a divorce specialist in a big legal firm and salted the wound by screwing him for a fortune in alimony. In Birkenhead Crown Court five years back, Harry had cross-examined Sibierski into hapless self-contradiction and secured an acquittal for a petty thief who regarded Walton Jail as his second home. Any hope the sergeant might have forgotten his humiliation was dispelled by a tight smirk as he introduced himself. The message couldn't have been clearer if Sibierski had worn a tee shirt proclaiming *Payback Time.*

'Last night my colleague DC Cusden asked about your movements after five o'clock yesterday evening. You told him you met someone in Widnes yesterday evening.'

Harry settled back in his chair. It was almost as comfortable as Juliet's sofa. The suite of interview rooms had been refurbished to a high specification, all light Scandinavian wood and walls washed in summery pastel shades. All it lacked was piped music and an escalator connecting Police HQ with the Paradise Project shopping development so that suspects could indulge in a little retail therapy in between interrogations.

'I said I went to meet someone. Not quite the same.'

Sibierski scrutinised Harry as though he'd found him on the sole of his shoe, following a stroll through a sewage farm.

'Legal quibbles already, Mr. Devlin?'

'Last time we met,' Harry said, 'we agreed it was important for investigating officers to be sticklers for accuracy.'

'You declined to tell DC Cusden who you were due to meet.'

'It didn't seem important.'

Sibierski shook his head in a pantomime of disapproval.

'You obstructed his inquiries.'

'It's no secret. Her name is Ka-Yu Cheung.'

'You'd arranged an appointment with her?'

'She rang me yesterday morning and asked to see me at six o'clock.'

'She was a client?'

'No, but we knew each other through work. She's employed by the firm that cares for the plants in our office. And her partner, Tom Gunter, was once a client.'

'Gunter, yes. You defended him on a charge of murder.'

'Until he changed lawyers.'

The smirk returned, as if to say: *good decision.*

'Did you bear him a grudge?'

'Of course not.'

'I never met a lawyer who liked to lose out on a fee.'

'It happens.'

'Why did Ms Cheung want to see you?'

'She didn't say.'

'Didn't you enquire?'

'She didn't want to talk on the phone. Said she'd explain when we met.'

'You invited her to come into your office?'

'She asked me to meet her at Widnes. The West Bank.'

'There's a public house close to the river. I've sunk a few pints there in my time. Did you arrange to meet in the bar?'

'No, at Runcorn Bridge. Or to be more exact, underneath it.'

Sibierski's black eyebrows twitched in mock-surprise. 'Do you arrange many client appointments under road bridges?'

'I told you, she wasn't a client. An acquaintance, that's all.'

'Funny place for a meeting.'

'Her choice, not mine.'

'Why would she want to meet there?'

'I assumed she wanted to speak to me in private. Away from prying eyes.'

'Sounds rather intimate.'

'If we talked in a pub, we might be seen or overheard.'

'Taking a risk, weren't you? Middle-aged man. *Respectable professional.*' Pleased with his ironic thrust, Sibierski winked at his fresh-faced DC, who gave a hasty nod of approval. 'Meeting a young woman in an out-of-the-way spot like that?'

'It's hardly remote. There are paths along the riverside, a promenade. Houses a stone's throw away.'

'But what if she made some sort of allegation about your behaviour? You'd be in trouble, wouldn't you?' He could barely restrain a snigger. 'Career on the line, reputation at risk?'

'Kay wasn't like that.'

'What was she like?'

'Intelligent. Attractive. Likeable.'

'Quite a paragon. Are you sure she was only an acquaintance?'

'I'd known her for years, since we took out a contract with Green and Pleasant to look after the plants in the office. I liked her. Describe her as a friend, if you like. We never socialised together.'

'I suppose Tom Gunter wouldn't have been happy if you had. Pity about her taste in men, eh?'

Harry couldn't resist it. 'We all make mistakes with the opposite sex, don't we, Sergeant?'

Sibierski sucked in his cheeks and the young DC winced, waiting for the explosion. But it didn't come.

'And did you make a mistake with her, Mr. Devlin?'

'Such as?'

'Did you try it on with her yesterday evening?'

'I never even saw Kay. I arrived more than half an hour late, due to the demonstration.'

'Oh yeah, the moaning farmers.' Sibierski had urban grime in his genes, and he wrinkled his nose to indicate his contempt for the rural lobby.

'When I couldn't see her, I walked around either side of the bridge, but there was no sign. Then Wayne Saxelby called to say that Jim had been attacked and I rushed off to the hospital.'

'Were you shagging Ka-Yu Cheung?'

Harry leaned over the table towards Sibierski until the stink of unfiltered Woodbines made him want to throw up.

'Fuck off.'

The DC shuffled in his chair, no doubt wishing he was back in the sixth form, but Sibierski bared his teeth in a grin. A collector's item, probably the closest he'd ever come to punching the air with glee.

'Oh dear. Struck a nerve, have I?'

'She's dead.' Harry bit his tongue, trying to control his temper. 'I'd like to think you would concentrate on finding whoever killed her rather than amusing yourself at my expense.'

'Touchy, Mr. Devlin. I'm only doing my job.' His voice sank to a whisper. 'As for Ms Cheung being dead, you don't need to remind me. Two hours ago, I saw her naked body on a cold slab. The man who killed her mutilated her after death and left her body under a thicket for the flies to feast on. Nothing amusing about what I saw in that mortuary, I promise you.'

Harry stared at the wall behind Sibierski's head, picturing in his mind that pretty, timid woman. *Harry, can you spare a minute?* Remembering her phone call. *I need to talk to you.*

'So you deny being in a relationship with Ms Cheung?'

There's nobody else I trust.

Shit. She'd relied on him, and he'd let her down, without even knowing.

His throat was dry. 'Of course.'

'You've never had sex with her?'

'No.'

'Never asked her for sex?'

'No.'

'You didn't argue with her before you took the phone call from Mr. Saxelby and lose your temper—like you did a minute ago?'

'No.'

'Easily done. It can happen in an instant. The red mist descends and suddenly you find yourself out of control….'

'There was never anything sexual between us. I want whoever killed her caught, and quickly.'

Sibierski licked his lips. 'Where were you on Sunday night?'

The change of tack flummoxed Harry. He felt his cheeks reddening, though he wasn't sure what he was being accused of.

'For God's sake, what's this all about? I was at home. I was due in court first thing Monday morning. By eleven o'clock I was in bed.'

'Can anyone corroborate that?'

Harry clenched his fist. Sunday night, yes. When Lee Welch was murdered. No question, Sibierski was loving every moment of this.

'No.'

'Well, well.' Sibierski straightened. 'All right, you're free to go.'

Harry was tempted to say *thanks for nothing*, but he kept his mouth shut. As he reached the door, Sibierski said, 'Oh, just one more thing.'

'You've being watching too many repeats of *Columbo*.'

'The shoes you wore when you went to Runcorn Bridge. We'd like to examine them, if you don't mind.'

Harry couldn't stifle a grunt of exasperation. 'For God's sake. Do me a favour.'

A slow smile crept across Sibierski's saturnine features, like a trespasser tip-toeing through a bomb site.

'All right, I will. I don't often say this, Mr. Devlin, but I'd like to offer you a bit of free advice for next time we meet.' He wagged his forefinger. 'If I were you, I'd hire a decent lawyer.'

◇◇◇

'Sibierski is as unpleasant as he's ugly,' Carmel said. 'And that's saying something.'

They were facing each other across a table in the hospital cafeteria, a chocolate muffin and a cup of tepid coffee in front of each of them. Jim was still unconscious, but Carmel's mood was bright, verging on febrile. He guessed the doctors had given her something to stave off the blues.

'What's the latest?'

'This afternoon, I called a couple of friends in high places.' Carmel fiddled with an ear-ring, a habit when her mind worked overtime. 'The smart money says that Kay was killed by the same man who murdered Denise Onuoha and Lee Welch.'

Harry had dreaded this ever since Sibierski said that the corpse had been mutilated.

'He strangled her and then cut out her tongue?'

'You didn't hear it from me, okay? If the Chief Executive of the Authority finds out I've said anything to you, I'll be the next one to lose a tongue.'

'Why would Sibierski waste time questioning me?'

A long pause.

'I hate to break this to you, Harry dear, but you're bound to be a suspect.'

'You can't be serious.'

One look at her face told him she *was* serious. The room felt airless. His shirt was sweaty and he needed a shower. He'd assumed that, once Sibierski had his fun, the focus would turn to Tom Gunter. A dead woman's lover must be the prime suspect. But if the case was linked to the other murders, the kaleidoscope shifted.

'Sibierski didn't tell me when she was killed.'

'The forensic boys are keeping their options open at present. All I know is that you were in the vicinity of the crime scene at roughly the right time.'

'Who found the body?'

'An elderly mongrel-walker.' Carmel shivered. 'Remind me never to get a dog. Throw them a stick and they fetch back a bit of rotting flesh.'

A wave of nausea swept over him. 'Kay's tongue was left at the scene too?'

Carmel nodded. 'Whatever else he is, he isn't a souvenir hunter.'

'What does Tom Gunter have to say for himself?'

'Nothing yet. He's disappeared. When officers turned up at the Marina flat to break the news of Kay's death, there was no sign of him.'

Harry banged his fist on the table. 'Case solved.'

'Not so fast. Remember what I said about the murders being linked.'

'If you're looking for a serial killer, he must be a candidate,' Harry said. 'Come to think of it, I saw him the day Lee Welch's body was found. He seemed to have a lot on his mind.'

'Doesn't mean he killed those women, Harry.'

'Why would he vanish, then?'

'Wouldn't you, in his shoes? Come on, Harry. As soon as he got wind that Kay was dead, he'll have panicked. A man with his criminal CV is bound to attract suspicion. Anyway, there's another development. The SIO has called in Professor Maeve Hopes for expert assistance.'

'Were there no psychics or tea-leaf readers available?'

'We know she's a media tart, but the PR people are desperate to keep the journalists onside until there's a positive lead. She's a specialist in serial killings. The Bridlington Butcher, the Horsham Whisperer, you name it.'

'So what does her crystal ball reveal?'

'She says the likely culprit is a white male, operating in a geographical area he knows like the back of his hand. A loner with an over-active imagination, introverted and insecure. Apparently quite normal in everyday life…'

'Narrows it down to a hundred thousand or so.'

'You did ask.'

Harry bit into his muffin as savagely as if it were Sibierski's wagging forefinger. 'Kay's murder doesn't make sense. Denise and Lee were escort girls.'

Carmel sighed. 'You're not going to like this.'

Her sorrowful expression bothered him.

'Please don't tell me…'

'Yes, your friend Kay was on the books of Cultural Companions.'

He almost choked on the last of his muffin 'I don't believe you.'

'Sorry.'

He closed his eyes.

'I know you liked her. But she signed up with them a fort-night back.'

'Gunter must have forced her into it,' he muttered.

'Maybe. But they've rented a pricey new apartment. He worked as a freelance and didn't have a guaranteed income. As for Kay, you don't earn a fortune feeding and watering potted plants.'

He cast his mind back to Monday morning and Kay's embar-rassment when she told him they'd moved to the city. He'd assumed she was aware that Tom had delivered the note about his death on Midsummer's Eve. But something very different had been on her mind.

'She wasn't obliged to offer favours to clients,' Carmel said. 'I told you, the foot-soldiers who manage the agency for Casper May and Malachy Needham take pains to make it clear to girls and punters alike that money changes hands only in return for the pleasure of attractive female company. Anything more intimate is strictly forbidden.'

'But?'

'What consenting adults get up to in their own time is their own business. The agency claims to be an equal opportunities employer, though I doubt if that extends as far as recruiting fat women with bad breath.'

'Perhaps Kay took the bosses at face value and some bloke was dis-appointed when she didn't let him have his wicked way with her.'

'You could be right. Chances are, that's what lies behind these killings. A violent inadequate who takes out his frustrations on vulnerable women.'

'Not me, though.'

'Definitely not you, Harry.' She took a sip of coffee, then pulled a face because it was cold. 'It would save a lot of grief if you were as well organised as Casper May and came up with an alibi for the murders.'

He shook his head. 'I was on my own in the flat.'

'You ought to get out more.'

'I finish up in enough trouble as it is. Imagine the chaos if I actually tried to enjoy myself.'

For the first time since the attack on Jim, she burst into laughter. Slightly too loud.

'Poor Harry. But I'm glad you finished with Juliet May.'

His mobile chirped, saving him from the need to answer. 'Hello?'

'This is Ceri Hussain.'

He swallowed hard. He hadn't expected her to call, let alone so soon.

'How are you?'

'I'm fine. Is this a bad time to call?'

'I'm at the hospital. I don't know whether you heard…'

'About Jim Crusoe? It's the talk of the city. Dreadful news. That's why I called, to see how he is.'

Of course. She was being kind. Not wanting to make another date.

'They've operated on him.'

'Will he be all right?'

'We're waiting for word from the doctors.'

'I'll be thinking of you both.' A pause. 'I wondered…'

'Yes?'

'I did enjoy the other night. Things must be rough for you at the moment.'

He let her words hang, not knowing what to say.

'You'll be very busy, but if you felt like getting together for a coffee sometime. Or a bite to eat…'

'I'd love that.' He couldn't believe she was making the move, and felt himself colouring under Carmel's inquisitive gaze. 'When would suit you?'

'Oh, I'm at your disposal. My social life is a bit of a waste land these days. I realise this evening is too short notice, but if you...'

Seize the moment. 'No, that would be fine. Absolutely fine. Shall we say seven thirty, at The Lido?'

'Lovely. See you then.'

He switched off the phone and took a breath.

'Sorry about that.'

Carmel said, 'Who was it?'

'Um...nobody special.'

'Harry Devlin, I've known you too long to let you prevaricate. One minute, you crack on that you're Billy No Mates, the next you fix up a secret tryst. Spill the beans.'

'No tryst. That was Ceri Hussain. And before you start, we're not seeing each other. Not the way you mean.'

'You're blushing like a nun in a night club!' she said in triumph. 'Well, well, you sly dog. Got into her knickers yet?'

'A couple of evenings back I took her to watch a film at the Alhambra, that's all.'

Carmel gave a theatrical sigh. 'I suppose you haven't called her since? When are you taking her out for a slap-up meal?'

'Tonight.' Conscience pricked him. 'I'm sorry. It's selfish of me to go wining and dining when Jim is in intensive care.'

'Don't be silly. You need a break, you were up half the night and you've been flogging your guts out all day.'

Well, not quite all day. Better not mention his afternoon excursion to Juliet's penthouse, let alone the drama of his hasty exit.

'No, I'll ring Ceri back and rearrange.'

'Don't you dare.'

'I can't leave you to cope on your own.'

'I hope you're not suggesting I can't hack it? No way will I let you mess up on this. Jim wouldn't want that, either. If Ceri is keen, strike while the iron is hot. And don't waste the evening chatting over the Borth case.'

The Borth case, yes. Harry's mind strayed down a fresh track. Aled Borth fitted Maeve Hopes' profile, but so did thousands of men. The difference was, Borth had known one of the dead girls. Perhaps more than one.

'You look miles away.' She waved him towards the door. 'You don't have to hang around here, you know. It may be hours before there's any news about Jim. Why don't you go home and get ready for your night out? You deserve it.'

'I don't want to leave you on your own.'

'I'll be fine. Promise.'

'Sorry if I seem distracted. I'll call you later to see how he is.'

'It's good to be distracted sometimes.'

At the door, he hesitated. 'It's not thoughts of Ceri that are distracting me. Honest.'

'What, then?'

'I don't suppose your contacts have confirmed whether Borth was a client of Cultural Companions?'

Carmel shook her head. 'Give them time. There are a lot of leads to follow in a case like this. Most of them going nowhere.'

'I don't want to believe that I acted for the man who killed Kay. But there's something else.'

'Tell me.'

'On the morning of the inquest, Borth came into the office. He bumped into my secretary.'

'Amazing Grace?'

'I'm sure they knew each other. Nothing was said but they both seemed embarrassed by the encounter.'

Carmel's mouth opened. 'You don't think she's another escort girl? Keeping company with men who have spooky tastes?'

'I'm not sure what I think any more.' His mouth was dry. 'But if she is on the books of Cultural Companions—I don't want her to finish up as the next victim.'

Chapter Fourteen

In the square-shouldered shadow cast by the Liver Building, Harry waited at the crossing for the lights to change. The brown stonework of John Newton House gleamed in the early evening sun. Gulls swooped and whirled overhead, and the Strand echoed with the hoot and roar of cars dodging traffic cones beside the brand new highway to the river's edge. Another skyscraper had begun to soar beyond a freshly built hotel. Invisible behind a security fence, diggers roared like caged animals. The earth was moving, the landscape he'd known all his life changing before his eyes. The city had needed a facelift; he hoped it wouldn't turn into a heart transplant.

Victor was alone behind the desk at ground level, absorbed in a paperback. On the cover, figures in white paper suits gathered behind a yellow tape marked POLICE—DO NOT CROSS. Wasn't living above a scene of crime enough for him?

They exchanged grunts of acknowledgment. On the fifth floor, reception was deserted. The palms and ferns seemed to droop, as though mourning for the woman who had cared for them. When he reached Sylvia's room, he found her locking the door.

'You're working late.'

'I wanted to make sure that everything was under control. I didn't expect to see you again today. Any news about Jim?'

He shook his head. 'You'll be the first to know once Carmel and I hear anything from the medics.'

She sniffed hard. The mask she'd worn all day was flaky at the edges. Her face was pink and blotched, as though she'd shed tears when she thought no-one was around to see.

'Harry, who would do such a thing?'

'He was mugged.'

'You don't believe that. Why would a mugger take such a risk, hiding in a secure underground car park? How would he know the security cameras were on the blink?'

'The city's full of people who take chances. Even when they're not stoned out of their minds, they don't think like you and me.'

Sylvia's mouth set in an obstinate line. 'There are so many easy pickings round here. Offices where you can walk straight in. Why go to the trouble of lurking down in that dark and dusty basement? There must be something more to it.'

'Such as?'

'This message you received about Midsummer's Eve. Might that be connected?'

He blinked. 'How do you know about that?'

'Oh, Harry.' She scolded like a mother who'd caught her son surfing pornographic websites. 'Do you imagine you can keep a secret in this place?'

Hard to believe that he'd once congratulated himself for keeping his affair with Juliet quiet. How naïve could he be?

'Not really. So Jim couldn't keep his mouth shut?'

'He was worried for you.'

'You could have fooled me.'

'He didn't want you to stress out over it. But it bothered him.'

'It was a joke.'

'Foretelling your death? No, that's scary.'

'I'm still in one piece.'

'It isn't Midsummer's Eve yet. And Jim isn't in one piece any more, is he?'

Her voice trembled. Afraid she was about to cry again, he rested his hand on her shoulder and felt bone under the thin cotton top. She choked back a sob.

'And then there's poor Kay. Such a sweet girl. To think that she and I were chatting only the other afternoon.'

'What did you talk about?'

'Nothing special.' Sylvia frowned. 'She seemed out of sorts. Wound-up.'

'What was wrong?'

'I asked about her new flat. I thought she'd be thrilled. But she didn't want to talk about it.'

'Where did they get the money from?'

'You know what young people are like, Harry.' She tutted like a censorious grandmother. 'Live now, pay later. It was all very different when we were kids.'

'They rented, they didn't buy.'

'Even so, the landlord would ask for money in advance. Where would they find the cash? Tom never seems to hold a job down for long. From what Kay has told me, he'd rather stay at home with a curry, watching soccer on satellite TV, or go out to watch the trains at Lime Street Station while she's out working her fingers to the bone.'

'So they hadn't won the lottery?'

'Kay would have mentioned anything like that. She confided in me sometimes. Her mother was dead, you know, and she'd fallen out with her sister. I think she needed an older woman to talk to.'

He nodded; Sylvia was a good listener. 'What sort of things did she confide?'

She drew away from him. 'Woman's talk, Harry. Private stuff.'

About sex, then.

'Nothing that gives you any understanding of why she was murdered, then?'

'Good Heavens, no! Who would want to kill a nice girl like that? The murderer must be a maniac, that's all I can say.' There was a catch in her voice. 'It's like a nightmare. Harry—what's happening?'

'The police will sort it,' he said, with more confidence than he felt.

'What did they say to you?'

'Not much.' This wouldn't be a good moment to mention that Sibierski wanted him to provide an alibi. 'They seem to think there's a link with a couple of other murders.'

'The woman who was found on Waterloo beach? And the other one, a few weeks ago?'

He nodded. 'Let's wait and see. In the meantime, I'll take good care of myself. Promise.'

'You'd better, Harry. We can't afford to lose you as well.'

'You won't be rid of me that easily, don't worry.'

She folded her arms, fighting for control. 'So what brings you to my room at this time of evening?'

'I wanted to check our personnel records.'

A gallows smile. 'Don't tell me you've had a sudden crisis of conscience about those overdue staff appraisals?'

'I'd like to check our file on Grace.'

She made a performance of consulting her wristwatch. 'At this time of day? What's wrong?'

'Probably nothing. No need for you to wait. I have a spare key to the filing cabinet.'

'Harry, you can trust me.'

He gazed into her anxious eyes. Sylvia was a rock, but even rocks wear to sand. With Jim on the danger list, she had enough to fret about. He couldn't burden her with his fear that Grace might not only be a part-time escort, but also the next target for a brutal serial killer.

'The morning of the Borth inquest, Grace met the client for the first time. I had the impression that they knew each other, but neither of them said anything.'

'What's unusual about that?'

'They seemed…I dunno, embarrassed? Unwilling to acknowledge each other. So I was curious to find out more about her background. Did we take up references?'

'They were excellent. But what does that mean? References only tell you what the referees want you to know.'

She led him into her room and unlocked the three-drawer cabinet where she stored confidential staff records and handed over a buff folder.

He leafed through the documents. Agency terms of business, evidence of qualifications, and a two page curriculum vitae. Grace was Liverpool born and bred; after leaving school at sixteen, she'd studied at secretarial college and spent a couple of years travelling the world before starting work. Following spells typing for senior officials at first the University and then Merseyside Police, she'd spent most of her career working in the legal profession. Even before becoming a temp three years ago, the longest she'd spent in the same job was eighteen months. She'd worked in most of the law firms in the city, two of which had provided glowing testimonials, as well as the coroner's office and the magistrates' court.

'She's a butterfly.' Sylvia's tone made it clear this was not a good thing.

'Maybe she likes variety.'

'Maybe she's looking for something she'll never find.'

Aren't we all? Harry kept his mouth shut. His eye had been caught by Grace's home address. 13 Oram Avenue, Waterloo.

'You look surprised,' Sylvia said.

'Sorry, I've raised a false alarm,' he said. 'Grace's home is a quarter of a mile from Aled Borth's. For all I know, she's a regular at the Alhambra.'

Sylvia raised her eyebrows, but slipped the folder back in its place and said nothing. He could tell she wasn't convinced. Neither was he, really. Even if Grace and Borth might be neighbours, that didn't explain why they'd been so shocked to see each other.

◇◇◇

As the lift doors closed on Sylvia, he went in search of Gina Paget. She was mopping the floor in the kitchen area, elbows pumping with a furious rhythm. She'd sprayed into the air a citrus fragrance so fierce that he almost choked. When he coughed, she gave a little gasp. She spun round to face him, her cheeks bright red.

'You shouldn't sneak up on people like that!'

'Sorry. I meant…'

'Okay, okay, I didn't mean to bite your head off.' She wiped her hands on her overall. 'You can understand why I'm jumpy. There's been another, hasn't there?'

He knew at once what she meant. 'Yes.'

'The radio news only said a woman had been killed, but one of the girls says that the victim came to work here sometimes. Looked after plants.'

'Your grapevine's very efficient.'

'Everyone knows everyone else's business, don't they?'

'Uh-huh.' As Sylvia said, you couldn't keep secrets. How long before Wayne Saxelby started dining out on the story of how he'd rescued Harry from the balcony? He could imagine him bragging: *tiptoed along like bloody Blondin, he'd have broken his neck if I hadn't hauled him in.* 'Her name was Kay. How much do you know about her?'

'I never met her. But one of the Lithuanian girls who works on the first floor has a friend who knew her.'

'They were escorts?'

'So your grapevine's working too.' Gina stabbed her mop into the bucket. 'Don't tread on that floor, it's slippery. You could break your neck.'

'Nowhere's safe,' he said softly.

'The man who's doing this needs to be stopped. They said on the radio that the police have brought in a top profiler. About bloody time.'

'The profiler can't conjure up a suspect out of thin air.'

'Maybe there's a suspect closer than we think.'

'What makes you say that?'

She bent closer to him, and lowered her voice, although he was sure there was nobody else around. 'The girls have been talking.'

'And?'

'They told the supervisor they may go on strike unless something's done about Victor Creepy.'

'They're not saying he's murdered three women?'

'Why not? He soaks himself in all this forensic bollocks, he knows how to kill without leaving a trace. They reckon that's how he's evaded detection all this time. You can take that look off your face, Harry Devlin. I'm not saying I go along with the rest of them. If I did, I wouldn't still be at work here. But you have to admit, it makes a lot of sense.'

He shook his head. 'Victor has an alibi for the murder of Kay.'

'How can you be sure?'

'You heard my partner Jim Crusoe was attacked last night?'

'In the basement, yes. Mugged, wasn't he?'

'I haven't a clue what happened.'

She shivered. 'Imagine, something so close to us here. Poor man, it must have happened not long after I left.'

'Don't you remember seeing Victor? He and a friend were here when Jim was discovered in the car park and stayed for the rest of the evening after the police arrived.'

'I suppose so.' She didn't seem thrilled that Victor was off the hook. 'But you'll never persuade the girls he hasn't got something to hide.'

'How do you mean?'

'Why does he guard those keys of his like they were the crown jewels?'

'I'm glad to hear there's some kind of security here.'

'He's obsessive about it. Even Lou's duplicate set isn't complete.'

'I didn't know that.'

'There are lots of things us cleaners know that you important bosses don't.'

That I can believe. 'Go on, surprise me.'

Her voice dropped to conspiratorial pitch. 'Lou fancies our supervisor. She'd run a mile if it ever got serious, but it's not a bad idea to make friends with the bloke on the desk. Lou doesn't really like Victor. He says being interested in all this crime scene stuff isn't healthy, though I suppose his real gripe is that he doesn't like being told what to do. He even blames Victor for what happened to your partner.'

Harry stiffened. 'How come?'

'He reckons it was Victor who fucked up the security cameras.'

'You're kidding.'

'It wouldn't be difficult for someone with the right know-how. And Victor worked as an electrician for years, he says.'

Harry didn't know that. Again he realised how little he understood about the people he spoke to every day of his working life; even compared to a woman who cleaned here for a few hours each night.

'These keys, does he keep them on him all the time?'

'When he's on duty, yes. When he isn't, they stay in his flat.'

'Yes, I've seen the rack they hang on, on the wall inside the front door.'

'Wouldn't it be fascinating if we could lay our hands on those keys?' she breathed.

When he nodded, she burst into laughter, as much from surprise as delight.

'I can make it happen, you know.'

'How?'

'There's a girl called Irena, she cleans the offices on the first floor. She's Lithuanian and she doesn't like Victor. I'm sure she'd help.'

'How could she lay her hands on the keys?'

'All we need her to do is borrow them for five minutes. She can make an impression and then put them back in their place. Victor won't be any the wiser.'

'But if he's paranoid about security…'

She tapped the side of her nose. 'Irena's an artist among shoplifters. You should see her wardrobe, she must be the best dressed cleaner in the North of England. And she's never paid for a single garment. It's like magic, what she does. Trust me, Victor will never know his keys have disappeared.'

◇◇◇

'Heard the news about the latest murder?' Ceri Hussain asked.

Harry swallowed the last mouthful of marinated Tuscan beef. Topped with flakes of Parmesan cheese. He'd never be a gourmet, but even he could tell that the food was excellent.

'Uh-huh.'

'And you know the victim?'

They had chosen a secluded corner at The Lido, a Venetian-themed restaurant overlooking the waters of Albert Dock. Waiters kitted out as gondoliers with stripey shirts and straw hats; on the table, red roses blooming out of a vase of Murano glass. Gaudy carnival masks hung from the walls, Vivaldi played in the background. Until now they had kept the conversation casual. Ceri looked good in a slickly tailored khaki jacket with a white vest underneath. He relished being with her, couldn't help feeling flattered by the concentration she bestowed on him.

'Her name is Kay Cheung.'

'Tom Gunter's girlfriend,' Ceri muttered.

He cleared his throat. Now for the tricky bit. 'I ought to tell you, the police have questioned me about her killing. Officially, I'm a suspect.'

In the flickering candle-light, Ceri's expression was as sombre as when she brought in verdicts on the how, why and when of death.

'That's absurd.'

'Perhaps I should have told you before I asked you to have dinner with me. I don't want to wreck your reputation.'

'Never mind that, Harry. What are they thinking of?'

'Kay asked to see me yesterday evening.'

'Why?'

'She wouldn't discuss it on the phone. We arranged to meet in Widnes, by the road bridge. Where she was killed. I turned up late because Farmers4Justice blocked the road, and she was nowhere to be seen. For all I know, the poor woman was already dead by then. Cards on the table, Ceri. Stan Sibierski suggested her rejection of my sexual advances drove me to murder.'

'For goodness sake! I know Sibierski, he's a buffoon. Pay no attention.'

'Thanks for the vote of confidence.' He gave her a crooked grin. 'But feel free to leave now if you wish.'

'I wouldn't dream of it.' She hesitated. 'Harry, I don't want to break confidences.'

'Of course not,' he said, pricking up his ears.

'Widnes falls outside my jurisdiction, but the rumour mill is working overtime. Ken Porterfield is always first with any news. He still has plenty of friends in the police. The story goes that they are linking this death to the two other murders. Denise Onuoha and Lee Welch.'

He nodded. 'Same m.o. Same signature.'

She peered at him. 'Do you know what the murderer's signature is?'

'He…cuts out their tongues.'

He came close to gagging as he forced out the words. Nobody deserved to die like that. But Kay, of all people? He remembered seeing her that last time, doing what she loved, caring for the plants. When he thought about how she had been violated, he wanted to scream with rage. She'd trusted him, she had nobody else—and he'd let her down.

Ceri spoke so quietly that he had to strain to hear. 'I gather she worked as an escort, like Denise and Lee.'

'He forced her into it!'

'Tom Gunter?'

'Who else?'

'You can't know that for certain.'

'Nothing else makes sense. Kay was a lovely young woman. If it wasn't for Gunter screwing up her life…'

'There's nothing you could do.'

'I should have found out why she wanted to see me. If only I'd…'

'Believe me, Harry, you can't live by *if onlys*. If I ever doubted that, Ricky's death made me sure.'

He didn't say anything for a few seconds. Her husband's suicide was still a raw memory for her. He mustn't make it worse.

'I hear Gunter has disappeared.'

'You're as well informed as Ken Porterfield.'

'It comes from a lifetime of nosiness,' he said, striving for a lighter note.

'You obviously have friends in the police too.'

He pushed his plate to one side. 'Stan Sibierski isn't one of them.'

'Sorry, I didn't mean to pry.'

'No problem.' But even with Ceri, he wouldn't be drawn. He mustn't compromise Carmel Sutcliffe by hinting she had been indiscreet.

'As for Gunter, Ken tells me that he has an alibi for the Onuoha case.'

It didn't mean much. Alibis were bought and sold in Merseyside all the time. Soon, no doubt, they would become a staple of internet auctions.

'Provided by a friend?'

'Harry, you're a cynic.'

'Years of experience, that's all. I suppose Tom leaned on someone to cover for him.'

'No, he did much better than that.'

'Go on. Surprise me.'

'Tom was in police custody when Denise was murdered.'

'Meaning what, exactly? In jail? Out wearing an electronic tag while he washed old people's cars as part of his community service?'

'It couldn't be more straightforward. He was held in a cell overnight.'

He swore under his breath. 'What happened?'

'An argument with a bloke in a pub escalated into a fight and Tom pulled a knife. A couple of the other man's mates knocked seven bells out of him and took the knife. The police were called and when Tom started being stroppy, they locked him up. He got off with a caution, but there's no way he could have murdered

Denise. The timings can't be made to fit. If the same man killed all three women, you can be sure it wasn't Tom Gunter.'

'Could Tom have found out how Denise was murdered?'

'Out of the question. The police have kept this very tight. There's no way he could have known.'

Her certainty was compelling. He felt his shoulders droop.

'So Tom is in the clear?'

''Fraid so.'

Kay's murder made sense as a dismal domestic crime. Her lover was violent, easy to imagine a quarrel getting out of hand. But if Kay was simply one more entry in a long list of victims, she'd lost her life through the most ridiculous of reasons. She'd found herself in the wrong place at the wrong time. A place where she'd meant to meet him. Would it have been different if he'd set off earlier, if the Strand hadn't been clogged with the demonstration?

'Why would he do a runner, then?'

'We know it's a serial killing,' she said patiently. 'We know he has an alibi for the first crime. But Tom doesn't have a clue. He'll be holed up somewhere, probably petrified about what will happen to him, innocent or not.'

Tom, in hiding and afraid? Maybe there was some justice. But not enough.

'Which means we have to look elsewhere for our murderer?'

'I don't like this any more than you do. But the police have to face facts. A serial killer is at work.'

'I gather that Maeve Hopes has been called in to contribute her expertise.'

'Such as it is,' Ceri murmured. 'The professor and I spent twelve months on a committee investigating evidence in criminal cases.'

'I bet that was fun?'

'I finished up thinking she cared more about her own profile than any criminal's. If the police are consulting her, they must be desperate.' She ran a hand through her thick hair. 'Sorry, do I sound like a jealous bitch?'

He shook his head. She'd only drunk a single glass of wine, but he'd never heard her speak so frankly before. He hoped her candour meant she trusted him.

'Of course not. I've never met the Professor and already I've formed a deep prejudice against her. As for the police, they have three murders to investigate. Three separate crime scenes. There must be loads of trace evidence. DNA, whatever. They will latch on to a suspect soon.'

'Maybe.'

A swarthy gondolier whose deep Mediterranean tan didn't quite match his broad Scouse accent refilled their glasses and took dessert orders. When he had departed, Harry said, 'I expected you to be more optimistic.'

'Disillusioned by a thousand post-mortems, I'm afraid. The truth is, I've lived with death for a long time. Too long.'

Her melancholy dismayed him. She'd always struck him as so strong, so assured. And now she spoke as if tempted to toss it all away.

'You work so hard to help bereaved families to come to terms with loss. I've seen you in action, remember. It's your vocation. Everyone admires what you've achieved.'

'Nothing lasts forever.'

'Ceri…'

'Sorry, I shouldn't burden you.' She drank some more Marzemino. '*In vino veritas,* perhaps.'

'You're not burdening me.'

'Your partner's lying in hospital, desperately ill. You don't need me sounding off with self-indulgent angst on top of that. All I'm saying is, don't take it for granted that the police will solve this case soon. Chances are, they'll never find who murdered the girls.'

'The kind of man who commits this crime never knows when to stop.'

'Not true, I'm afraid. Think of Jack the Ripper, the Hammersmith murderer, the Zodiac case. The list goes on. Serial killers who stopped before they were caught.'

'Or killed themselves first.'

Ceri considered this for a long time before giving a shrug of impatience. 'Who knows?'

'I have to believe justice will be done.'

'Oh, Harry. And you an experienced lawyer. When will you learn?'

As if to soften the harshness of her words, she stretched a slim hand across the table and laid it on his. A few days ago, he might have dreamed of this. A candle-lit dinner with Ceri Hussain, her cool skin touching his. Yet death and disaster had brought them together. Be careful what you wish for.

In his jacket pocket, his mobile trilled and gently, he withdrew his hand. Carmel's mobile number shone on the screen. He could tell from her voice that she was trying not to let her hopes rise too high too soon.

'The surgeon's pleased with how the operation went. He says Jim's shown amazing resilience.'

'That's wonderful.' He knew the crunch would come when his partner woke up. Would he still be the same man they'd known for so long?

'As for Amazing Grace, I've put out feelers. The word is that she isn't on the books of the escort agency.'

'Thank God for that.'

'You could do with some good news. Talking of which, are you enjoying the coroner's company?'

He threw a quick glance at Ceri. She was savouring the last of her wine, casting a thoughtful eye over framed prints of the Piazza San Marco and the wooden bridge at Accademia.

'Definitely.'

A throaty chuckle. 'Have a lovely night.'

'Speak to you tomorrow.'

When he'd rung off, Ceri smiled. 'Good news about Jim Crusoe?'

'It's early days.' He took a breath. 'Another thing. It concerns Aled Borth.'

She frowned. 'Tell me.'

He described Grace's brief encounter in the office with Borth and his fear that she might be a potential victim. As he talked, he became aware that Ceri's attention had begun to wander.

'You think Borth might be the murderer?'

'I don't know what to think.'

'And this secretary of yours, she's called Grace?'

'Grace Samuels, that's right.'

'Grace Samuels! She used to work for me, did you know?'

'Her c.v. said she once worked in the coroner's office. I meant to ask if it was before your time.'

'Not quite. We overlapped by a couple of months. An unusual character, Grace, but a first-class secretary. Intelligent and well-organised. Unfortunately, her parents died soon after she began working for me, and after that, she lost the plot. Wanted a change.'

She sounded as though she didn't have much patience with people who wanted a change, let alone those who lost the plot. He'd met few women as single-minded about their work as Ceri Hussain. Throwing herself into her job must have helped her to deal with her husband's death. But maybe she'd come to realise that there's no pleasure in all work and no play.

'She's temping now. I guess it suits her, but she doesn't mix with the other staff. They find her rather strange.'

'Is it any wonder? All that pagan nonsense.'

'Pagan nonsense?'

'Didn't you know? After the death of her mum and dad, she got into nature worship. God knows what it involves. Dancing round Stonehenge skyclad on Midsummer's Eve, for all I know.'

'Midsummer's Eve?'

She stared at him. 'What…oh, you're not wondering if Grace sent you that message, are you?'

◇◇◇

'Grace just wouldn't behave like that,' Ceri said as they left the restaurant. 'Besides, why would she?'

'I suppose you're right.' Harry exhaled. 'I may not be the best boss in the world, but I'm not quite bad enough for the staff to wish me dead.'

She laughed. 'I'm sure they love working for you.'

Darkness had fallen. In the distance, drunken delegates to the John Lennon Convention were caterwauling *Imagine* as they made their way back to their hotels.

Harry walked to the edge of the river and looked across towards the lights of Wirral shining in the blackness.

'The longest day,' Ceri said, 'and it's nearly over.'

'Did you know, Midsummer is one of those quarter days of the legal calendar when servants were hired and rent and rates were due? I suppose I shouldn't worry. The true significance of Midsummer's Eve is legal, not pagan.'

'Now I know everything,' she said softly, and leaned towards him.

But the moment was ruined as he missed his footing on the cobbled walkway. They had polished off a couple of bottles of wine as they chatted through the meal. Just as well Ceri had arrived in a taxi; it wouldn't do for a coroner to drink and drive.

'I ought to call a cab,' she said, when she'd stopped laughing.

He caught a hesitation in the words. At once his legs felt weak. Nothing to do with the alcohol this time. His head was clear enough for him to see that a door had opened. Wait a few seconds and it would shut again.

Take your chance.

'Would you like to come back for coffee?'

She stopped to consider him. Her face was in shadows and he couldn't read her expression.

'We've just had coffee.'

Blown it. Oh God. He shouldn't have tempted fate by tidying up the mess in his flat before he met her at The Lido.

'I mean…I've enjoyed your company.'

She brushed his shoulder with her fingertips. 'And I've enjoyed yours, Harry. Thank you.'

'So…?'

She laughed. 'As it happens, I could use another shot of caffeine. It's a shame to rush off. But I mustn't stay too late.'

'No, no, of course, that's fine.' He tried not to stammer with delight. 'My place is only a stone's throw away. I can ring for a cab when you're ready to go.'

'Thanks.'

Before he knew what was happening, she'd linked her arm with his and they were heading for Empire Dock. The evening air was mellow, her touch felt warm and close. How long since he'd last brought a woman back home? His life was slipping like sand through his fingers. A week ago he'd dreamt he had driven his car into a sea of mud in the middle of nowhere. When he put his foot down, the wheels spun, but the car didn't move. He woke in a cold sweat, but he was living the dream. He was trapped in his work and needed to escape.

'You're very quiet,' Ceri said.

'Sorry.'

'No need to apologise. Let's enjoy the evening.'

Her closeness made him light-headed, in a way the booze never could. As he unlocked his front door, panic seized him. What if his unknown enemy had trashed his home while he'd been out, and sprayed it with graffiti about death on Midsummer's Eve?

But the flat was silent and untouched. He padded into the kitchen and poured coffee into a filter. Over his shoulder he saw her kneeling down to take a look at his music collection.

'Choose whatever you like,' he said.

'I have a soft spot for Elvis Costello.'

As the coffee machine chugged, the flat filled with the raw vocal of *What's Her Name Today?* Dark words wrestling with a lush melody. As she settled on the sofa and kicked off her shoes, his stomach fluttered. Her mood seemed fragile. Even at the end of a meal as long and leisurely as a trip down the Grand Canal, he'd seen the way she turned and twisted her napkin as they talked, squeezing it into a tight little ball. Probably this was the first time she'd been alone with a man like this since her husband's terrible death. How to avoid the one false move that would ruin everything?

He poured the coffees. She took off her jacket and folded it over a chair. He sat next to her on the sofa, and she half-turned to face him. For a few minutes they small-talked, but he hardly knew what he was saying. Her skin was pale; he was conscious of the swell of her breasts beneath the white vest. Thank God he'd had a few drinks, otherwise his nerves would stretch to breaking point. He might have been an infant paddler straying out of his depth, excited yet fearful of being washed away by a tidal wave. Every now and then, her dark eyes met his; she yielded a trace of a smile, but no clue to what was in her mind.

He put down his cup and dared to rest his hand on her arm. Touching it so lightly that it might almost be an accident. She didn't pull away. Her leg moved, grazed against his.

'Thank you, Harry,' she whispered.

Their faces moved closer together. Within moments they were kissing, her tongue hot and hungry on his. Her fingers slipped inside his shirt and she began to undo the buttons. He brushed against her breast and she gave a little gasp. His hand moved under her vest, felt the hardness of her vertebrae beneath the smooth skin, worked its way round until it reached the stiffening nipple and she gave a little cry.

At once she was on top of him. Pushing him beneath her with unexpected strength. Panting hard. His arms were wrapped around her back and he caressed her spine. She stared down at his face, but he wasn't sure she could see him. It was as if she were gazing through a telescope into the far distance.

'Ceri…'

She'd seen something through the telescope, something that frightened her. Horror filled the dark eyes and she jerked up and away from him.

Next moment she was standing up, grabbing at her jacket. He felt as though he'd been kicked in the kidneys. He'd tried to be so careful and still he'd got it wrong.

'I can't do this.' Her voice was throaty, unrecognisable. 'Sorry.'

'What is it?'

She pulled on her shoes. 'It's not you, Harry. It's me. And it's Ricky.'

Ricky, the husband who had chased women, suffered depression, failed in business, and finally killed himself. How long would his memory suffocate her?

He clambered off the sofa and stood in front of her. 'Please talk to me.'

'Ricky felt rejected. It made him angry and ashamed, made him behave in a way I would never have believed.'

'He shouldn't have done what he did.'

She bowed her head, then sucked air into her lungs and looked him in the eye. Her face was dark with grief.

'You don't understand what I'm saying.'

'Try me.'

His cheeks burned. She couldn't guess how desperate he was not to be rejected too.

'I must go now.'

'But…'

'No buts. Please, Harry.'

It wasn't going to happen between them after all. He inhaled the warm air. Time to admit defeat. Show a bit of dignity.

'I'll see you out.'

'No need.' In two minutes she'd aged ten years. 'Sorry, sorry, sorry.'

The door closed behind her and Harry slumped on to the sofa. His heart pounded, his head throbbed. He felt sick with anger and despair.

'It's not you.'

The story of my fucking life.

The Fifth Day

Chapter Fifteen

In a dream, his footsteps slapped weathered stone steps as he
fled from someone whose face he could not see. At the bottom
of the stairs, his path was barred by a mahogany door set within
a Gothic arch. He rummaged through his pockets, but he'd lost
the key. It must have fallen out as he ran. Too late to go back
and hunt for it. He hammered his fists against the iron-strapped
planks until his knuckles bled, but nobody came. From the
other side of the door came a faint sound. Muffled music, but
he couldn't make out a melody. Thirty feet above his head, a
steel door slammed. Heavy boots crashed down the steps, he
heard heavy breathing. There was no way out.

He jabbed at the door and, by a miracle, it swung open,
smooth and silent on an oiled hinge. A long stride took him into
the chamber on the other side. He spun round and saw an iron
bolt gleaming in the candle-light. Crashing it home, he gave a
gasp of relief. At last he was safe from his unknown foe.

High above his head, an organ played. Discordant sounds, a
weird pastiche of a funeral march. Swivelling, he was confronted
by a dozen leering revellers in a semi-circle. They wore red cloaks
and their faces were disguised by Venetian masks. Shafts of light
caught a plague-doctor's scythe-like nose, the colourful squint
of a Harlequin cat, a Cubist face smudged by tears, a beast with
bared teeth frozen in mid-howl.

His eyes smarted, his sinuses ached. The air was thick with
smoky incense. He was in a basement, eerie and unfamiliar. A

trail of dark smears on the stone flags led into darkness. The masked figures began to moan and keen. Their chant was word-less, rhythmic, threatening. From the midst of the semi-circle, the plague-doctor beckoned him. Harry sensed that something lay beyond the revellers, something hidden and grotesque.

He took a pace forward and peered through the holes in the masks. It felt like gazing into the souls of the creatures who confronted him. He recognised the pale eyes of Victor Creevey. The Cubist mask belonged to Barney Eagleson, the man who embalmed the dead for a living. The beast with bared teeth was Casper May, and the Harlequin cat his wife. Juliet's small mouth formed into a smile but he knew better than to let her fool him once again. Any moment now, she would spit and scratch.

The plague-doctor cackled and unsheathed a claw. A knife glittered in the gloom. Harry had seen that blade before, Tom Gunter had caressed it in the gardens of the Parish Church. With a jolt of dismay, he realised that the mournful brown eyes behind the mask did not belong to Tom. The plague-doctor was Ceri Hussain.

Harry was mesmerised. He couldn't move, he was at the mercy of the creature with the cruel beak. But the plague-doctor merely stepped aside, to permit a glimpse of what lay beyond. A mortuary slab, with a slender figure in a plain white gown stretched out upon it. A woman with long dark hair.

'Ka-Yu?'

As he whispered her name, the woman began to stir. So she was not dead after all. Her upper body rose, her arm reached out. She turned to look at him.

Her olive face was perfect and unmarked, her eyes heavy-lidded, as though the sound of his voice had roused her from a long, untroubled slumber.

'Ka-Yu, can you hear me?'

But when she opened her mouth to answer, no sound came. Nothing was there but a black void. He caught a glimpse of a hacked-off stump and his stomach heaved.

Ka-Yu had no tongue.

◇◇◇

He woke in a sweat and ran to the bathroom. When he tried to be sick, nothing happened, so he stripped off and walked under an icy shower, desperate to sluice away the memory of Kay's mutilated mouth. As soon as he'd towelled himself dry, he went to the kitchen and made himself a pot of Columbian Roast. Though he couldn't stop yawning, there was no sense in going to bed. He hadn't a chance of sleep.

Ceri's departure had left him numb. The first gulp of coffee scalded his throat, but he didn't care. He needed to feel something, needed to have a purpose, a mystery to solve. This wasn't just about him, or Midsummer's Eve. Kay was dead, Jim barely alive, and Carmel's heart was close to breaking.

He switched on the television for the early news. In the absence of a quick arrest in the hunt for Ka-Yu Cheung's killer, they fell back on words of wisdom from Maeve Hopes. She was wearing a little black dress, perhaps out of respect for the deceased, perhaps because it showed her slim figure to considerable advantage. Harry's eyes were drawn to her beaky nose. Like the plague-doctor in his dream.

'Most serial killings are solved because the culprit makes a mistake.' She gave the camera an encouraging smile. 'For all we know, he has already left the tell-tale clue that will lead the police to his door.'

Pray God she was right. He dared not share Ceri's pessimism, dared not persuade himself that the murderer would never be caught. Or that he would only be caught if another woman died.

◇◇◇

'Jim had a quiet night.' Carmel's voice kept breaking up on the mobile, yet for all her weariness, this morning she sounded less desolate. 'The nurse seems pleased, though I'm not counting any chickens. I'm about to nip over to the office for an hour, and catch up on some urgent stuff.'

'Practise the art of delegation. Nobody's indispensable. And you must be exhausted.'

'You must be joking. No way do I want the Police Authority to figure out that I'm dispensable. Otherwise I might finish up working for you again. Besides, you want the inside track on the murders, don't you?'

'But…'

'Anyway, if nobody's indispensable, why are you already in the office? You never used to start this early. Surely you're too long in the tooth to become a workaholic?'

'Thanks, you know how to make me feel good. As it happens, there's a lot to do.'

'Don't give me that, Harry Devlin. Why haven't you told me how you got on last night? I expect a full report. Unexpurgated.'

'Don't hold your breath. There's not much to tell.'

'That I don't believe.'

He exhaled. 'It wasn't a success, actually. I'm not sure we'll be seeing each other again.'

'I knew she wasn't perfect,' Carmel said. 'She must be a stupid cow to give you the cold shoulder.'

'It wasn't…'

'Come on, Harry. We're mates, aren't we? I insist on hearing all the gory details.'

'You really don't want to know.'

'Bollocks.' Her voice softened. 'Without Jim to talk to at the moment, you're the man in my life, do you realise? Now, tell me all about it.'

'There isn't…'

'Harry, you're putty in my hands. Always have been. Get used to it.'

'We had a lovely meal, and talked about Grace…'

'You're out on a date and you start discussing your secretary?'

'Listen, you'll enjoy this. According to Ceri, Grace is a pagan worshipper.'

'Amazing Grace?' Carmel sounded startled and gleeful in equal measure. 'You're kidding!'

'Not a word of a lie. As for Tom Gunter, Ceri has heard that he's on the run. But he has a cast-iron alibi for the Onuoha killing.'

'Yeah, my mate on the inquiry team told me. It's a bummer, frankly. If we're talking serial murder, Tom isn't our man.'

'Ceri reckons that he's disappeared out of panic rather than guilt.'

'Unless he's dead too.'

Harry hadn't considered this possibility. 'Suicide out of remorse? The only way a man like that kills himself is if he sees there's no way out.'

'Suppose he knew who killed Kay. What if she took a cab to Widnes, as she intended, but he followed her? Witnesses at the Marina say she left the flat at five o'clock, on foot. Perhaps she didn't want to be spotted getting into a cab in case Tom asked them if they'd seen her. Within a couple of minutes, he was back home. Maybe he'd been keeping an eye on her. His car was outside and he jumped straight into it and drove off. Nobody saw him return—very irritating. What's the point of nosey neighbours if they don't keep a permanent vigil by their front window?'

'Did he come back to the flat later on, then?'

'Must have done. The car's parked there again.'

'Anything to suggest that he won't be back in a hurry?'

'A team of detectives searched the flat. There's no ready cash lying around, so he probably took it with him. Some of his stuff has been taken away for forensic checks, to see if they can be linked to the scene where Kay was killed. But we mustn't jump to conclusions. If he witnessed the murder, he may have taken fright. Or confronted the killer and come off worst. Or tried his hand at blackmail and been murdered for his pains.'

'I never knew you had such a fertile imagination.'

She said quietly, 'The truth is, I don't much care whether Tom Gunter is dead or alive. But the guessing game takes my mind off what happened to Jim.'

'Thanks for telling me all this stuff.'

'Time to change the subject, Harry. I want to know more about your date with the Coroner.'

'There isn't much more to tell. Except that I invited her back to the flat for coffee, and she said yes.'

'Wow. Progress at last!'

'Not really. I thought something was going to happen between us, but she changed her mind at the last minute. Made her excuses and left. All very embarrassing.'

'Oh shit, Harry. I'm sorry.'

'Nothing to be sorry about. The woman lost her husband not long ago. She's still grieving, it's only to be expected. I was crass.'

'You're not crass,' Carmel said. 'At least, not where women are concerned.'

'Is that a compliment?'

'It is, actually. So you didn't arrange to meet again?'

'Uh-uh.'

'Send her flowers, keep in touch. Faint heart never won fair coroner.'

His eyes strayed to the latest advice from the desk calendar. *Life is ours to be spent, not saved.*

'She's not ready for a new relationship.'

'Give her time.' Another pause. 'You're ready, aren't you?'

He'd not even asked himself the question until now. But he knew the answer.

◇◇◇

'Something wrong?' Wayne Saxelby asked.

'Jim's in intensive care. Apart from that, everything's hunky-dory.'

At once Harry regretted the brusque reply. Wayne had dropped in to ask after Jim and boast about the new podcast he was about to download on to his website. Harry was in no mood for conversation, but he shouldn't take his temper out on the man who had saved his partner.

Thankfully, Wayne had a hide as thick as a tabloid editor's. His tone was more-in-sorrow-than-anger.

'You can't fool me, my friend. Something's bugging you. I can read you like a book.'

Like one of those trashy paperback thrillers you love hung unspoken in the air. Harry sighed. Wayne's ego had never seemed to allow for an interest in other people. The possibility that management consultancy had transformed him into a perceptive judge of character was almost too much to bear.

Harry shrugged. 'I had a date yesterday evening. Things didn't go as I'd hoped. That's all.'

'Not with Juliet May, by any chance?'

Harry reddened. 'No.'

'There's someone new in your life?'

'Doesn't look like it after last night.'

'Plenty more fish in the sea, eh?' Wayne shook his head. 'I dropped lucky with Tamara, I suppose. Luckier than I deserve.'

Harry stifled the temptation to say *too right*. 'Yeah, well. Easy come, easy go'

'Tell you what.' Wayne leaned forward, as if about to disclose a state secret. 'Tamara's due home on Saturday evening. I've organised a surprise party to welcome her back. Just a few friends. You must come along. I'd love you to meet her.'

'Thanks, I appreciate it.' Although a social bash with Wayne, Tamara and their celebrity chums held as much appeal as a night on the razzle at Guantanamo Bay, it would hardly be tactful to say so. 'I wouldn't like to butt in.'

'Nonsense! Tamara's not the ditzy blonde you may think from watching *Celebrities without Shame*.'

Harry would rather have his teeth pulled out than watch *Celebrities without Shame*, but even so Wayne had managed to wrong-foot him. He'd bestowed a great honour with the party invite.

'Of course not,' he said hastily, before it dawned on him that this wasn't an entirely tactful reply. 'I'm really very grateful.'

'No need. Tell you what, spare an hour of your evening, that's all. I'll pick you up, it's no trouble.'

'Very kind, but…'

'That's settled, then.' Wayne pursed his lips. 'I'd suggest you bring your date along too, but…'

'I don't think so.'

'Let's be honest, your love life was never exactly plain sailing, was it? Nothing new there. Why so twitchy all of a sudden? Surely this isn't anything to do with this murder at Widnes? Suzanne said you've been interviewed by the police.'

Bloody Suzanne and her big mouth. 'There's a rumour that Kay Cheung's murder is linked to a couple of others.'

'It might be an idea to confide in someone. A trouble shared, and all that.'

'Sorry, Wayne, I don't have anything to tell you.'

'All right, suit yourself.' He hauled himself up from the chair. 'Let me know if you change your mind. You might not believe it, but maybe I can help.'

Harry doubted it. But as Wayne reached the door, he looked so disgruntled that Harry's conscience wouldn't allow him to let the man go without another word.

'Thanks.' He cleared his throat. 'And not just for what you did for Jim. I was bloody glad to catch you at home yesterday. Must have been a shock seeing me outside your window.'

Wayne's features relaxed into the familiar grin. 'You're not kidding. Opening the blinds only to find Harry Devlin peering into my living room? It's the stuff nightmares are made of. For a moment there, I thought someone had filled my lunchtime sandwich with magic mushrooms. You should have seen your face. You looked as though someone wanted you dead.'

'Casper May is a…'

'This isn't about Casper May, though, is it?' Wayne peered at Harry with naked curiosity. 'Sorry, but I just don't buy that. It makes no sense. There's someone else you're afraid of.'

Harry shrugged. 'It's a long list, starting with the taxman, my accountant…'

'You don't fool me,' Wayne murmured. 'There's a good deal you aren't telling me. But if you want to hug your secrets to yourself, fine. Just remember, if you want to talk any time, give me a call.'

Harry made up his mind. 'All right. You're throwing the party on Saturday. Midsummer's Eve. That's the day I'm meant to die.'

◇◇◇

'It's bizarre,' Wayne said for the third time. 'I mean, who would want to kill *you*?'

He made it sound like a particularly unambitious choice of victim. Harry almost felt offended.

'Your guess is as good as mine.'

'I mean, have you anything special planned for Midsummer's Eve?'

'Doing the laundry and washing the car will be as exciting as it gets.'

Wayne frowned, as if grappling with a sudoku of infinite complexity. 'Might that date be an anniversary of some kind?'

'If so, it's passed me by.'

'It must have some significance, Harry. What else could it be?'

'Something to do with pagan traditions?' Harry hesitated. 'It's a ridiculous idea, of course, but I might consult Grace. Someone told me she's a pagan worshipper.'

Wayne's eyes widened. 'Seriously? Now, that is amazing. I had no idea. Though she is a bit flaky?'

'Eccentric, perhaps. Intelligent, certainly.'

'She's a loner. I've noticed she doesn't mix with the rest of your staff.'

'Nothing wrong with being a loner.'

'True. I suppose you could say that you and I are both loners, too.'

'Until Tamara comes back?'

Wayne sighed. 'I miss her, that's for sure.'

'Must be difficult for you.'

'At least I know she'll be coming back soon.' Wayne studied his shoes. 'In some ways, I miss my mother even more.'

'She's dead?' When Wayne worked for Crusoe and Devlin, he'd talked about her a lot. He went to visit her at an old people's home four times a week, regular as clockwork. 'I'm sorry to hear it.'

Wayne bowed his head. 'It happened three years back, soon after I left the firm. A dreadful shock. She seemed so fit and well when I last saw her, the day before.'

'The home where she lived,' Harry said. 'In Crosby, wasn't it?'

'That's right. The Indian Summer Care Home.'

Harry stared. 'The place owned by Malachy Needham?'

'Yes, why do you ask?'

◇◇◇

While Grace caught up with the filing, Harry tinkered with a draft plea in mitigation. The case was open-and-shut: his client had been caught by a speed camera, driving at seventy miles an hour through a thirty-limit in road-works on the M58. The mitigating factor was that the man was late for a conference where he was due to deliver a keynote speech. Harry only hoped that the prosecution didn't cotton on that the conference topic was 'Making Health and Safety Integral to our Everyday Lives'.

He wondered about the Indian Summer Care Home. Two unexpected deaths didn't even amount to a coincidence. Mrs. Saxelby and Nesta Borth had died years apart and the truth was that old people's lives did often end in homes, however scrupulous the care.

Wayne Saxelby was an only child, and when he talked about his mother's death, a tear came to his eye, something Harry had never seen before. He realised that he'd never made sufficient effort to get to know Wayne; there was more to him than just an ego bigger than Ben Nevis.

Wayne didn't disguise his bitterness at the loss of his mother, not least because he said his father had never recovered and died twelve months after his wife. But his anger wasn't directed towards Malachy Needham. If he had any reason to doubt that she had died of a massive coronary, he gave no hint of it. He even volunteered that Needham's staff had done their best for the old lady.

Wayne hadn't been with her at the end, and that had left him with a sense of guilt. Harry empathised; every now and then, he felt a twinge himself. Guilt about his parents, his wife, his half-brother. It was as though he'd been slapdash, losing those close to him while he looked the other way. Perhaps there ought to be a criminal misdemeanour of living without due care and attention.

Grace closed the bottom drawer of the filing cabinet and turned round. She was wearing a see-through cheesecloth top with a vest underneath and evidently no bra. Her skirt was floaty, her sandals displayed slender feet and small toes with chipped pink varnish.

'Any news of Mr. Crusoe?'

She was the only person in the firm who didn't call Jim by his first name. When Harry said that Jim was holding his own, she gave a cautious smile.

'I prayed for him last night.'

Harry's knowledge of paganism didn't extend much beyond a mild fascination with *The Wicker Man*. Now was as good a time as any to get his secretary talking. She had a natural reserve and he'd not learned much about her. How little he really knew about the people he spent so much of his life with. Even Sylvia, he'd never guessed she carried a torch for Jim.

'Thanks, Grace. As it happens, your name cropped up in conversation yesterday evening.' A flush came to the woman's pale cheeks. 'No need for your ears to burn. I was chatting to the Coroner. She told me that you used to work for her. Said how sorry she was when you left.'

Grace bowed her head. 'That was a difficult time for me. My mother and father had recently died.'

'I'm sorry.' A wild thought flashed into his head. More untimely deaths at the Indian Summer Care Home? 'Was it…very sudden?'

'Very. They'd gone on a golfing holiday in the Algarve and the coach they were travelling in took a bend too fast. Five people died, including the driver.'

His sympathy was mixed with relief. Better abandon all thoughts of a previously unsuspected series of mysterious deaths under Malachy Needham's baleful eye. He got up and perched on the side of his desk. Grace stood in front of him, resting her hands on the back of a chair. Her musky fragrance was overpowering.

'Tough to cope with a double tragedy like that.'

'They were only in their mid-sixties, they'd looked forward to a long and happy retirement together. What happened was so cruel, so pointless…it made me question things. Dad was a sidesman at the local church, Mum arranged the flowers for the altar. I wondered why their God hadn't kept them safe.'

He detected a spark of resentment in those last few words. Like Wayne Saxelby, she hadn't stopped grieving.

'Ceri Hussain mentioned that after they died, you…'

'Lost the plot? It's true. I was an only child, and solitary. Very close to my parents. They had me late in life and I was the apple of their eye. When they were taken from me, I felt cut adrift. I wasn't in a relationship at the time. For the previous five years, I'd…'

'Yes?'

'Well, I'd been involved with a married man, I'm afraid. He was a barrister in one of the local chambers. I won't mention his name. He was desperate to be appointed Queen's Counsel and he was frightened that a breath of scandal would scupper his chances. When it came to choosing me or taking silk, it wasn't much of a contest. He dumped me a few weeks before I started work at the Coroner's Court.'

'I'm sorry,' he said again.

'Don't be. Something good did come out of the tragedy.'

'Tell me.'

'I needed something fresh in my life, and Wicca came to my rescue.'

'Ceri Hussain mentioned that.'

'She didn't approve. I made the mistake of confiding in her. I liked her and I'd seen how she behaved in court, how sensitive she was to bereaved families. I thought she'd realise what I was going through, the sheer physical effort of simply climbing out of bed and catching the bus to get in for work every morning. When all I wanted to do was to hide under the bed clothes and hope the rest of the world would go away.'

'She's a good listener.'

'Don't get me wrong, Ceri is a decent woman. But she's a ruthless perfectionist, she likes everything to be just so. Remember, she's both a lawyer and a medic, she's trained to believe in a rational universe, where you can't take anything on trust without evidence to back it up.'

Ceri hadn't seemed too rational last night, but perhaps that was the point. She must have despised herself for not turning down his invitation to come back for coffee. His thoughts strayed to their brief encounter on the sofa, and he had to drag his attention back to Grace.

'...and death doesn't mean as much to her as it does to most of us. I suppose it's because that's what her job is all about. Murder, suicide, accident, it's all in a day's work to Ceri Hussain.'

'She takes her job seriously.'

'Yes, but she's trying to create order from chaos. Finding solutions to unanswered questions. Bringing in a verdict, closing the argument. She saw Wicca as my comfort blanket, and that meant she wrote me off as weak and illogical. Not like her, in other words. After that, I never had the courage to talk intimately to her again.'

'I'm sorry.'

'I didn't know she was a friend of yours.'

'We are...acquaintances, that's all.'

Grace scanned his face for clues. 'Of course, you appeared in front of her the other morning.'

'Yes, in the Borth case.'

He thought her eyelids flickered at the name. Might as well put the question.

'You know Aled Borth?'

No mistaking the flinch this time. Or the hunch of her shoulders under the flimsy top. She was on the defensive; he was sure she didn't want to talk about Aled Borth.

'What makes you say that?'

'You bumped into him on the morning of the inquest, remember?'

'Oh yes, you were there.' She hesitated, and he guessed she was calculating how to respond. 'Did he mention that we'd met before?'

'Not in so many words, but…'

'But?'

'You tell me.'

'Honestly, you don't want to know.'

'Try me.'

'Shouldn't we both be getting on with our work?'

'It can wait. Aled Borth interests me.'

'I can't imagine why.'

He waved at the chair. 'Take the weight off your feet.'

'If you insist.' She moved around the chair. 'At least you're easier to talk to than Ceri Hussain.'

'Aled Borth?' he prompted.

'I'd no idea that was what he was called,' she said. 'If I had, I'd have recognised it the first time you asked me to work on the inquest file. But in our Circle, we take our names from Mother Nature. Aled Borth joined a year ago, but I knew him as Greenleaf.'

Greenleaf?

Somehow Harry kept a straight face. It was a skill developed over years of listening to hardened recidivists assuring magistrates that they'd be starting a new job on Monday and were determined to stay out of trouble in future.

'It soon became clear that he wasn't genuinely interested in our belief systems. He seemed to treat the Circle as a kind of niche dating agency. I presume he expected us to rip our clothes off at the first glimpse of a full moon.'

'Did you get to know him?'

'I kept my distance. One or two of the other women took pity on him, but they soon discovered he was only interested in one thing. And it wasn't exploring his spirituality. We're a collective, we don't have an established hierarchy or priesthood, paganism isn't about rules. But he started making a nuisance of himself. After a few weeks, one of the men took him aside and suggested it would be better for him to leave.'

'And that was the last you saw of him?'

'Until he turned up here the other day. I don't know which of us was more embarrassed, him or me.'

'If you didn't even know his real name, I suppose you didn't find out much else about him?'

'Not really.' She wrinkled her brow. 'He struck me as rather mean. Mind you, he was chronically short of money. I remember him complaining once about his mother. He said she was drinking away his inheritance. If you ask me, all that fuss he made about her supposedly being poisoned was nothing to do with wanting justice done. My bet is, Greenleaf felt ashamed for wishing her dead and wanted to find somewhere else to lay the blame.'

Harry guessed she was right. Aled Borth had persuaded himself that he was a faithful son, determined to protect the reputation of a fine old lady who rarely touched a drop of alcohol. Pure fantasy. Whatever other crimes he might have committed, Malachy Needham surely hadn't murdered Nesta Borth or Mrs. Saxelby. There wasn't a business case for killing the residents of the Indian Summer Care Home. All he cared about was money.

With Kay Cheung, it was different. Someone had strangled her and hacked out her tongue. She deserved justice. Harry was determined to make sure she got it.

Chapter Sixteen

As the door closed behind his secretary, Harry recalled Kay murmuring to the potted palms as she fed and watered them. She was a gentle woman, content with the simple things. He couldn't believe she'd been happy to work as an escort, for all the ostensible respectability of Cultural Companions. Had her revulsion at a client's demands led to her death?

He called Sylvia in and asked what she knew about Kay. Needless to say, she'd learned far more than Harry ever had.

'Her sister is a photographer. She's ten years older, and quite successful, I think. They fell out because she didn't approve of Tom Gunter.'

'A woman of sound judgment, then.'

'Absolutely. Though it was such a pity. The two of them were never close. When the parents died, the sister was reluctant to take responsibility for Kay. Kay went her own way, but when she became involved with Tom, the sister was furious. After that, they hardly ever spoke to each other.'

'So it's not likely the sister can cast any light on Kay's death?'

Sylvia frowned. 'Shouldn't you leave all this to the police?'

'You know me.'

'Too well.'

'I'm curious, that's all.'

'Curiosity will kill you one day, Harry. After what happened to Jim…'

'This is nothing to do with what happened to Jim.'

The moment he said it, he wondered if it was true. But it must be, surely?

'All right.' She shook her head, resigned to the inevitable. 'The sister is called Rosamund Chow. She changed her name when she began to make her way in photography. If you want to talk to her, she may be up at St James' Gardens.'

Harry was startled. 'By the Cathedral?'

'Yes, I read in the *Daily Post* that she's exhibiting her photographs there.' Sylvia shivered. 'I didn't much like the sound of the show. She calls it *Aspects of Death*.'

◇◇◇

'Where better to display photographs about death than in an old cemetery?' Rosamund Chow asked.

Good question and Harry didn't have an answer. They were standing under a large gazebo of green canvas in St James' Gardens, sheltering from the drizzle. The awesome bulk of the Anglican Cathedral loomed up in front of them, but Harry had eyes only for the pictures on display.

The photographs were black and white. He found the spare images unsettling. Faces twisted with grief, men and women dressed in black gathered around an open tomb, a body on a mortuary table, covered in a shroud.

Rosamund Chow waved him to sit down on a plastic chair next to a table covered in leaflets about her work. She was a short, dumpy woman who kept her hair in a tight bun and wore a plain white blouse and grey skirt. Her manner was brisk and business-like and everything she said suggested an uncompromising intelligence. Harry detected no trace of Kay's habitual anxiety to please, but the shower had deterred visitors to the exhibition, and once he'd explained that he was the friend Kay had arranged to meet on the day she died, she was willing to talk. She'd already told him that she was married to an accountant and lived in leafy, upmarket Woolton. Harry had met her husband at the professional networking events that Jim insisted he attend. He was an affable fellow, and Harry suspected that Rosamund wore the trousers. Hard to imagine that she and Kay ever had much in common beyond a blood-tie.

'It is one of the differences between the Chinese mind-set and the Anglo-Saxon,' she said. 'There is not such a taboo about death. We think about it a lot. Perhaps…perhaps it will make it easier for me to come to terms with this ghastly thing. Though right at this moment, I cannot be sure.'

'Did you see much of Kay?'

'We last met twelve months ago. I bumped into her in the city centre. She was going to an office to see to their plants, and I was off to see my husband for a bite of lunch at the Athenaeum. We talked for a few minutes, but I'm afraid it was all very super-ficial. Kay knew that I disliked Tom Gunter. He could twist her around his little finger, but with me she could be stubborn. No way did she want me to have the satisfaction of saying, "I told you so." Neither of us mentioned his name, but he was there in spirit, standing right between us.'

'What did you know about their relationship?'

'Let me speak candidly, Mr. Devlin. Never mind *de mortuis.* Kay was a sweet, innocent girl, but she wasn't strong and at times, I'm afraid, she didn't behave in a particularly intelligent way. She chose her men badly, and although I only ever met Gunter the once, that was enough. Paul and I never wanted to have anything to do with him again. He was obviously unreliable and had a hair-trigger temper. I have little doubt that he beat Kay if she displeased him. But she didn't have the backbone to walk out. Does that sound harsh? To say that she was perversely loyal might be kinder. Even when he was charged with murder, she stood by her man. You were his solicitor, you say, you must be aware that she actually believed he was a victim of mistaken identity.'

'The case against him fell apart. Once he'd sacked me, that is.'

Rosamund Chow snorted. 'Legal jiggery-pokery, I expect you were too honest to indulge in it. Of course, from Kay's perspec-tive, her loyalty was vindicated. How ridiculous is human nature. Poor Kay had an endless capacity to deceive herself.'

Rain smacked against the gazebo's canvas roof and Harry turned his collar up against the gathering wind. The gardens occupied a scooped-out site, once a quarry and later a burial ground, and they formed a cool, quiet and mysterious oasis close to the heart of the city. Close to the gazebo, the cylindrical Huskisson Memorial honoured the man killed by Stephenson's 'Rocket'. Behind was Liverpool's very own spa, a spring of water said to be drinkable, though Harry had never chanced it. Above were sloping Ramps, down which hearses once travelled to deliver the dead to their final resting place. Catacombs were cut into the sandstone cliff, old tombstones lined the pathways. Reminders of mortality were everywhere. Including the occasional needle discarded by the junkies and prostitutes who sometimes crept in here at night.

'You never spoke to her after that meeting?'

'I did not say that, Mr. Devlin.' Her tone was precise, verging on pernickety. Harry suspected that having Rosamund as an elder sister might be a challenge for anyone. 'We didn't keep in close touch, but Paul and I are Christians and our faith has become the cornerstone of our lives. We are born again, you might say. I came to realise that I let Kay down. I was older and wiser and I should have kept her safe from men like Gunter. I failed her.'

'I feel the same,' he blurted out. 'That message she left for me…'

'You must not reproach yourself. You were a friend, but I was her flesh and blood. For years, I was preoccupied with carving out my own path. I adopted a new professional name, met Paul and married him. There wasn't any room in my life for a younger sister.'

'Did you contact her?'

'Belatedly, yes. I rang her up ten days ago and tried to explain that I wanted to make amends for my past mistakes. She told me she and Gunter had moved into a flat at the Marina. It was a step up for them, but she seemed unhappy. I wondered where the money was coming from. Nowhere good, I suppose. I suggested we meet for a coffee, but she put me off.'

'And that was the last time you heard from her?'

'No, Mr. Devlin. She left a message on my voicemail on the morning she was murdered. I told the police about it, of course.'

'What did she say?'

A flicker of pain creased Rosamund Chow's stern face, and Harry's heart went out to her.

'She asked me to call her. Her last words were: *you were right.* About Tom Gunter, I presume.'

'Did you ring back?'

'No, I was too busy with the exhibition. I thought it would keep. Besides, I wanted to savour what she had said. I'm afraid it is one of my sins, Mr. Devlin. I very much enjoy being proved right. But of course, in the long run this has not made me feel happy at all.'

She sniffed hard, although Harry saw no sign of tears. He looked away while she blew her nose, at a photograph of two old Indian men, contemplating the blackened remains of a funeral pyre.

'I must pray for the Lord's forgiveness,' she said in a muffled voice. 'While I absorbed myself in death, I neglected life.'

◇◇◇

'If there's a serial killer at work,' Harry said as he sipped a half of Cain's, 'you can bet that he has a history. These people don't spring out of nowhere, fully formed as sadistic murderers. There's a build-up. Clues in their past. Previous crimes, they…'

'All right, all right.' Carmel raised her hands in mock-surrender. 'You're starting to sound like Maeve Hopes. When you get a bee in your bonnet, there's no stopping you. Jim used to say the same. "If only Harry worked as hard as he…"'

Her voice faltered as she realised she'd used the past tense. 'I mean, he'll say it again the minute I tell him the latest.'

'Yes, he will,' Harry said quietly.

For a minute or so, neither of them spoke. They were in the saloon bar of the Burning Deck, across the road from the General. It was a cramped little pub which did a roaring trade thanks to the families of patients who felt in need of something stronger than tea, coffee or squash in the hospital cafeteria. The place owed its name to an almost forgotten daughter of Liverpool, Felicia Hemans. She'd been a chum of Wordsworth and at one time her verse earned her a reputation second only to Byron's. But her fame hadn't lasted. These days her poetry was remembered by a single phrase from 'Casabianca': *The boy stood on the burning deck, whence all but he had fled.*

Some days, Harry could imagine exactly how that boy must have felt.

'Kay was different from Denise and Lee. Too gentle and quiet for anyone to describe her as bubbly and fun-loving. Even if Denise and Lee were killed by a client who lost it, Kay wouldn't arrange to meet a client at the same time as she was supposed to be seeing me.'

Carmel tasted her white wine and pulled a face. 'Yuck. Too sweet. Like Kay Cheung, eh? She doesn't fit the typical profile of an escort. Cultural Companions say she'd only been out with a couple of men. The team is checking up on them, of course.'

'I wonder if she was killed for some other reason than the first two victims.'

'But the m.o. is identical. That's the complication.'

'What have you found out about Borth?'

'Not much. I need to tread with care. The SIO won't take kindly to an in-house lawyer poking her nose in. There's a strict line between legal and operational, you know that.'

'You'll wrap him around your little finger.'

'As of now, this is the highest profile investigation in the North of England. We're under pressure. The media are screaming that Denise's murder wasn't taken seriously because she was an escort.'

'Isn't it true?'

'Not true and not fair. There simply wasn't enough evidence for the team to get their teeth into. Everyone is focused on achieving a result. The people at the top won't want to be distracted.'

'If you don't ask, you don't find out.'

Carmel pushed her glass to one side. 'Okay, okay, anything to get you off my case.'

'Thanks.' A thought struck him. 'What about the forensics? Were all the women strangled in exactly the same way?'

'Manually, yes. There were fingernail marks on the throat of Denise Onuoha, but they haven't been matched to a suspect. Lee Welch's neck was bruised, but there wasn't much forensic evidence. Same with Kay Cheung. But he may have made a mistake in his latest choice of crime scene. Forensic clues don't last long on a beach, but grassy areas are different. Footwear impressions were found close to Kay's body that look interesting.'

Harry finished his drink. 'Sibierski insisted on checking my shoe size.'

'He's just pulling your plonker, Harry. These prints came from size 11 trainers.'

'My feet are size 9.'

'Phew, got away with it, eh? If we can find a match to these impressions, we're in business.'

Harry breathed in. Not so long ago, his lungs would have choked up in a place like this, but the smoking ban had cleansed the atmosphere. Now there was only the smell of stale beer to clog up your nasal passages.

'How did the murderer cut out the women's tongues?'

'With no great expertise.' She made a face. 'Messy. Horrible, actually. He used a common type of Swiss army knife. We haven't found the weapon, or weapons. Maybe he used the self-same knife each time, maybe not. There are thousands of those knives out there.'

'Yeah, I saw one recently,' Harry said. 'Tom Gunter threatened me with it.'

◇◇◇

'You took a risk, confronting him,' Carmel said five minutes later.

'It wasn't as if we were strangers. I once acted for him, don't forget.'

'All the more reason to watch your step.'

'Thanks for your confidence in my client management skills.'

'Fools rush in, and all that.' She coloured. 'Sorry, that sounds cruel. Listen, Harry. I know you mean well.'

'That sounds worse.'

'It's just that…with Jim in such a state, I need you to look after yourself.'

'We can't wrap ourselves up in cotton wool. Jim wasn't poking his nose into anybody else's business, was he?'

'But…'

'No buts,' he said, rising to his feet. 'I must get along. Things to do.'

'There's no stopping you, is there?' she said in weary resignation.

He touched her warm hand. 'After what happened to Jim and Kay? Nothing at all.'

◇◇◇

His next destination was Pretty Street, in Waterloo. Aled Borth's cottage propped up the end of an ancient terraced row in a featureless one way thoroughfare five minutes from the waterfront. The street name was presumably the brainchild of Victorian city fathers with a keen sense of humour, but Aled's neighbours had done their best to live up to it. Their small front gardens were neat confections of coloured pebbles and shrubs hardy enough to withstand the icy blast from the waterfront. In contrast, Aled's patch of ground resembled a 'before' shot in a garden makeover programme. It was covered with old, broken concrete; nettles, bindweed and couch grass had colonised the cracks. Harry made his way from the broken wooden gate to Aled's front door. The curtains upstairs and down were drawn.

There was no bell, only a rusting iron knocker. Harry smacked the door with it half a dozen times, but no reply. He couldn't hear a sound from inside. Not a curtain twitched. If Borth was hiding in there, he was keeping very still.

A stout woman in her seventies emerged from the house next door, wheeling a tartan shopping trolley. She stared at Harry as if he was an extra-terrestrial with more than his fair share of tentacles.

'You're not looking for Mr. Borth, are you?'

'He doesn't seem to be at home.'

The woman gave a loud sniff. 'Heaven only knows what that one gets up to. Coming and going at all hours of the day and night, there's no rhyme or reason to it. I never knew decent folk keep such peculiar hours, that's for sure. Come to that, I've lived next door to him for more years than I care to remember, but I've never known him have a caller.'

She paused for a moment, as if to ratchet up her disapproval. 'I mean to say, not a *male* caller.'

Harry hazarded a jocular grin. 'A bit of a ladies' man, is he?'

This time her sniff sounded more like a bomb blast. 'I wouldn't call them *ladies.*'

Harry tried to look shocked, but he felt a surge of excitement. If Borth had a habit of paying for female company, over time his demands might have become increasingly exotic. He might have wanted to take what wasn't for sale. Even in the sober environment of the coroner's court, he'd not been able to control his temper. Alone with an unwilling or scornful escort girl, the impulse to indulge his fantasies by force might have become too strong to resist.

The woman glared at Harry's grey pinstripe. After crawling round Juliet May's balcony, he'd dropped off his court suit at the cleaners. This one was Asda rather than Armani, but at least it was a suit and that alone created grounds for suspicion in Pretty Street.

'You're not a debt collector, by any chance? I mean, he's forever complaining that he's short of money and he still owes me for a pint of milk from a month ago.'

'No, I'm his solicitor.' It was more or less true, though Harry could not conceive that Borth would ever consult him again.

'His solicitor?' The way the woman scowled, Harry might have confessed to being a paedophile. 'No wonder he's on his uppers if he's had to pay legal fees. My son Brian has just been involved in a court case. Lawyers? Money-grabbing blood-suckers, that's what he calls them.'

Harry tried to compose his features into an expression neither vampiric nor avaricious. 'Any idea where Aled Borth might be?'

'At that blinking picture-house, like as not. He spends half his life there. I don't see the point, myself. Why go to the cinema when you can watch television in the comfort of your own front room?'

◇◇◇

In the June daylight, the turrets and the towers of the Alhambra seemed even more at odds with their surroundings than on a cold winter's night. Two men chatted in a foreign language as they unloaded boxes from a white van outside the kebab house, while a gang of truanting kids kicked a football at a goal chalked on a brick wall. Harry strolled up the steps to the cinema entrance. The main door was closed, but when he pushed, it yielded to his touch.

Every other time he'd stood in the foyer, fellow movie-goers had milled around the kiosk and box office, and the air was thick with the aroma of popcorn and fruit gums. Now the Alhambra's interior was graveyard-quiet, with chandeliers unlit and the windows shuttered. Everything was dark, from the densely patterned carpet to the oak panelling on the walls. His skin felt clammy and uncomfortable, and his shoulders stiffened with tension.

The silence was shattered as a venerable organ roared into life. In the auditorium, someone was playing the Alhambra's lovingly restored Mighty Wurlitzer. Harry recognised the frenzied rhythms of *The Phantom of the Opera.*

It had to be Aled Borth.

Harry took a pace forward, then paused. He was about to confront the man on his home ground, with nobody to call on for help. What if Aled were a serial killer? But the organist didn't frighten him. Ka-Yu Cheung was dead and her murderer must be found and that was all he cared about. When he strode past the kiosk and kicked open the door to the auditorium, the music shuddered to a halt.

The lights were up in the movie theatre. Stretched between two Doric columns, an amber curtain concealed the vast screen. There wasn't a soul in the fifteen hundred red plush tip-up seats of the stalls and circle. Crouched like a crab over the keys of the Mighty Wurlitzer was Aled Borth.

'Hello, Aled.'

An unforgiving glare illuminated Aled's bald patch. He was wearing tweed trousers with threadbare knees and dirty carpet slippers. As Harry walked up to him, the whiff of old beer was as strong as in the saloon of the Burning Deck. When Aled turned, the goldfish eyes behind the spectacles were dull with drink.

'What do you want?'

'I'd like to ask you one or two questions.'

'Nothing to say.'

'You knew Lee Welch.'

'Lee Welch?'

Aled's voice trembled with fear. The feeble attempt to feign ignorance would not convince a child.

'The girl who was murdered. Whose body was found on the beach, a stone's throw from here.'

'Oh, yes. I read about it.'

'And you recognised her name, didn't you?'

'So what?'

'You knew her.'

'I knew her mother.'

'Her *mother*?'

'Yeah, she worked in the Co-op with my Mum, donkey's years ago.'

It was like that heart-sinking moment when a witness you're cross-examining comes up with an answer that takes your breath away. Yet Aled hadn't hesitated; he gave no sign of making up something that sounded plausible. And hadn't Gina spoken of Lee's mother having a job in a shop?

'You met her again recently, didn't you? In very different circumstances.'

Aled looked away. 'I…dunno what you're talking about.'

'I think you do. She was an escort girl and you hired her. Want to tell me the full story?'

'You must be bloody joking.'

'Or would you rather explain to the police instead?'

'Who do you think you are? You're my fucking solicitor!'

'That's history,' Harry said softly. 'What matters is that I knew the latest girl to die. Her name was Ka-Yu Cheung and she never had the joy in life she deserved. Whoever killed her took away any chance she might find something better.'

'I don't know what you're talking about. Are you making some kind of threat?' Aled struggled to his feet, his demeanour a pastiche of injured dignity. 'You're right, I ought to call the police!'

'Chances are you'll speak to them any time now.'

Aled jabbed a forefinger hard into Harry's midriff. He scarcely felt it—at last, an upside to putting on a few pounds.

'Why are you persecuting me?'

'You were a client of Lee Welch's. Easy to prove, these agencies keep records, they like to show that they operate above board. Anything the girls agree with the clients is nothing to do with them, blah, blah.'

'I told you, she grew up here. Her mother…'

'Did she tease you, was that why you lost it?'

'No!' Aled's breath was coming in short gasps. 'I would never hurt her. She's the sort who made enemies. It could have been…'

'Enemies? She'd been down in London, she hadn't had much time to make enemies back here.'

'Not true. She was sly and greedy, and…'

'You really didn't like her, did you?'

'Listen, all I did was pay for her time. Where's the harm? I just like to talk to the girls, that's all. Lee was happy the last time I saw her. She told me she was going to be rich.'

'Oh yeah?'

'There was something she'd overheard at work. She did a bit of cleaning and she knew something that someone wanted to keep dark. Lee said they would pay good money to keep her mouth shut.'

'You're making it up. You haven't had a proper relationship for God knows how long, so you make do with prostitutes. But what…'

'You bastard!'

Aled lunged at him, fists swinging. He caught Harry a glancing blow on the temple and within a moment, both of them were on the floor, grappling with more stubbornness than science. What Aled lacked in strength, he made up for in bloody-minded rage. He hauled himself up and started stabbing at Harry's eyes with short, grubby fingers. Harry struggled to push the man's hand away from his face, not meaning to inflict pain, just to avoid it. He didn't want to hurt Aled, whatever he might have done to Kay and the others. He loathed violence, his passionate hatred of it had brought him here, to this renovated picture palace and a bizarre wrestling match.

Suddenly he heard the clatter of a big man's footsteps, and then Sid Rankin's voice, hoarse with astonishment.

'My God, now I've seen everything. A cinema organist trying to poke a solicitor's eyes out!'

Aled moaned, and rolled off Harry's stomach. When Harry shifted position, his ribs hurt. In the melee, he'd bitten his own tongue. It seemed to take an age before he could stand upright. Aled was huddled up a couple of feet away, his back wedged against the Mighty Wurlitzer. His spectacles lay on the floor, the glass crushed beyond repair. Tears trickled down his cheeks, moistening the thread veins.

'All I did was talk to the girls,' he muttered.

Harry gulped in air. Aled was a dirty old man in more ways than one. He'd admitted to hiring escorts, but it was a long way short of proof that he was a murderer.

'Why should I believe you?'

'Because it's true. A…a cultural companion, that's what I wanted. Someone I could pay to be my friend for an hour or two.'

Sid looked as dazed as if he was the one who'd come off worst in a bare-knuckle fight. Harry would have laughed if his ribs could take the strain.

'Come on, you two. What's going on? I mean, am I dreaming this?'

Harry wiped dusty hands on his trousers. At this rate, he'd need to take out a second mortgage to afford his dry cleaning bill.

'It's not what you think,' he said.

'Harry,' Sid said, 'you really don't want to know what I think.'

◇◇◇

'Another fine mess you got yourself into,' Carmel said.

They were together again at the General, in reception at A&E. Harry's ribs kept aching and he'd decided to have them checked out. The nurse gave him a once-over and announced that although she couldn't find anything worse than a bit of bruising, he ought to have a precautionary X-ray, just in case.

'It wasn't in vain,' Harry insisted. 'Aled Borth admitted he knew Lee Welch.'

'Takes us no further forward.'

'Did you find out any more?'

Carmel nodded. 'Do you want the good news or the bad news?'

'I reckon I'm due some good news.'

'All right, you were spot on. Aled Borth has a history. Six months ago he was cautioned for kerb-crawling in Toxteth.'

'It's a progression.' Harry dug his nails into his palm. 'He picked girls up on the streets until police surveillance made it uncomfortable. After that, he turned to hiring girls from escort agencies.'

Carmel sighed. 'Ready for the bad news?'

'Break it to me gently.'

'Ever since Denise Onuoha was murdered, the team has been checking up on past offenders with a history of association with prostitutes. Painstaking work. They have traced the movements of hundreds of men. Including Aled Borth.'

'That's not bad news.'

'Depends on your point of view. When Denise was killed, Aled was playing his organ. No rude jokes, please. There was a soiree at the Alhambra and he performed selections from the days of silent movies. He couldn't have made it across the river until long after midnight, by which time Denise was probably dead.'

'It's not a water-tight alibi. What about the night Kay died?'

'Aled arrived at the cinema at six fifteen, for a screening at seven. No way could he have killed her at Widnes and hot-footed it back to Waterloo in time. You'll never guess what film was showing.'

'Go on.'

'*The Trouble with Harry*,' Carmel chortled. 'They ought to re-make it as a documentary.'

'So did he have an alibi for Lee Welch's murder?'

'Not as far as we know. But if the crimes form a series, he must be in the clear. Are you suggesting Aled was able to ascertain the murderer's m.o. and copy it in killing Lee? How could he do that?'

His last sight of Aled Borth stayed in his mind. Squeezed into a foetal ball against the cinema organ, Aled had sobbed himself into incoherence. Suppose he was telling the truth, and the reason he tried to wheedle his way into the pagan circle, and then hired escort girls when that didn't work out, was that he craved female company, *any* female company, once his mother left for the Indian Summer Care Home, to spend her twilight days in a booze-soaked reverie?

'Are you okay?' Carmel asked.

'Sore ribs, that's all.' The pangs of conscience hurt more. He didn't like Aled, but he wished he hadn't made a sad life even harder to bear. 'Surely the murders must all have been committed by the same person?'

'That's the assumption the SIO has made. But…'

'Forget Aled. What if someone else knew the killer's signature?'

'You read my mind, Harry darling.' She smiled sweetly. 'Which in itself I find rather perturbing.'

'A copycat with access to the inquiry might have killed Lee,' he said, chasing after the train of thought, 'or Kay. Or even both of them.'

'That assumes confidential information leaked from the inquiry team.'

'Par for the course.'

'Cynic. The SIO made every effort to contain the key facts on a need-to-know basis.'

He shrugged. 'But you knew. And I knew.'

'Don't rub it in. I shouldn't have opened my big mouth.'

'I'm glad you trusted me. But not everyone who needed to know will have been discreet.'

The nurse appeared. 'Ready, Mr. Devlin?'

A thought grabbed him and he said to Carmel, 'I'm not talking about the investigating officers. Even in a highly sensitive murder case, there are people on the fringes who find out important stuff. Such as the fact that the victims' tongues were cut out.'

The nurse opened her eyes very wide. 'I'm sorry?'

Neither of them paid her any attention. 'Who do you have in mind?' Carmel asked.

'The pathologist. The paramedics who moved the body. Staff from the undertakers.' He paused. 'A mobile embalmer, for instance.'

◇◇◇

Carmel told him she'd never heard of Barney Eagleson, but she agreed it was worth asking a few questions; even if he wasn't the killer, if he'd been indiscreet, more people might know about the M.O. than the police believed. The X-ray revealed that Harry's ribs were not broken, and within half an hour he was in his car, crawling back to the waterfront. Traffic inched through endless roadworks, past huge and colourful billboards bragging about the millions spent on what the authorities, with a stab at irony, had dubbed the City Centre Movement Strategy. He shut out the grumbling engines and impatient horns by turning up the volume for an old favourite track. Dionne Warwick's definitive *Walk on By*. The chorus might have been the city engineer's advice to frustrated motorists.

When at last he reached John Newton House, Lou was engaged in his usual colloquy at the welcome desk with W.H. Auden. Harry gathered that they were unhappy with the recent performances of the England football team, and had much smarter ideas about players, formation, and tactics than the wildly overpaid team coach.

'Is Victor around?'

Lou shook his head. 'Gone out on the piss with his mate.'

'Barney Eagleson?'

'The bloke who looks like he's got TB, that's right.'

'Any idea where they are?'

'Sorry, mate.'

'Or when Victor might be back?'

'As long as he's back to relieve me at six, that's all that matters, isn't it?'

The entrance doors swung open and Wayne Saxelby strolled in. 'Harry, just the man!'

Harry's heart sank. 'Hi, Wayne.'

'Were your ears burning? I've been in touch with the Chief Executive of LIC.'

'LIC?'

'Liverpool Innovators' Centre. They make grants available for local businesses at the cutting edge.'

'I'm not sure we qualify.'

'Use your imagination! I pitched this idea of the firm developing an interactive web presence. You can combine a blog with online client satisfaction surveys and a chat room for members of your personal network.'

'I'd worry too much about what they might chat about. As for client satisfaction…'

'Look forward, not back! I'll include detailed proposals and costings in my report. It should be with you on Monday.' Wayne beamed. 'See, I'm assuming you make it past Midsummer's Eve.'

'I appreciate your confidence. Anyway, I'd better be getting back.'

'Sure, don't let me stop you.' Wayne lowered his voice and cast a glance towards the desk, but chewing gum and football talk occupied Lou's full attention. 'By the way, I had a thought. Your message about Midsummer's Eve. Might it have been sent by Casper May?'

'Why would he bother? We've only been tenants for a fortnight. It's too early for us to fall behind with the rent.'

The lift doors opened and Wayne waved Harry in. As they moved from the ground floor, he tapped the side of his nose. His know-all expression made Harry want to kick him. Not for the first time, he forced himself to remember that he was in the man's debt.

'Suppose Casper got wind of the fact that you and his ex-wife are more than just good friends?'

'I told you…'

'Harry, we're both men of the world. All I'd suggest is this. Might be an idea to give the lady a wide berth for a while. Know what I mean?'

The lift doors opened at the fifth floor and Harry escaped without another word. But as he exchanged a few words with Suzanne, his mind raced. That photograph in Juliet's penthouse, of the couple walking up to the door of the Adelphi. The woman had reminded him of someone and he'd remembered who it was.

The moment he was back in his room, he did an internet search against the name of Denise Onuoha. Sure enough, he came up with the news stories about her murder. And the old picture of the victim as a schoolgirl. He closed his eyes. Yes, he was sure of it now. The woman in the photograph was Denise.

Her hair was different and her outfit glamorous, but the similarities were unmistakable. Juliet kept a photograph of a woman who had been strangled.

Had Ceri conducted the inquest on Denise, was that a link? The inquest would have been adjourned pending further inquires, but a verdict of murder by person or persons unknown was inevitable, unless and until the culprit was found.

The door to his office opened and Grace looked in and asked if he would like a cup of tea. He nodded, but didn't speak. His head was too cluttered. One damn thing after another.

As his thoughts roamed, he opened his inbox and scrolled through his emails. The name of one sender stood out.

Ka-Yu Cheung.

His heart almost stopped.

A message from a dead woman?

Hardly daring to touch his mouse, he scanned the words on the screen.

Harry, you will only receive this email if I'm in trouble. Tom showed me how to delay sending a message, and how to recall one that has already been sent.

I hate to say it, but Tom is sick of me. Whatever I do to please him, it's never enough.

I'm scared. I overheard him talking on the phone when he didn't realise I'd just got back home from work. What he said was terrifying. He's done something bad, that's how he found the rent for our new apartment. This time he is in too deep to get away with it.

Now he has guessed that I know too much. The way he looks at me frightens me to death. I'm pretty sure he's bugged our phone. He has the skills. So he knows I want to talk to you.

He has a knife, and he's ready to use it.

If someone doesn't stop him, he'll kill someone else.

Chapter Seventeen

Tears pricked his eyes as he dialled Carmel's number. A lecturer at college once said he had too much imagination for a lawyer, and it was true. He found it easy to picture Kay trembling as she typed with two fingers, and to smell her fear as she listened for her lover's footsteps. She must have sent the email shortly before her death. They might be her last words, before the life was squeezed out of her and her tongue wagged no more.

That bastard Gunter.

Carmel's voice murmured in his ear. 'Harry, darling. Found the Maltese Falcon yet?'

'I may have found out who killed Ka-Yu Cheung.'

When he told her about the email, she whistled. 'So, you reckon it's the obvious suspect, after all?'

'Usually the way, isn't it? Despite the fact that her tongue was cut out and Tom had an alibi for the Onuoha murder.'

'Are you suggesting a coincidence?'

'Or two people conspiring to commit a series of crimes? If Tom killed Kay, what about Denise?'

He hesitated as soon as he mentioned Denise's name. The photograph. He didn't want to cause a rumpus with Juliet—or her ex-husband—without a very good reason. He must think things through before he told Carmel that Juliet kept a snap of the first victim in her magazine rack. There might be an entirely innocent explanation, but he hadn't the faintest idea what it was.

'I found out something else when I rang HQ a few minutes ago. The forensic people have matched Tom Gunter's trainers to the footprints where Kay Cheung's body was found.'

'Is that conclusive?'

'Not when we hear from counsel for the defence, I expect, but even so. A huge search for him is underway. The senior officers reckon he may not have gone far. He left his car at the Marina, so he doesn't have his own transport unless he's stolen someone else's motor. There's a chance he may be hanging out with friends or in some dark corner of the city.'

Harry had a sick feeling in the pit of his stomach. He was sure that Tom had killed Kay. Presumably he'd accessed her emails or found out about the meeting at Runcorn Bridge and decided he had to shut her up for good. *The Woman Who Knew Too Much.* If Kay hadn't blown the whistle on her lover, she might still be alive. Something else for him to feel guilty about.

'If I hadn't…'

'Listen, it's not your fault,' Carmel interrupted.

'If you're right, it would make a nice change, wouldn't it?'

'Don't blame yourself. Kay called because she trusted you and there was nobody else she could rely on. She turned to you because you're honest, and you were on her side.'

'Much good it did her.'

'Don't beat yourself up over this, Harry. Please, I have enough on my plate. Jim's making progress, but he's not out of the wood yet.'

'Sorry. I'm being self-indulgent.'

'No, you just can't help getting involved. Only trouble is, if you get involved with murder cases…'

'I know, I know.'

'What I don't understand is, you've been on your best behaviour for years, then all of a sudden, it's like a dam bursting.' She paused. 'Is this anything to do with that baloney about Midsummer's Eve?'

'No, I've almost forgotten about that.'

The moment he said it, he realised it wasn't true. He took another glance at the desk calendar. *The best thing about the future is that it only comes one day at a time.* Not much consolation when the date was 22 June.

Tomorrow was Midsummer's Eve.

◇◇◇

When the phone rang half an hour later, he snatched it from its cradle.

'I said I didn't want any calls.'

Suzanne said, 'The Coroner is on. She says it's personal. And urgent. I'll tell her you're too busy, shall I?'

Ceri. Personal. Urgent. For once, Suzanne had pressed all the right buttons.

'No, no. Put her through, please.'

'Are you sure?' Suzanne gloated. 'I mean, I wouldn't want to disturb you in the middle of important business.'

'I'm sorry I snapped. You did the right thing.'

'It's just that…'

'Please, could you put her through?'

She heaved a sigh to convey patience tried beyond endurance, and a moment later he heard the voice of Ceri Hussain. Tense, unsure, quite unlike the calm and authoritative Coroner he'd listened to in court.

'Harry…is it convenient? I…I don't want to interrupt you if you're busy.'

'I'm glad to be interrupted,' he said. 'At least, by you.'

'That's sweet of you. Harry, I…I wanted to apologise. For the other night.'

'No need, honestly. Forget about it, please.'

'No, I shouldn't have messed you about like that.'

'I shouldn't have asked you back.'

'But I was glad when you did. I wanted to…be with you. And then suddenly it became too much. I felt overwhelmed, but I handled it wretchedly. I'm hoping we can still be friends? I'd like to stay in touch, if that's all right with you.'

'That would be wonderful.'

'So, how are things? Did you talk to Grace about the pagans?'

He found himself telling her the story of his search for Aled Borth and their bizarre encounter at the Waterloo Alhambra.

'My God. Mr. Borth, a serial killer?'

'I don't think so. He's a sad specimen, but I got it wrong. There's no real harm in him. His alibis are impeccable.'

'You watch, it'll be as I said. My hunch is, the police are nowhere near finding the man who killed those poor girls.'

'There may be more than one murderer. Tom Gunter is in the frame for the murder of Kay Cheung.'

'Tom Gunter? I don't believe it.'

'There's supposed to be evidence linking him to the site where Kay's body was found.'

He heard a sharp intake of breath. 'You mean it was a domestic?'

'Not so much a crime of passion, more a crime of uncontrollable rage.'

'But he's another suspect with an alibi the police couldn't break.'

'Exactly. He couldn't have murdered Denise Onuoha. So two separate killers must have been at work.'

'You're saying someone else murdered Lee and Denise?'

'Yes, though that doesn't explain how Tom Gunter was able to copy the original m.o..'

'There must be some mistake.'

'No mistake, Ceri. Information has leaked, though God knows how it reached him.'

'He's an IT expert, do you think he hacked into the police computer system?'

A very long shot, Harry thought. As Ceri spoke, he'd suddenly had the glimmer of an explanation for the mystery.

'He may have talked to someone on the periphery of the investigation.'

'I can't believe anyone in the police would gossip with a man like Gunter.'

'Agreed.' Harry pictured Barney Eagleson's knowing smile. 'But I can think of someone else who might.'

'Are you serious?'

'It's the man who first told me what the murderer's signature is. Barney Eagleson.'

'The embalmer?'

'You know him?' As soon as he said it, he realised it was a stupid question.

'Of course, in my job I come across undertakers and embalmers all the time. But I can't believe…'

'He's an odd character.'

'Harry, you need to be careful.' He was touched by the anxiety in her voice. 'Better leave this to the experts. The police have the resources, they know what they are doing.'

'You said yourself, they might never find whoever strangled those girls.'

He could almost hear the fatalistic shrug. 'Well, Harry, if your mind's made up, I'm sure I won't change it. You have a reputation for being persistent.'

'Speaking of which, would you like to get together again sometime?'

Another pause. 'Harry, I'm…I mean, I really enjoy your company.'

'That's good enough for me.'

'It's not long since Ricky died,' she said softly. 'I persuaded myself I was getting past the worst. But…some days it feels as if I'll never get past it.'

'You will. You'll never forget him, but you'll get over the pain. Trust me, I've been there.'

'I don't deserve your kindness,' she said.

Before he could argue, she'd put down the phone.

Five minutes after Sylvia and Grace said goodnight, Gina Paget arrived at his door. Her eyes shone, her smile gleamed with excitement, her hands were tucked behind her back, as if she were a fond parent concealing a birthday gift.

'It's worked like a dream!'

'You have the key?'

'Ta-da!' With a flourish she opened her palm to reveal a small key. 'It's all thanks to Irena. She's a magician.'

'How did she get it?'

'Don't ask,' Gina giggled. 'Let's just say she didn't have to sleep with horrible old Victor. Apparently he was scared to death when she came on to him. Told him he was her dream husband and he could have a lovely Lithuanian bride without even needing to give his credit card details online. All in broken English and with explicit hand gestures, naturally.'

'Naturally.' Harry laughed. 'I owe her. And you.'

'Let's say we're quits after you bought me that drink the other night. And Irena wants you to represent her if she is ever nicked by a store detective. Though it would take a Sherlock Holmes, she's that good. Deal?'

'Deal.' He held out his hand for the key, but she shook her head.

'I'm coming down to the basement with you.'

'I don't think so, Gina.'

'Oh yes, I am. Nobody's going to stop me from seeing what Victor Creepy gets up to behind closed roller shutters.'

'We can't be sure it's safe. Christ knows what's going on in the basement. If anything.'

'I don't see you picking up the phone to beg the police to rush over here. Are you saying I can't come with you because I'm a woman?'

Game, set and match. 'Of course not.'

'Well, then.' She checked her watch. 'I spoke to Lou. He thinks Victor has nipped out for a drink with his pal, but we don't have much time. Victor's supposed to take over on the desk at six, and he may be back in the building before then. Let's get moving.'

As they waited for the lift, Harry asked himself what they were moving towards. He had no evidence that Barney Eagleson knew Tom Gunter, far less that he'd shared inside information with him. Victor Creevey knew that Denise's tongue had been cut out, yet there was no reason to believe that he and Tom had met.

Even so. Someone had battered Jim in the basement, a crime lacking motive and logic. If Jim had stumbled across something untoward in the basement, the attack made more sense. And if Barney, or Victor, was responsible for what had happened to his partner, Harry meant to make them pay.

'Are you angry?' Gina asked in a small voice as the lift doors opened.

'Why do you ask?'

'It's written all over your face.'

He mustered a careful smile. 'Just as well you're coming along. You can be a restraining influence.'

'Mmmm.' A cheeky grin. 'I like a man who gets carried away. Especially a solicitor, you're supposed to be so discreet and well-behaved.'

'You obviously haven't met many solicitors. Here we are. Ground level.'

Lou and W.H. Auden were still absorbed in football talk at the welcome desk. Harry and Gina tip-toed across the floor and made it through the door to the basement without earning a glance from the *concierge*. His usefulness was on a par with the clapped-out CCTV, and for once Harry was delighted. He'd dreamed up several explanations about why he and a young female cleaner wanted to sneak off to the basement of the building and none of them would have fooled a toddler.

Gina stood with her back to the door, and whispered, 'Made it!'

'So far.' Harry cast a glance at the entrance to Victor's home. No sign of life. 'Shall we go downstairs?'

He took the steps one at a time, trying not to make a sound. It wasn't long after five, and someone might be in the car park, ready to leave for home. Or Wayne Saxelby might be lurking there, after a trip to see a client. When they reached the bottom of the stairs, he peeped around the edge of the door, but saw nothing. The basement was deserted.

'Come on.'

Gina tried the key in the lock of the roller shutter. It lifted without a sound.

'It's well oiled,' she whispered. 'Must be in regular use. That Irena, she's brilliant. He never noticed, you know. When she turned up at his door and invited herself in, he was too busy fending her off to realise she'd slipped the keys into her pocket. According to Irena, when he realised she was nude beneath her overall, his eyes nearly popped out of his head. He was scared stiff and really made it clear that he didn't want to know. But she made an impression of the key to give to the locksmith and put it back on the hook when she called back a few minutes later. Old Creepy was so desperate to get rid of her, he never guessed a thing.'

'Sure about that?'

'Trust me, I'm a cleaning lady.'

Behind the shutter was an unlit passageway, running along the rear of the car park. Harry stepped into it.

'Do you want to wait here, so that you can sound the alarm if I run into trouble?'

'All right, if you want to play the hero,' Gina murmured, 'but won't you need a torch?'

'I didn't bring one.'

She gazed at the ceiling before producing a pencil-sized light with an exaggerated flourish. 'Here.'

'Gina, you think of everything.'

'You bet.' She winked at him. 'Mind how you go.'

The torch cast a narrow shaft of light between the unpainted brick walls of the passageway. The air smelled musty, the stone flags underfoot were hard and uneven. No sign of the hole in the floor that, according to Victor, had caused the place to be shut off for safety reasons. On the right hand side were doors set into archways. Harry remembered his dream about the people in masks. No music this time, just the distant scurrying of tiny feet. Even in the heart of a built-up city, rats were never far away.

The doors had iron handles caked in dust. He tried to turn one, but it did not budge. Ahead, the passage made a ninety-degree turn. He edged to the end of the wall on his right and poked his head around the corner. The way forward was blocked by another door, this time made of steel. It might have been the entrance to a bank vault, except that the door did not sit flush on the ground. Through the gap he saw light coming from within. Not daylight, but low-wattage bulb with a reddish glow.

Unless someone had been careless, the room behind was occupied. Harry held his breath.

Was that a faint noise? He strained his ears. Yes, he could hear a sound, almost like hands clapping.

He shuffled up to the door. The noise on the other side became louder.

Suddenly he heard a shriek of pain.

No time to think, or shout to Gina to summon help. Someone was being hurt, he was sure of it. He put his shoulder against the door and heaved against it with his whole body weight.

The door wasn't locked, and it gave way at once. His momentum propelled him inside and his legs gave way under him. As he clambered to his feet, he kept blinking hard to adjust to the light shed by a dim red bulb suspended from the ceiling.

But it would take more than an instant to adjust to what he saw.

Victor Creevey was stripped to his garish mauve underpants. He'd taken off his glasses and his puny chest glistened with sweat. His right hand clutched a knotted cord.

Tied to the wall by leather straps was a skinny, naked man with a mass of thick black hair and a nose stud. Barney Eagleson, it had to be. His skin gleamed; it was as well oiled as the shutter outside. Half a dozen dark weals striped his back.

On a table in the corner of the room lay the men's clothes and a bunch of keys. Together with a couple of whips, a black hood with slits for eyes, and assorted accessories to cater for every conceivable fancy of the do-it-yourself S&M enthusiast. And on the ground was an outline of a man, chalked in much greater anatomical detail than ever found at a crime scene. His hands were bound above his head.

Harry didn't know whether to laugh or cry. He'd spent the last couple of weeks working five floors above a makeshift torture chamber.

◇◇◇

'Where's the harm?' Victor Creevey repeated. 'It's a free country.'

His horror at Harry's arrival had given way to a stubborn defiance. He'd morphed into a militant trade unionist, insisting on the right to strike. In his case, with a knotted cord.

Harry jerked a thumb towards Barney Eagleson's damaged flesh. Although Victor had unstrapped him, Barney was sitting on his haunches, head buried in his hands. He was making unhappy noises.

'Tell him that.'

'Barney? The man's embarrassed, that's all, and who can blame him? We're consenting adults, Harry, that's all that matters.'

'You told me how slaves used to be chained up here in olden times. Not much has changed, eh?'

'Except that it's a game,' Victor hissed. 'You ought to know the law better than me. Everything we do here is perfectly legal and above board. Barney and I have our human rights, same as everybody. We're not hurting anyone. At least not anyone else.'

'You fixed the CCTV so that nobody could watch what you were up to. Without tapes and television, you could come and go as you pleased.'

'We live in a surveillance society, Harry. What happened to civil liberties?'

'Jim Crusoe's still in intensive care. If we'd had watchable footage of the man who attacked him…'

'I couldn't have foreseen that, Harry.'

'No?'

'Look, I'm sorry.' Victor's mulish expression suggested he seldom said sorry. 'But it wasn't me who hit your partner.'

'How can I be sure that he didn't stumble on this room, that you didn't attack him in a state of panic?'

Victor's voice rose as stubbornness dissolved into astonishment. 'You can't be serious! I wouldn't hurt a fly.'

Harry jerked a thumb towards Barney. He was still whimpering.

'Really?'

'That's different. It's…about pleasure as well as pain.'

'You have to be the prime suspect.'

'Whoever attacked your partner came close to committing murder.' Victor folded his thin arms in a gesture of wounded dignity. 'The poor man almost died.'

'I bet your first thought was for yourself. Whether the police would find out about your little game.'

Victor exhaled. 'I managed to fob the constable off. Told him the key to the shutter was lost. He didn't ask any more questions. Quite right, too. Interfering down here wouldn't have helped find the man who left Jim for dead.'

'If you didn't do it, have you any idea who did?'

'Not the foggiest. Barney and I planned to have a session down here later that evening, after a couple of drinks at the Stapledon. Of course, the emergency services swarming all over put paid to that.'

'I bet.'

'This is the first time Barney and I have come back here since then.' Victor's tone became self-righteous. 'Out of respect, you might say.'

Harry grunted. No wonder Irena had startled Victor when she'd revealed she had nothing on beneath her overall. Women didn't have much to fear from him.

'Each to his own, my friend.' Victor puffed out his pigeon chest.

'Yeah, right.'

Time to face facts. Neither Victor nor Barney had murdered the escort girls, and Harry couldn't imagine either of them bashing Jim over the head. As Victor said, their thirst for violence was strictly make-believe.

'Listen, it would be a miserable world if we all had the same tastes. '

Harry glanced at the assorted plugs, clamps and whips on the table. 'I guess so.'

'No need to be sarky. S&M is becoming as respectable as an interest in forensic science.'

'I suppose Casper May has no idea of what's happening in his premises?'

Victor's face turned the shade of a tomato. 'Listen, Harry, it's no skin off his nose. You won't mention this little incident, I hope. You're not a vindictive man, I'm sure, and it would be more than my job's worth.'

'No,' he said wearily. 'I don't owe Casper May any favours. I don't think anything in our lease forces me to tell him.'

'Thanks, Harry. You're a man of integrity. You can keep confidences.'

'Speaking of which, who else knows that the murdered women had their tongues cut out?'

The change of tack startled the two men. Barney said, 'I dropped a hint the other evening, it was wrong of me, I know. But I swear I haven't mentioned it to anyone other than Victor here.'

Victor attempted the expression of a virtuous seeker after knowledge. 'And that's only because of my academic interest in crime scene investigations.'

'Oh really?'

'Yes, really. Neither of us have breathed a word, have we, Barney?'

'I would never do anything to compromise an investigation,' the embalmer said. 'Gossiping about an ongoing case would be the quickest way to wreck my career.'

Harry would take some convincing, but it was clear that the two men had bared their souls enough for one night. He wasn't about to drag an admission from either of them.

Victor wanted to change the subject. 'One question, though. I'm always so careful to lock the shutter behind us. It excites Barney, you know. The thought that one day we might be locked in. Entombed forever in our own torture dungeon.'

'Yeah, well, whatever turns you on.'

'So how did you get in here?'

Harry heard footsteps approaching down the dark passage and within moments Gina appeared in the doorway. For a nanosecond it was as if she couldn't comprehend the scene that greeted her eyes.

'I heard…oh, Jesus.'

As her voice died away, Victor closed his eyes in despair. Barney peeped at her through his hands and gave a panicky yelp.

Harry sighed. 'The answer to your question is that I needed help. And I'm sorry, gentlemen, but I'm not sure that keeping this quiet is going to be easy.'

Chapter Eighteen

Ten minutes later, Harry and Gina were waiting for the lift to take them back upstairs. Victor had told Lou he could go home, before disappearing back to his flat to help Barney wash the last of the oil off his angular frame. Nobody was manning the desk, but given the events of the past few days, who cared?

'I'll ask Irena to keep stumm,' Gina said. 'Mind you, Victor is so unpopular with the girls, he'll have to make it worth Irena's while.'

'If he has any sense, he'll start hunting through the Situations Vacant column. He won't want to hang around if our landlord finds out what he's been up to.'

'The landlord is the bloke we met in the bar? He looked about as sympathetic as a claw hammer. It can't be a picnic for your lady friend, being married to a man like that. No wonder she took a shine to you.'

'Until this week, I hadn't seen her for years.' Harry hoped he wasn't protesting too much.

'Oh yeah?'

The lift doors opened, and Wayne Saxelby's tanned face beamed out at them. There was no getting away from him. He gave Gina an interested glance and hailed Harry with his customary exuberance.

'Good evening, Harry. Aren't you going to introduce me?'

'Gina, this is Wayne Saxelby.' She gave him a mock-curtsey. 'Wayne, meet Gina Paget. Gina works for Culture City Cleaners.'

'I recognise the uniform.' Wayne grinned as he shook her hand. 'Good to see you liaising closely with the staff, Harry. You've anticipated one of the recommendations in my report.'

'Report?' Gina asked.

'Wayne is a management consultant,' Harry said. 'He lives in the penthouse on the top floor, but he and I go back years. He's helping us develop our business plan and marketing strategies.'

'Lovely,' she said in a baffled tone.

Wayne said, 'Have you heard? It was on the radio half an hour ago, the police want to question Tom Gunter about the death of his girlfriend. They reckon he's still in Merseyside, but they warned the public not to approach him. He's described as dangerous.'

Gina said, 'Who is Tom Gunter?'

'You don't want to know.'

'Of course I do.'

'Last Monday, he threatened Harry with a knife in the church gardens at the back here.'

She dug Harry in the ribs. 'You never mentioned that! I didn't realise solicitors lead such exciting lives.'

'Believe me,' Wayne chortled. 'You don't want to kid yourself that this fellow is your typical Liverpudlian lawyer. They broke the mould when they made Harry Devlin.'

'Yeah, well, thanks for the testimonial.' Bored with waiting for passengers, the lift doors had closed. Harry pressed the button again. 'I'd better be getting on.'

'Any more news about Midsummer's Eve?' Wayne asked.

Harry followed Gina into the lift carriage. 'I decided it must be a hoax.'

Wayne tutted. 'You don't want to take it lightly. Someone is threatening you. It's as if there's some special significance to Midsummer's Eve.'

Harry pressed for his floor. 'If so, it's escaped me so far.'

'You need to work on it. Think harder. Are you sure Tom Gunter didn't send the note?'

Harry cast his mind back to his last meeting with Tom. He'd been so sure that the man's startled reaction was genuine. Might he have misread it? His calamitous experience with Ceri Hussain the other night was proof, if it were needed, of his flair for getting the wrong idea.

As the lift doors closed, he offered a helpless shrug and Wayne shook his head, like a teacher disappointed with a dunce.

'He has the gift of the gab, your friend,' Gina said. 'I bet he thinks he can charm the birds off the trees.'

Harry said nothing. He was in no mood to heap praise on Wayne's way with women. Not that he was jealous, of course. And not that he wanted Gina for himself, either. She was too young for him, and he wasn't her type.

In the confines of the lift, the sour whiff of bleach on her overall was unmistakable, but when she treated him to a naughty-girl smile, he couldn't help laughing with pleasure.

'Honestly, I thought I was going to die when I walked into that dungeon. I mean, Lee and I once did a photo-shoot in a studio in Soho that was kitted out like that. But you don't expect to come across S&M in a city office block.'

'It's common enough, but in a different way,' he said as the lift stopped. 'Meetings with auditors, taxmen and people from the Law Society. But there's not much pleasure and an excess of pain.'

She put her hands on her hips. 'I suppose I'd better finish vacuuming floors.'

'Come out for a drink with me.'

He said it on the spur of the moment, but as soon as he spoke, he knew he craved company. Was there much difference between him and the likes of Aled Borth and Victor Creevey? They all wanted to keep loneliness at bay.

'Give me fifteen minutes to tidy up. And tidy myself.'

'See you later.'

'Is it all right if I bring Irena along too?'

'Perfect.'

'She's got a taste for double vodkas and a thirst like a docker. Better visit the cashpoint first.'

'Your wish is my command.'

She gave him a sidelong glance. 'Don't tempt me, Harry.'

◇◇◇

He phoned Carmel to find she was in high spirits. Although Jim was groggy, the doctors seemed hopeful that he would make a good recovery.

'They say you can't predict a case like this. So much depends on how the patient wakes up. You can have weird experiences when you're unconscious for so long, it must be frightening. He'll need to undergo tests, but he recognised me. We talked for ten minutes before he dozed off again.'

'When can I see him?'

'Tomorrow morning would be good. The poor man doesn't remember anything about the assault. He didn't see anyone, as far as he can recall. Sounds as though someone was hiding down there and hit him before he had a clue what was happening. The police are no nearer to finding who did it. They've checked out the usual suspects in mugging cases, but no joy. I wondered…'

'What?'

'Don't take this the wrong way, but it occurred to me that whoever hit Jim might have been targeting you. Perhaps they realised their mistake, that's why they didn't finish him off.'

'I never use the car park. Anyone who knew me would see they'd got the wrong man.'

'What if someone was hired to attack you, someone you'd never met?'

'With no means of identifying me? So they might have left for dead anyone who happened along? It doesn't stack up.' He paused. 'And I'm not thrilled with the idea that someone was hired to smash my brain to a pulp.'

'Sorry, I'm just flailing around for an explanation.' She paused. 'Have you heard the latest about Gunter?'

'That the police have issued an appeal for sightings? Wayne Saxelby told me. He even made me wonder if I was mistaken, and Tom was responsible for that nonsense about Midsummer's Eve.'

'Suppose someone else paid him to frighten you?'

Harry frowned at the telephone. 'You like this idea that I have an unseen enemy with a secret grudge and money to burn?'

'Just thinking aloud.'

There was a knock at the door and Gina appeared. She'd changed out of her overall into a smock top with ruched sleeves and indigo skinny jeans. She looked set for a night on the town, with her thick gold belt, gold bangle, gold wedges and matching bag. A moment later, she was joined by another young woman with a high pony tail. Irena was dark and pretty, in a red halter neck top that left little to the imagination. No wonder Victor had been distracted when Irena showed up on his doorstep, even if he was immune to her sexual charms.

'Harry, are you all right?' Carmel asked.

Gina beckoned him with her forefinger.

'Seldom better,' he said.

◇◇◇

The big screens in the Stapledon were alive with *The Blob*. A young Steve McQueen urged folk in his home town to beware of being gobbled up by an extra-terrestrial blancmange. Like all alien menaces, the pink gelatinous goo was impervious to bullets, but possessed a single, quirky weak spot. Steve was about to discover that he could melt it by judicious use of a fire extinguisher. If only Harry's anonymous adversary were so easily tracked down and vaporised.

He bought the drinks and joined the two women at a corner table. Irena's command of English might be erratic, but by gesture as well as word she was making clear beyond doubt her opinion of Victor Creevey.

'I wanted to ask you about Lee Welch,' he said. 'She'd come into money unexpectedly.'

Gina nodded. 'Found herself a rich bloke, I suppose. A sugar daddy.'

'Might she have wanted you to think so?'

'Of course. We were mates, but that didn't stop her wanting to make me jealous. She liked to keep one step ahead of me.'

Not many people would stay one step ahead of Gina, he thought. 'The money may not have come from an admirer. I've heard she'd found out someone's guilty secret.'

Her eyes widened. 'You mean she was a blackmailer?'

'She may not have thought of it quite like that. But if my source is reliable, the answer is yes.'

Gina winked at Irena. 'Don't you love the way lawyers talk? So, is your source reliable?'

He cast his mind back to Aled Borth, weeping on the floor of the Waterloo Alhambra. 'Not usually. But it's worth asking a few questions. Supposedly Lee obtained this information while she was at work. Did she drop a hint?'

'No, she enjoyed being mysterious.' Gina shivered with distaste. 'I didn't want to know anything about her clients, or what she got up to with them. I was disappointed in her. When we were in London, we could both have made a lot of money if we'd taken up the offers we were made. But we didn't.'

'Why did she change her mind when she got back home?'

Gina took a sip of Chablis. 'If you ask me, she'd given up on making it as an actor. Not that Lee would ever admit it, but a lot of girls are out there, all with the same dream. We'd tried and failed in London. I think she'd decided that if she wanted a cushy life, she had to marry a rich man. Until he walked into her life, she was willing to grab any chance of making a few quid that came her way.'

'Where did she work as a cleaner?'

'Now you're asking. Half the offices in the city, I guess. Lee wasn't like me, she hated cleaning. Never took a pride in the work. And she liked variety. I doubt if she lasted in any one place more than a fortnight.'

Irena had finished her vodka and lime. She wiped her lips and said, 'We work in same place some days.'

'You and Lee?' Harry asked. 'Which places?'

Irena looked sorrowfully at her empty glass.

'Another?'

Irena smiled. So did Gina.

As Harry waited to be served at the bar, the Blob oozed through a projectionist's room, while hysterical cinemagoers fled for the exits. Almost as bizarre as his encounter with Aled Borth at the Alhambra.

He felt a tap on his shoulder.

'We must stop meeting like this.'

Juliet. Once upon a time, the sound of her voice would have made his knees weak with lust for her. These days, desire was stifled by anxiety. She was playing a game, and he didn't know the rules. But one good cliché deserved another.

'Do you come here often?'

She threw a glance towards the door to the VIP lounge. Following her eyes, he saw Casper May and Malachy Needham, deep in conversation.

'Malachy has a stake in this place. It's a goldmine. He's offered Casper a slice of the action.'

'To go along with the cleaning company and Cultural Companions?'

A girl with flame-coloured hair and a dress even skimpier than Irena's joined the two men. She draped a hand over Needham's shoulder and offered him a drink from her glass of Pimm's. As he sipped, she kept her eyes locked on Casper.

'Between you and me,' Juliet said, 'business isn't all those two share.'

'Don't tell me, she's a Cultural Companion?'

Juliet snorted. 'Don't be fooled by the butter-wouldn't-melt smile. She's a tart from Toxteth, hand-picked by Malachy. But she makes eyes at Casper, like all the rest.'

'So what? You and Casper aren't married any longer. You're both footloose and fancy free. And you have Jude the Obscure Actor to keep you entertained.'

'Jude and I have split.'

'Sorry to hear that.'

'Don't be. Poor Jude, he has the brain of a rhino and he's about as sensitive.' She finished her gin and tonic and banged the glass down on the counter. It wasn't her first drink of the evening, for sure. 'Full marks for energy and physique, but that's not enough. I like a man to have a little imagination.'

When the girl behind the counter tired of flirting with a beefy colleague and at last took Harry's order, he found himself asking Juliet if she wanted a drink. It was only good manners.

'Another gin, and go easy on the tonic.' The barmaid turned to busy herself with the drinks and Juliet frowned at her pert twenty-year old backside. 'I lied to you about Jude because I wanted to see if you'd be jealous.'

Harry shifted from one foot to another. It wasn't in Juliet's nature to make herself vulnerable. The gin was talking and he wasn't sure where this might lead. Nowhere safe, was his guess.

'You don't need me to be jealous.'

'You reckon?' She smiled. 'And if you accuse me of fishing for compliments, you'll be dead right.'

'You've got everything you could want. Looks, money, personality.'

She leaned against him and murmured, 'What I have is never enough.'

He handed his money to the barmaid. 'You don't need me, Juliet.'

'You let yourself into my penthouse and left the key there. What was all that about?'

'Your mention of the photograph puzzled me. I thought I'd check it out. But you'd made a mistake. Casper came back sooner than expected. So I let myself out on to the balcony.'

'For fuck's sake, Harry. It's a wonder you're still in one piece.'

'It's okay, I'm not scared of heights. Only of falling.'

'How did you get down?'

'I talked my way into the penthouse at the back. Lucky that Tamara's boyfriend was in.'

'Really?' She raised her eyebrows.

'What I really wanted to know is the story behind the photograph.'

She put a finger to her lips. 'Ah, that would be telling.'

'You can tell me.'

'It's a long story, and not very edifying. Let's forget it, shall we?'

'Sorry, Juliet, no can do. The woman is Denise Onuoha, isn't that right?'

Her gaze hardened. She might have had too much to drink, but she hadn't lost all control.

'Let it go, Harry. It's nothing to do with you.'

'Who is the man in the photograph?'

'Doesn't matter. It was months ago.'

'I want to know his name, and what the photograph means.'

'You should know better than to interfere with Casper's business. You got away with interfering with me. Time to quit while you're ahead.'

'I'm not into quitting.'

She rolled her eyes. 'There's something almost admirable about your stupidity, Harry.'

'Thanks for those kind words.'

'Don't think I under-estimate you. People do it all the time. But you never give up, do you?'

He shook his head.

'I have to go. Thanks for the drink.'

For a moment he was tempted to seize her arm and demand again the truth about the photograph. But there was nothing to be gained from causing a scene. As he threaded through the crowd, three glasses balanced between his hands, he felt Juliet's gaze burn into his back. He looked straight ahead towards the two young women, sitting beneath a mural from *Forbidden Planet*. It depicted the spooky laboratory of the long-dead Krell, store of even more accumulated wisdom than the Liverpool Legal Group members' library.

'So you worked with Lee Welch?' he prompted, as Irena tilted her glass.

'Sometimes,' she said, smacking her lips.

'And Denise Onuoha?'

'I met her once, at our…what to say, HQ? Not a nice girl. Lee knew her better than me.'

'Where did you work with her?'

'Stalagmite Insurance. Quality Accountants Limited.' She scratched her nose as she thought back. 'And Culture Cleaners Company. The HQ.'

'In Tithebarn Street?'

'Yes.' Irena wiggled her index finger and made a face, a parody of wiping a shelf and finding it caked with dust. 'Not good, huh? The main place of a cleaning firm and it is covered in dirt?'

Harry nodded towards the VIP lounge. Juliet had joined Casper, Malachy and the young blonde outside the door. The men were still talking, the women exchanged hostile glances but didn't speak.

'See the men over there?'

'Uh-huh.'

'You work for them. Casper May and Malachy Needham, they are in charge of Culture City Cleaners.'

'Yes, yes, I recognise.'

'Did Lee know them?'

A shrug. 'I don't know for sure, mister. I guess so.'

'They also own Cultural Companions, the agency which hired Lee as an escort.'

Irena nodded. 'Lee asked if I wanted to make easy money that way.'

'And?'

She gave a thumbs-down sign, 'Not for me, mister.'

Gina dug her elbow into Harry's ribs and whispered, 'Look who's coming over here.'

Juliet had tired of being ignored by her ex-husband and glared at by a girl half her age and was weaving through the throng, unsteady yet determined in her progress. Harry swore under his breath. His shoulders tautened with tension. He'd never imagined the day would come when all he wanted of Juliet was for her to leave him alone.

No chance of that. She arrived at their table and subjected the two women to a searching gaze. Harry felt himself reddening. But Gina and Irena weren't fazed.

'I'm surprised you lingered at the bar,' Juliet said. 'When you have such lovely companions to look after. This young lady, I've met before, but her pretty friend I don't know. Won't you introduce me?'

After they had said hello, Gina whispered in Irena's ear and the Lithuanian girl smiled.

'So, you are wife of the man we work for?'

'You're with Culture City Cleaners?'

Gina nodded. 'So was Lee Welch, my friend. The girl who died.'

'Died?'

'Murdered.' Gina's voice sharpened. 'You must have seen it in the papers. They found her body on the beach at Waterloo. She worked for Cultural Companions, as well '

Juliet pursed her lips. 'Oh yes?'

'She heard something she wasn't meant to hear. Poor Lee, she was nosey. Loved to eavesdrop. Someone was willing to pay to keep her quiet.' Harry kicked her leg under the table, but there was no stopping her in full flow. 'Perhaps it was cheaper to shut her up permanently.'

'Meaning what, exactly?'

'I guess it was someone she worked for,' Gina said softly. 'Someone who could afford to buy her silence. Someone ruthless, someone violent.'

'I've had enough of this.' Juliet made a dismissive gesture with her hand. She still wore her wedding ring, Harry noticed. 'I'm going home.'

'Goodnight,' Harry said.

Her eyes rested on him and for an instant he wondered if she was going to ask him to come back with her. But she didn't say another word, just gave him a curt nod and stumbled off towards the exit.

Gina and her friend exchanged amused glances. They'd probably written her off as some old lush. But it was a mistake to under-estimate Juliet May.

He finished his drink. Something Juliet had said nagged at the back of his mind, but the harder he racked his brains, the further away the memory skipped. It would come back running if he managed a decent night's sleep. Chances were, it didn't matter anyway.

His eye caught the sinister shades of black and blue shades in the mural and he remembered the story of the Krell. For all their knowledge and sophistication, their whole race had been wiped out in a single night of frenzy and terror. Destroyed when they unleashed the power of their dark, subconscious desires.

◇◇◇

Darkness was falling as Harry made his way through the car park to his flat in Empire Dock. Gina had failed to talk him into a night on the town. He was flattered when she asked him to tag along, but it wasn't a good idea. They were too young. Suppose he got lucky? He'd had a few drinks, but not enough to deceive himself. If he finished up in bed with one of the girls, it wouldn't make them happier in the long run. He was weary and his head throbbed and he needed to be on his own.

Hard to believe only twenty four hours had passed since he'd strolled along this same path with Ceri. What was she up to tonight combing through post-mortem reports? Work was a displacement activity, it took her mind off the loss of her husband. He needed to give her time and space to sort herself out. Trouble was, once she'd sorted herself out, would she give him a second glance?

Lights danced on the blackness of the Mersey, but Empire Dock was full of shadows. Was Tom Gunter lurking somewhere, ready to strike with fist or knife? Harry asked himself if Tom might have attacked Jim Crusoe, but it didn't add up. Nothing did.

Including Ceri's take on Tom. She was a shrewd judge, but when he'd appeared in her court, Tom Gunter had made an impression on her that Harry didn't fully comprehend. When she talked about him, disdain was tinged with something else. Was it awe?

He remembered her saying, 'He kept himself under perfect control.' He hadn't noticed it at the time, but there was a hint of admiration in her voice. She was so controlled herself. Controlled and, perhaps, controlling. She was a coroner, accustomed to being in charge. To exercising her power to making sure justice was done. Justice as she saw it, that is.

It was raining again, and he quickened his pace towards the apartment block. While he waited for the lift, he decided he could use a hot shower. Wash the day away. Tomorrow morning, he'd visit the hospital and talk to Jim. Something to look forward to.

As he walked down the corridor, he spotted something that had been pushed half-way under his front door. He bent down to pick it up.

A single sheet of paper. It bore two words in a crude and childish hand.

Midsummer's Eve.

He ripped the paper into tiny shreds and fumbled with his key in the lock. His hand was shaking, and the door wouldn't open. He closed his eyes, and uttered a few quiet words of prayer.

Midsummer's Eve was ninety minutes away.

The Sixth Day

Chapter Nineteen

Harry slept badly, jerking into wakefulness time after time as the night crawled on. His thoughts darted down avenues that led nowhere. His eyes itched and his body was stiff as he stretched under the duvet. No chance of rest until Midsummer's Eve had come and gone.

For once he was up before his alarm screamed. He drew the bedroom curtains and opened the window. Midsummer's Eve, but the sky was the colour of slate and the air felt damp. Some things never changed. A June Saturday in Liverpool wouldn't be the same without the imminent threat of a downpour.

A helicopter engine droned, somewhere out of sight. In the distance, the ferry chugged past the site of the new cruise liner terminal, otherwise the river was empty. Once giant ships had filled it. Even the last act of the American Civil War was played out here, when the *Shenandoah* lowered and furled its flag for the last time in the Mersey. The captain preferred to surrender to the Royal Navy rather than face the humiliation back home. Pub quiz facts surfaced from the trivia pool in Harry's brain. The first shot of the war was fired by a cannon from Duke Street, and the warship *Alabama* was built at Cammell Lairds' yard to wreak havoc along American shores, sinking Union ships and capturing their crew. Forever cussed, Liverpool gave aid and comfort to the Confederacy even when the cause was lost. Long after abolition in Britain, the slave trade provided rich pickings for the city's cotton merchants.

Slavery. Wherever he turned, there was no escape from reminders of the way people were bought and sold. It hadn't ended with the *Shenandoah*. He thought about the foreign girls brought to England to scrub floors and, if they were pretty enough, to keep the company of any man willing to pay. Denise Onuoha and Lee Welch were naïve young women who dreamed of fame and fortune and finished up dead on a beach, their ambitions scattered like grains of sand.

He hadn't known Denise or Lee, but his gorge rose at the thought of Kay, lying dead in a thicket beneath Runcorn Bridge. Murdered by a man she loved and who cared so little about her that he made her sell herself in the weeks before he ended her life.

It was as if he'd stared all week at a Magic Eye picture and failed to decode the image concealed within the elaborate pattern. While he stood at the window, the breeze blew his ideas around. Tom was a killer, and Ceri could no longer deny it. Yet she'd seemed to want to defend the man.

'The police are nowhere near finding the man who killed those poor girls,' she'd said. And then: 'Tom Gunter? I don't believe it.'

Did she fancy Tom? He succumbed to a pang of jealousy, but told himself it was absurd. She wasn't the type to go for a bit of rough and besides, she knew Tom was a borderline sociopath. Yet she didn't want Harry to suspect him of the murders, so much was clear. She'd done her best to nudge his attention elsewhere.

Had she found him attractive, allowed him to touch the same smooth skin that Harry had caressed? She'd talked of her husband suffering rejection, but he'd assumed she meant her obsession with her job, instead of her man. Surely she'd not betrayed Ricky by sleeping with Tom Gunter?

Yet Tom had come into money, more than he could make from booting up a few computers. If he'd had an affair with the Coroner, he might have blackmailed her afterwards into paying him to keep quiet.

Kay's last message was stamped on his brain.

I overheard him talking on the phone…What he said was terrifying. He's done something bad, that's how he found the rent for our new apartment. This time he is in too deep to get away with it.

If someone doesn't stop him, he'll kill someone else.

Who was Kay afraid that Tom might kill—Ceri Hussain, if she refused to fork out any more blackmail money?

No, no, no. He couldn't accept that Ceri had slept with Tom, but he was worried about what she might have done. He yearned to talk his suspicions through with her, see if she could persuade him that he'd deceived himself. It wouldn't be the first time. But if he turned up at her house, chances were that she'd slam the door in his face. Why hadn't he seen it until now? Beneath the courtroom calm, she was frightened.

◇◇◇

He showered and guzzled a couple of slices of burnt toast with marmalade before ringing Carmel. The moment he heard her cheery hello, he offered up a prayer. She sounded happy. Jim must be on the mend.

'The nurse said you can see him this morning. If you're free.'

'I'll be right over.'

'Are you on your own?'

'Yes, why?'

'I wondered if Ceri might be with you.'

'She's still mourning her husband.'

'Ricky Hussain? Come on.' Carmel clicked her tongue. 'I mean, I'm sorry he's dead, but…'

'But what?'

A heavy sigh. 'I told you what he was like. One of those men who never mastered the art of eye contact. He didn't understand that breasts don't have eyes.'

'You really disliked him, didn't you?'

'Frankly, Ceri was far too good for him. When he chatted me up that time, I asked what his wife would think and he said she wouldn't even notice, she was so preoccupied with her high-powered job.' Carmel snorted. 'According to Ricky, she spent too much time with the dead, not enough with the living. He wasn't much good as a salesman, he certainly didn't close the deal with me.'

Harry squeezed the phone in his palm until his hand hurt. 'She's never recovered from his death.'

'It's the guilt. If only she'd paid less attention to her work, and more to him, he might be alive to this day.'

'You can't live by if onlys.' Ceri had said exactly that on the phone.

'True.' She sounded surprised by his harshness. 'Have you heard about Tom Gunter?'

'Heard what?'

'They've found him.'

Harry clenched his fist. 'Where?'

'Not half a mile away from your place. Around midnight, a teenage girl spotted a man skulking around the Salthouse. She saw he had a knife in his hand. When she hared off towards the Strand, he gave chase, but she ran faster. She's a sprinter in the county team and she managed to raise the alarm. Within five minutes the man was cornered at the Salthouse Quarter site.'

'Why do they think it's Tom?'

'The description fits. Even in Liverpool, there aren't too many men with knives hiding out in deserted building sites on any given evening.'

'Have they arrested him?'

'No, he's hiding there, threatening to kill anyone who goes near. The negotiators have been trying all night. The Strand is closed, the whole area is cordoned off.'

Hence the helicopter. He could still hear its distant buzz. The police must be desperate to make sure that their man didn't get away. Easier said than done. The Salthouse was a vast, soot-stained warren that stood on the other side of the road from the born again dock buildings. The salt traders had deserted it long ago and for years the complex had housed a motley gathering of ship-repairers, chandlers and assorted leftovers from the city's maritime hey-day. When the last business shut its doors, the Salthouse was left to moulder. Eighteen months back, it had disappeared behind a huge grey hoarding as a consortium of developers set about transforming it into yet another shopping mall. But the builders had gone on strike over a pay dispute and a couple of months back, work on the site had come to a halt.

'Not a bad place to hole up for a few days if you didn't want to be found.'

'He couldn't stay there forever. Sounds like the moment he decided to make a move, he gave himself away. Once they've caught him, they'll lock him up and throw away the key.'

So Kay would be granted justice. Forensic evidence was less easy to intimidate than a witness who was short of money. Harry drummed his fingers on the breakfast bar. In his mind he pictured Tom walking towards the police, hands in the air. Defeated, finished. But where did this leave Ceri?

He didn't understand that breasts don't have eyes.

'Are you still there?'

'Sorry, wool-gathering. See you shortly.'

He put down the phone. Half of him thought it was a eureka moment, the other half wondered why he hadn't realised sooner.

The man in the photograph outside the Adelphi must be Ricky Hussain. He'd been admiring Denise Onuoha's ample charms on their way into the Adelphi. Presumably he'd booked a luxury suite for the evening, the better to enjoy his paid-for escort while Ceri remained preoccupied with the dead.

The owners of Cultural Companions must keep their staff under surveillance. Knowledge was power, and the information that the Coroner's husband had hired an escort and taken her to a hotel was worth a small fortune.

No wonder Ricky Hussain had killed himself.

◇◇◇

Within five minutes he was outside Empire Dock. The obvious thing to do if he was to head straight for the hospital was to pick up his car, turn left out of Empire Dock, and keep clear of any drama down the road at the Salthouse. Of course, he couldn't contemplate the obvious thing. He'd go for a walk before he visited Jim.

His path took him past the elegant curves of the nearly-completed Arena and a gathering of cranes. Tall, green and angular, they resembled alien creatures, visitors from a distant galaxy. Invisible workmen hammered behind the fence. A new Liverpool was taking shape before his eyes.

As soon as he reached the Strand, he saw the barrier across the road. The Salthouse Quarter was a couple of hundred metres further down. Yellow tape and red cones spanned all six lanes of the highway. A couple of paramedics stood next to an ambulance. Beyond them, unmarked white cars and vans formed a blockade. Blue lights flashed, walkie-talkies crackled. Someone was talking through a loudspeaker, but Harry couldn't make out the words. The helicopter swooped low over the Salthouse, then whirled back towards the river.

He crossed the road and headed for the maze of streets behind the Strand and Jamaica Street. They were crammed with small industrial units, silent and shuttered because it was Saturday morning. He didn't have a game plan, but there was nothing new about that. The atmosphere was clammy and it had started raining again. His shirt was thin and he wished he'd brought a jacket to keep his shoulders dry.

He imagined Tom Gunter hiding in the overgrown remains of the Salthouse at dead of night, wondering what to do next. Even though Tom hadn't lasted five minutes in the army, he'd probably picked up a few survival skills. He'd spent most of his life in Merseyside and there was nowhere obvious for him to run. He'd have heard small creatures scurry by in the dark, and the quiet drip of water seeping from holes in the roof and walls. Some men would find the hopelessness of it impossible to bear. But Tom would never surrender to the warmth of a prison cell with satellite TV and all mod cons. Not with a life sentence stretching out ahead of him. No wonder there was a stand-off. Tom Gunter never gave an inch.

The rain fell harder as Harry walked down a narrow street skirting a patch of waste ground. Ahead of him stood the fence at the rear of the Salthouse Quarter. Ten feet high and topped with razor wire. If he strained his eyes, he could make out the wording of large red and white posters on the grey boards. They warned that the site was protected by 24/7 security. Had the guards been skiving or sleeping when Tom broke in? Most likely, the money to pay them had run out. He saw more yellow tape, more unmarked vehicles, more police officers with frames made chunky by body armour. Several men and women carried guns. The air was sour with tension.

For a moment Harry felt sorry for Tom Gunter. With such force ranged against him, the man didn't stand a chance. Harry's default emotion was to side with the underdog. But when he remembered how Tom had defiled Kay's mouth post-mortem, any sliver of sympathy was washed away.

A tubby ginger-haired constable, panting and out of condition, ran towards him.

'You can't go any further, sir.'

'What's happening?'

Sometimes it bothered him, how easy he found it to act stupid. In unkind moments, Jim would say he had a head start.

'It's an incident, sir,' the constable said, as though that answered every question. His voice was scratchy with suppressed anxiety. 'If you wouldn't mind moving along.'

'An incident involving Tom Gunter?'

The constable took a step towards him. 'Now what do you know about…?'

At that moment, a door in the fence began to open. Harry pointed towards it and the young policeman stiffened. A skinny figure in black skipped out. His movements were jumpy and familiar. In his right hand, he held something. Harry thought he recognised the handle of the Swiss army knife he'd pulled in St Nicholas Gardens.

One of the police officers shouted through a loudspeaker. 'Armed police! Put your weapon down!'

'Get back!' the young constable hissed.

Harry saw Tom Gunter lift his right arm. Jesus, he was about to throw the knife.

He dived for the cover of a low brick wall. The impact of hitting uneven, stony ground jarred his whole body, but pain dissolved in the roar of an explosion that ripped the air. As he blinked dust out of his eyes, police officers yelled, but he couldn't make out the words. Another explosion rocked everything, made the world seem to shift out of kilter.

For a horrifying moment, a man shrieked in agony.

And then came silence. The desolate quiet of horror sinking into stunned men and women.

A few moments passed, though Harry felt as though an hour passed. He heard people begin to move around and call to each other. His elbows and knees hurt, but he was still alive. He raised his head and saw armed men and women moving in the distance, heard people shouting, as if to reassure each other.

'The shots didn't hit him!'

'He pulled the knife.'

'Did he cut his own throat?'

'The fucking scumbag.'

'He's not moving.'

He turned to the young constable.

'Once upon a time, I was Tom Gunter's solicitor.'

The constable's voice trembled. 'I don't think he'll be giving you any more business, sir.'

Chapter Twenty

Seagulls soared over Empire Dock. They cried out loud, but weren't mourning Tom Gunter. Nor was Harry as he limped back to his car, trying to get his head round what had happened.

Tom must have tired of the waiting game and decided to make a break for it. Perhaps he was past caring what happened next. The moment he ignored the police warning, he was doomed. If he hadn't killed himself, they'd have done the job for him. Harry remembered the final scene of *Butch Cassidy and the Sundance Kid*, a favourite film. He hummed the poignant melody that accompanied the last frozen frame.

What should he feel—relief, satisfaction, pleasure? Kay had been avenged, justice done. Gunter was callous, and the world better off without him. Yet he could not delight in the death of another human being.

And what of Ceri, might Tom's death break her heart?

At the door to the underground car park, he whipped his mobile out of his pocket on an impulse and dialled her number. Straight to voicemail. She sounded calm and in complete control.

'This is Ceri Hussain. Please leave a message after the tone and I'll get back to you as soon as possible.'

No time to compose an elegant message. He found himself gabbling like a teenager on a first date.

'Ceri, this is Harry Devlin. I have to tell you, Tom Gunter is dead. The police cornered him and he committed suicide.'

Like Ricky Hussain, he thought, as he switched off the phone. Frustration gnawed at him like a hungry rat, nibbling his stomach. He wished he'd not been so abrupt. He didn't want to speculate about how she would take the news. One thing was for sure; no way would she conduct Tom's inquest.

◇◇◇

'Heard the news about Tom?' he asked Carmel as he walked into the waiting room at the General.

She nodded. 'I've just come off the phone. Good riddance. There has to be an inquiry, but the officers should be in the clear. From what I hear, we carried out a textbook operation.'

'I suppose it's for the best.'

'Too right, after what he did to Kay Cheung…'

'We're absolutely certain that he did kill her?'

'The footprint evidence is strong, but there's more. The CSIs have linked him to Lee Welch.'

'What?'

'Yep. They've finally recovered a fingerprint from her skin using superglue. It matches with Tom's records.'

He stared. 'I don't understand.'

'Well…'

Her expression said it all. It didn't matter whether he understood. All that counted was the evidence.

'Tom was in a relationship with Kay. She said in her email to me that he was sick of her. It might have suited him to kill her and hope that the case was linked to a murder that he couldn't have committed. But what connection did he have with Lee?'

'That's for the investigating team to figure out. Remember, he'd used prostitutes in the past. My two cents is, he hired Lee and then they fell out. Perhaps he decided not to pay for her services.'

'Denise Onuoha was killed in the same way as the other two. Strangled, tongue cut out, body left on a beach or a river bank. Yet Tom had a perfect alibi. He couldn't have killed Denise.'

'From the look in your eye, I deduce you have a theory.'

'I hope I'm wrong.'

'That's not like you. Are you going to share your ideas?'

'Not until I've had a private conversation with someone.' He folded his arms. 'So how do you explain it all?'

She gave him an exasperated look. 'It's not my job to explain it, Harry. Thank God I'm just a humble lawyer. Now, are you ready for a word with Jim?'

They set off down the corridor that smelled of antiseptic. Jim was tucked up in bed in a small private room with a picture of Coniston Water on the wall. His head had been shaved and his skin was the same dull shade as the sky outside. He seemed shrunken and old, but he was alive, and nothing else mattered. Although his lips were pale, a faint smile played on them.

'Harry,' he said in a thin voice. 'Why aren't you minding the shop?'

'It's Saturday.'

'What sort of excuse is that?'

Harry sat by the side of the bed and clasped his partner's hand. 'You had me worried there.'

'You don't get rid of me that easily.'

'The doctors said you might undergo a personality change.'

'Don't get your hopes up. I still keep the parking space.'

'Attention deficit syndrome, it's common enough after a blow on the head.'

'I'm not bothered. You've suffered from it for years.'

'So how does it feel, having a near-death experience?'

'Remember when we were at the College of Law, listening to endless lectures on the law of landlord and tenant? They were ideal preparation.'

◇◇◇

'He looks good,' Harry said when they were back in the little room.

'Relatively speaking.' Carmel was fighting to keep her emotions in check.

'It's going to be okay.'

'I think so, Harry.'

As she hugged him tight, he said, 'Can you do me a favour?'

'You can always ask.'

'I want to find out something about Lee Welch.'

'Go on, break it to me gently.'

'Did she ever work as a cleaner at the Coroner's Court?'

Her lips compressed into a thin line. 'What's this all about?'

'Call me when you find the answer. Please?'

'Where are you going?'

'I told you, I need to talk to someone.'

◇◇◇

Outside, the hospital car park was jam-packed as usual. Dodging between the vehicles that circled, vulture-like, in search of a free space, he switched his phone back on. Better see if Ceri had called while he was inside with Carmel and Jim.

Sure enough, she'd recorded a message.

'I'm so sorry, I've ruined everything. Please don't think too badly of me. Everyone else will.' She sounded weary and beaten. 'Thanks for your kindness, Harry. I wish I hadn't put myself out of reach.'

Hands shaking, he rang her number.

'This is Ceri Hussain. Please leave a message…'

Shit.

He raced to his car.

◇◇◇

'Ken Porterfield.' The coroner's officer sounded stern. Probably Harry had interrupted him in the middle of sinking a pre-lunch pint.

'Listen,' he hissed into the mobile, 'have you spoken to Ceri Hussain today?'

'No, but why do you ask? Is anything wrong?'

'Can you tell me Ceri's home address?'

'Why do you want to know?'

'I want you to meet me there.'

'At the Coroner's house?' His tone suggested that Harry was proposing a joint assault on the Vatican. 'What on earth for?'

'I'm worried sick. I think…something may have happened to her.'

◇◇◇

Carmel called as he queued at the lights at the end of Jericho Lane.

'Culture City Cleaners has a contract to clean the Coroner's Court.'

He swore in fury. Never had he been so sorry to solve a mystery.

'What's wrong, Harry?'

'Everything.'

'Tell me.'

'Later. What about Lee Welch? Did she work on the contract?'

'Yep, you were spot on. She was on the evening shift there for a few weeks earlier this year.'

He gripped the steering wheel so hard his hands hurt. 'Fucking hell.'

'What does this all mean?'

'Trouble,' he muttered, as amber turned to green and he turned in the direction of Sefton Park. 'Big bloody trouble.'

◇◇◇

Ceri Hussain's house was a smart detached at the end of a tree-lined cul-de-sac. Pleasant, nondescript, the sort of place where nothing bad ever happens. Ken Porterfield lived on the far side of the park, a five minute stroll away. He had already arrived by the time Harry turned into Bullough Walk. Although it had stopped raining, a grey mackintosh was draped over his bulky shoulders. As he peered at a ground floor window with its curtains drawn, he looked more like a nosey neighbour than a one-time vice cop.

'You'd better not be having a laugh.' For once there was no hint of amusement in Ken's voice. 'It'll be more than my life's worth if you've brought me out on a wild goose chase. If the Coroner turns up and catches us prying…'

'Listen to this.'

Harry put his mobile to Ken's ear and played back the message that Ceri had recorded. As he listened, Ken's face crumpled like a used crisp packet.

'Bugger me, Harry. It sounds like…'

'Goodbye?'

'Well…I mean, what is going on?'

'It's a long story. First things first. We need to find her.'

They followed the brick path that led around the house. In the neat garden at the rear, hydrangeas bloomed, pink and blue. Ivy and a deep purple clematis scrambled up a freshly painted white trellis. A sparrow supped at a bird table carved from stone, reached by stepping stones across a square of lawn. There were hanging baskets filled with lobelia and petunias. All very ordinary, an English suburban garden. The only sound came from a distant hedge trimmer. The house was silent. Ceri might be having a well-deserved Saturday morning lie-in, but Harry doubted it. His stomach felt queasy, as if he'd swallowed a mouthful of something rotten.

'We have to break in.'

Ken puffed out his cheeks. 'Can't do that, Harry. The Coroner's house? We'd need a bloody good reason to smash her back window in.'

'If the shit hits the fan, you can blame me.'

'I'll blame you anyway.'

'That's settled, then.'

'She might have gone shopping.'

Harry nodded towards the gabled garage. Through its back window he made out the sleek contours of Ceri's red BMW.

'On foot?'

'Why not? She's not a bloody invalid.'

'You don't really believe she's out shopping. She's not answering her mobile, yet she once told me she keeps it switched on 24/7.'

'It comes with the territory, when you're City Coroner. An unexplained death may occur at any time of day or night.'

'Ever known her blip off the radar like this before?'

Ken shook her head. 'She's obsessive about making herself available, I never knew a woman so committed to her work.'

'Well, then.'

'Hold your horses. Her mobile might be malfunctioning or out of range.' Ken shifted from foot to foot. 'What if this turns out to be a false alarm?'

'What if we forget about it and go back home, and then it turns out this wasn't a false alarm?'

'Speaking of alarms, suppose we set off her security system and the police show up?'

'I'm a defence lawyer and you have more mates on the force than the Chief Constable. If we can't talk our way out of it…'

Ken weighed this up. 'All right, you silver-tongued bastard. You win.'

Harry pointed to a kitchen window. It didn't seem completely shut. The sash had stuck.

'Reckon that's the best bet?'

'You should have been a burglar.'

'Maybe one day, if staying on the right side of the law doesn't work out.'

Ken shook his head. 'I really don't know what to make of you.'

'Just get us inside the house, mate, I'll jump on the psychiatrist's couch later.'

'It's going to be tight.' Ken patted his stomach. 'I wish now I'd said no to that second helping of steak and kidney pud last night.'

It must have been imagination, but Harry thought he could hear the relentless tick, tick, tick of his own wrist watch.

'Let's do it.'

It took Ken less than thirty seconds to force open the lower window. So much for home security. First he helped Harry climb up and haul himself inside, and then with much grunting and swearing he managed to squeeze his own bulk over the sink and granite-topped breakfast bar and into the kitchen.

'Just don't have a heart attack,' Harry muttered. 'It's not a good time.'

'No way,' Ken panted. 'I've not got round to changing my will since Elsie left me and I moved in with Sharon. I'm buggered if I'm going to keel over and let that old battleaxe inherit.'

Everything was tidy. No unwashed breakfast things, no lingering smell of bacon or coffee. Spice jars were arrayed in a rack, a telephone sat in its cradle. On the wall was a photograph in a chrome frame of a couple in a churchyard. Ceri, gorgeous in a white wedding dress, and a self-consciously handsome man with a carnation in the buttonhole of his three-piece suit. His arm was draped around Ceri's bare shoulder, his demeanour possessive.

Ricky Hussain in happier times. Years before someone else had photographed him, taking Denise Onuoha into the Adelphi.

Next to a cork notice-board, half a dozen keys were arrayed in a rack. No spaces remained for any that Ceri might have taken with her. It looked as though she hadn't left the house.

No time to lose.

'Ceri!' he bellowed. 'This is Harry Devlin!'

'If she is in here, you'll frighten the poor woman to death,' Ken grumbled as he dusted his trousers.

Harry wiped his brow. He was sweating hard, and not just from the exertion of clambering in through the window.

'Frightening her is the least of my worries.'

The internal kitchen door was shut. He threw it open and hurried into the hallway. The first door he opened was a walk-in cupboard. The second gave on to the living room. Someone was lying on the sofa. He glimpsed dark, familiar hair and bare feet hanging over the arm-rest.

'Ceri!'

He ran in and crouched on the carpet beside the sofa. His knees still hurt, but it didn't matter. She was wearing a claret and blue striped rugby shirt and black corduroy jeans. Her feet were slender, her toenails unpainted. Her eyes were closed and for a sickening moment, he thought she was dead. But she was still breathing, though it was a rough and laboured sound.

He seized her wrist. In his hand it seemed so fragile, it might break at any moment.

'Wake up! Wake up!'

She groaned, and saliva trickled from the corner of her mouth. He'd never before seen her without a dab of lipstick. But you wouldn't bother with lippy, would you, the day you meant to kill yourself?

Ken's heavy tread came up behind him. 'She's taken an overdose. The silly cow, what's going on here?'

Harry glanced up at a couple of empty packets of pills on a coffee table near the sofa. There was a bottle of whisky, too, and an empty tumbler. He could smell the drink on her. She'd swallowed the tablets and alcohol, then lain down on the cushions, waiting to die.

'What are you waiting for?' he snapped. 'Dial 999.'

Colour had drained from the big man's face. 'Right you are.'

As Ken headed back for the kitchen, Harry hooked his arm round Ceri. Cradling her, he choked back a sob.

'Talk to me.'

Her head moved, as if in a feeble gesture of dissent, and her eyes opened a fraction. Her gaze lacked focus and he wasn't sure if she was seeing him, or some horrid image from a nightmare. Harry heard Ken bellowing into the phone. He shut out the noise. He must keep Ceri awake until help arrived.

'Please, say something.'

The pale lips twitched. She'd tried to speak, but he couldn't catch the words. He bent closer.

'What is it? Tell me.'

Her skin was puffy. He'd never seen her look her age before. As he held her tight, he felt her breasts against his arm. What wouldn't he have given for such intimacy a couple of nights back? But never like this, when she'd chosen death instead of life.

'It's Harry. Come on, everything's going to be all right, I promise.'

He uttered the lie without a second thought. But a lie it was. Ceri's life would never be all right again.

Her lips moved again. 'Mur....'

'What?'

'Mur..murder.'

So this was it.

She wanted to confess.

Chapter Twenty-one

Ceri's eyes closed and her head slumped against his hand. Was she losing the fight?

'Murder?' He shook her hard. 'Ceri, please!'

Ken lumbered back into the room. 'They should be here soon. Look, why has the Coroner taken an overdose?'

'She paid Tom Gunter to kill Lee Welch.'

'For fuck's sake! Have you lost your mind?'

Harry was holding her tight. 'No, but Ceri did.'

She stirred in his arms. 'I…I worked too hard. Ricky couldn't cope…'

'Prozac wasn't enough to make him feel good, was it? He hired prostitutes. Escorts.'

A frail hand flapped towards a bookcase opposite the door. Ceri's literary taste was sober and respectable. Thomas Hardy side-by-side with hardbacks of Margaret Attwood and Annie Proulx. Not a lurid paperback thriller in sight. Propped up against a Folio Society box set of novels by Trollope was a large brown envelope. In elegant script, verging on calligraphy, she'd written *Harry Devlin*.

Ken picked up the envelope and passed it to Harry without a word. Four sheets of notepaper covered in the neat handwriting slipped out, together with a photograph. Another copy of the shot of Ricky Hussain taking Denise Onuoha into the Adelphi. He turned it over. On the back someone had written *Nesta Borth inquest—verdict natural causes.*

A message from Malachy; perhaps Casper had a hand in it too. As a threat, it was laughably unnecessary once Professor Afridi showed up. Poor Ceri. She must have been afraid that Lee Welch had sent her the photograph and was putting on the squeeze. Ceri probably thought the girl was Malachy Needham's lover, hence the attempt to clear his name.

Harry said softly, 'Lee knew you'd covered up for Ricky, didn't she?'

Ceri strained to speak. Veins stood out on her forehead. Her voice rasped.

'He…he'd told me he'd killed her. Because she laughed when he couldn't…'

'He took Denise Onuoha to a beach one night and then she mocked him because he couldn't get an erection?'

A nod of the head.

So it came down to this. The injured pride of a loser who made the mistake of marrying a perfectionist. For a habitual womaniser, an escort girl's contempt must have been the last straw.

'He strangled her, then cut out her tongue?'

'Yes.'

Ken swore again. All at once he looked old and past it.

'Lee eavesdropped when you were talking to Ricky?'

'He told me he…wanted to die. Pay the price. I told him… not to be stupid.'

Harry glanced at the whisky bottle and the empty pill packets. Stupid was right.

Ceri whispered, 'By the time I got home…'

'Ricky was dead. Meanwhile Lee had heard enough to demand money to keep her mouth shut. I suppose you knew she was an escort, too? Denise probably confided in her about seeing Ricky.'

'I was…in so deep.'

Undeniably true. The City Coroner had encouraged her husband to cover up his murder of a prostitute. If word got out, her career would be destroyed. She'd be lucky to stay out of prison herself.

She'd been struck by Tom Gunter's callous determination to save his skin. Maybe he could help to save hers. He had a track record of getting away with murder. Through discreet enquiries it would be easy to discover that he'd been in custody on the night Ricky killed Denise. A stroke of fortune—Tom could make it look as though the same man had strangled and mutilated both girls.

Problem solved.

He said in a whisper, 'You panicked?'

She inclined her head, though if they'd been in court, she would have rebuked him for such a leading question.

Her lips parted, as though she intended a mirthless smile. 'Too much gin.'

'So you offered Tom a small fortune to kill Lee?'

'The next day,' she croaked, 'I changed my mind. Too late.'

'Yes, far too late. He'd have joined the queue of blackmailers, if you hadn't gone through with it.'

So she'd stuck to her plan. Tom strangled Lee and chopped out her tongue. Nobody would believe Ricky had killed Denise once an identical crime occurred after his suicide. The morning after the murder, Harry confronted Tom in St Nicholas Gardens. No wonder he seemed so out of it. His jerky gait had reminded Harry of a marionette, but he'd never guessed Ceri was pulling the strings.

'I saw Tom on Monday. On his way to collect the rest of his fee from you, I suppose. Did he mention our encounter?'

'Uh-huh.'

Ken said, 'The ambulance is here.'

The coroner's officer had stationed himself by the window that looked down the cul-de-sac. Soon the paramedics would take charge. Harry stood up, but his legs felt flimsy, and he'd lost his sense of balance. He needed to clutch on to the bookshelf for support.

Ceri closed her eyes. Guilt must have played havoc with her nerves, knowing that he'd acted for Tom, and was notorious for his unhealthy fascination with murder. She needed to get closer to him. Already he believed Tom to be a killer. What if he started sniffing around?

And to think that he'd felt flattered by her interest in him.

◇◇◇

The moment he arrived back at his flat, he tore off his trainers and threw himself on to his bed. His body ached as if he'd crawled away from ten rounds in a bare-knuckle fight. On Monday, when Tom Gunter decided not to kick his head in, he'd experienced a giddy rush of excitement. From then on, he'd suffered a non-stop pounding.

The paramedics had rushed Ceri to A&E and the police had taken custody of her suicide note. He'd only read it once, but the story was emblazoned on his mind. When Ken Porterfield had asked if he was all right, he'd said of course. It wasn't true, and they both knew it, but Ken understood that he needed to be left on his own. When he drove home, the car veered along Jericho Lane and through the old Festival Gardens as though he'd had too much to drink.

He'd worked out most of the story and her note filled in the blanks. After Tom killed Lee, his mood became volatile. He was sick of Kay, and had forced her to become an escort simply to prove he could bend her to his will. He bugged their phone and heard her arrange to meet Harry. He'd followed her to the riverbank and strangled her. His final betrayal was to cut out her tongue. He wanted to make the police think it wasn't a domestic, but a third series killing. But those size 11 footprints gave him away.

When he called Ceri, she said she couldn't cope with the guilt. He threatened to cut her tongue out too, but she told him the killing must stop, whatever price she had to pay. He changed his tune and said that if she kept quiet, everything would be fine. But Harry was a wild card, and once the police had cornered Tom, she knew it was finished. When they checked Tom's belongings, they'd be able to trace the cash to her.

You see, I'm not a very efficient criminal. It was crazy, why did I fool myself that I could get away with such wickedness?

'God alone knows, Ceri,' Harry muttered to himself. 'God alone knows.'

He tried to think himself into her head and understand the fuzzy desperation that had driven her to squander everything. In the note, she said she'd cared for him—and why indulge in deception when she was about to die? But she'd deceived him more than once and he was no longer sure what to believe.

The clock on his bedside table sounded louder than usual as it ticked off time. When the hour chimed, he opened his eyes and contemplated the ceiling. It could do with a lick of paint. Yet did it matter if the bedroom looked shabby? After the Ceri Hussain fiasco, he wouldn't bring anyone back here in a hurry.

The doorbell rang. Joints protesting, he heaved himself off the bed and padded into the hallway. The way things were going, he wouldn't have been surprised to be confronted by the Grim Reaper, scythe in hand. When he peered through the spyhole and saw Carmel Sutcliffe standing on his threshold, his shoulders slumped as the tension seeped out of him and he let out a gasp of relief as he opened the door. To his dismay, he felt a pricking at his eyes.

She stared. 'Who were you expecting, Ceri Hussain?'

That did it. He felt a fat tear run down his cheek.

◇◇◇

'Me and my big mouth,' she said ten minutes later.

They were on the sofa and she had her arm round him. He felt her fingers brush his neck and hair. Her breath was soft and sweet.

'You weren't to know.'

'Ceri was too good to be true. But I would never have…'

'I've told you the story,' he snapped. 'Let's not talk about it any more.'

'Okay.' But she couldn't let it go. 'Why on earth did I ever feel envious of Ceri Hussain?'

Good question. Envy never made sense to Harry. Greed he could understand, sloth certainly, lust beyond a doubt. But why waste your life worrying about what others had? You never saw inside their souls, never felt the private agonies they endured. It wasn't only in nightmares that people you thought you knew wore disguise.

While Carmel made them both a pot of tea, he chose a CD at random and Karen Carpenter's melancholy voice crooned about people playing games, but fooling only themselves. We are lost in a masquerade, she sang. Plaintive, lovely Karen, she too had died young. Wealth and fame hadn't been enough, and she'd starved herself until her heart could no longer bear the strain.

He looked at Carmel out of the corner of his eye. Her nose was beaky, her skin had blemishes, and yet an air of sensuality clung to her. She'd worked for him, she lived with his business partner, he counted her as a friend, and yet did he know her so much better than Ceri? How easy to take friends and acquaintances for granted. Because they were always there, you never gave them the consideration they deserved. He needed a little distance to put his thoughts in order and he edged along the sofa, away from her.

'Why did you come here?'

She frowned. 'Why do you think?'

He took a breath. Mustn't succumb to paranoia. You had to take risks and give your trust. Even if people you trusted sometimes let you down.

'Sorry. I don't mean to seem ungrateful.'

'I wanted to make sure you were all right. You might not have liked Tom Gunter, but to watch him die…'

'It was over in an instant.'

'Even so. I was concerned for you—and that was before I heard about Ceri.'

'Thanks.'

She looked him in the eye. 'This week, I came close to losing Jim. I couldn't bear it if anything happened to you.'

◇◇◇

The phone wailed five minutes after Carmel left. He picked up the receiver and crushed it against his palm at the sound of a familiar voice, a voice that kept creeping into his mind, a trespasser he could never quite evict.

'This is Juliet.'

'Hi.'

'You don't sound thrilled to hear me.'

'It's been a…difficult day.'

'Well, it's about to get better.'

Unlikely, Harry thought. He kept quiet.

'Are you still there?'

'Yes.'

'You're very monosyllabic, sweetie. Are you doing anything special tonight?'

'Well…'

'You really ought to get out more. I'm going to make you an offer you can't refuse.'

'Yes?'

'Remember, this isn't any ordinary Saturday night.'

'What do you mean?'

'Surely you haven't forgotten? This is Midsummer's Eve.'

Chapter Twenty-two

'Sorry, Juliet,' he said. 'Prior engagement.'

'What exactly is this prior engagement?'

Her voice sounded as sharp as a chainsaw. How had he never noticed this before?

'It's supposed to be a secret.'

'You and I don't have secrets from each other.'

It wasn't true, but he said, 'Tamara's homecoming party.'

'Tamara's what?'

'Your neighbour,' he reminded her. 'Lives with Wayne Saxelby in the other penthouse? She flies back to the UK this evening and Wayne is throwing a surprise party for her. He asked me along. My guess is that he's afraid she'll have found someone new while she was away filming.'

'Is this some kind of joke?' Her scorn startled him. 'Harry Devlin whiling away Midsummer's Eve with his celebrity chums?'

'I didn't mean to start a debate about my social life,' he snapped.

'Or your fantasies?'

'I told you before. Since you and I stopped seeing each other, I've moved on.'

'I'm asking you to take me out to dinner and you come up with the most ridiculous excuse I've ever heard.'

'Sorry you're not impressed. I've been invited to a party, that's all.'

'You must be out of…fuck, there's someone at the door. Casper must have forgotten something.'

'Yeah, he's forgotten you two aren't married any more. Best of luck, Juliet.'

'I'll get rid of him.'

'Good plan.'

'Give me ten minutes, and I'll call you back.'

'Don't bother.'

'Harry.' He pictured her cheeks turning crimson as she fought to keep her temper. 'Listen to me.'

'It's too late for that, Juliet.'

'You don't understand.'

'That's where you're wrong. Enjoy Midsummer's Eve.'

He rang off before she could put the phone down on him.

◇◇◇

He called the hospital, seeking news of Ceri rather than Jim. Beyond learning that she was still alive, he found out nothing about her condition or chances of survival. A weary nurse came close to telling him he had no right to intrude. Ceri might have addressed her suicide note to him, but he had no claim on her.

Would she want to be saved? Even if she made it, the overdose might have damaged her permanently. No chance now of covering up her complicity in the murder of Lee Welch. She didn't deserve to escape retribution—she was the Coroner, she should strive for justice and truth, not put her own selfish interests ahead of common humanity. What Tom had done to Lee, let alone Kay Cheung, was savage and inexcusable. Yet he couldn't bring himself to loathe Ceri for her weakness. Everyone was fallible. One disaster in her life had led to another, simple as that.

If Ceri survived, he couldn't imagine the hell she would endure. Someone who had commanded such respect and envy could never come to terms with humiliation and disgrace. One grey morning, he supposed, a prison officer would unlock the door of her cell, and find she'd finally succeeded in killing herself. Happened all the time. Fred West and Harold Shipman were only the tip of the iceberg. In these civilised days, there was no need for public executioners—it was left to murderers' initiative to hang themselves.

The phone rang again. Bloody Juliet. He ground his teeth, rehearsing his riposte if she harped on about Midsummer's Eve.

Half-way across the room, he stopped in his tracks. Suppose it was Juliet who haunted him, teasing him with that forecast of his death on Midsunmer's Eve? She lived in John Newton House, it would be simplicity itself to drop into the office last Monday morning and leave the mock-obituary for him to find. A resident in the block could easily nip down to the fifth floor and trash his room when no-one else was around.

To think that she might betray him filled him with nausea. They'd cared for each other once, what motive could she have? He couldn't believe she was jealous, simply because he'd taken a pretty girl to the Stapledon for a drink. Juliet had so much, it would be absurd for her to envy a wannabe actress who'd ended up as a cleaning lady.

Besides, the note about Midsummer's Eve arrived before she'd bumped into him in Gina Paget's company. If Juliet hated him, there must be some other reason.

The answering machine kicked in.

'This is Wayne.' He sounded as though the stress of preparing for the party had stretched his nerves. 'Sorry to nag, but I thought I'd better ring to check you haven't forgotten…'

Harry grabbed the receiver. 'Sorry. I was…in the other room.'

'Are you all right? You sound frazzled.'

'It's been…quite a day.'

'Your mobile's been switched off this afternoon and you were out earlier on,' Wayne reproached him. 'I left a message asking you to give me a ring.'

Harry hadn't noticed the machine blinking red when he'd arrived back home and collapsed on to the bed. After seeing Tom shot and finding Ceri on the verge of death, the last thing on his mind was who might have called.

'If you don't mind, I'll give the party a miss. With Jim in hospital, there's so much to do.'

'You're not on the duty solicitor roster this weekend, Sylvia told me. Do come, I've told Tamara all about you. She's looking forward to seeing you. My old boss, she can't believe it.'

Neither did Harry. No way would Tamara Dighton have the slightest interest in meeting a downmarket Liverpool brief. Wayne simply couldn't help shooting a line. This was all about Wayne's ego, Harry was sure. *Look at me, you once said I'd never make it in the legal profession, but look at us now. I've made a success of my life. I have all the money I need and a gorgeous lover too.*

'Honestly, I'm knackered. I'd be embarrassed to meet all your smart friends and then nod off in a corner after the first drink.'

'It wouldn't be the first time you'd embarrassed yourself.'

'Nothing personal, but I need to chill out for an hour or two. Tell you what, if I feel less like a zombie after I've had a kip, I'll show up at the penthouse later. Okay?'

'The party isn't at the penthouse,' Wayne said, with exaggerated patience. 'I told you, I want this to be a surprise. If you like, I'll give you a lift there.'

'Thanks. I'll give you a ring if I'm up for it.'

'See you later, then.'

The moment Wayne rang off, Harry felt his conscience nag. He wasn't in the mood for socialising, but the man had saved Jim's life and he owed him for that. If Wayne wanted to brag about his rich and glamorous lifestyle, where was the harm?

The phone trilled again. He glared at it, and didn't move.

On the answering machine, Juliet's voice sounded loud and bossy, reminding him of a long-ago history teacher he'd irked through his vague grasp of the causes of the Civil War.

'Harry, will you pick up the phone?' Even a bad line couldn't muffle the harshness of her tone. 'I know you're there.'

He folded his arms. Time for Juliet to get it into her skull that he wasn't going to dance to her tune. He pictured her lips forming into a thin, angry line.

'I've got rid of Casper. He wanted me to sign some papers, that's all. Come on, answer the bloody phone. Are you afraid I've turned into some kind of stalker?'

'Well,' he muttered to himself, 'now you mention it…'

'You shouldn't do this, you make me feel as though I'm a sad old bitch, with nothing better to do than chase after something that died long ago.'

He shrugged at the phone. Whatever her game, he wasn't playing.

'I like you, Harry. We can still be friends. It hurts me to see you being taken for a fool.'

Provoked, he snatched the receiver.

'Juliet, it's over.'

'You don't understand what I'm trying to tell you.'

'And you're not listening to me. No hard feelings, but I don't think we should see each other any more.'

The bell rang as she started to speak.

'Sorry, I have to go.'

'Don't you dare hang up!'

For the second time in half an hour, he banged down the phone on her. Through the spyhole in the door, he saw Gina. She was wearing a blue corduroy cap, stripey top and microscopic skirt.

As he opened the door, she grinned and said, 'Like the outfit?'

'Makes a change from the white overall. You look like one of David Hemmings' girls in *Blow Up*.'

'Never heard of him, but I'll take it as a compliment.'

'He was a beautiful young man and the film was a classic of sixties cinema.'

'Fascinating.' She mimed a yawn. 'Are you inviting me in, or what?'

'Sorry, come through.' He led the way into the living room. 'It's great to see you.'

'I like your flat.' She tossed her cap to one side, kicked off her shoes and jumped on to the sofa overlooking the Mersey panorama. 'Oh my God, what a fantastic view.'

He dragged his gaze away from her slender, bare legs.

'Too right. So what brings you here?'

'My Saturday job. I'm a guide on the Swinging Sixties Tour. We start at the Cavern Club and finish up by the Yellow Submarine in Albert Dock.'

He blinked. 'How many jobs do you have?'

'Got to keep the wolf from the door. The pay's better for going out with randy old men. But I'd rather skivvy than live on a fat executive's credit card. Besides, this is a lot less dangerous.'

'The man who killed your friend is dead.'

She nodded. 'Lee can rest in peace at last. I heard the news on the radio before I came out. Good riddance, that's what I say. The tourists started getting twitchy when they saw the police cars at the Salthouse. I did my best to persuade them that murder isn't an occupational hazard in downtown Liverpool.'

'It's sorted now.'

'You're pale. Is anything wrong?'

'I was on the spot when the murderer cut his own throat.'

Her eyes widened, making her look like a startled fourteen-year old. Those dodgy film-makers in Soho must have loved her innocence. Thank God she'd escaped from them and come home to Liverpool.

'You poor thing.'

'His name was Tom Gunter. Once upon a time, I acted for him. He was recommended to me by a girl I knew. His partner, Kay Cheung. Tom murdered her as well as Lee.'

'Don't forget the other girl, Denise.'

'No.' He shook his head. 'Someone else killed her.'

'You're kidding!'

'It's a long story.'

He would not say a word about Ceri. Right now he wanted to forget what had happened and just enjoy Gina's company.

She stretched luxuriantly on the sofa. 'I'm not in a hurry.'

'Can I get you a drink?'

'Any chance of a glass of wine? After two hours of being nice to tourists with hearing aids, I could do with a drink.'

'The best I can do is supermarket Chablis, I'm afraid.'

'Fine by me.'

She followed him into the kitchen and chattered as he faffed around in search of a corkscrew. 'So this is your bachelor pad? Your own private kingdom. Bet you love coming back here and getting away from it all.'

'How did you know where I lived?'

'You told me you had a flat in Empire Dock. The chap on the desk downstairs gave me directions. I think he took a shine to me.'

'When you're wearing a skirt as short as a belt, it would take a monk not to tell you anything you wanted to know.'

'Depends on the monk,' she grinned. 'I think Victor Creepy would be immune to my charms, don't you?'

He poured the drinks. 'What brings you here?'

'I was at a loose end and I didn't have anything else to do. Sorry, does that sound unkind? I didn't mean it.' She sampled the wine. 'I just thought I'd see if you were around. But I'll piss off if you're busy.'

'Does it look like it?' He breathed out. 'Hey, I'm really glad you came. Though you should be swanning off with some hunk who's half my age.'

'I ditched the last hunk ten days ago. He didn't understand, sometimes I just want to talk.'

'Talking's all I'm good for, right now.'

Back in the living room, he fished a John Lennon CD out of the rack. *Mind Games*. After his conversations with Juliet, it seemed appropriate. The woman was trying to mess with his head, but he couldn't figure out why. As Gina talked about her plans for the future, he half-expected the phone to ring again, but by the time he'd finished his first glass of wine, he'd begun to relax. He needed to put Tom and Ceri out of his head. Maybe Gina would accompany him to the party Wayne was throwing for Tamara. But a quiet meal in Albert Dock and a few more drinks appealed even more.

Out the Blue was playing when the doorbell rang.

'Expecting a visitor?' Gina asked.

'Probably the bloke in the next door flat. He moved in a month ago and he keeps borrowing my speakers. Can't imagine why he doesn't buy a set himself, he's loaded.'

'Perhaps he's lonely.'

'He's a party animal, out every night of the week.'

'People aren't always the way they seem. Take it from me, I'm a cleaning lady. I see life in the raw.'

The bell shrilled again, loud and insistent.

'Better see what he wants.'

Harry didn't bother to check the spyhole. Big mistake. As the door opened, he found himself staring at Juliet. Never had a trout pout looked so menacing. She swung her silver handbag as a constable might twirl his truncheon.

'Since you hung up on me twice, I thought I'd better turn up in person.'

'This isn't a good time.'

She made an exasperated noise and stuck a foot in his door. 'This will only take five minutes. Then I'll piss off out of your life forever, if that's what you want.'

All things considered, it wasn't a bad offer. But there was a snag.

'I'm not alone.'

'Let me guess.' The elegant eyebrows arched. 'The Premises Regeneration Executive is paying a visit?'

'She's a friend.'

'Is that why you took an hour to answer the door, because you were scrambling back into your pants?'

'Does it matter?'

'Frankly, my dear, I couldn't give a damn. You see, I'm not quite the jealous old maid that you take me for.'

'It's not that…'

'Five minutes is all I ask. There's something you need to know.'

'You win.' He stood to one side and waved her through. 'Five minutes it is.'

She marched into the living room as Gina started to fill the two glasses from the wine bottle. Her gaze measured the younger woman's legs, took in the scattered shoes and corduroy cap.

'Very cosy.'

Gina offered a teacher's pet smile. 'Mrs. May. You still use your married name, don't you? Harry, can you fetch another glass?'

'I'm not stopping.' Juliet was glacial. 'No wine, thanks all the same. Sorry to interrupt your tete a tete.'

'What is it you wanted to tell me?' Harry asked.

'This stuff about Tamara's party. You were making it up, were you? An easy way to fob me off when I suggested we might get together?'

'Nonsense. Wayne invited me along. He and I go back a long way. He used to work for us before he took up consultancy.'

'What sort of a consultancy?'

'Usual kind. Charges people a fortune to tell them what they already know.'

'He's taking you for a ride.'

'He spouts a lot of bullshit, sure. It's part of the job description. Don't worry, Jim and I know what he's like.'

'You think so?'

'What are you getting at?'

'If he's told you that Tamara's his latest squeeze, then he's having a laugh.'

'You mean she's dumped him?'

'Harry, get real. Why would Tamara Dighton, a woman who can take her pick, look twice at a sleazeball like Wayne Saxelby?'

'It takes all sorts.'

'Oh, for fuck's sake. Casper introduced me to Tamara when she came to look round John Newton House. She was with a drop-dead gorgeous Greek footballer who plays for one of the big clubs. She told us that she wouldn't move in for a while because she'd be filming in the Caribbean. Wayne never lived with her in that penthouse.'

'He lives there now.'

'Only until tomorrow.'

Harry stared. 'Seriously?'

'Seriously. Tamara told Casper and me about it. Wayne turned up at some press conference she gave. Said he was a businessman with a sideline as a backer of independent films. He wanted to spend a quiet fortnight down by the waterfront in Liverpool, researching potential storylines and cutting a few deals. According to Tamara, he hated hotels, and preferred to be on his own in a luxury apartment. Long story short, he persuaded her to let him take care of her brand new flat while she was away.'

'And she agreed?'

'Why not? He wasn't asking for money, and didn't seem short of it. She hadn't got round to filling the place with prized possessions so there was nothing to steal. It suited her to have someone keeping an eye on the place while it stood empty. She's nervous about security.'

'Jesus.' Harry's throat was dry. 'You're saying Wayne is a glorified house-sitter?'

'Got it in one.'

He shook his head, remembering the bareness of the penthouse when Wayne had let him in through the balcony window. He'd put it down to a fashionably minimalist taste in interior décor.

'And she didn't check up on him?'

'Did you and Jim?'

'That's different.'

'Don't kid yourself. I've talked to him myself, don't forget. He's a plausible charmer, knows exactly what buttons to press. Chutzpah takes you a long way in this life. He told Tamara he wanted to keep a low profile while he was in Liverpool. Never mind Capital of Culture, he said, this is a city of vultures. He reckoned a bunch of losers and wannabes would pester him for investment if they knew he was sniffing around, with money to spend.'

Harry shifted from foot to foot. 'Even if Wayne was lying when he said he and Tamara were an item, why would…?'

'I told you, Midsummer's Eve just happens to be his last night in the penthouse. Tamara isn't due back for another week. I asked Casper for her mobile number. Call her if you want, check this out for yourself.'

'I might just do that.'

'The real question is this. Why would Wayne Saxelby invite you to a homecoming party for someone he hardly knows, and who isn't even coming home?'

Midsummer's Eve, Harry thought, it keeps coming back to Midsummer's Eve. The words that had haunted him since Monday last hummed in his brain.

Died suddenly.

Another phrase sprang to mind, from his encounter with Wayne, moments after his confrontation with Tom Gunter in St Nicholas Gardens. His first instinct had been right all along. The innocence of the question was belied by that vulpine smile.

'Did you get my message?'

Chapter Twenty-three

Harry gave Gina a frayed grin. 'I could do with another drink.'

She picked up the bottle and said to Juliet, 'Will you change your mind, Mrs. May?'

Juliet shook her head. 'My five minutes are up, I think.'

'Why did you come here to tell me this?' Harry asked.

'Because there's something weird about him. When you mentioned this party, it was obvious that if you weren't lying to me, he was lying to you. And I've known you long enough to understand that even when you do lie, it doesn't come easily. Wayne Saxelby is different. Whenever I bump into him in the building, he's always showing off. I know a thing or two about rich businessmen. Casper and Malachy Needham, whatever you may think about them, they're the real deal. If Wayne Saxelby is a successful entrepreneur, then my name's Mother Teresa.'

'Just because he's told a few lies, it doesn't mean there's any harm in him.'

'Come off it, Harry. You're not pleading before the magistrates now.' She fiddled with the buckle of her bag. 'You know what I wondered?'

He held her gaze. 'Is this about the attack on Jim Crusoe?'

'Got it in one. I like Jim, though I'm not sure he likes me. He didn't deserve to have his skull cracked open. And when you've just moved into a nice new flat, you don't like to think that extreme violence has been inflicted a few floors below. It shouldn't happen. Casper's spitting feathers.'

Gina said to Harry, 'Why would Wayne beat your partner up?'

'A good question, my dear,' Juliet said. 'Perhaps you can help him find a few of the answers.'

'You have Tamara's number?' Harry asked.

Juliet fished in the silver bag and retrieved her mobile. It was small and pink and glitzy. She thumbed the keys and read out a number which Harry wrote down.

'I'll leave you to it. When Casper came round earlier on, he changed his mind about this evening and offered to take me out for a meal instead. So I need to go back and get ready.'

'Thanks.' All at once, Harry felt embarrassed. 'It was good of you to come round. I'm sorry I...'

She clasped his hand for a moment, then let it go. 'Not another word, please. Don't worry, I can see myself out.'

'Goodbye, Mrs. May,' Gina said.

'Goodbye, Gina.' Juliet paused. 'Look after him, won't you? I promise you one thing, with Harry Devlin, there's never a dull moment. Unless you hate films and music and mysteries, that is.'

◇◇◇

Five minutes later, he was surfing the net at his desk in the small study, clicking the mouse fast and often enough to make his wrist ache. The homepage of Wayne Saxelby's website was elegantly designed, but when he tried to access the link to Client Testimonials, the screen filled with the message *Page Not Found*. To listen to Wayne talk, you'd assume countless prospective clients beat a path to his door, but the web-counter showed only a handful of hits in the past thirty days. Tamara's fans had set up half a dozen online sites in her honour, but none mentioned Wayne. Six months ago, in a blaze of publicity, she'd split up with a rock singer with a cocaine habit, and since then she'd had a succession of wealthy admirers. Not a management consultant among them. Of course, Wayne might have dodged the gossip columnists. But Harry couldn't see it. Wayne, resist the chance to preen in front of the paparazzi?

Gina stood at his shoulder, her breath warm against his neck. In the compact room, he was aware of the closeness of her body to his, and of a delicate freesia scent.

'He dresses well. Designer clothes, none of your chain store crap.'

'He drives a BMW too. But what does that really prove? He can persuade people to offer him finance, that's all.'

'If he's brilliant at what he does…'

'He talks a good game. Jim and I should have realised when he offered us consultancy services for nothing. No such thing as a free lunch.'

'You didn't pay him?'

'His story was that it made business sense from his perspective. If we liked his initial work, we would cough up to engage him longer-term, and hey presto! He'd have gained a foothold in the legal services sector. But let's face it, Crusoe and Devlin aren't anyone's idea of a trophy client.'

'You fell for his smooth talk.'

Harry sighed. 'I suppose it suited us to think that Wayne had no hard feelings after he finished working for us.'

'What happened?'

When he'd told her the story, she said, 'He blames you for destroying his dream.'

'It was his parents' dream, he made that clear. They wanted their boy to be a solicitor. A respectable professional. But he was always something of a Walter Mitty.'

'Walter who?'

'I'll tell you another time.' He checked his watch. 'I ought to ring Tamara Dighton. Even if she's a late riser, it must be close to mid-day in sunny Barbados or wherever.'

He switched off the PC and went back to the living room to pick up the phone. Gina squatted on the floor, legs tucked beneath her.

Presently a distant voice on a bad line said, 'Yah?'

'Tamara Dighton?'

'Yah.'

He conjured up a picture of a sun-kissed beach, waves lapping the sandy shore, Tamara in a bikini as tiny as it was expensive. A world apart from New Brighton, in more ways than one.

'My name is Devlin and I'm ringing from Liverpool. Your landlord here, Casper May, is a friend of mine.' He crossed his fingers behind his back. 'I wanted to know if you need another house-sitter.'

'I'm coming back to England on Wednesday.'

'To Liverpool?'

'Yah.'

'And Wayne Saxelby is moving out tomorrow?'

'Look, what is this? Are you from the *Mail*?'

'Absolutely not.' A fervent note entered his voice. 'I just wondered about how you came to know Wayne Saxelby.'

'He showed up at a party and introduced himself…look, I know he backs film-makers, but there's nothing between him and me, if that's what you're thinking.'

'You aren't close friends?'

'He said he'd keep me in mind if he found a suitable vehicle for my talents while he was in the city. He's in the business, and he's keeping an eye on my flat for me while I'm away. I mean, there's a little man who's supposed to look after the building, but he lives downstairs, it's not the same.' A pause. 'Look, you are from the *Mail*, aren't you?'

The drawl was fading, and he detected a hint of native Scouse.

Harry contrived an elaborate sigh. 'All right, Ms Dighton, there's no fooling you. But if you were willing to talk to me on an exclusive basis…'

'Speak to my agent,' she said. 'He handles all that kind of thing. I've got better things to do right now. Like having a swim.'

He heard a click as she put down the phone.

'Well?' Gina demanded.

'Juliet was spot on.'

'What are you going to do?'

He banged the phone back on its stand and clenched his fist. Anger was rising to the surface. 'If he's responsible for putting Jim in intensive care…'

'You're a solicitor,' she said quickly. 'You can't take the law into your own hands. Tell the police.'

'Tell them what?'

'That Wayne isn't the man he pretends to be.'

'If people were locked up on that basis, we'd need a prison on every street corner. Police officers like evidence. If he did attack Jim, he's covered his tracks. Posed as a rescuer, the man who saved Jim's life.'

'Scumbag,' she said. 'Is there something to accuse him of?'

'Inviting me to a party that isn't going to happen?'

'If he's leaving tomorrow, we have to do something.'

'We?' He considered her eager, up-turned face. 'This is my problem, not yours.'

'I want to help. I mean, what's this so-called party about? I'd say he wants to lure you down to the basement or somewhere and beat you up too.'

'Or worse.'

Died suddenly.

'Is there anything in the penthouse that might prove what he's done?'

Harry shrugged. 'He must have typed the announcement of my death on his beloved laptop. Presumably he deleted the document…'

'I bet it can be retrieved.'

'Two problems with that. First, even if I can establish he typed the notice, that doesn't prove he hit Jim over the head. Second, we can't break into the penthouse and trawl through his laptop. We don't know his passwords…'

'Details!' She waved them away with an airy gesture. 'Can't you forget you're a cautious solicitor for a moment? If we can get into the flat, who knows what we will find? At least we can nick the laptop and ask an expert to do the hard work.'

'You're incorrigible.'

'Nice word, hope it's a compliment. Hey, you never know what else we may find. Besides, we have to start somewhere. Probably with another drink. Shall I pour?'

He couldn't help grinning. 'All right.'

'Listen,' she said, clutching the bottle like an offensive weapon, 'it shouldn't be so difficult. The man's more or less stalking you, right? If you can gather some of your precious evidence from the penthouse, you will be able to make a complaint to the police.'

'Under the Protection from Harassment Act?'

'Whatever.'

'Maybe you're the one who ought to be a solicitor.'

'Only if all else fails.' She poured until the glasses overflowed. He was starting to realise she didn't have much restraint. 'Come on, it's worth a shot.'

Harry shook his head. He'd already broken into one home today with disastrous results. 'I don't think so, Gina.'

'Worried about breaking and entering?'

'Among other things.'

'It's not a problem. Victor Creevey's master key will let us into the penthouse.'

'How do you propose we get hold of that?'

'Let's ask him for it.' She nodded towards the window. 'I can see him at this very moment. Strolling along the waterfront with his chum.'

Harry picked up his glass and moved to join her. Victor and Barney were fifty yards away, sauntering along the riverside from the direction of Albert Dock, pausing every now and then to glance across the Mersey. Their bodies kept touching, as if by chance. They looked content in each other's company.

'So—are you up for it?'

The wine worked its magic. Her enthusiasm was impossible to resist.

'Okay. You win.'

◇◇◇

Victor froze as he caught sight of Harry and Gina hurrying towards him, trainers pattering on the stone walkway. Barney had reverted to languid mode, and merely raised his thick black eyebrows.

'What do you want?'

'Keep your hair on, Victor.' He was conscious of Gina by his side, stifling a giggle as she contemplated the building manager's bald patch. 'This isn't about what happened in the basement. That's just between ourselves.'

Victor's eyes became tiny slits. Maybe Crippen looked as hunted as this when Inspector Dew turned up on his doorstep to ask about the disappearance of his wife.

'Well, then?'

'Wayne Saxelby. I'm told he's house-sitting for Tamara Dighton.'

Victor's jaw dropped. 'You weren't supposed to know.'

'I've had a conversation with Juliet May. Interesting. Wayne spun me the line that he was Tamara's latest boyfriend. Load of bollocks, isn't it?'

'He's doing some consultancy work for you and Jim Crusoe, right? He took me into his confidence, but I promised to keep my mouth shut.'

'Time to break that promise, Victor.'

Victor frowned. 'He said his business was getting off the ground and he was desperate to create the image of the man who had everything. Showing off, I suppose. But I admired his honesty.'

'Oh yeah?'

'He's full of talk, I grant you. But he's a likeable guy. Quite a charmer.'

Barney made a scornful noise.

'Presumably money changed hands?'

'What if it did?' Victor's default tone remained righteous indignation. 'No law against it, is there?'

'At this precise moment, I couldn't care less about the bloody law. Wayne has spun us all a line. He's not the man he seems.'

'Told you,' Barney said unexpectedly. 'I never liked the cut of his jib. It wasn't jealousy, despite what you said. The one time we met, I could see he wasn't to be trusted.'

'What has this got to do with me?' Victor demanded.

'I want to take a look inside that penthouse. Gina tells me you have a master key?'

Victor scowled at the girl. 'I can't jeopardise security, if that's what you're suggesting. It's out of the question.'

'Remember the CCTV cameras?' Harry muttered. 'I'll be upfront with you, Victor. I think Wayne knows more about the attack on Jim than he's admitted.'

'You can't imagine he'd hurt your partner! It's utter nonsense.'

'Is it? He's the only person known to be on the scene. The only one with a possible motive.'

'Such as?'

'He used to work for us.'

'He mentioned that. Said how far he'd moved on since then. Are you jealous of his success?'

'We allowed him to resign rather than be sacked. Maybe he holds that against us.'

'I don't believe it!'

'I do.' Barney's hair was blowing in the breeze. 'He's a creep.'

As Victor gave his lover a reproachful glance, Harry said, 'We need the key for an hour, maximum.'

'Sorry, it's more than my job's worth.'

Gina shot a glance at Barney. 'Which is precisely what, if Casper May finds out about your fun and games in the basement?'

'Where's the harm, Victor?' Barney murmured. 'Who cares if Harry here has a little…poke around?'

'You two have caused me a lot of grief,' Victor said. 'As a matter of fact, you might like to know that I've handed in my resignation. I've agreed to work out one month's notice. Barney and I will move to Manchester. We have friends in the Gay Village, so don't think you can threaten me.'

'You're relaxed if I have a word with Casper May, then?' Harry said.

Victor spat on to the paving stones. 'I'll get you the key.'

'Shall we come with you?'

'No need.' He nodded towards the bulk of Empire Dock. 'You live in one of those flats, don't you? I'll drop it off in a quarter of an hour.'

◇◇◇

'What next?' Gina asked when they were back inside.

Harry reached for the phone. 'We need to make sure that we aren't interrupted while we scout round the penthouse.'

His call was answered at the second ring. 'Wayne Saxelby.'

'This is Harry. I've changed my mind about coming to the party.'

'You have? Terrific!' Wayne sounded as though Leonardo DiCaprio had promised to drop by. 'I was going to call you again, try and twist your arm. You'll be glad you came.'

'And I have some good news. Jim Crusoe has regained consciousness and he's sitting up and saying a few words.'

'Fantastic! I'm so pleased.'

'But there's one thing that's rather odd. While Carmel was out of the room, he said something strange about what happened down in the basement, the night he was attacked.'

'What do you mean?'

'I don't want to talk on the telephone. But since you were there that night, I'd like to discuss it with you.'

'Why not now?'

'It's very…sensitive. I'd rather do it face to face.'

'Mysterious.' Wayne hesitated. 'Okay, let's talk before Tamara's party.'

'Are you collecting her from the airport?'

'No…' Harry supposed Wayne was making it up as he went along. 'She's booked a cab. Of course I've said nothing to her about the party. I'll pick you up from Empire Dock, it's not out of my way. We can have a natter over a beer before the fun starts.'

'Actually, I need to talk to Carmel, as well.'

Wayne became doubtful. 'What about?'

'I'll explain later.'

'I don't…'

'Let's meet at the pub opposite the hospital.'

'The Burning Deck?'

'Say in half an hour?'

'No, it's not convenient. Let me collect you and bring you here first.'

'Sorry, can't manage that. I've already arranged for Carmel to join us at the Burning Deck later. It would be useful if you and I had a private chat first.'

'But…'

'It's important, Wayne. You'll understand when I've explained everything.'

Gina grinned at him and gave a nod of encouragement. She was almost dancing with excitement.

'This is all most peculiar.' Wayne was unhappy. 'What is…?'

'See you in the saloon bar.' Harry had become as keen on interrupting as a political interviewer. 'Don't be late.'

As he put down the phone, Gina applauded.

'Oh my God! You ought to be an actor yourself.'

'Believe me, I dredged up some of the corniest B-movie lines I could remember.' He parodied breathlessness. '*I don't want to talk about it on the telephone.*'

Her eyes sparkled. The wine had taken hold.

'Here's another one for you. How about *he's swallowed the bait?*'

◇◇◇

Victor turned up ten minutes later than promised, but his mood had lightened. He handed over the key with a ceremonial flourish.

'Barney and I are off to the Stapledon for a couple of drinks, followed by a meal. You'll have a free run this evening.'

'An hour is all I need.'

'On my way back, I thought I saw Wayne Saxelby in Water Street, hailing a black cab.'

Harry and Gina exchanged glances. 'Excellent.'

'I still think you're barking up the wrong tree. He might have a lot to say for himself, but he always struck me as a decent fellow.'

'Barney seems less sure.'

Victor treated them to a libidinous wink. 'It's no bad thing to keep a young man on his toes. If you get my meaning.'

'I'll leave the key behind the front desk.'

'Hope you find what you're looking for.' Victor glanced over his shoulder on his way out. 'Though I'd lay odds that it's a wild goose chase.'

When the door closed behind him, Gina said, 'Wayne Saxelby won't hang around in the Burning Deck when he realises you aren't going to show up. We'd better get moving.'

'You don't have to come. For a solicitor to trespass in someone else's home is bad enough, but…'

'For a cleaning lady, it's all in a day's work. No arguing, Harry. You can't keep me out of this now. If you talk like a schoolteacher, I'll never speak to you again.'

'I wouldn't want that.'

'Me neither.' She slapped him playfully on the backside. 'Come on.'

'We shouldn't have polished off all that wine.'

'Once we're done in John Newton House, I expect you to buy another bottle.'

◇◇◇

He felt light-headed as they walked along the Strand. Partly the effect of booze on an empty stomach, partly the adrenaline rush of venturing into the unknown. He shouldn't be doing this, far less bringing Gina along. But he couldn't help himself. Beneath the giddiness, his insides churned with rage. Jim had been battered to the brink of death, and now it seemed that Wayne Saxelby was responsible. Nothing could excuse the attack on Jim, nothing at all. Whoever did it deserved to be hunted down and made to pay the price.

'Are you all right?' Gina asked as they crossed the road at the lights.

'Fine, why do you ask?'

'There's an odd look on your face. I've never seen it before.'

'What sort of look?'

'I dunno, sort of hard and intense. *Focused*, I suppose.'

'Yeah, you won't see me looking focused that often. Not in the office, for sure. Ask Jim Crusoe, he'll be the first to say so.'

They arrived at John Newton House and Harry let them in. The lobby was quiet, but for the never-ending gush of the waterfall. Victor had abandoned the desk with its forlorn array of blank screens. The lift whisked them up to the top floor. He remembered his last visit here, and his expulsion on to the balcony. It seemed to belong to a different lifetime. When Wayne Saxelby still acted like a saviour. Before Ceri Hussain tried to kill herself.

As they stepped out on to the landing, he realised that he was exhausted. The events of the day had taken a toll, and the booze hadn't helped.

'Are you okay?' she asked again.

The silence up here was eerie. Down the corridor was the door to Juliet's penthouse, but she was out with Casper. He imagined Wayne in the saloon bar, consulting his watch and drumming his fingers on the table in irritation.

'Never better.'

Untrue, but who cared? He fitted Victor's key in the lock. It turned easily and the door to Tamara Dighton's penthouse slid open.

The place was as tidy as he remembered from his last visit. Ahead of them, the door to the room where Wayne kept his laptop stood ajar.

'Lead the way,' Gina whispered.

'No need to keep your voice down,' he said. 'There's nobody around.'

He strode forward, pushed at the door and moved into the room.

The moment he stepped inside, something hit his head with tremendous force. He felt a searing pain and lost his balance, groping blindly for something to hold on to as he crashed to the floor.

Gina screamed and he heard rapid footsteps. Then she screamed again, in agony this time.

'Nobody around?' Wayne Saxelby's voice enquired as his head swam. 'Uh-uh, Harry. Wrong again.'

Chapter Twenty-four

As he came round, everything was fuzzy. His face was wet and his head hurt. He felt dried blood on his cheeks, and he wanted to groan. But he couldn't make a sound. Adhesive tape stretched tight over his mouth.

He prised open his eyes, only to find that he was in the dark. Flickering candle-light relieved the blackness, but he didn't have a clue where he was. A long way from Tamara Dighton's penthouse, for sure. The atmosphere was dank and he heard a sound like a leaky tap. The plop, plop, plop, of rainwater from a roof he couldn't see.

He was underground, in a cave or tunnel, couldn't be sure which. His ankles were bound together by thin strands of wire that bit into his flesh, and his wrists were tied behind his back. He'd been trussed up and dumped on a floor that was damp, cold and rocky.

This must be what it felt like to be a slave. Not in control, your life no longer your own. At the mercy of others.

As his eyes adjusted to the feeble illumination, he glimpsed a sodden, bunched-up towel lying on stony ground, inches from his feet. No wonder his face was moist. The towel had been wiped over it.

'Harry.'

Somewhere in the shadows, Wayne Saxelby whispered his name. He might have been greeting a lover as she awoke from her slumbers. Harry heard footsteps and saw the familiar face in the candle's flame. Wayne ripped the tape from his lips with a force that made his eyes fill with tears.

'Harry,' Wayne said again.

'Uh?'

Harry's voice creaked like a cellar door. He felt as though he'd spent the whole day knocking back the booze, not just shared a single bottle of cheap plonk with Gina Paget.

Shit. Gina, what had happened to her?

'Sorry about the bang on the head. I needed to make sure I could transport you here without your making a nuisance of yourself. You will behave for me, won't you?'

Harry remained motionless.

Wayne stamped on his ankle.

'Won't you?' Wayne repeated.

Harry made a fractional movement of his head.

'I'm prepared to punish misbehaviour, make no mistake. I'm in no hurry. There are hours to go before the end of Midsummer's Eve. I won't knock you unconscious again. It would defeat the whole object if you finished up a cabbage. As Jim nearly did. I've been looking forward to this, and I'd hate to mess up at the last moment. You'll have a splitting headache, of course. But don't fret. That won't last for too long.'

Wayne bent down again, and Harry saw him fumble in a shoulder bag. He pulled out a flask and put it to his lips. When he'd torn the gag from Harry's mouth, his breath had smelled of whisky. He needed Dutch courage to do whatever he had in mind.

'Ah, that's better. Don't get your hopes up, I'm not pissed out of my brain. Just…excited. I feel like a traveller at the end of a long journey. I suppose you'd like to know where I've brought you and why?'

Harry didn't move.

'You don't fool me, Harry. Your curiosity is the stuff of legend. Welcome to the Waterloo Railway Tunnel. My father brought me here when I was a boy. It was built to connect Edge Hill Station with the docks. The Philistines of British Rail closed the Waterloo thirty-odd years ago, a wicked waste. Now they want to use it again.'

Harry recalled the news coverage. The Waterloo Tunnel might be opened up to ease traffic congestion. Pity this was Saturday night, and there was no chance of Merseytravel engineers shinning down a vent to rescue him.

'Look,' Wayne said. 'I'll shine my torch.'

A thin beam danced along stone walls, catching the tails of stalactites that slithered down from the roof. Two arched openings gave into short passageways, beyond was a brick-lined chamber. Ahead, the tunnel curved away and disappeared into darkness.

'Smoke flues and a boiler room.' Wayne sounded like a tour guide. 'Round the corner is the shaft where I brought you down. There's all sorts of debris too, even an old smashed-up wagon. You'd never believe the things that are left to lie and rot for years underground.'

He paused and said. 'My father died on Midsummer's Eve, you know. Same day of the year as my mother, but twelve months later.'

The torch beam wobbled. Wayne's hands must be trembling. Harry caught sight of Gina. She was tied up, like him, and her thin frame was wedged against the opposite wall of the tunnel. She was still in her stripey top and absurdly short skirt. Her legs were spread and the beam lingered on a glimpse of white thighs and dark knickers. Her head lolled on her left shoulder, her eyes were shut, and her mouth sealed with tape. Harry couldn't tell whether she was awake or sleeping, alive or dead.

'Why did you have to bring her along?' Wayne asked. 'It's your fault she has to suffer too. Collateral damage.'

To the best of Harry's knowledge, Wayne had never kept a girlfriend for long. Yet he'd pretended to be Tamara Dighton's lover. How careless to fall for his fantasy.

A few yards further down the tunnel, steel glinted in the torchlight. The beam jinked over a bulky piece of equipment, tempting him to guess what it might be. Then Wayne switched off the torch and the moment was gone.

'My parents were married for years before I came along. Mum had one miscarriage after another. My birth was like a miracle, she said. I was the apple of their eye. You'll say they spoiled me, but I wanted to please them. I scraped through the degree and law finals, but after that it got even harder. Which is why I ended up working for you and Jim. The bottom of the barrel.'

Wayne shook his head. 'I was desperate to keep my clients happy. That's why I told Mrs. Birch I'd negotiated such a good settlement. I meant to repay the money once I'd sorted out a loan. I was the loser, not her. You and Jim could have turned a blind eye. Nobody would have been any the wiser if you hadn't made such a fuss.'

Until the next time, Harry thought. But he kept his mouth clamped shut.

'Mum was desperately ill by then. Dad couldn't cope, that's why she moved into the Home. You told me I was finished with the firm and I wrote out my resignation rather than be sacked. Afterwards, I drove for miles round Wirral, wondering how I'd break the news to my parents. My mobile was switched off when Dad was frantically trying to ring me, to ask me to join him at Mum's bedside. I should have been there, it was my duty as a son. I finally turned up after the ambulance had taken her body to the mortuary. It was Midsummer's Eve. Not that you will remember.'

No, Harry hadn't the faintest recollection. His only concern had been sorting out the mess that Wayne left behind. He hadn't known that Mrs. Saxelby was sick.

'When I lost her, I sort of crumbled. No job, no money. I'd failed and let my parents down. I got it into my head that if I'd kept my job with Crusoe and Devlin, Mum might have lived.'

Better say something.

'Sorry,' Harry muttered.

Wayne didn't seem to hear. 'You know why I loathe hospitals? Because I've seen too much of them. The psychiatrists worried about me, they thought I was a danger to myself. Especially after Dad died. He killed himself, did I mention that?'

Harry shook his head. He didn't know what was coming next, but was sure he wouldn't like it.

'He never got over Mum's death, of course. They didn't spend a single night apart in forty years of marriage. Want to know how he died?'

Harry was more concerned about the girl who lay a few feet away, hidden in the darkness. He must save Gina, even if it cost his own life. But though the wire bindings felt crude and inexpertly fastened, he could not work himself free. At least not while Wayne watched him. And he dared not squirm out of the glow cast by the candle-light.

Wayne took a step forward. His fist was balled.

'You do want to know, don't you?'

Harry nodded.

'He was a carpenter by trade, he'd served a long apprenticeship. A real craftsman, that was Dad. He took a pride in his work.'

Gina groaned and Wayne spun round. The torch beam fell on her pale face. It was made ugly by a grimace of pain.

'Coming round? Good, I want you to hear this too.'

'Let her go,' Harry mumbled.

'Even by your standards,' Wayne said, 'that's a very stupid request. Tell you what. She can die first. Trust me, I'm doing her a favour.'

Gina groaned again and Wayne slapped her on the cheek. The coarse sound of his hand on her skin echoed in the tunnel.

'Where was I? Oh yes, my father. While I was in and out of mental hospital, he spent a lot of his time in the garden shed. His private kingdom, where he used to make bird tables and such-like. I had no idea what he was doing in there. Next Midsummer's Eve, I found out.'

Harry waited.

'I'd been to see my psychiatrist. She thought I was making progress. I'd not talked to Dad about the anniversary of Mum's death. I hoped the day would pass without him saying how much he missed her. Kidding myself, of course.'

Wayne cleared his throat. 'The minute I got back home, I knew something was wrong. You know how it is?'

Harry nodded. Less than twelve hours had passed since he and Ken Porterfield had broken into Ceri Hussain's house. Since then, his life had changed, not once, but twice.

'I found him in the living room. His body was in one place, but his head had rolled across the floor. What he'd built in his shed was a purpose-made guillotine. Marvellous craftsmanship, with a timer and the sharpest blade I'd ever seen. He bent under the blade and pulled the switch, and everything worked, exactly as he'd planned.'

Harry swallowed hard as Ceri's voice murmured in his brain.

'People find all sorts of imaginative ways to kill themselves. In the past two or three years alone, we've had death by antifreeze poisoning, by circular saw, even by a home-made guillotine.'

'You're honoured,' Wayne said. 'I've never spoken about my father's death before. That worried the psychiatrist, she thought I wasn't dealing with it. I was hospitalised for six months after Dad decapitated himself. Until it dawned on me there was one way I could make things right.'

He frowned at the memory. 'I realised you and Jim were to blame for everything. Okay, I wasn't the world's best solicitor, but work gives us self-respect, and you robbed me of mine. Mum was poorly, but you'd stopped me from being with her when she passed away. And I hold you responsible for what happened to Dad. A whole family, destroyed. What gave you the right?'

'Sorry,' Harry said again.

'Too late. I decided a long time ago that I didn't want to live. Suicide runs in families, they say, and I guess it's true. But it stuck in my gullet that, if I killed myself, you'd carry on without a care in the world. As if you weren't to blame.'

Harry's heart pounded. With infinite caution, he tested the wire ties that held his wrists behind his back. There was some give, but nothing like enough. If he tried to free himself, Wayne would be on to him straight away. A phrase from their conversation in Tamara's flat stuck in his mind.

'Best of luck, Harry. I have this feeling you're going to need it if you keep sticking your neck out.'

No wonder Wayne had smiled.

'You talk a lot about justice, Harry. As it happens, I'm with you one hundred per cent. That's why I decided you should face a spot of poetic justice yourself.'

The torch beam danced again, to allow Harry a proper look at the apparatus he'd glimpsed.

In the middle of the tunnel was a rickety old table. On top of it stood a wooden guillotine. The glint of steel in the light came from the blade. Wayne was right, its cutting edge was as sharp as any Harry had seen.

He retched convulsively. Wayne pulled a face and switched off the torch. He picked up the towel to mop Harry's jaw.

'This isn't going to be pleasant, get used to it. You'd never believe how hard it was, persuading the Coroner's office to let me have the guillotine back. But it's my property, I was sole heir to my father's estate. And since you insisted on bringing the girl along, I thought she should be the first to test the blade. Give you an idea of what lies in store.'

'Don't,' he whispered. 'Please.'

'Begging, eh? I ought to thank you, really. You gave a purpose to my life. I managed to pull myself together well enough to create a new identity, without even changing my name. You'd be surprised how easy it is to convince people that you are rich and successful. Of course, I took risks. It's what entrepreneurs do. Trust me, I read management books till the bullshit was leaking out of my ears.'

Harry was thinking about Gina. How to get her out of this in one piece?

'Persuading Tamara to let me house-sit for her was a stroke of luck. It was easier to be on the spot as Midsummer's Eve drew near. I always wanted this to be your last day. There's a symmetry about it. I wanted to rattle your cage, make you realise something bad was going to happen. The fake press clipping about your death, the message on your home answering machine, the mess I made of your room. Childish, perhaps, but I knew your imagination would fill in the gaps.'

'And Jim?'

Wayne frowned. 'He has no imagination whatsoever, no point in twisting his tail. I didn't much care whether he lived or died. The only essential was that, if he survived, he shouldn't be able to identify me. As Fate would have it, Victor Creevey called on me. He dropped a hint that you were planning to visit when you thought I was safely away at the Burning Deck.'

Bloody Victor. He'd lied about seeing Wayne catch a cab, as well.

'My only fear was that someone would spot me dumping you both down the tunnel vent. It's a quiet spot, and covered in undergrowth, but you can never be sure someone won't stick their nose in. Thank goodness, there wasn't a hitch. I've spent a fortnight flirting with Victor, and today it paid off. He's really taken a dislike to you, Harry. You ought to be more careful about making so many enemies.'

Wayne paused for breath, and gave a cheerful wink as he pointed towards the darkness and the guillotine.

'Too late for that now, though, eh?'

Harry made a sudden effort to squeeze out of his bonds, but he couldn't free himself. In an instant, Wayne punched his face and shoved him back onto the ground.

He couldn't help whimpering. His cheek hurt like hell. The bone must be broken.

'Not a good boy. Next time you do something silly, your fingers go under the guillotine. Probably some other bits too. Don't provoke me, Harry. You can't guess the times I've rehearsed this. Not that it's as easy to practise tying someone up with wire. Behave while I light another candle.'

A match flared in the darkness.

'Look past the guillotine,' Wayne instructed. 'See the gap in the floor of the tunnel?'

Harry followed his gaze.

'That hole leads to a disused sewer. It's a ten foot drop, and the channel's filled with water. Take a look at your final resting place. They won't find you for ages. Or your head. Maybe not even when work starts on renovating the tunnel. Who knows, you may finish up beneath a brand new rail track.'

'And you?' Harry muttered.

'I'll climb back up to ground level and wander along the Northern Line until the last express is due. I'll step in front of it, and everything will be done and dusted.'

Harry turned his head back to look at Wayne. Behind him, Gina had her eyes wide open. A frantic light shone in them. When she shifted her arms, he understood her meaning.

He must distract Wayne's attention, if only for a split second.

He took a breath, and uttered a high-pitched scream of agony. It didn't require much imagination. Every inch of his body seemed on fire.

'What the fuck?'

Wayne bent towards him, face contorted in fury. As he moved, Harry saw Gina launch herself at their captor. Her legs were still tied together, but her hands were free. She kicked Wayne, and he lost his balance. As he flailed with arms outstretched, trying not to fall to the ground, she stabbed her fingers into his eyes.

Wayne yelled with pain.

Harry summoned his last ounce of energy and lashed at Wayne's temple with his bound legs. Wayne gasped, but heaved himself away from Gina's frantic assault. She was spitting and flailing and gouging. In his confusion, Wayne crashed into the table behind him.

The guillotine came crashing down and Wayne made a desperate effort to dodge the falling blade. He slipped and went head over heels. Harry heard a strangled cry and a thudding splash.

Wayne had disappeared into the hole in the ground.

Gina pulled off the wires that tied her ankles. It took a couple of seconds, while Harry struggled to free himself. She flung her small frame at him and unfastened his wrists and legs. As he rubbed his arms to relieve the numbness, she tore off the tape that covered her mouth.

'Amazing,' he gasped. 'How did you manage that?'

In the feeble candle-light, her face was dirty and he was sure she was choking back tears, but from somewhere within she conjured up a smile of triumph.

'Don't forget, you're talking to Harriet Houdini.'

The Seventh Day

Chapter Twenty-five

A blustery evening on the beach at Waterloo. The Iron Men stared out to sea, but kept their thoughts to themselves. Harry and Gina limped across the sand, making for nowhere in particular. They'd been patched up in Casualty the previous night, and although Harry's head throbbed where Wayne had struck it, the doctors reckoned the concussion had done no lasting harm. The rest of his body felt sore and old, but he'd live.

Unlike Wayne. The fall into the sewer had broken his neck.

The sky was beautiful, with the last lingering light of day. Red, yellow and orange hues cast reflections that shimmered upon the dark water. The motionless shadows stood at intervals along the beach, as far as the eye could see.

'I love the statues,' Gina said. 'I like to imagine they are alive.'

They'd driven here from the hospital. Ceri had slipped into a coma. The overdose had damaged her liver beyond repair, and the doctors didn't expect her to live. Jim was taking tentative steps along the road to recovery. Carmel had been thrilled to meet Gina; she'd got it into her head that at last Harry had found a girlfriend. She didn't understand.

Gina had come back with him to Empire Dock on Saturday night. After what had happened in the tunnel, neither of them wanted to be alone. He'd taken the sofa, she'd had his bed. No question of their making love; they'd been too bruised and weary for anything but sleep.

'What did Mrs. May want?' Gina asked.

Juliet had called round at the flat earlier, and he'd answered the door in his dressing gown.

'Just checking that you're still in one piece.'

'For the time being.'

'I'm glad.' She cocked an ear as Gina padded around in the living room. 'Do I gather you have company?'

'Uh-huh.'

She mustered a smile. 'Look after yourself.'

'And you.' As she turned away down the corridor, he called out, 'Thanks for yesterday.'

'It was nothing,' Juliet said, without looking back.

As the sun slid towards the horizon, Gina's hand touched his. The words and rhythms of that old favourite song jangled in his brain. He'd last heard it at the Alhambra, whose turrets he could see poking above the houses, pointing to the heavens. He'd been accompanied by Ceri Hussain. It felt like a scene from another lifetime.

He clasped Gina's fingers, and whispered the words.

'As long as I gaze on Waterloo Sunset,
I am in paradise.'

Author's note

I must record my gratitude to those friends, clients, and colleagues who have offered help of many different kinds with this book. As a Liverpool-based solicitor writing about another Liverpool-based solicitor, I am keen to make the point that Harry Devlin's life is not mine; and a good thing too. Similarly, his Liverpool is in some respects a fictional construct. As before, I have taken liberties with the real city and its topography, both for the purposes of the story and in the hope of avoiding even accidental collisions between the real and imaginary worlds. So, for example, John Newton House, the Stapledon Bar, the Waterloo Alhambra, the Indian Summer Care Home, the Liverpool General Hospital, the Burning Deck, and the Salthouse Quarter are fictitious. The Liverpool Police Authority is an invention, not to be confused with the Merseyside Police Authority; however, the real City Coroner does work in the Cotton Exchange, and the gardens of St Nicholas Church and Liverpool Cathedral are fascinating oases in the city centre. Antony Gormley's Iron Men have so far survived all attempts to evict them from the Sefton shores, and there were indeed, at the time of writing, plans to re-open the Waterloo railway tunnel. A number of other real-life landmarks are mentioned, including (to give its precisely correct name) the Britannia Adelphi Hotel. It goes without saying that all the characters and organisations taking an active part in the story-line are my inventions and not intended to have even a vague resemblance to any counterparts in real life, but as a lawyer, I cannot resist the temptation to say it anyway, and to add that any resemblance that might exist is wholly coincidental.

A good many people—too many for them all to be listed—have given of their time and expertise to answer my innumerable questions and requests for support. However, I would like to express special thanks to some of them. Andre Rebello, HM Coroner for Liverpool, generously provided me with extensive insight into the life and work of a modern coroner and made interesting suggestions which influenced my account of the inquest into the death of Nesta Borth. My discussions with Andre left me with enormous admiration for the challenging, yet exceptionally important work that coroners do. Philip Tarleton, managing director of Meade, King, Robinson & Co Ltd, and Denis Maxwell gave assistance which helped me to create John Newton House. Francis Cassidy, chief executive of Crosby Plaza Cinema, Rupert Hoare, until his recent retirement the Dean of Liverpool Cathedral, and Neil Scales, chief executive and director general of Merseytravel, all gave me the benefit of their knowledge and expertise, while Mai Lin Li of Kirklees Libraries supplied insights which helped with the portrayal of Ka-Yu's life. Margaret Jackson and John Hollingsworth of Aintree Hospital provided background know-how for the hospital scenes. Paul Charles, a fellow crime writer and musicians' agent, persuaded Ray Davies, the legendary composer of 'Waterloo Sunset', to grant permission to reproduce a portion of the lyrics. Ann Cleeves, Rosa Plant and Juliet Doyle were among those who made valuable comments on aspects of the manuscript. My agent Mandy Little, my British publisher Susie Dunlop, my American editor Barbara Peters and my American publisher Rob Rosenwald, were all as supportive as ever. So were my long-suffering family: my wife Helena, my son Jonathan and my daughter Catherine. Jonathan deserves special thanks, in particular for his work on designing and maintaining my website, www.martinedwardsbooks.com.

Martin Edwards

To receive a free catalog of Poisoned Pen Press titles, please contact us in one of the following ways:

Phone: 1-800-421-3976
Facsimile: 1-480-949-1707
Email: info@poisonedpenpress.com
Website: www.poisonedpenpress.com

Poisoned Pen Press
6962 E. First Ave. Ste. 103
Scottsdale, AZ 85251